Praise for *Magick & Mayhem*

"Magic, Merlin, and murder are a great mix for this debut cozy. Up to her ears in problems, both magickal and mortal, Kailyn's a fun and adventuresome heroine I loved watching. Crafting a spell, summoning a familiar, and solving a murder shouldn't be this hard—or this fun."
—**Lynn Cahoon**, *New York Times* and *USA Today* bestselling author

"Sharon Pape's *Magick & Mayhem* is spellbinding, with magical prose, a wizardly plot, and a charming sleuth who, while attempting to protect a cast of sometimes difficult and always surprising characters, has a penchant for accidentally revealing her own powers and secrets to exactly the wrong people."
—**Janet Bolin**, Agatha-nominated author of the national bestselling Threadville Mysteries

"*Magick & Mayhem* is a charming, must-read mystery with enchanting characters. A fun and entertaining page turner that I couldn't put down."
—**Rose Pressey**, *USA Today* bestselling author

Other Books by Sharon Pape

Sketcher in the Rye

Alibis and Amethysts

Sketch a Falling Star

To Sketch a Thief

Sketch Me if You Can

Magick & Mayhem

An Abracadabra Mystery

Sharon Pape

LYRICAL UNDERGROUND
Kensington Publishing Corp.
www.kensingtonbooks.com

LYRICAL UNDERGROUND BOOKS are published by

Kensington Publishing Corp.
119 West 40th Street
New York, NY 10018

All Kensington titles, imprints, and distributed lines are available at special quantity discounts for bulk purchases for sales promotion, premiums, fund-raising, educational, or institutional use.

Special book excerpts or customized printings can also be created to fit specific needs. For details, write or phone the office of the Kensington Sales Manager: Kensington Publishing Corp., 119 West 40th Street, New York, NY 10018. Attn. Sales Department. Phone: 1-800-221-2647.

Lyrical Underground and Lyrical Underground logo Reg. US Pat. & TM Off.

First Electronic Edition: May 2017
eISBN-13: 978-1-5161-0055-2
eISBN-10: 1-5161-0055-7

First Print Edition: May 2017
ISBN-13: 978-1-5161-0056-9
ISBN-10: 1-5161-0056-5

Printed in the United States of America

To my family, both the two-legged and four-legged members.
You are the center of my universe.

"Those who don't believe in magic will never find it."
—ROALD DAHL

Chapter 1

"You need to summon a familiar of your own," my grandmother Bronwen said. Her voice was easy to recognize, despite the fact that it emanated from a small, amorphous cloud of energy hovering above my new computer. Both she and my mother had been steadfast in their refusal to buy into the technology age, so when she popped out of the ether that morning, I expected a tirade against the computer that now occupied the desk behind the counter. It took me a few seconds to realize that my recent purchase wasn't the subject of her visit. I briefly considered telling her the computer was my familiar, but I didn't think she would see the humor in it.

"Hand-me-downs never work properly," she went on. "Surely we've taught you better."

"Besides," my mother chimed in, from a second cloud that appeared beside Bronwen's, "my Sashkatu is ancient, and the five others aren't worth the cost of their kibble."

"Morgana!" my grandmother scolded, "you mustn't write them off that way. You summoned them and they came. They're our responsibility now. I mean Kailyn's," she muttered. "I keep forgetting that we're dead. In any case, it's entirely possible the problem was more yours than theirs anyway."

I held my breath, hoping my mother might finally realize that arguing about such things was pointless. I'd thought death would mellow the two of them, but so far they'd proven me wrong. Maybe the sudden, unexpected nature of their passing had left their souls on edge, and once they adjusted to their new circumstances they'd put their earthbound bickering behind them. Then again, maybe not. I'd always suspected they enjoyed the verbal sparring far too much to give it up.

"What exactly do you mean it's my fault?" my mother asked indignantly, dashing my hopes. "*You* didn't have any better success at restoring our mojo than the cats or I did."

"*I'd* been semi-retired for three years," Bronwen sputtered. "*You'd* taken the reins of the business!" The chimes over the front door jangled like a bell ending a boxing round.

"Hey, we have company," I hissed at them. "Make yourselves scarce!" They vanished without a second to spare as a middle-aged couple ambled up to the counter. I was grateful I didn't have to explain the presence of clouds in my store.

The woman's eyes were flitting around the shop with anticipation, but her companion looked like a child who'd been dragged to the dentist. I made a mental note to buy a comfortable chair for the men who were coerced into making the trip.

"Welcome to Abracadabra," I greeted them, trying to shake off the negative energy my family had left in their wake. "Take your time browsing. If you have any questions, I'll be happy to answer them. There are some baskets at the far end of the counter to make shopping easier." I'd talked my mother and grandmother into buying lovely wicker baskets instead of the ubiquitous plastic ones available in all the grocery and drugstore chains. They cost more, but they were more fitting for our shop.

The woman thanked me and went to take one, her husband grumbling, "How much do you plan on buying here?"

"Well, I'm sure you don't want to drive up here again anytime soon," she said sweetly as she started down the first of the four narrow aisles. I'd heard the warning in her undertone, but I doubted that he had. Back in my early teens, I'd realized there were certain subtleties of mood in women's speech that often eluded men.

I sat down behind the computer to finish setting up my online banking account. Although the shop wasn't large, it took most people half an hour or more to browse through all the lotions, potions, unguents, and creams with intriguing names and mystical purposes. Until about fifty years ago, the inventory had been smaller, meant specifically for those who were practiced in the arts of sorcery and witchcraft, but that was before tourists discovered our quaint little town of New Camel, New York. My enterprising grandmother had seized the opportunity to add a line of the health and beauty products our family had been whipping up for our own use as far back as anyone could remember. It didn't take long before word of mouth brought a steady stream of customers to our door. The other merchants in the town prospered as well. A couple of bed and breakfasts opened to accommodate visitors who wanted to spend the night. One local resident was able to drum up enough financial support to open a small ski resort nearby. Snow is never in short supply around here in winter.

When the couple returned to the counter, the woman was beaming with success. Her husband was carrying the basket, now piled high with our most popular products. He looked as close to dying of boredom as anyone I'd ever seen. He yawned widely, without bothering to cover his mouth.

"You ought to have a website so people could order your products online," he groused as I rang up his wife's purchases. "You're way out here in the boonies, no public transportation, hard to get to from everywhere. It's a miracle you have any customers at all."

Not a miracle, I wanted to say, just a little magic. But that was one secret ingredient we never talked too much about. "Thanks for the advice," I said instead. "I'll definitely look into it." I had considered going ahead with a website after I inherited the shop, but although Morgana and Bronwen were deceased, they hadn't totally passed on. The thought of arguing with them about it on a daily, if not hourly, basis quickly shut down my enthusiasm for the project. Besides, I was still euphoric about finally having a computer on the premises.

"My friends all swear by your products," the woman said with a smile. "So I had to try them for myself. I told Robert here that we'd make the trip into a bit of a vacation, but for him if there's no golf, it's not a vacation." She sighed and searched my face for some empathy. I nodded and smiled back, though I was finding it hard to relate to her problem. She could have left Robert home and driven here alone or with friends. Maybe it was simply the difference between her generation and mine. Had it been me, I would have preferred to make the trip alone. But then, I've had strong, self-sufficient women as role models all my life. My father left when I was five, and my grandfather, years before my birth. Morgana and Bronwen had carried on as if they'd never really expected their spouses to make the final cut.

Robert took the shopping bag I held out to them. "We should

have been on the road fifteen minutes ago," he said to his wife, who was looking at a display of candles infused with healing oils.

"I love your shop," she said as he hooked his arm through hers and propelled her out the door. He pulled it shut behind them so hard that he startled Sashkatu, who'd been sleeping in the spill of sunlight on the windowsill behind me. The cat regarded me with regal contempt as if I'd been the source of the disturbance. Although he was fifteen, his black coat had kept its luster, and his emerald eyes were as sharp and bright as ever. If he pined for my mother, he kept it to himself and slept right through her visits from the other side. When he was done glowering at me, he sighed and laid his head down on the tufted goose-down cushion Morgana had made to ease his arthritic joints. Fortunately the five other cats didn't seem to mind being left back in the house during the workday. I didn't want to think about the destruction they could wreak on the shop's inventory with one high-energy game of chase. If I were to follow Bronwen's advice and summon my own familiar, there would be seven cats to deal with and a bigger bill for cat food and other feline necessities. I kicked that decision to an already-crowded back burner in my mind and prepared to close up for the night.

I was ready when my Aunt Tilly came through the connecting door from her shop, Tea and Empathy. She was my mother's younger sister and my one remaining relative, aside from a few distant cousins somewhere in the wilds of Pennsylvania. Although I loved Tilly dearly, she tended to be a bit scattered and eccentric. According to my grandmother, she was hands down the best psychic our family had ever produced.

She padded up to the counter in one of the frothy Hawaiian muumuus she'd taken to wearing after menopause settled in with some extra pounds. Her ballet flats dangled from her left fingertips and the turban she often wore at work was still perched on her head. She thought it lent her an air of mysticism. I thought it made her look like a Hawaiian swami with identity issues, but I would never tell her that.

"Did you want to wear the turban to see the attorney?" I asked, because I'd never seen her wear it outside the shop.

"Oh my," she said, plucking it off her short red hair and giggling. "Silly me—I forgot I had it on." I laughed too, because even as a child I'd thought of her as Silly Tilly. She plopped the turban onto the counter and finger-combed her curls. I beckoned my purse from the shelf behind the counter and was actually surprised when it popped up and floated into my hand. These days my magick was far from a certainty.

While I set the security code, Tilly slipped on her shoes. My little blue Prius was parked outside at the curb. Tilly climbed, or more accurately fell, into the passenger seat. I tucked in the edges of her dress and shut the door, before hopping behind the wheel.

Jim Harkens, who handled our family's legal matters, shared a small, one-story office building with the town's only dentist. It was less than a three-minute drive from our shops, hardly worth taking the car. But Tilly had arthritis in her hips and corns on her feet. My mother had tried everything in her bag of tricks, but the ailments had proven impervious to her spells and potions. So we drove to our appointment.

When we pulled into the parking lot behind the building, Jim's big white SUV was the only vehicle there. I pulled into one of the diagonal spots and helped my aunt out of the car. Jim's office suite was off the short common hallway on the left. We opened his door and walked past Ronnie's unoccupied desk. She was Jim's receptionist, secretary, and paralegal all rolled into one. Since she only worked until four, we saw ourselves down to Jim's office. I knocked on the closed door. There was no response, but it wouldn't be the first time I'd found him asleep, his padded chair angled back and his feet propped up on his desk. Although he was on the brink of fifty, he'd confided to me recently that early retirement was beckoning with a Siren's call. I knocked again, then tried turning the knob. Since it was unlocked, I walked in, Tilly right on my heels. The room was dark, bits of sunlight creeping in around the edges of the closed blinds. When I stopped to let my eyes adjust, Tilly slammed into me and sent us both sprawling. If Jim had been awake to see our little vaudeville act, he would have enjoyed a good laugh. But he must have been sleeping soundly.

"Are you okay, Aunt Tilly?" I asked, doing a quick appraisal of my own condition. My left knee had taken the brunt of the fall, and although it hurt, I didn't think it was broken.

"I'm okay, dear. Just had the wind knocked out of me," Tilly said. "Guess I have more than enough padding these days."

Unfortunately she'd landed diagonally across my lower back and legs, softening her fall, but grinding me into the coarse, commercial-grade carpeting. As my eyes accommodated to the darkness, I could see that Jim's chair was empty. Maybe he'd gone to use the bathroom in the outer hallway. I was gathering myself to stand up, when I realized he hadn't gone anywhere. He was inches from where I lay, and even in the dim light I could see what looked like a dark bloody halo around his head.

Chapter 2

I felt Tilly's weight shift on me as if she was preparing to get up. By her silence, it was clear she hadn't realized we weren't alone on the floor. Dealing with my own upside-down emotions would have to wait. There were things that needed doing. "Don't move," I said to her.

"Nonsense," she replied, "I told you I wasn't hurt." She tried to leverage herself off the floor and me.

"Don't move," I repeated, "this may be a crime scene." She immediately flopped back down, knocking the breath from my lungs in the process.

"Crime scene?" Her voice rose a shrill octave. For someone who could predict the occurrence of future events, you'd think she'd be less startled, or at least less panic-stricken, by the horrors that can crop up in life. But you'd be wrong. "What do you mean? Kailyn, what's going on?"

"I need you to calm down," I said, trying to keep my own voice even. "We're not in any danger." Although I couldn't know that for certain, a screaming Tilly wouldn't help no matter what the situation was. Besides, I was reasonably sure that if Jim was murdered and the killer was still in his office, we'd already be dead too. *Focus,* I told myself. I knew we had to do our best not to disturb the crime scene, but in spite of all the blood, a little voice in my head was insisting that I check to see if Jim might somehow be alive. I was on my stomach where I'd fallen, but I was close enough to touch him. Trying not to think about what I was doing, I reached over the pool of blood and found his face and neck. The skin was too cool to the touch, but I felt for his carotid artery anyway. I'd never actually done it before, except on myself as a matter of curiosity. What little knowledge I had on the subject, came from watching TV shows. I held my breath to steady myself and walked my fingers along his neck to the spot below his chin where his pulse should have been. Nothing. I checked all over that part of his neck to be sure I hadn't missed it. Jim was truly gone. Tears welled up in my eyes. I dashed them away with my hand. No time for that now. Focus. The best thing I could do for him was not trample any possible clues that might lead the police to his killer. "Okay, Tilly," I said, forcing the words through the tightness in my throat, "I want you to crawl backward to the doorway, but don't get up until I get the lights on. I don't want you to trip over anything and hurt yourself."

Without argument, my aunt hoisted herself off me and did exactly as I asked. "I want to know what's going on, Kailyn," she demanded once she reached the threshold. "Stop treating me like a child for goodness sakes. I won't fall apart."

By then I'd gotten to my feet and found the light switch. The overhead lights flashed on, illuminating the awful scene we'd literally stumbled upon. What I hadn't been able to see in the darkness was the small, round bullet hole in the center of Jim's forehead.

Tilly screamed long and hard as she struggled to her feet. "Sorry, sorry," she gasped when she finally came up for air. "I didn't mean to do that. I'm perfectly fine now, really I am. It was the shock of seeing him lying there like that." She was rocking back and forth on her heels and shivering like a dog in a thunderstorm.

"I know," I said, putting my arm around her quaking shoulders to steady and comfort her. The contact made me feel a bit better too. "Now I'm going to walk you over to Ronnie's desk. You can sit in her chair while I call the police."

"Yes, yes, that's what I should do," she mumbled, allowing me to guide her with my arm around what had once been her waist. After she was seated, I took a minute to try to compose myself. Jim was dead, but my heart ached for Elise, his wife and my best friend. For the shock awaiting her and their two boys. It wasn't as if he'd been suffering through a long illness or was known to have had heart problems. There was nothing in their shared history to prepare them for this.

Once I felt able to speak sensibly, I used the phone on Ronnie's desk to dial 911.

Although New Camel was too small to have a police force of its own, the county kept two officers here on a split shift. They were head-quartered in a small, repurposed bungalow near the center of town. The men were rotated out on a three-month basis, because it was considered too cushy a gig to be permanent. Cushy or not, I'd heard that most of the officers complained of boredom. Until today, the only crime we'd had in the past five years was one pickpocket, one burglary, a counterfeit hundred-dollar bill and the occasional trespasser. I was about to shake things up for sure.

"Officer Curtis, what's the nature of your emergency?" He sounded like I'd taken him away from something more interesting. I heard a baseball announcer in the background.

"This is Kailyn Wilde," I said. "I'm calling to report a murder at thirty-five Main Street. It's our attorney, Jim Hastings."

"Did you say *murder?*" He sounded cynical, as though he thought my call was a practical joke. "Are you aware that it's a crime to file a phony report?"

"I assure you there is a dead body here," I replied stiffly. I almost said something less polite, but this was about Jim, not me.

Curtis didn't seem convinced. "You have to stay there until I arrive, you know. If you're not there, I'll come looking for you. We don't take hoaxes lightly."

"Neither do I, Officer. My aunt and I will be here waiting." Maybe it was the mention of my aunt that rang true, but Officer Curtis was immediately more civil.

"Thank you, ma'am. I'll be there in five minutes." It took him two. He arrived with lights whirling and siren blaring as if he'd actually needed to make it through heavy traffic. In this town, heavy traffic was five cars lined up at a red light.

Tilly had recovered, for the most part, by the time Curtis strode in. He looked maybe thirty, stood about five ten with hazel eyes and light brown hair that had probably been haystack blonde when he was a kid. After a brief exchange, during which I learned his first name was Paul, I led him into Jim's office. He squatted beside the body and felt for a pulse like I had. Apparently satisfied that the victim was indeed beyond help, he stood up and looked around the office before turning to me.

"Why don't we go back and join your aunt," he said to my relief. Jim was my first experience with death, minus the trappings a funeral home provides. The initial shock of discovering him had started to fade and with it, the protective numbness. Standing there at the exact spot where he'd died was becoming harder by the moment. At least Elise had been spared that.

"After you called, I alerted county," he said once we'd rejoined Tilly. "A detective is on his way here along with a forensic unit. I'll be staying until they arrive to protect the crime scene. The detective will want to take your statements. Have either of you touched anything since you got here?" Tilly blanched, and I had a pretty good idea why. While Curtis and I were in Jim's office, she'd no doubt gone through Ronnie's desk drawers. She likes to snoop. She's the guest who peeks in the medicine chest and, given the opportunity, rifles through personal papers on your desk. To her credit, she doesn't have a malicious bone in her body, so anything she finds that would be gossip-worthy is never passed to a third party. She's as true to her own code of ethics as any man or woman of the cloth.

"Yes, we have," I said to divert his attention from her sudden pallor, "because we had no idea we were walking into a crime scene. We touched the doorknobs for starters."

Curtis's lips tugged up in a sheepish smile that almost made me forgive his telephone manners. "Yeah," he said, "how else would you have gotten in here?" I had a feeling this was his first murder too. "It doesn't matter," he went on. "I'm sure the detective is going to take your prints."

"Are we automatically suspects?" I asked. "Why would I have called you if one of us had killed him?"

"It wouldn't be the first time a killer called the cops to throw suspicion off him- or herself."

"Oh," I said, "I didn't think of that. I guess I wouldn't make a very good criminal."

"Look, regardless of whether or not you're suspects, they'd need your prints in order to exclude them from the forensic results."

"I like that reason a whole lot better," I said, though it didn't completely ease my mind.

We spent a few more minutes in awkward conversation before Detective Max Duggan arrived. He and Curtis acknowledged each other, then the patrolman took care of introducing him to us. Duggan took out a little pad and a pen and jotted down our names. He was a good decade older than Curtis, his no-nonsense buzz cut already seeded with gray. His nose looked as if it had been broken a time or two and left to heal on its own; a scar bisected one shaggy eyebrow. If I didn't know better, I'd have thought he was a prize fighter or a drill sergeant.

Curtis escorted him to Jim's office. He returned a few minutes later and said a quick goodbye to us. On his way out, he collided with a gurney piloted by a woman who looked too young for the job. I realized that was something my mother used to say. Twenty-eight and I was sounding like the establishment. Atop the gurney was a folded, black body bag and what I assumed was a forensics case. The woman asked where she could find the crime scene. I pointed the way down to Jim's office.

"I'm getting hungry," Tilly whispered after she walked away. "I wonder how much longer they're going to keep us." No matter the circumstances, you could depend on my aunt's appetite. In grief or joy, fear or illness, it was the one constant no matter what life threw her way. I found that crumb of normalcy very welcome. I walked around the desk to give her a hug. Since she was still seated, I had to make do with putting my arms around her shoulders and giving them a squeeze. "I think it's going to be a while yet," I said.

"I don't suppose they'd let us order a pizza?" she asked wistfully. Leave it to my aunt to put a smile in my heart under the worst circumstances. A moment later the detective returned.

"Okay ladies," he said. "I'm going to ask you some questions so we can try to figure out exactly what happened here." He consulted his memo pad and then looked up at me. "Ms. Wilde, how about I start with you? We can sit over in that little alcove near the door."

It wasn't exactly an invitation I could refuse, so I followed him into the nook that served as a waiting room. He asked how well I'd known Jim and for how long. Why I'd come to the office that afternoon with my aunt. If I was aware of any problems Jim was having, financial or personal. If I'd heard anyone complain about him or his services. I wasn't much help. Although I'd known him most of my life, in a small town way, it was his wife with whom I was close. I hadn't had any direct dealings with him as an attorney, until Bronwen and Morgana died.

"Do you know who worked here with him or for him?"

"As far as I know it was only Ronnie, Rhonda Platt. She was his one employee, his girl Friday. She's been here as far back as I can remember. Jim didn't have any business partners I know of."

"Was Rhonda here when you arrived?" Duggan asked.

"No. She usually leaves at four, and we didn't get here until a little after five."

He looked up from his pad. "You knew Rhonda wouldn't be here when you made the appointment?"

I knew exactly what he was thinking, but I could hardly refuse to answer his question on the grounds that it might incriminate me. Just saying those words was sure to raise whatever suspicions he already harbored. "Well yes," I said with as much poise as I could cobble together. "My aunt and I each run a business here in town and we don't close until five. Jim is always kind enough to wait for us."

"I see." Duggan jotted more notes. "You see anyone else coming or going when you were here?"

"No."

The detective led me step-by-step from the moment we got out of my car, until my 911 call. When he'd run out of questions, I had one of my own. "Who's going to tell Elise what's happened?"

"I'll be doing that as soon as I leave here."

"Is it okay if I'm there with her?"

"Afraid not," he said.

I hadn't expected his response. "Why not?" I blurted out. "She's going to need someone there for support."

"I understand your concern, but until we know more, I have to talk to her alone."

"You don't mean talk, do you? You mean question her."

"I have a job to do," he said in a don't-push-it tone of voice. "Now please tell your aunt to come in here."

Tilly's complexion had turned a little gray in my absence, whether from nerves or a plummeting glucose level, I couldn't tell. We switched places. I sat in Ronnie's chair and she went into the alcove with the detective. Fifteen minutes later, Duggan asked the crime scene investigator to take our prints.

"Detective, do you really think we could commit murder?" Tilly asked in a reedy voice, one hand over her heart as if she was making a pledge to our innocence.

"It's standard police procedure, for the purpose of exclusion, ma'am," he told her, echoing Curtis's words. His tone had become almost kindly. Maybe he was worried that Tilly might have a heart attack and further complicate his evening. Since I knew Tilly better,

I suspected that her overriding concern at that moment had more to do with satisfying her hunger and less to do with any cardiac condition.

The fingerprinting was done with a digital scan that was quick and clean. Once it was over, Duggan told us we could go. "But don't leave town," he added as we walked out the door. If it was an attempt at humor, an accompanying smile or wink would have helped. On its own, the trite warning had a chilling effect.

"That man's never going to win any congeniality contests," Tilly muttered as we walked to my car.

"Congeniality probably isn't in his job description," I said, trying to short-circuit any further discussion of his personality. But I could see by Tilly's expression that she was revving for a comeback. I dove in with a new topic. "Do you want to stop somewhere for a quick dinner?"

"Oh," she said, her train of thought instantly derailed. "How about that new Italian place—Salami's or something?"

"I think you mean Saldano's." Had this been any other day, I would have been tickled by Tilly's habit of reading half a word and adlibbing the rest with what she thought it should be. But today wasn't any other day, and laughter was definitely not an option on my personal menu. In fact I was pretty sure the eating and digesting options were off the table too. Agitation had that effect on me. As I drove the few blocks to the restaurant, I wondered how I'd be able to sit idly by, waiting for the police to find the killer. And how I was going to help Elise through the tragedy that was about to turn her world upside-down.

Chapter 3

After taking Tilly home, I brought Sashkatu back to my house and fed all the cats. Then I drove to Elise's house. Duggan's unmarked car was in her driveway. A few neighbors were standing on their front lawns, ostensibly watching their kids play ball in the street, but no doubt also curious about the unfamiliar car and the cut of the man who went into the Harkens' house. Maybe it was my state of mind, but they looked like vultures waiting for their chance at the carrion.

I parked at the curb, determined to wait for the detective to leave no matter how long it took. Elise had to be in shock. How could she be expected to comfort her boys in such a state? By the time Duggan emerged, I'd been on the brink of trying a spell to hurry him on his way. I was almost disappointed that it didn't come to that. He saw me waiting and gave me a stiff nod of consent that I didn't bother to acknowledge. I was out of my car and onto the porch before he'd backed out of the driveway.

The storm door, with its summer screen, was closed, but unlocked. Beyond it, the front door was wide open. I walked in without ringing the bell or knocking and found Elise and her sons huddled together on the sectional in the family room. She looked up at me, her face blank, her eyes dry but unfocused. *Shell-shocked* was the word that came into my head. The boys, eleven-year-old Noah and fourteen-year-old Zach, were sobbing, their faces red, their eyelids puffy. Noah hiccupped between sobs. I went over to them, knelt on the floor, and stretched my arms around the three of them the best I could.

"Does your family know?" I asked softly. Elise shook her head. "Okay, I'm going to call them. But first, can I get you water or anything?" She shook her head again. I went into the kitchen, found her address book, and started making calls. Her older sister, Gayle, lived two hours away. Her parents were in Florida, her brother in Maine. Gayle was out the door, into her car, and on her way before we hung up. Elise's brother told me he'd make the more difficult calls to Jim's family.

Gayle came through the door in record time and the sisters fell into each other's arms. I left them together in the living room and went back to the boys in the family room. I asked if I could make them something to eat. They both declined. When I suggested having pizza delivered, Noah looked at his older brother for guidance. "All right," Zach said, "I guess I could eat a slice."

Noah nodded solemnly. "I guess I could eat a slice too." The pizza was delivered warm and fragrant. We even talked Elise into eating a few bites. Afterward, I cleaned up the kitchen and hung out with the boys until they were ready for the refuge sleep could provide.

I got home after midnight, slept fitfully, and was up before dawn. A knot of anxiety had taken up residence in my stomach. There was no point in adding caffeine for it to feed on, so I skipped my morning cup of coffee. It was too early to get ready for work or make phone calls, but keeping busy calmed me. Never a problem when you owned a house. I cleaned out the refrigerator and reorganized the linen closet. But when I looked at the clock, it seemed to have moved one tick forward, two tocks back. I gave up and hit the shower. After toweling dry, I peered at myself in the mirror. I'd be thirty in less than two years, and so far the family recipes were doing their job, holding back any signs of that momentous occasion.

Genetics had dealt me a favorable hand overall. I had my mother's oval face and high cheekbones and my father's dark coloring. Bronwen claimed I had her mouth and nose, but my lips were not as full, my nose not as straight. I'd been told more than once that I had an exotic look, which I took to mean I wasn't everyone's cup of tea. It didn't bother me. I'd never coveted a beauty queen's tiara. I combed my hair and pulled it back in a large barrette at the nape of my neck, brushed black mascara on my lashes and blush on my cheeks. Then I shimmied into one of my sundresses and padded back down to the kitchen to force-feed myself breakfast. I settled on an English muffin, because it seemed basic enough for my stomach to tolerate.

By then the cats were up and about. I noticed they were acting a little off, less tolerant of each other, more demanding of my attention. Maybe they were picking up on my edginess. Two of them tried to follow Sashki and me out the door when we were leaving for the shop. Sashkatu swatted at them as he walked out, his tail high in the air in a feline snub.

He and I made the short trek down my walk and across the lane that separated the front of my house from the back of Abracadabra. Once inside, Sashki climbed his custom-built stairway to the windowsill, stretched out on his cushion, and, with a sound somewhere between a purr and a deeper groan of satisfaction, promptly fell asleep. Two years earlier, when he'd started having problems jumping up on things, my mother had hired a well-known carpenter in the area to build him several sets of steps. The distance between the risers was calculated to be a perfect match for the length of his legs. One set stayed in the shop, the other two in the house. They all had wheels and little parking brakes to ensure that they wouldn't roll when in use on the hardwood. Sashkatu had always been a bit of a diva, but lately if any of the other cats tried to use his steps he literally had a hissy fit.

I'd always loved the shop, which, according to family lore, had been established by a British ancestor well before the Revolutionary War. I didn't know much more about its history or my family's, for that matter, because my mind always wandered off when my mother tried to impart it all to me. I was sure there'd be plenty of time to learn the boring details. I certainly never expected to lose most of my links to the past as soon or as suddenly as I did. I guess my mother understood how unpredictable life could be and how easily one could run out of time.

When I was a child, the shop had seemed older than time and full of delightful, ancient mysteries. Although I was no longer in awe of its secrets, I still felt cosseted and safe within its walls. Built of fieldstone, with a wonderful, arched wooden door, Abracadabra stood out from the other quaint shops of New Camel like a diamond in a display of dull quartz. My favorite part of the shop had always been the mullioned windows on either side of the door, the panes of glass separated into diamonds by black wooden dividers. Being there was usually enough to center me. But that day, my mind kept rocketing back and forth between Jim's murder, Elise's grief and the fact that Tilly and I were suspects.

There was a time not long ago, when the shop was always bustling with customers and keeping busy wasn't a problem. I looked around me, needing some distraction. There wasn't a mote of dust to be cleaned away. All the bills that were due had been paid. I peeked in the connecting door to Tilly's shop. If she wasn't with a customer, I'd ask her to brew up a pot of tea for us. She made her own special blends, and the one she called the *soul soother* I'd found helpful in trying times. But my aunt was be-turbaned and absorbed in reading someone's palm. Truth be told, Tilly didn't need palms, crystal balls, head bumps, or tarot cards to give someone a reading. They were merely props that set the stage and added drama to what would other-wise have been a simple, straightforward reading that took five minutes or less. No one wanted to pay a hundred dollars for a five-minute soliloquy. They wanted the whole shebang. Almost everyone who came for "the show" also stayed for the proper English Tea she served at an additional price. It came complete with tiny crust-less sandwiches, scones with jam and clotted cream, imported from England, and an assortment of little pastries. The odds were Tilly would be busy with her client for another hour or more.

As it turned out, I shouldn't have worried about keeping myself occupied. As soon as I returned to my desk, the doorbells jingled. I looked up to find Beverly Ruppert marching toward me with the look of a woman on a mission. Beverly considered herself a friend of the family, although none of us have ever shared that opinion. She was also a regular in the shop. She swore by our neck cream and the fine line-erasing balm, but that morning she didn't look at all like a happy customer.

"Hi Beverly," I said, wondering what had put her in such a dour mood. "How are you?"

"Not well," she said. "The last bottle of erasing balm I bought isn't working. There must be something missing from the formula. Look." She leaned across the counter and turned her head so that I could see the problem for myself. What I saw were tiny lines radiating from the outside corner of her eye. Since I hadn't seen her at such close range when the balm *was* supposedly working, I had no means of comparison. "Have you been sticking to Morgana's formula?" she asked before I could explain that to her.

"I certainly intend to, but the bottle you're using was made by my mother. I haven't run through enough of her stock yet to make a new batch."

Beverly was clearly unsettled by this news. "Oh," she said, momentarily at a loss for words. "How . . . how is this possible then? I've never had a problem with any of your products before. Could Morgana have made a mistake with the formula? Could one of the ingredients be ineffective or expired?"

"I wish I knew," I said. The complaints we'd been getting involved different products at different times and appeared to be so random that we'd all been stumped. That was why my mother had started looking for a new familiar. It wasn't the kind of thing we talked about with friends and customers. Although some may have wondered if we were actual sorcerers, no one had ever asked us point-blank, which probably meant they didn't really want to know. "If you'd like to try a different bottle, please help yourself," I offered.

"Thank you," Beverly said, immediately going off to grab one. "I suppose I shouldn't be focused on such a trivial problem," she went on when she returned to the counter. "It seems like everything is going wrong in this town lately. First that horrible accident that killed your mom and grandmother, and now Jim murdered right in his own office."

"The ME hasn't made that determination yet," I pointed out.

"Maybe not, but I talked to Lou, from the cleaners across the street from Jim's office, and he saw the cops and crime scene investigators carrying tons of stuff out—computers and boxes full of who knows what. They don't do that when a person dies of natural causes," Beverly summed up with an air of authority. "And you and poor Tilly—" her voice lurched to a stop with dramatic angst. "I can't begin to imagine how you're coping, after finding him like that. It must have been so awful." There was a definite, question-like uptick at the end of her sentence.

"If you don't mind, I'd rather not talk about it," I said.

"Well sure, I understand completely."

I gave her a little smile of appreciation, although she'd sounded more disappointed than understanding.

"Jim was my attorney at one time, but I also knew him and his family from church. This has to be so hard for Elise and the kids." She looked at me with eyebrows arched as if once again hoping I'd share. "Jim was such a nice man," she went on when I didn't rise to her bait, "a pillar of the community, as they say. I can't imagine who would have wanted to kill him. I don't suppose you heard anything around town recently that might point to a possible killer?"

I shook my head instead of saying what was on my tongue, namely that any rumors of that sort would most likely have originated with her. I was trying to think of a polite way to end our conversation when dear Aunt Tilly arrived by way of the connecting door. She shambled up to the counter where we stood, sans turban and barefoot, in deference to her corns. Although my heart lifted at her appearance, it went into freefall once I saw her expression. It looked like another problem was about to wash up on my already overcrowded shore.

She and Beverly exchanged perfunctory greetings. I knew Tilly wasn't fond of her for a laundry list of reasons, not the least of which was the way she always tried to grub a free reading whenever she bumped into my aunt.

"There she is, the poor dear," Beverly said, reaching out to put her arm around Tilly's floral-print shoulders.

Tilly foiled the attempt with a nimble enough side-step to the right. "Hello Bev, how are you?"

"Shouldn't *you* be telling me?" she asked, chuckling at her own cleverness. The line might have been funny the first time she'd used it, but by time ninety-four, it had definitely lost its luster.

Tilly's brows lowered over her eyes in a dark frown that was rare for her. "I get the feeling there's some kind of electrical trouble at your house," she said ominously. All that was missing were some ominous chords in the background.

Beverly's eyes widened. "Oh no, oh my goodness; I'd better get back home. Thank you," she said, plucking her free erasing balm off the counter before running out the door.

I turned to Tilly. "Is there really a problem at her house?"

"I have no idea; I just needed to get rid of her." The grim line of Tilly's mouth kept me from laughing.

"What's wrong?"

"It happened again. I wasn't able to do a proper reading on my last client."

It had happened once before, five months ago. "Do you think it's being caused by the same thing that's been messing with our mojo here?" I was still finding it difficult to say *my* instead of *our,* when talking about Abracadabra.

"I hope not," Tilly said with a sigh. "If it keeps happening, rumors will start spreading, and I can kiss my reputation, clientele, and income goodbye."

"Everyone has an off day now and then. You can always say you were fighting a bug."

"I suppose," she said without much conviction.

The first time the problem cropped up, my mother and grandmother had tried to remedy the situation. And for five months it seemed like they had. "Maybe the spell they used wore off and you're in need of a booster shot," I suggested. I didn't mention the possibility that the last time the problem may have gone away on its own and not because of their help. That would mean having to wait it out, and patience was not Tilly's strong suit. "Do you remember what spell they used the last time?"

Tilly wagged her head dismally. "I meant to write it down, because Morgana and Bronwen were awful about keeping their files updated. But I guess I was so relieved to be functioning properly, I dove back into work and never quite got around to it."

"Not to worry," I said, managing to keep my tone light, although the odds of my finding it had plummeted to the sub-basement. I didn't have anything close to the experience that my mother and grandmother had had. I was like an intern suddenly left in charge of a complex corporation when the auditors are about to arrive. There was always a chance my efforts could make matters worse. "I should be able to figure it out," I went on in the spirit of positive thinking. I had to try. I couldn't bear to see my usually buoyant aunt so despondent. My one ace in the hole was the possibility that one of our dearly departed might pop in for a chat or a rant. Either would do as long as I had the opportunity to ask about the spell they'd used. I'd tried summoning them a couple of times since they'd been gone, but never received a timely response or a visit. "Is it possible the client was blocking you?" I asked. It wouldn't make much sense, but I wanted to be sure we covered all the bases. I was constantly amazed by the things people did.

"I've never had a client come in for a reading who had something to hide."

"You can tell the difference between your loss of ability and someone blocking your ability?"

"Absolutely. That first time and again today, it was like an electrical brownout in that part of my brain. But when a person blocks me, my mind feels as if it's hit a stone wall."

Last resort. "Have you ever tried the spell to make a malady disappear?" I asked.

"You don't mean the Abracadabra," she said as if I'd suggested an old wives' tale. Although it was the name of our shop, we'd never had much success with the spell. I'd once proposed changing the name, but was quickly shot down by my three elders, who reminded me that the name had been handed down through countless generations. It was sacrosanct. End of discussion.

"It can't hurt to try it," I said, "until we come up with something better."

"I write the word on a piece of paper, then go to the next line and write it again, leaving off one letter. I keep doing that until there are no letters left."

"Right. It should look like an upside-down triangle."

"Then I roll up the paper and wear it in a locket around my neck," she said in a monotone, like a child reciting something learned by rote. "And the problem is supposed to disappear the way the word did."

"Exactly," I said trying to rouse her enthusiasm. Spells don't work if you don't believe in them. "Why don't you go home, put your feet up and give it a shot." She was clearly in no state to help me search through the haystack of papers that passed for my mother's filing system. Years ago, Morgana had bought a cabinet and folders to organize everything, but she'd never actually gotten around to transferring any of the paperwork into it. Stuffed into plastic bags, it was all still crowded into the narrow coat closet in the shop.

Tilly, who was generally quick to volunteer for any project, ambled off without argument, which told me my instincts about her state of mind were correct. A moment after she disappeared into her shop to close up for the day, my front door opened and Elise walked in.

She was the last person I'd expected to see in my shop. "Is anything wrong?" I asked, grabbing her in a hug. "Sorry, talk about a stupid question."

She gave me a lopsided smile. "I know you meant is anything *else* wrong? Thankfully no, but I needed a few minutes of sanctuary. I'm exhausted." She let herself fall back against the counter. "There are too many decisions to make at a time when I'm not thinking clearly. You went through it with your mom and grandmother, so you understand." I nodded. "And my house is in a whirlwind. I can't tell from one minute to the next how many people are there. Family from my side, family from Jim's. They've been driving in and flying in since early this morning. More are arriving all the time."

"Do you want to go into my house where you can sit? Or there's the desk chair behind the counter." One of these days I really had to get another chair for the shop.

"This is fine. I can't stay long." She put her hand to her mouth as if she'd realized we might not be alone. "Is there anyone here?" she whispered.

"Nope."

She sighed. "On top of everything else, Duggan came back this morning with more questions. Did I know if Jim had any enemies? The only one I could think of was Edward Silver, the dentist. They weren't friends anymore, but I hardly think he would kill Jim."

"Did Duggan think it could have been a robbery gone bad?" I asked.

"As far as I know, Jim never kept cash or valuables in the office, but a random thief wouldn't know that. Duggan wanted me to go over there with him to see if anything was missing. Ronnie offered to go instead. She has a much better idea of what's supposed to be there and she wants to tie up some legal odds and ends anyway. To be honest, I'm not ready to face the office yet." Easy to understand. Jim was murdered there. The blood-stained carpet would still be there to mark the spot where he'd died. She was quiet for a moment. "Did the office look to you like it had been ransacked?" she asked. "Like the killer was looking for something in particular?"

Now that I thought about it, aside from the hideous bloodstain, the office had looked as clean and tidy as on my previous visits. No one had rifled through drawers, upended furniture, or strewn papers around. There was a good chance the intruder had come to Jim's office with nothing less than murder in mind. I shook my head. "No, it was the same as always. Did the detective say if they found any clues? Anything useful?"

Elise put her hand to her forehead. "I can't believe I didn't tell you right away. My head is a sieve. They found a gun in the garbage bin behind the building. Once forensics has a chance to run their tests, they'll know if it's . . . if it's the murder weapon." Elise stammered over the last words.

It had to be the right gun. What were the odds it was another random gun someone happened to throw away behind Jim's office on the day he was shot to death? "If it is the murder weapon, it should lead the police in the direction of the killer, instead of focusing on you," I said. At the very least, the forensic results should put us all a bit lower on Duggan's suspect list. Then why wasn't I feeling more upbeat about the discovery?

Elise looked at her watch. "I'd better get home before my family sends out the militia to find me. I turned off my phone when I left the house. By now I'm sure someone's noticed I'm missing."

Business dropped off a couple of hours before closing. It was a perfect time to search for the spell my mother had used on Tilly in the past. I went over to the closet and dragged out the first of five large plastic bags. After I dumped the papers onto the counter, I started picking my way through the hodgepodge. There were receipts, recipes, spells, ideas for recombinant spells, photos, and scraps of paper with random numbers and names. I felt as if I was rifling through the attic of my mother's brain. This was going to take a lot longer than I'd originally thought, and there was no guarantee I would ever find what I was looking for.

I was well into the sorting of papers when it struck me why I wasn't more pleased to hear about the gun that was found.

Its location bothered me. What self-respecting killer would casually toss a murder weapon into a garbage bin so close to the scene of his crime? After giving it some thought, I came up with three possible reasons that would make sense. The killer panicked and wanted to get rid of the gun before the police caught up with him; or he was on an ego trip, daring the police to find him; or he was trying to frame someone else for the crime. The third option seemed the most likely to me. If I was right, any fingerprints found on the gun wouldn't belong to the killer, but to the person he wanted to frame.

Chapter 4

Ronnie Platt called at eight the next morning, with profuse apologies for the earliness of the hour. I assured her we'd been up for a while, with the exception of Sashkatu, who was on the fast track to setting a Guinness world record for most hours slept by a cat. The rest of my clowder was assembled in the kitchen with me, busy licking out the remnants of each other's breakfast bowls, while I worked on my second cup of coffee.

"I asked Detective Duggan if I could go into the office this morning to tie up some things now that Jim . . . isn't there," Ronnie said with a catch in her voice. "He wasn't thrilled, but I explained that a law firm isn't like a dry cleaners or a grocery store. Legal matters have to be addressed in a timely manner. I need to file court papers, contact clients, give them their files, and recommend other attorneys in the area."

"Then they've finished investigating the, uh, the scene?" I asked. We were both avoiding the more specific words, as if Jim might somehow return to life if we didn't say *dead* or *murder* aloud.

"No, they're sending Officer Curtis along to make sure I don't disturb things."

"Do you want me to come in with Tilly to sign those papers?" I asked, thinking that was why she'd called. I wouldn't have minded taking a closer look around the place now that Jim had been relocated to the ME's office. Maybe I'd find a clue that had escaped everyone else's notice, a clue that would bring the case to a swift conclusion. To my mother's and grandmother's chagrin, I'd grown up with my nose buried in mysteries. When I wasn't reading about detectives, I was on the lookout for a mystery I could solve, a search that went woefully unfulfilled. So it came as no surprise that the prospect of trying my own hand at detective work immediately appealed to me. Besides, where could I find a more motivated sleuth?

"Actually I thought I'd stop by your shop on my way home," Ronnie was saying. "If that's all right."

It took an effort to yank my mind back to our conversation. "Oh . . . sure," I said, more disappointed than I had any right to be. "Whatever is easier for you."

"Great, I'll be there about four."

After we said goodbye, I lingered over my cooling coffee, convincing myself it didn't matter if I couldn't get back into the crime scene right away. I could still take an active role in investigating the case. Surely I'd learned a thing or two from all those mystery books, a sort of reading osmosis. In any case, I couldn't see any downside to giving it a try.

I spilled the dregs of the coffee into the sink and went upstairs to get dressed for the day. If there wasn't exactly a spring to my step, there was at least a more hopeful feeling in my gut. By the time I was ready to leave the house, Sashkatu had finally roused himself. I found him in the kitchen, lying beside his bowl with the disdainful look of a sovereign whose needs are not being met. He narrowed his eyes at me and uttered a raspy "meow," which I figured was "off with her head." I decided to take his food out to the shop with us, because the other cats would expect to be fed again if they saw him eating. Besides, he'd become a slow eater in his dotage, and I was already late in opening for the day. I doubted there would be customers ready to knock down my door, but it hadn't always been that way, and I still had hopes of turning things around.

It occurred to me that I still hadn't summoned a familiar of my own. How many cats did it take to make one a crazy, cat lady? I suspected I was already teetering on the brink. Maybe I should try for another species. Maybe a dog? I'd pined for a dog as a kid. Now that I didn't have to please anyone but myself, why shouldn't I have one? I would have to wait until the moon was full for the spell to work, though. I hadn't been paying much attention to the night sky lately, but I knew I could find the answer on the Internet. If Morgana or Bronwen had been privy to my thoughts, they would have pointed out that computers made us lazy and alienated us from nature. If I'd been monitoring the night sky, instead of my computer screen, I would already know the answer. I conceded that imaginary round to them.

I commuted the fifty feet across my front lawn and the road to the back of the shop, the grass dense and springy beneath my sandals. Sashkatu ambled behind me like a lazy shadow. Although he'd always been, first and foremost, my mother's cat, we'd had a lot of good times together back when he and I were younger. Whenever I sat down to read, he would curl up in my lap and I'd read aloud to him. I know he enjoyed hearing the soft drone of my voice, even if he didn't understand the words. He'd purr and preen and sigh deep, peaceful sighs that resonated inside me. The memory brought with it a bittersweet, nostalgic ache for what had been and would never be again. Back then my family had been whole, although minus the men, a protective circle within which I didn't have a care in the world. Okay, that wasn't entirely true. In my teens, I'd raged against my mother's injustices, feeling like I had no options in my life. That I'd been born into my family for one reason—to continue the lineage. But Morgana was smart. She let me go to college in Vermont to "find myself." I changed majors five times, spent my junior year in England, and finally graduated with a bachelor of science in botany. Still searching for myself, I found my way back home. From what my grandmother told me that first day back, I'd followed my mother's journey to a surprising degree.

I unlocked the back door of the shop, turned off the security system, and waited for Sashkatu to saunter in. Then I set the bowl of cat food on the floor behind the counter, because he'd always preferred dining in private. When I opened the front door for business, no one trampled me in their rush to come in.

Abracadabra was located in an ideal spot on a corner of Main Street at the center of town. According to Bronwen, it had been there long before the rest of the town, which slowly grew up around it over the years. Across the narrow side street, Lorelei Donovan, known to us all as Lolly, was sweeping the sidewalk in front of her fudge shop. We waved to each other. I'd always thought she was the perfect proprietor for a candy store. She was in her seventies now, with a ready smile, rosy cheeks, and an ample roundness from sampling more of her stock than was strictly necessary. She also taught classes in making fudge, which Tilly and I had once attended. What I remember most from the experience was how much we laughed.

"I hope we get a good crop today," Lolly said, beaming with her usual good humor.

"Crop?" I repeated.

"We have that bus tour due in at eleven."

"Wow, it completely slipped my mind." It was a good thing she'd reminded me or the tour group might have caught me in the middle of an avalanche of my mother's papers. I'd planned to go through more of the bags, but that would have to wait until the bus left. With the current financial state of my business, I couldn't afford to put off a single potential customer by appearing less than a hundred percent attentive.

"With all you've been through lately, my dear," Lolly said, "it's a wonder you remember to put one foot in front of the other." She wagged her head in sympathy.

"Thanks for the heads-up. I hope it's a good day for both of us!"

Lolly wished me the same, and I hurried back inside to straighten up. How could I have forgotten about the bus tour? A substantial part of the shop's revenue came from the busloads of people who came to New Camel on one-day excursions. They helped spread the word about our town and that brought in more tourists. Abracadabra and Tea and Empathy were always two of the most popular shops. In fact, it was rare for anyone to leave without making a purchase from me. At the very least, anything procured in an "authentic magick shop," which was how we were listed in the tour guides, would serve as a great conversation piece when the tourists returned home.

My spirits buoyed by the prospect, I nearly flew around the shop, straightening jars and bottles, wiping away dust and spider webs that had appeared overnight as if by a magick of their own. Having licked his bowl clean, Sashkatu was enthroned on his tufted windowsill, watching me with what I could swear was amusement. The ends of his tiny lips were canted up, and there was a definite twinkle of mirth in his eyes. If he could speak, he'd surely be quoting Shakespeare to me, something along the lines of, "Lord what fools these mortals be."

"You should be glad you don't have opposable thumbs," I told him, "or I'd have you cleaning to earn your keep." Never the fool, himself, Sashkatu closed his eyes and snuggled deeper into the eiderdown. By the time the bus arrived, the shop was sparkling, and I was ready to be a cheerleader for all things magickal.

This time the tourists were middle-aged and older women, part of a church group that hailed from Buffalo, which was east of us. They were chatty and curious, remarking to one another about the beauty products, which they hadn't expected to find in my shop, and asking me countless questions about the uses of the more esoteric items like dragon sticks and pulverized lodestones. At least a half dozen of the women were sorely disappointed to learn that Tilly was ill, which is what she'd instructed me to say when she'd decided not to open her shop again until she was healed. No pressure, Kailyn.

The women told me they'd made the trek to New Camel primarily for the purpose of having a reading with Tilly. I guess it was a good thing that my aunt never made appointments in advance and took clients on a first-come-first-served basis. No guarantees meant fewer complaints. And since she was "ill," they all seemed to realize that complaining would hardly be the productive or generous way to handle their dismay.

The bus was scheduled to depart promptly at three o'clock, and I was grateful it wasn't an hour later. After ushering the last customer out the door, I collapsed into the chair at my desk. There was no denying how much the day's revenue was going to help my bottom line, but I hadn't known that standing at the register could wear you out this way. Watching Morgana and Bronwen from the sidelines, or working alongside them, the job had seemed like easy money for a minimum of effort. But since they'd been gone, I'd been given a crash course in reality. And the store's hours were only one part of the business. There were books to reconcile, bills to pay, and products to prepare, some of which required ingredients only found in the wild. Our shop had long been considered the source of essential elements by other, "lesser" witches, wizards, and sorcerers, as Bronwen had always referred to them. During my rebellious years, I'd called her out for being so pretentious. "It's not pretension," she'd replied, "it's simply a fact."

Sashkatu stepped down from his soft perch onto my shoulder and from there jumped into my lap, making me realize I'd better cut back on his food now that he wasn't getting much exercise—make that any exercise. He'd slept through the hectic day, opening his eyes occasionally to survey his domain and see if he was missing out on anything important—like food. Sitting for the first time in hours, I was aware of how thirsty and hungry I was. My morning coffee was the one thing I'd consumed all day. Under normal circumstances, I would have popped into Tilly's shop for a quick scone, but she was elsewhere awaiting her cure. I stroked Sashkatu's silky coat, wondering if there might still be some leftovers from her last day at work. No harm in looking. The cat's ears pricked forward as if he'd read my thoughts. I set him on the floor, and he led the way to the connecting door. I flicked on the lights and went into the small kitchen where Tilly often prepared the goodies for her teas. There was a paper plate on the counter holding two scones. My stomach gurgled as I peeled back the plastic wrap covering them. One blueberry, one cranberry pecan. I took the plate. No point in having to come back. Sashkatu was delighted with my decision. He serenaded me with his entire repertoire of sounds on our way back to Abracadabra. How could I put him on a diet today and then eat the scones right in front of him? His diet would have to wait until tomorrow. I was clearly an enabler. We were almost done sharing the second scone when Ronnie Platt walked in.

I brushed the last crumbs into the wastebasket as she came up to the counter, carrying a large messenger bag. Without her usually flawless makeup, she looked like a faded copy of herself. I'd never actually met her until after Morgana and Bronwen died, although I had answered the phone once or twice when she'd called from Jim's office to talk to them. I knew through the small town grapevine that she'd started working for Jim straight out of college. And there she'd stayed for the past fifteen years. Although she hadn't been related to him by blood or marriage, she'd probably spent as much time with him as his family had. His sudden death had to be tough on her too. I offered my condolences.

She managed a thin smile as she hoisted the messenger bag onto the counter. It landed with such a thud that it might have been filled with rocks instead of papers. "Thank you, Kailyn. You're the first person to acknowledge my loss. Jim wasn't only my employer, he was also my mentor, my friend"—she gave a self-conscious laugh— "my work husband. I believe that's the phrase they use these days. Don't get me wrong, I'm not saying I should be treated like part of his family. But it's nice to know that someone realizes this is hard for me too."

I nodded and waited an extra moment out of respect before changing the subject to business. "You need me to sign those papers, right?"

"I know you had an appointment with Jim to do that," Ronnie said, opening the messenger bag. "The problem is that I'm not qualified to go forward with much of anything on my own." After a few seconds of rummaging through its contents, she withdrew a manila folder with *Wilde* typed neatly on the tab. "This is your mom's paper file and there's a thumb drive in the pocket with the information on it as well. I included the names of a few attorneys in the area, ones Jim knew and recommended in the past when he couldn't take on more work. I'm sure any one of them will be able to handle your legal affairs properly."

I thanked her and took the folder, stowing it on the shelf behind the counter where I kept my handbag. "It must have been uncomfortable for you at the office today," I said to make conversation, because she didn't seem ready to leave now that she'd taken care of business.

"It felt all wrong without Jim there," she said. "Almost like I was trespassing where I didn't belong. And Curtis—I know he had a job to do—but he was watching me like a hawk. No, make that a vulture. I think he would have followed me into the bathroom if it hadn't been off the public hallway."

"Duggan interviewed me and my aunt right after we found Jim," I said in the spirit of commiseration. "I'd never even gotten a parking ticket before and suddenly I was one motive away from being accused of murder."

"When he came to my house that night to tell me about Jim, I was in a state of shock," she said. "But he started right in asking me all these questions. I couldn't think straight. I mean, what if he misconstrued something I said? I was afraid he was going to slap on the handcuffs and cart me off to jail." I could feel the confusion and panic of that night rolling off her as she spoke. It was a good thing she was venting it. She needed to calm down before she got back in her car. The distracted driver who'd killed my mother and grandmother was still fresh in my mind. "I've already got one strike against me," Ronnie was saying. "Opportunity."

"Same with us. But Duggan's a pro. He'll find the killer." Or I will. I sounded a lot more confident than I felt. It wasn't easy with gloom and doom nearly choking the air out of the shop. "The police still need to prove motive, and none of us had one." Assuming she was telling the truth.

"I'm worried about Elise," she said, apparently determined to keep fretting. "I overheard Curtis on the phone with Duggan today. I was busy printing and photocopying, so he probably thought I couldn't hear him over the noise. They were talking about the gun they found, and I could swear he said, 'it was Jim's?' like he couldn't believe what Duggan was telling him."

That hit me hard. If Jim owned the gun that was used to kill him, it begged the question of who'd had access to it. Elise must have popped to the top of Duggan's leaderboard. "Do you know if they found any prints on the gun?"

"I didn't hear anything about that," she said, "but I'm surprised the ME hasn't issued his findings yet on the cause of death. A bullet in the head seems pretty cut and dry."

"He must be waiting for all the tests to come back. I'm sure they have a certain protocol to follow."

"I suppose." She lifted the messenger bag off the counter. "Do you know if the plans for Jim's funeral have been finalized yet?"

"I'm glad you reminded me. It's been a crazy day. I told Elise I'd call some people for her, and you're on my list." I gave her the details about the wake, scheduled for that night and the funeral, scheduled for the next morning. Then she left to finish her rounds. I planned to attend both, to support Elise as well as to trawl for clues. It wasn't often you found most of New Camel gathered in one place.

Chapter 5

After feeding the cats and cleaning out the litter boxes, I jumped in the shower, then changed into a black pencil skirt and white blouse that seemed more appropriate for a wake than the pink-and-green peasant dress I'd been wearing. I exchanged my silver, high-heeled sandals for black peep-toes and drove to the next block to pick up Tilly. After Uncle Albert died, she'd remained in the house where they'd lived. My mother and grandmother had tried to coax her into moving when the house next to ours came up for sale, but she'd stood firm. She preferred to stay where she was—it was home. Besides, it was only a block away. By the time I'd grown into adulthood, I realized she'd made the right decision. The bickering between my mother and Bronwen was bad enough; adding another personality to the mix would have been catastrophic. I think all the cats would have left home, and I wouldn't have been far behind them. Although I loved and missed the family matriarchs, I didn't miss the drama. Had they lived, I'd probably be looking for a house of my own about now.

Tilly was waiting for me on her porch swing. She hated wearing black, so she'd opted for her one muumuu in sedate earth tones that did a nice job of setting off her fiery red hair. But the look must have been too minimalist to suit her, because gold bangles bedecked her wrists and gold hoops hung from her earlobes.

Once we were on our way, I primed Tilly to be alert for bits of conversation that might provide clues to Jim's killer or suggest a path I could follow in my investigation. Tilly thought that was a dandy idea. She'd lurk in the shadows and tiptoe around on little cat toes. No one would catch on to what she was doing. *Stealthy* would be her watchword. The images her words brought to mind immediately made me regret enlisting her help.

The parking lot of the funeral home was almost full when we arrived. I wanted to believe it was a tribute to how well Jim had been respected and liked by the community, but I knew it was also because of the manner in which he'd died. Nothing newsworthy ever happened in our town, unless you counted the annual Camel's Day Fair, so I was sure plenty of the people were there to learn more about Jim's murder and the life that had led to it. For all I knew, the killer himself—or herself—would put in an appearance to deflect suspicion and to find out if he or she was on anyone's radar yet.

Walking up to the front door of the funeral home, we had to maneuver around groups of middle and high school kids who populated the path and lawns, some laughing and flirting as if they were at a social event. I remembered being their age and believing that death was something that happened only to old people. It was sad to think that Jim's kids would no longer be carefree in that way. When we stepped inside, the mood changed instantly. There was no doubt that we'd entered a place for solemn ritual. The thick carpeting absorbed the sound of our footsteps and the soft lights were kind to eyes red from grieving.

We had no trouble finding the room where Jim lay in repose. Although there were ushers standing by, all we had to do was follow the people ahead of us. We wended our way through the crowd that had spilled out of the Harkens' room into the wide hallway, pausing to exchange whispered greetings with everyone we knew. Between Tilly and me, that covered a good eighty percent of those in attendance, which made our progress slow. Inside the visitation room, we made our way down the center aisle to Elise, who was standing beside the closed casket, with her two boys, stiff and straight in their suits. Elise looked calm and composed as she accepted condolences from the people ahead of us. She was as pretty as ever, her delicate features perfectly framed by the chin-length cut of her auburn hair. She had a quiet elegance about her even when she was in sweatpants.

When I finally came face to face with her, we hugged and held onto each other for a few extra beats. Noah and Zach were dry-eyed, but pale. When I hugged Zach he was very still, his jaw clenched fiercely, determined not to show emotion in front of his friends. My hug was no more than a brief, gentle pressure before I moved on.

With Noah, I felt his breath catch in his chest as I hugged him. I knew if I didn't walk away quickly, he would start crying in the safety of my arms. I'd been the boys' babysitter for a long time and I still came "to keep Noah company," as we put it, when no one else was at home. It was part of a beautiful circle that had started with Elise as my sitter when I was young. At that time, the twelve years between us was huge, but after I reached adulthood, those years meant nothing.

Following me, Tilly pulled Elise into a tight embrace, nearly smothering her in silk muumuu. No doubt fearing a similar fate, both boys stretched out their right hands well before she reached them. Thankfully, Tilly was astute enough to understand. As we moved away to make space for the next visitors, I took a quick survey of the room. Many of the pews were filled with people engaged in muted conversation. There was no way we could slide in and out of rows to listen for an interesting topic, without being obvious about it. Our best bet was to circulate among those assembled in the hallway. I was a little surprised to find that the number of people out there had increased during the ten minutes we'd been in the room. Stealthy Tilly gave me a wink and set off on her fact-finding mission. I started working the other half of the hall, meandering around the knots of people and checking my watch as if I was waiting for someone to arrive, in case anyone wondered what I was doing. Pretty much everyone was talking about Jim and the way he'd died. A few expressed concern for Elise, who now had the added burden of being a single parent. Then I heard Beverly Ruppert remark, in a whisper loud enough to turn nearby heads, that she knew for a fact not everything had been "peachy keen" lately in the Harkens' household. Even if I hadn't recognized her voice, she was the only adult I knew who would use a phrase like *peachy keen.*

"Really? How do you know that?" I inquired as I joined her circle. It took all of my willpower to say it like I couldn't wait to hear all the sordid details and not like I wanted to flog her for spreading malicious gossip about Jim and his family.

Beverly turned to me with the look of the cat who'd nabbed the canary and was roasting it for lunch. "I happen to know a lot of people and I'm privy to a lot of secrets."

"Not so fast," said Connie Milhouse, "you can't drop a bomb like that and not elaborate." I was grateful she'd stepped in. I didn't want the discussion to deteriorate into a verbal sniping match between

Beverly and me. The three others in the group chimed in with similar comments. Under normal circumstances, I would have excused myself from such a distasteful discussion, but these were hardly normal circumstances. I was on a mission to find out whatever I could.

"Okay, okay," Beverly said, acquiescing like a diva agreeing to an encore. "I have a friend whose cleaning lady also works for the Harkens." She paused for what I assumed was dramatic effect. "And she overheard Jim and Elise arguing. They were trying to keep their voices down, but she caught a few key words that made her think the late Mr. Harkens may have been fooling around with another woman."

Seeing the smug expression on her face, I finally lost it. Regardless of whether she had more to reveal, I couldn't listen to her for another moment. "A few key words?" I repeated in a steely whisper. "He *may* have been fooling around? Seriously? Maybe you should be less interested in what's going on in other households and more concerned with how people will talk about you when you're gone." I turned sharply on my heel and strode off, leaving Beverly with her mouth hanging open in shock. I was so distracted that I plowed headlong into Detective Duggan.

"Whoa there, Ms. Wilde," Duggan said, putting his arms out to stop me. He was standing at the edge of the crowd with Officer Curtis and a man I'd never seen before.

"Oh sorry, sorry." I said, slamming on my brakes. I wobbled for a moment, but caught my balance before I fell flat on my face. "It's so crowded in here, it's hard to navigate."

"No harm done, though that woman you snapped at might not agree. That's quite a hot temper you've got there."

"And as you just saw, I walk away from situations that provoke it." I gave myself a gold star for having recovered my composure so quickly. From his position beside the detective, Curtis broke into a boyish grin. It was one of those smiles that makes you want to smile back, but I shot down the impulse. I didn't want Duggan to get the idea I was taking Jim's death too lightly.

The stranger held out his hand. "Roger Westfield," he said. "I don't think we've met." He was tall and reedy with wavy brown hair that dipped onto his forehead and would have benefitted from a stylist's attention. My guess was science teacher or CPA.

I took his hand and was about to introduce myself when Duggan cut in. "I was getting to it," he muttered like a child who's been reminded of his manners. "Kailyn Wilde, Dr. Roger Westfield, ME for Schuyler County."

By then our handshake was going on for too long. "Nice to meet you Dr. Westfield," I said quickly, withdrawing my hand before the moment became any more awkward. I couldn't quite picture him cutting up bodies. But what did I know? My experience with medical examiners up until then was based purely on TV shows.

"Ms. Wilde and her aunt are the ones who discovered Harkens' body," Duggan was saying. "Your aunt didn't come with you tonight?" he asked me, as if we were casual friends having a chat.

"She's here, down the hall mingling," I replied. "I need to be getting her home though. So, if you'll excuse me . . ."

"We'll see you around." Duggan said.

Not if I see you first, I thought and clamped my jaw shut to keep the words from spilling out. I did a quick one-eighty, checked for other road blocks, and headed off in Tilly's direction.

"I'm afraid I didn't hear much that was worthwhile," Tilly said once we were back in my car, "but I poked about in the auras of some people and found more dark stuff than I would have imagined. Gave me the willies."

"Guilt?"

"Yeah, along with about a dozen different things that have nothing to do with Jim. It was all an impenetrable morass. I couldn't see anything specific." She sighed and shrugged her shoulders. "Besides, I can't trust my reading of auras or anything else until I've fully recovered."

To be fair, I don't think Tilly was consciously trying to pile on the pressure, but that didn't stop me from feeling it. I promised myself I'd go through the rest of my mother's papers in the morning. I still had one important chore to attend to before I went to sleep.

I dropped Tilly at her house and pulled into my driveway a minute later. The moon was full and platinum bright above me as I walked to the front door and let myself inside. The perfect night for summoning my familiar. Although it had been a long day, I was energized by the prospect of performing the ritual. I changed into my old jeans and a T-shirt and spent the next two hours scrubbing down the house, although I kept it pretty clean on a daily basis. Either Morgana and Bronwen had shown me by example that was the proper way to live, or I'd come by the clean-freak gene more organically. I'd often envied Tilly, who didn't share our compulsion. Not that her home was dirty. But it wasn't surprising to find her breakfast dishes still in the sink at bedtime or the odd hair ball rolling along the floor like tumbleweed, courtesy of her familiar, Isenbale, a huge Maine coon.

When my house was sparkling, I filled the deep soaker tub with warm salt water and immersed myself in it up to my neck. I felt all the tension flow from my body into the water and a delicious peace settle over me. I might have stayed there for hours if the water hadn't started to cool and my pesky conscience hadn't kept nagging at me to get on with the summoning. Putting it off until tomorrow would mean having to clean the house again from top to bottom and I certainly didn't want to sign on for that. So I loofahed myself until my skin was a bright, tingling pink, then dressed in a clean cotton shift and lit a patchouli-infused candle. Candle in hand, I opened the front door of the house and peeked out to see if anyone was around. Fortunately it was late enough that my closest neighbors were asleep or watching TV. I flung the door wide and stood on the threshold to cast the spell.

> "Come to me, my canine friend,
> with a love that will not end.
> Paws and tail and deep brown eyes,
> loyal and gentle, sweet and wise."

There was no hard and fast rule about how long it would take for the spell to work, so I sat down on the floor in the doorway to begin my vigil. Ten minutes passed, fifteen, twenty. I kept thinking I should have bought a fly swatter to keep the flying insects out of the house. After an hour, I was scratching at mosquito bites and too exhausted to keep my eyes open. I could lie down for a while on the doorsill and run the risk of someone finding me still there in the morning, bitten to a pulp, or I could lock up the house and crawl into bed. Bed won out. If my familiar was coming tonight, I hoped he, or she, had a bark loud enough to wake me.

As it happened, I slept undisturbed, the five cats arrayed around me. Sashkatu had sole claim to the pillow next to me, which is where he'd always slept when Morgana was alive. Since I'd started using the master bedroom, he seemed content enough to remain there with me. My first night in that bed, one of the other cats tried to usurp his spot and received a good boxing for his efforts. Sashkatu might be old, but he was still feisty enough to defend his territory.

I opened my eyes to daylight and looked around me. The cats were pretty much where they'd been when I'd fallen asleep, which was unusual. With the exception of Sashki, most nights they played their own version of musical chairs. Perhaps my exhaustion had been contagious. I lay there an extra minute or two, listening for a bark, a plaintive cry, the scratching of nails on the door. Nothing. Apparently this was going to take longer than I'd anticipated.

The funeral began at ten o'clock sharp, the attendance half of what it had been for the wake. Tilly and I were among the few friends who accompanied the family to the cemetery, where the graveside service was mercifully short. Elise maintained her poise, but the facade was showing strain. Her eyes were red-rimmed and her pallor almost ghostly. She had her arms around her children, and her sister and brother had their arms around her. I sent thoughts of solace to comfort them all. I hadn't expected to learn anything more than I had at the wake and I was right. Funerals tend to be more somber, people not as given to chat or gossip when so starkly reminded of their own mortality.

By the time Sashki and I opened the shop, it was noon. If my familiar had arrived while I was gone, I hoped he or she would be savvy enough to find me and patient enough to wait for me. Of course, a familiar who wasn't would probably be lacking some other critical skills as well. In spite of that wisdom, I found myself looking out the window every five minutes. I took another bag of my mother's papers out of the closet and sat down at the counter, determined to keep busy and find the spell that might help Tilly. I was interrupted a few times by local customers, but by midafternoon I'd made my way through the rest of the bags. Unfortunately I had nothing to show for my efforts, unless you counted the recipe for my mother's quiche, which I'd been hunting for in the kitchen, of all places, and the phone number of our plumber.

I tugged the door to the coat closet open without leaving my chair. Emboldened by my success, I sent the bags back to the closet the same way. Halfway there they bumped into each other and the next thing I knew, a hurricane of papers was flying around the shop. I'd have to clean things up by good, old manual labor. It took me fifteen minutes to collect all the papers and stuff them into the bags, then deposit them in the closet. I was walking back to my desk, when a resounding crash made the floor beneath my feet vibrate. Startled from sleep, Sashkatu sprang up and lost his footing on the tufting of his cushion. I managed to catch him as he plunged toward the floor, for which I was treated to half a dozen frantic scratches.

As the worst of the noise faded away, I heard the continuing crinkle of breaking glass. There was only one place it could be coming from—the storeroom. But what could have knocked over the heavy shelving units in there? It occurred to me that I should be armed with a weapon of some sort, because intruders were seldom law-abiding citizens, and I clearly couldn't rely on my telekinetic skills alone. The most lethal thing in the shop was the broom and it was in the storeroom with my uninvited guest. I debated calling 911, but I'd had enough of the police for a while.

I headed for the storeroom as quietly as possible and listened at the door. When I didn't hear anything more, I cracked it open enough to peek inside. Like so many giant dominoes, the four steel units had toppled onto one another, throwing dozens upon dozens of glass jars to shatter on the cement floor, their contents merging into a muddy sludge that was oozing toward me. Standing in the middle of all the chaos, was an elderly man with disheveled white hair and a scraggly beard. He was thin and frail-looking, dressed in a dingy white shirt and baggy pants held up by a drawstring waist, all of which made him look like a scarecrow. Then I noticed that blood was trickling from the bottoms of his bare feet onto the jagged glass that surrounded him. He'd been staring at the floor as if wondering how he could navigate his way to the door without slicing himself to ribbons.

"Ah, Mistress," he said when he saw me, "would you kindly tell me what place this be?"

Mistress? Had this guy taken a wrong turn on his way to a Renaissance Faire? He was doing a pretty good job with the British accent, but where was the rest of his costume? And why was he here? Had he broken in during the night? Then why hadn't the alarm been triggered? The questions were quickly piling up, and I needed to start getting some answers. I considered grabbing the broom and sweeping a path to him, but decided to leave the glass between us as a deterrent for now. Not that he seemed at all dangerous. In fact, he looked more confused about the situation than I was.

"Let's start off with you telling me who you are," I said in my best no-nonsense tone.

His unruly gray brows pinched together in a frown. "Do you truly not know?"

"Truly," I replied, making no effort to mask the sarcasm.

"Mayhap it is my garb that is confounding." He leaned from the waist in a graceful bow. "Dear girl, I am Merlin, of course."

Chapter 6

I couldn't say anything for a minute. I opened my mouth, then closed it, speechless. Did this man really expect me to believe he was the legendary wizard? He looked more like a Don Quixote wannabe. On the other hand, he *had* managed to get through my locks and security system. "Nice to meet you, Merlin," I said, playing along. "How did you get in here?"

"I find myself as puzzled as you, my lady. One moment I was off to the woods to pick mushrooms for my dinner and the next I found myself in this room. I assure you that I never travel far from home clad in such slovenly attire," he added in dismay.

Terrific, it appeared that neither of us knew anything. "Do you know what caused my storage units to fall?" I asked, thinking he looked far too old and frail to have knocked down more than a couple of jars.

"I cannot be certain," he said, "but I believe them to have been a casualty of the same energy wave that brought me here."

An energy wave? Now he sounded like a refugee from *Star Trek.* It occurred to me that he might have been conked on the head when the steel shelving fell. But from where I stood, I couldn't see any blood in the rat's nest of his hair, and I knew from experience that scalp wounds bleed like crazy. I considered my options. I could drive him to the nearest hospital or better still, call for an ambulance. They would take him off my hands and check him out physically as well as mentally. So why was I hesitating? In spite of the implausibility of what he'd said, something about him must have struck me as genuine. After all, implausibility doesn't hold as much sway with me as it might your average person. My entire family could be considered a study in the implausible.

While I was arguing with myself, Merlin had begun to shiver. I decided to take him back home and make him a cup of hot tea. I needed to look at his feet anyway to assess how badly he was hurt. I could clean and bandage simple cuts, but for something worse I'd have to get him to an ER. "I'm going to clear a path for you," I told him, gingerly picking my way through the glass shards to the nearest corner of the room where I kept the broom and cleaning supplies. I swept the glass to the side as I made my way to him, explaining why I wanted to take him to my house.

"What is an ER?" he asked warily.

"It's the part of a hospital where people go when they're injured."

"No," he said tightly, his jaw clenched and the veins at his temples standing out against his pale skin. "No hospital!"

Maybe he had escaped a psychiatric facility after all. "I mean a regular hospital where they can take care of your feet," I added.

"Doctors can kill a man faster than the plague. I can minister to my own wounds. How do you think I have lived to this ripe age?" I had no idea what to say to change his mind, and there was no point in pressing him about it until I'd seen the state of his wounds. "Does St. John's Wort grow in this clime?" he asked. "What about the *Cinnamomum camphora* tree? I will need both for a liniment."

It was becoming more and more difficult to believe that this elderly man was merely pretending to be Merlin. Unless he was a botanist or a warlock, how would he have come by his knowledge of healing plants? Get a grip, Kailyn, I scolded myself. He's some wacky old fool who's probably in need of his medication. "To the best of my knowledge, that tree grows in warmer places than here," I told him, "but I do have some St. John's Wort flowers up front in the shop. I'm afraid the rest is on the floor here, along with most of my stock."

Merlin straightened his shoulders and lifted his chin, which seemed to make him grow in stature. "As I may be to blame for the destruction, I will make complete restitution for your loss," he said in an imperious tone.

"I appreciate the thought, but most of this stuff has to be harvested in the wild."

"I'm well-versed in these botanicals and I will see to it that your shop is returned to its former state with alacrity."

I was about to tell him that an apology would be sufficient, but I had a feeling that apologies weren't part of his repertoire, or he would have offered me one by now. In spite of his unkempt appearance, there was definitely something regal about him. As I led the way down the cleared path to the hallway, I glanced over my shoulder to see how he was doing. He was trying to tough it out and minimize his limp, but the pain was plainly written on his face.

"Wait right here while I get the St. John's," I said. I left him to run up front. I locked the shop door and grabbed a jar with the yellow flowers floating in olive oil. I stroked Sashkatu's back to wake him gently. "Time to go home," I told him. He looked up at me, bleary-eyed, but then his whiskers twitched and he came completely awake and alert. Without further prodding or a single stretch of his limbs, he scooted down the stairs and made a beeline for the hall. I had to run to keep up with him. When we reached Merlin, he uttered a meow that was more like a chirrup of joy and wound his body around and through Merlin's legs with so much pressure that he knocked the old man off balance. Merlin fell back against the wall, but when he saw me, he pulled himself upright again with a grimace of pain and determination. He didn't seem at all surprised or put off by Sashki's over-the-top greeting.

I explained again that I was going to take him back to my house. He nodded and followed me to the rear door at the end of the hallway. I tried, without success, to make Sashkatu back off before he tripped Merlin and made an ER visit a necessity. Merlin mumbled something I didn't understand. Sashki instantly stopped making figure eights and looked up at the old man as if awaiting further instructions. My head was caught in a riptide of questions. Could this old man really be Merlin? How could he be? Could he have traveled through time and space? Or just from the closest psychiatric ward?

I set the security system, opened the door and the three of us stepped outside. I laced my arm through his, so he didn't have to put as much weight on his feet. He started to pull away, but then must have thought better of it. We made our way slowly across the lawn, with me on one side of him and Sashkatu on the other.

I didn't expect any of the cats to greet us. They always know when a stranger enters their realm and they stay hidden until they deem the newcomer worthy of their time and effort. To my surprise, all five of them were waiting at the door when I ushered Merlin inside. They ignored me completely as they jockeyed for position around him, hissing and swatting at one another. Sashkatu, who never deigned to become involved in the other cats' squabbles, joined in the frenzy as if he considered Merlin his personal property. Merlin reached down to stroke each of them, murmuring words I couldn't make out. It wasn't English, at least not modern English. But whatever he said to them, brought immediate results. The cats' behavior changed as if he had flipped a switch inside them. They patiently took turns rubbing against his legs, purring like little engines. I was amazed to see Sashkatu interact with the other cats as though they were his equals. I'd have to remember to ask Merlin his secret. But attending to his feet was the first item on my agenda. Finding out his real name and address, so that I could get him back where he belonged, was the second.

I took him into the bathroom and had him sit on the edge of the bathtub. I sat on the floor to get a good look at the soles of his feet. The cuts were mostly slits, but it was difficult to tell how deep they went. I took it as a good sign that they'd stopped bleeding on their own. Of course there was a chance they might start again when I cleaned them, but if I didn't, he'd be courting infection. The cats had followed us and were sitting in an orderly group beyond the doorway. I'd never known cats to keep all four paws on the ground for this length of time. Merlin didn't seem at all amazed by their behavior. The bathroom, on the other hand, had his undivided attention. He asked me a dozen questions about the various fixtures and appliances, while I was busy gathering gauze, surgical tape, and scissors.

"This is all quite remarkable," he said, as wide-eyed as a child visiting his first candy store. "Does everyone have such conveniences?"

I was filling Bronwen's old foot basin with warm, soapy water. "In this country, most people do." I wanted to kick myself the moment the words left my mouth.

"I take it your reference is to England," he said.

"Sure," I agreed, "let's go with that." I wasn't prepared to give him a summary of world history and geography since the Middle Ages or whenever it was that Merlin was supposed to have lived. Before he could come up with another question, I asked him to put his feet in the basin. "It may sting a bit at first, but it's the easiest way to clean the cuts. He gave the basin a thorough appraisal before dipping the tips of his toes into the water. When nothing terrible happened, he immersed both feet. After a minute, a serene expression settled over his features. I let him enjoy what may have been his first foot bath, until the water started to cool.

"Might there be a mortar and pestle I can use to prepare a poultice?" he asked, taking the towel from me to dry his own feet. I went into the kitchen to find a set. Even in the twenty-first century the primitive mortar and pestle were often better suited to a sorcerer's needs than any modern gadget. While I was in there I set a kettle of water to boil on the stove. Then I brought the tools and the jar of St. John's Wort flowers back to Merlin, who had used my absence to further explore the workings of the toilet. He'd removed the top from the water tank and was fiddling with the flush handle with the curiosity and delight of a child.

"Remarkable," he proclaimed, then got busy using the pestle to mash the oily flowers into a paste. "Judging by the materials in your shop, I take it you, yourself, are practiced in the art of sorcery."

"Yes, but hardly in the same league as the great Merlin. I would love to see you in action," I added, thinking that his abilities, or lack of them, would help clear up the issue of his identity. In spite of my growing suspicion that he was, in fact, the famous wizard, I wasn't willing to become an acolyte without some verifiable proof.

Merlin's lips curved up in a little smile as if he knew what I was thinking. "In due time," he replied, "in due time." Once he'd applied the poultice to his feet, I wrapped gauze around them and secured it with surgical tape. I was congratulating myself on my latent nursing abilities when I realized that if he kept walking around without shoes, the bandages and his wounds would quickly become dirty. I rummaged around in my dresser until I found him a pair of my old tube socks. The fit wasn't great, because his feet were long and knobby, but they would do until I could find a more suitable pair. When I offered my hand to help him up, he pushed it aside, managing to stand on his own.

The kettle had gone from whistling to screeching like a banshee, by the time I plucked it off the stove. Merlin stood in the middle of the kitchen, rotating like a clumsy ballerina, as he tried to take it all in. If he'd been intrigued by the bathroom, the kitchen rendered him nearly catatonic. Worried that he might pass out after all he'd been through, I urged him to have a seat at the table. The cats had followed us and were now arrayed in a circle around him.

Merlin watched me pour the hot water into two mugs, add the tea bags, set out milk, sugar, honey, lemon, and a plate of Oreos, all without asking a single question. I knew it was only a matter of time before he regained his senses and the floodgates burst open. I offered him the cookies. Chewing might slow him down and give me a chance to explain the wonders he was seeing. And they did. I was able to provide a basic explanation of how everything in the kitchen worked, without having him constantly interrupting me with additional questions.

"The tea is barely passable, but these pastries are a delight," he said smacking his lips. He was on his sixth Oreo when I heard the front door creak open. It was either a burglar or Tilly. She had her own key to what my family jokingly called "the ancestral home," where I now lived with the cats. "Aunt Tilly?" I called out, to be sure I didn't need to arm myself with a knife.

"It's me," her voice floated into the kitchen several seconds before she did. "Is everything okay? I went to your shop, but it was . . ." Her feet and tongue stopped dead at the kitchen doorway. Merlin, who'd just discovered the fun of twisting open an Oreo and licking the creamy filling, didn't bother to look up.

"Kailyn?" Tilly finally uttered, looking from me to him and back again.

"I'll explain more later, Tilly, but I'd like you to meet—" I stopped, momentarily stymied by how to introduce my guest. Was Merlin his first name or his last? Did he go by one name the way Elvis had? I decided to go with *Merlin,* since that was how he'd introduced himself to me. "Merlin"—I patted his arm to get his attention—"this is my aunt Matilda."

When he saw Tilly standing there, he jumped up, nearly toppling his chair in the process. "Pleased to make your acquaintance, my lady," he said with a bow and a mouth ringed with cookie crumbs. "I must say—your hair is of a most remarkable shade."

"Why thank you," Tilly beamed, recovering her composure enough to fluff her hairdo like a preening bird. "I see we're having tea?" Either she hadn't heard his name or she was too busy flirting to process it.

"I'll be glad to make you some," I said, "but it's store-bought." I tacked on the disclaimer, because my aunt was a tea snob. She brewed her own mixture and eschewed all tea that came in a bag. To her way of thinking, the tea bag was the first nail in the coffin of civilization. I wasn't crazy about it myself, but I kept it in the cabinet for emergencies like this, although I'd never actually imagined an emergency quite like Merlin.

"That's fine, dear," she replied, lowering herself daintily into the chair beside Merlin. And not fifteen minutes ago, I'd been thinking that this day couldn't get any more bizarre. When the water was hot, I poured her a cup and a refill for Merlin. Then I added more Oreos to the plate. They were Tilly's favorite too. Of the store-bought variety, she always pointed out.

She spent the next hour, happily answering an endless string of Merlin's questions, each answer leading inexorably to another question. Updating the man on the past fifteen hundred years could take a lifetime in itself. When she stopped long enough to sip her tea and make a face like she'd been poisoned, I seized the moment. "Merlin, it's been so nice getting to know you, but I'm sure there are people worried about you. I really have to get you back where you belong."

"I fear that will not be an easy task," he said with a heavy sigh. "As I told you earlier, I believe I was caught up in an energy wave that pulled me out of my time and into yours. And from what your lovely aunt has told me, I've landed in another part of the world as well. The irony of my situation is that I've devoted a good portion of my life attempting to travel through time, but never succeeding. Then, out of the blue, it happens all on its own. Mayhap, a delayed reaction to my efforts. But I have no idea how to reverse the process." He didn't seem particularly concerned about the problem.

Although I heard everything he said, what I took from it was the simple fact that I might well be stuck with him. Of course I still had to check all the hospitals in a twenty mile radius to be sure they weren't missing a patient. If those efforts came up empty, I could call the police, who would no doubt send him off to a hospital to be evaluated anyway. From there it was sure to be a quick trip to a locked psych ward. And there he might spend the rest of his days. If he was actually Merlin, how could I do that to him? In that moment, my decision was made. If he was able to convince me of his claim with a display of magick worthy of the renowned wizard, I would let him stay, at least until we had more time to sort things out.

Chapter 7

"What say you?" Merlin sputtered indignantly. "I am required to prove who I am?" I'd clearly taken him by surprise. Replete with Oreos, he had allowed himself to relax in spite of his current predicament of time and space. We were still seated around the kitchen table, our cups empty, with the exception of Tilly's, and the plate picked clean of cookies.

"My apologies," I scrambled to explain, "but before I invite you to stay here with me, I need to be sure I can trust you. The world is not a safe place today, in spite of how much we may have progressed since your time. In many ways, it's a lot more dangerous. In the past, you had to come face to face with the person you killed. Today someone on the other side of the world can steal your identity or blow up a city with the push of a button." Having lived hundreds of years before the discovery of basic electricity, Merlin was clearly having trouble understanding the concept. Before we got bogged down, answering endless questions, I tried another tack. "You told me earlier that you would show me your magick," I reminded him.

"Everything has a price," he grumbled. I wasn't sure if he was referring to the awful state of the modern world or the cost of proving himself to me, but it didn't matter. "Since I do remember agreeing to a display of my abilities," he went on, "so be it." He pushed his chair back and got to his feet. "Is there anything in particular you'd like me to do?"

My aunt sprang up from her seat, more nimbly than she had in years. "Glamour me."

"Tilly wait," I said, grabbing her arm as if that might actually stop her.

She pulled her arm free of my grasp and turned to Merlin. "Can you make me look like a fire-breathing dragon?"

I cringed. What if he couldn't reverse the spell, and she had to live the rest of her life appearing that way to the world? It would be a whole lot worse for business than having her psychic powers abridged. "Why not start with something simpler?" I suggested. "The poor man should have a chance to warm up. After all, he's probably got the worst case of jetlag in history." I went for the laugh, knowing that it was easier to win Tilly over with humor than with argument. While she mulled it over, I grabbed the napkin holder from the table. "Merlin, would you please make this look like a vase of flowers?"

Merlin looked from Tilly to me and scratched his head, clearly trying to decide to whom he owed his allegiance. Although he'd landed in my store, nearly destroying it in the process, Tilly of the red hair won out. "I'm perfectly capable of a little glamouring before I rest," he said with a bit of pique. And right then I realized my mistake. I'd challenged his machismo in front of a female admirer. Not much had changed in that respect, between his time and ours.

"Wait, don't you need your wand?" I knew I was grabbing at straws, but I hadn't seen one in his possession, so it was worth a shot.

His wooly eyebrows gathered into a frown. "I was whisked away from home so abruptly that I didn't have time to take anything with me. I suppose I should be grateful I wasn't naked at the time. No matter. The wand is helpful, but not always essential."

Not always essential—hardly words that engendered confidence, but they didn't seem to diminish Tilly's enthusiasm in the least. She was grinning from ear to ear like a kid going to the circus for the first time. Since I was out of arguments, I zipped my lips. If ever I could have used my mother's input, this was it.

"Should I be standing or seated?" Tilly asked. "I don't want to ruin the chair with my claws or scales."

"You won't actually be a dragon," I reminded her. "You'll just appear that way to anyone looking at you." I glanced at Merlin for corroboration, but he was staring into space, mumbling a string of words I didn't understand. He looked up finally with a satisfied expression, turned to Tilly and began the foreign sounding incantation. When he was finished, nothing had changed. Tilly was still Tilly in her floral muumuu. I thanked whatever angels were watching over us. Prematurely, as it happened. A moment later she morphed into a large, green dragon with flaring nostrils and malevolent yellow eyes. As fearsome as the creature looked, it was impossible to take it seriously, not just because I knew it was my aunt, but also because it was still wearing her muumuu, which could now pass for a bib. I started to giggle, which clearly irritated the Tilly-dragon. She opened her mouth, exhaling a flash of fire. It was getting way too real for me. "That's it, Merlin, enough," I said. "Reverse the spell."

Merlin had his head in the pantry. "Might there be more of those cookies?" he inquired.

"No, but I can go to the store and buy more of them, *after* you change my aunt back into herself." I knew how to drive a hard bargain.

"Yes, yes, very well." He left the pantry grudgingly to focus on the Tilly-dragon. He recited the spell. This time I knew to be more patient and wait a bit for the results. A minute passed and then five more. Merlin tried rewording the chant. Nothing happened. I was getting more worried by the second.

"Aha," Merlin said. "I know what I did wrong." He tried again, and again we waited. Still nothing. I wondered if I could be convicted for the murder of someone who'd technically been dead since the Middle Ages. Twenty minutes later, Merlin was frustrated, and I wasn't sure if I was more angry or scared. If this had been a film set, we would have been up to "take" thirty-two. The Tilly-dragon must have been awfully thirsty, because she sipped the rest of the distasteful tea, an act that looked ridiculous, given her present state. But I was all out of giggles.

After a brief respite, during which Merlin paced around the kitchen muttering, he stopped and threw his hands up. "How could I have forgotten to reverse the last phrase?! What has befallen my memory of late?"

"You knew you had memory problems, yet you still thought it was a good idea to try this?" My anger and my voice had reached the boiling point.

"I forgot," he responded. "That is what forgetting is about, after all."

"Do you remember what to do now?" I could have won an Oscar for keeping my temper under control.

"Behold," he said with the renewed confidence of a showman. On take thirty-two, he nailed it. A minute later Tilly was back to herself, asking if I'd taken a picture of her as a dragon. A picture? I'd been too busy worrying about her well-being to think of it. I'm not proud to admit that I lied and told her the camera wasn't capable of capturing such powerful magick.

"Have I passed your test?" Merlin asked with aplomb.

"Yes, you have." I'd thought about saying "no" to shake him up a bit for what he'd put me through. But the truth was that he had proven himself. I'd never met any witch, wizard, or sorcerer who could have done what he did, mistakes notwithstanding.

"Then might I lie down for a while? I believe I do suffer from that lagging malady you mentioned."

"You're welcome to rest at my house too," Tilly said sweetly before I could answer. "I have two empty bedrooms; you can have your pick."

Tired as he seemed, Merlin perked up at her offer. Had he been a dog, I'm certain that his ears would have stood at attention. "And where might that be?" he asked.

"The next block, but I have my car here."

"If it means getting to ride in one of your modern conveyances, I cannot refuse your kind offer. What a remarkable day this has been."

Tilly turned to me, happier than I'd seen her in days. "You don't mind, Kailyn, do you?"

I didn't have the heart to object. It stung a little that Merlin picked her over me, but only until I'd had a moment to think about it. The last thing I needed was the additional time and work he would add to my already complicated life. He wasn't a friend who'd dropped by for the weekend. We had no way of knowing how long he would be staying or, for that matter, if he would ever be able to return home. "No, of course not," I was able to say with complete honesty.

I saw them out to Tilly's car, a snazzy red Camaro she'd purchased on a whim two years earlier, despite the fact that she'd had some difficulty climbing in and out of the car in the showroom. To her credit, I never heard her utter a single word of regret or complaint about it.

As I waved them off, I heard the phone inside ringing. I ran in, colliding with the cats who were assembled at the door, hoping for Merlin's return. They scattered, tripping me and making it more difficult to avoid stepping on any paws. After I made it through the gauntlet without inflicting injury, the cats resumed their vigil at the door. They had a long night ahead of them. Sashkatu had retired to the top of the living room couch. From there he could keep an eye on the foyer in comfort. I grabbed the phone off the table beside the couch.

"I'm so glad you're home," Elise Harkens said in response to my hello. Her voice was so thin and raspy, she sounded as if she was being strangled.

"What's up" I asked.

"I don't know if you heard . . ."

"Heard what?"

"The killer used Jim's gun to murder him. So now I'm—"

"Elise," I interrupted her, "why don't you come over to my house so we can talk?" Given this new evidence, Duggan might have put a tap on her line. Elise arrived ten minutes later, looking more distraught than she had on the day Jim died. I picked my way through the cats to open the door for her, then led her around them into the living room. When we sat on the couch, Sashkatu took umbrage at having his space invaded. With a plaintive yowl, he climbed down from his perch, using my body as a stairway to the floor and whacking me in the nose with his sturdy tail on the way. It was probably intentional, but this was not the time to scold him.

"Tell me what happened," I said to Elise.

"Whenever I think things can't get any worse, they do," she said, tearing up.

"Maybe it's not that bad," I said, worried that it was. "Did Jim keep the gun at home or in his office?"

"As far as I know it's always been in the house. When Jim bought it nine, ten years ago, it was at the time of those break-ins around the area."

"I remember that. Didn't the police eventually catch the guys who were responsible?"

"Yes. Luckily, Jim never had to use the gun against an intruder. I'd almost forgotten about it until today. Knowing that Jim's killer is still on the loose, I figured I should keep it handy, you know, in case he tries to come after the boys or me. When I went to get it out of the lockbox, it was gone."

"Did Jim ever lend the gun to anyone?"

"No, that would be illegal. He would never do it. But he lost the key months ago and never got around to buying a new box.

"Then we have to assume the killer broke into your house to steal the gun."

"To frame me, right? Why else would someone do that?"

I tried to come up with another possibility, but nothing else made sense. "How many people knew you kept a gun in the house?"

Elise thought about it for a minute. "A few, unless Jim mentioned it to people when I wasn't with him. I'll make a list of the people I'm aware of."

"It's a start. Did you report the gun stolen yet?"

She shook her head. "I've been wracking my brain trying to figure out when there might have been a break-in, so I don't sound like a complete lame-brain when I talk to them. Who wouldn't know when they've been burglarized?"

"Do you always arm your security system?"

"We used to, when we first got it, also around the time of those burglaries. But after everything died down, we didn't put it on unless we were going out of town. I mean, this is tiny New Camel."

I understood her point. Living in New Camel, you felt safe. It was easy to forget about crime. If you weren't a member of my family, that is. Whether there was crime, war, or peace, we relied on protective wards for security. "Vigilance is the price we must pay for the powers that make us different," my grandmother used to say. "Never forget, Kailyn, we have not always been welcome." Not long before she and my mother died, they'd had a basic alarm system installed, because our magick had become too unpredictable.

"The killer must have stolen the gun recently," I said, thinking out loud. "He would have wanted to minimize the odds of Jim realizing the gun was gone. And when he stole it, he would have been careful not to mess up the house in any way that would have raised a red flag. Think back a couple of weeks. If the killer made any mistakes, they were probably small ones. Something you might have attributed to Jim or the boys."

Elise shook her head. "I never came home and found the door unlocked or the—" Her hand flew to her mouth, her eyes widened. "I know when it happened. Ten days ago I found one of the big kitchen windows open. I assumed it was my cleaning lady's fault, because she sometimes forgets to close and lock all the windows after she cleans them."

"But that actually could have been the cleaning lady's fault. So we still need some other clue to corroborate the fact it happened that day. Something small, a book out of place or items switched around in a closet, a drawer not closed all the way."

Elise's brow furrowed. "Wait—I blamed my boys for tracking mud onto my bedroom carpet right after it was cleaned. They swore they hadn't been in there, but I didn't believe them," she added sheepishly.

"Mud? I don't think we had any rain that week though."

"No, but our sprinklers were on and they make the flower bed under the kitchen windows muddy."

"Here's the problem," I said. "If I'm right, the killer wouldn't have left any evidence of being in the house. He would have cleaned up after himself." And I'd been doing so well up to that point. So much for trying to fill Nancy Drew's big shoes.

"The dirt was smeared as if the person tried to clean it," Elise said. "It's a lot easier to get up when it's dry. It vacuums right up. If you try to wipe up wet dirt, it leaves a mess."

Maybe there was still hope for me as a sleuth. "It could be the killer knew that, but didn't have the time to hang around and wait for it to dry. He left, hoping you wouldn't tie the mud to the break-in. And he got lucky. Was there mud anywhere else in the house?"

"I didn't see any, but the other floors are ceramic or hardwood, way easier to clean."

"All right, now that we've pinpointed the day it happened, you've got to call and report the theft."

"I know," Elise said miserably, "but it's sure going to sound like I'm making the whole thing up—a lame attempt at a defense if ever there was one."

"Think of it this way: once you report the gun stolen, they'll have to investigate it and then maybe they'll find the real killer."

"Oh, I'm sure they'll go through the motions. But in the end, there's a real possibility I'll go to prison, and my boys..." Tears filled her eyes and spilled down her cheeks. I handed her the small box of tissues from the coffee table in front of the couch. She pulled one out and dabbed at her eyes and nose with it. Then she set the box down next to her as if she thought she might need another one soon. I tried to think of something comforting to say, a reason to be optimistic, but nothing came to me. She was the one to break the silence. "When I called, it wasn't just to tell you about the gun," she said, absently kneading the tissue in her hands. "I wanted to know if there's a spell or potion that would make the killer come forward and confess, or . . . or one that would help Duggan find the guy? Would Aunt Tilly be able to read the killer's mind if she were in the same room with him?"

Elise and I had never spent much time talking about my family business, hers either, for that matter. Because of the large age gap between us, it wasn't until the last six years or so that we'd become close adult friends. During that time, I'd taught her some spells and whipped up some potions to help with a variety of things, from bee stings to her difficult mother-in-law. We didn't see it as odd or any different from asking a friend for help with algebra or advice on how to catch a guy's attention.

I put my hands over hers, hating to dash her hopes. "I wish it were that simple," I said. "If it were, I would have already done it. I can't cast a spell on an unknown individual and I doubt Duggan would be willing to let me practice magick on him for any reason. Unfortunately, Tilly can't read a person when there's something they're trying to hide."

Elise managed a half-hearted smile. "That's what I thought, but I had to ask. I had to be sure." We talked for a few more minutes about how the boys were doing, before she left to get back to them. To reach the door, she had to pick her way around the cats as if she were trying to avoid land mines.

The sound of the door closing drew Sashkatu out from wherever he'd been nursing his snit. He made his way directly to me and began weaving in and out of my legs, which generally meant he wanted my attention and would keep it up until he'd communicated his desire. I looked at my watch. Evening had snuck up on me. The other cats were still fixated on the door and the memory of Merlin, so it had been left to Sashkatu to remind me about dinner. I lined up their dishes on the counter and filled them with kibble and canned tuna with assembly-line efficiency Mr. Ford would have found impressive. Then I set five of them on the floor with fresh water. The sixth one I took into the first floor powder room for Sashkatu and left him to chow down in private. The smell of food had finally drawn the other cats into the kitchen.

I opened the refrigerator, looking for inspiration for my own dinner, but there wasn't much there to inspire even the most creative chef.

There were a couple of eggs, a lone apple, and a container of Chinese takeout that had to be at least two weeks old. I tossed it in the garbage, afraid to peek inside. Okay, that narrowed down my choices. Dinner was going to be an egg with an apple for dessert. No matter what new calamity tomorrow had in store for me, the day would also have to include a trip to the grocery store. I was cracking the egg on the side of a small fry pan when my mother popped in for a visit.

Chapter 8

"What on Earth is going on down there?" Morgana's voice was so loud and unexpected in the quiet house that I jumped, fumbling the egg for a moment before losing it to the floor.

"I wish you wouldn't sneak up on me like that," I said, grabbing a paper towel and stooping to clean up the mess before the cats had a chance to track it all over the house.

"I suppose you have a point," she replied, more irritated than apologetic. "How would you have me announce myself?"

"I don't know . . . whisper my name, float silently into sight, ring a little bell."

"I'll try to remember that," she agreed, still a bit huffy.

"Thank you. Is everything all right over there?" I asked, hoping to reset the tone of our conversation.

"Same old, same old," she said, which meant nothing to me, since she and my grandmother had never actually told me what it was like on the other side. Either they had no desire to talk about it, highly unlikely, or they'd been sworn to secrecy. Imparting information to the living was probably number one on the hit parade of sins when you reached the other side. Otherwise, we'd all know a lot more on the subject. "I'm here to talk about *you*," my mother went on. "Have things gotten worse?" Given how much had happened lately, I waited for her to be more specific. "I thought you were going to summon a familiar of your own."

"I did, last night," I said. It didn't seem possible that it had been less than twenty-four hours ago.

"And yet all you've managed to summon is some weird old man."

I almost didn't tell her, but then I realized she was bound to figure it out sooner or later and I'd have to account for my reticence on the subject. "He's not just any old man, Mom, he's Merlin."

Her laughter was a combination of a belly laugh and a crackle of electricity. I called it a *cackle with a crackle* when I described it to Tilly. "There is no way that old sad-sack is the mighty Merlin," Morgana managed to squeak out as her laughter subsided.

"Then I guess you didn't catch his little performance," I said offhandedly.

"What performance was that?"

"He glamoured your sister into a dragon."

"No way. Not possible."

"Green scales, yellow eyes, fire-breathing, the whole nine yards." Morgana didn't respond. I'd rendered her speechless for the first time in my life.

"Well, I'd have to see that to believe it," she pronounced, but with an uncharacteristic lack of conviction in her voice.

Priorities forced me to let the remark go unchallenged. As long as she was there, I had a couple of important questions to ask her and I didn't know when she might be summoned away. "Listen, mom, I can't find the spell you used to restore Tilly's powers the last time she lost them. Do you remember where you put it?" She suggested a series of places I could search, all of which I'd already tried. I asked her to let me know if she thought of anywhere else to look and then I moved on. "Would you happen to know any spells that could help me find a killer?"

She gasped. "A killer? In New Camel?!" I'd forgotten that she didn't know about Jim's death, so I quickly filled her in. "I'm gone for a lousy couple of months and everything comes apart at the seams," she muttered. "Please give Elise my heartfelt condolences— oh, you can't. Not without really freaking her out. This being dead business is very exasperating." I didn't point out that she would probably be adjusting better if she let go of her earthbound ties and embraced her new state of being. She had to be aware of that herself. Besides, I wasn't ready to let her go.

"Mom, do you know of such a spell?" I prompted when she didn't respond.

"I'm thinking. I'm thinking."

Several more minutes passed. "Nothing?"

"Sorry, murder is not something we ever encountered in New

Camel. Promise you'll be careful, Kailyn. I've got to run, your grand-mother's calling me. I'll try to get back to you if we come up with any-thing. I know, why don't you ask your friend Merlin for help?" she added dryly, managing to get in the last word.

Thinking about our conversation after she left, I realized she'd made a point that had eluded me. She'd immediately connected Mer-lin's appearance to my attempt to summon a familiar. She'd always been good at seeing the forest as well as the trees. But was it possible for a spell to go astray to such a huge degree? Under normal circum-stances, I wouldn't have bet on it, but then we'd lost "normal" months ago. My epiphany brought with it a stab of guilt. If she was right, Mer-lin's voyage through time might all be on me. And guilt brought along its old pal self-doubt. How was I going to help anyone if I was con-stantly worried about doing more harm than good?

Sometime during the night, my mesmerized cats finally gave up their vigil at the door and joined Sashkatu and me in bed. At least Merlin's hypnotic effect on them wasn't permanent. Although I'd gone to bed half expecting to be awakened by a frantic call from Tilly, I didn't hear from her until the next morning. When I saw her name on the caller ID I had no idea what awaited me. It turned out to be a pleasant surprise. I sure hadn't had my quota of those lately. Tilly sounded more cheerful than she'd been since losing Morgana and Bronwen. She gave me a detailed rundown of what she and Mer-lin had been doing since they'd left my house. She'd made grilled cheese sandwiches for their dinner and Merlin had gobbled up three. She could barely make them fast enough. To the best of her ability, she'd explained how everything in the house worked, from the com-puter and printer all the way down to the shower and electric tooth-brush. According to her, he was like a kid in a candy store on his first sugar high.

"Did you find out if he can restore your powers?" I asked, in case she hadn't thought of it. It didn't seem like an unreasonable request in exchange for his food and lodging.

"I did mention it," she said, "but I think he was too deep into cul-ture shock to hear me. I'll bring it up again later. I'm really calling to tell you that Merlin can stay here with me if you're planning to go into your shop today."

I did have to open the shop, since I'd been closed most of yester-

day. There was also the matter of cleaning up the mess in the storeroom and making a list of what needed to be replaced. Restocking certain items in my inventory was going to be the hardest part. Thinking
about it made my head spin. I was happy to accept her offer.

"Smart girl. I can guarantee you wouldn't get anything done with
Merlin there." She sounded as proud and exhausted as the mother of
a two-year-old, exploring the world around him. What we all took
for granted was as new and different to Merlin as if he'd come from
another planet entirely. "I'm enjoying having him as a house guest,"
Tilly went on. "Can you believe it? I'm actually hosting the greatest
sorcerer who ever lived." She went on about him for a full five minutes, gushing like a teenage girl over a rock star. Merlin probably
didn't know it, but he had his first groupie.

I put the TV on in the bedroom to hear the morning news while I
got ready for work. I was brushing my teeth when I heard the ABC
anchor say they were going live to a press conference in Schuyler
County for the ME's report on the shooting death in New Camel.
How sad, I thought, that it had taken murder for our little town to hit
the big time. I washed the toothpaste out of my mouth and ran into
the bedroom to watch. I was perched on the edge of the bed when
they cut away to a reporter who was standing off to one side of a
room crowded with journalists and cameramen, all jockeying for position. Whoever had estimated the size of the turnout and chosen the
room had failed miserably. Between the jostling, bobbing heads, I
caught a glimpse of a low stage at the front of the room. It was not
more than two feet off the ground with a podium front and center.

The din of dozens of voices made it difficult to hear what the reporter was saying, though he was practically eating his mike. He was
still talking when the cameraman cut away to focus on the stage. A
large, florid man, in a police uniform, his hair piece slightly askew,
had stepped up to the podium. The room hushed. He cleared his
throat and patted down the too-black toupee as if he felt something
wasn't quite right up there. Since he couldn't very well adjust it in
front of the cameras, he let his hand drop and started speaking. "For
those of you who don't already know me, I'm Police Chief Donald
Gimble. For starters, I want to assure all of you that we are doing
everything in our power to find the killer and bring him to justice as
swiftly as possible. At this point, I can't give you any particulars on
the case, because I don't want to jeopardize the investigation. I do

want to emphasize that if anyone has information that might be helpful, I urge you to call the hotline we've set up. Throughout this broad-
cast the number should be at the bottom of your screen. You can also
find it in the newspaper. Rest assured that you can remain anonymous.
Now I'd like to introduce the man you really came to hear today,
Schuyler County ME, Dr. Roger Westfield." A flurry of voices accompanied the ME as he walked onto the stage. Seeing him with a
white lab coat over his clothes, he looked a lot more like an ME than
he had at the wake. He and Gimble exchanged a few words before
the police chief clapped him on the shoulder and left the stage.

Westfield adjusted his wire-rimmed glasses, then consulted the
tablet he'd placed on the lectern. "There are still a couple of tests
pending," he began, looking out at the audience, "but I feel comfortable telling you today that Mr. Harkens died of a single gunshot
wound to the head. The bullet passed through and destroyed several
critical structures in the brain, before exiting the skull. Death would
have been instantaneous. After the remaining tests are in, I will be
able to provide a more complete report." Once it was clear that he
had nothing more to add, the reporters launched a barrage of questions at him. Clearly startled by the onslaught, he backed away from
the podium, stumbling over his own feet and nearly going down. At
the last moment, he won the battle with gravity and regained his balance. Gimble hustled back onto the stage like the cavalry coming to
the rescue. He held his arms up, then slowly brought them down,
hands open in a gesture that said, "Calm down, quiet down." At least
that's what it said to me. Not all the reporters seemed to get it, or they
got it and weren't ready to give up. I'd seen it happen before. Throw
enough questions at someone and they might answer a couple just to
get you to shut up. Not this time. Westfield stepped off the stage and
vanished into an anteroom. The camera cut back to the reporter, who
repeated the ME's statement for anyone in the audience who hadn't
understood it the first time. I turned off the TV, trying to decide what
my next move should be. Although I had lambasted Beverly for gos-
siping about Jim and Elise at the wake, I couldn't help but wonder if
there was any truth to her remarks. I had no intention of calling her to
find out. If Elise had known about Jim having an affair, I was sure
she would have told me. But what if he was having an affair and
Elise didn't know about it? There was one person I could ask, and
after I closed the shop for the day I intended to do that.

Chapter 9

When I called Ronnie, she suggested meeting at the Soda Jerk Café. I figured she was probably concerned about a possible tap on our phones too. The café is an adorable throwback to the soda shops of the 1950s, complete with poodle-skirted waitresses, green Formica table tops, and an old-fashioned juke box. They serve the basics for breakfast and lunch, but are best known for their over-the-top sundaes and ice cream sodas. Tourists love stopping in there as much as we townies do, often making it difficult to get a seat. With no bus tours scheduled for that day and less than an hour until closing time, the café was barely half full. I found Ronnie in a booth in a back corner, sipping a cup of coffee. We exchanged quick hellos as I slid in across from her. A teenage waitress immediately appeared to take my order.

"Coffee for me too," I said. She shrugged her shoulders and turned away. I was pretty sure that if her shoulders could talk they would have said "whatever."

"What's up?" Ronnie asked once we were alone.

I decided not to beat around the bush; it took too much time and energy. "There's a rumor making the rounds that Jim was having an affair. Do you know if there's any truth to it?"

Ronnie sighed. "I've heard that too. For all the years I knew Jim, he was the quintessential family man. He always made time to be at his kids' athletic events, plays, you name it. He put a lot of thought into what he bought Elise for her birthday, their anniversary, Christmas. Never asked me to do it instead. He was my role model for the perfect husband. It may be his fault that I'm still single," she said with a self-conscious laugh. "To answer your question, no, I don't believe the rumors."

The waitress stopped at our table long enough to set my coffee down, before going on to drop a check at another table. "I'm really glad to hear that," I said, adding a splash of milk to the coffee. "If there's any hard evidence Jim had a girlfriend, the police would have a motive to pin on Elise. A lack of motive may be the only reason they haven't arrested her yet."

"I know. I've been thinking the same thing."

I took a sip of my coffee. The Soda Jerk was definitely not known for its robust brew, but I'd forgotten how weak it was. I should have ordered an ice cream soda. "There is something else I wanted to ask you," I said.

"Ask away."

"It occurred to me that one logical suspect is the dentist who shared the building with Jim. How well did they get along?"

"They were friends in the beginning," she said. "They had dinners out with their wives, invited each other to their homes. But about five years ago they had a falling out."

"Do you know what it was about?"

"Do I ever. Edward Silver offered to pay me more if I left Jim and went to work for him."

"Whoa, that's a surefire way to sour a friendship."

"Oh yeah. When Jim found out, he went ballistic. I heard that he stormed into Silver's office in the middle of the day—with a packed waiting room—and demanded to see him. When the front desk couldn't calm Jim down, Silver finally came out. He ordered Jim to leave or he'd call the police. Jim left, but not before calling Silver a backstabbing thief, only in much more colorful terms. Everyone in the office heard him."

I understood Jim's anger. Trying to steal an employee was a crappy thing to do to a friend. But apparently it didn't end there. Silver started doing spiteful little things. Keying Jim's car, puncturing his tire. Jim was sure Silver was behind it, but he couldn't prove it. He was so sick of the whole thing, he talked about relocating, even though he still had a couple of years left on his lease.

I sipped my coffee that was now tepid as well as weak and pushed it away "I guess you never know what you're going to find when you look under some rocks. Does Duggan know about their history?"

"He does now, because at that first interview he asked me if Jim had any enemies I knew of." She pushed her cup aside too.

"What's your take on Silver?" I asked.

"To be honest, I doubt Silver has it in him to commit murder, but then I'm continually surprised by human nature. And not in a good way."

I'd hoped to hear something more definitive, but given Ronnie's ambiguous answer, the dentist was going to stay on my list of suspects for now. "Once the police get a look at Jim's client files, maybe they'll find a few more suspects, people who had axes to grind," I said. "No matter how great you are at your job, it's impossible to please everyone." If the police, or I, couldn't come up with more suspects, Elise was going to be the logical choice for scapegoat.

"They can't look at those files without getting each client's permission," Ronnie pointed out. "Attorney/client privilege survives death. At most, they can demand a list of Jim's clients, which they've already done."

"Promise not to laugh," I said, feeling a bit foolish over what I was about to admit, "but I've decided to do some investigating of my own." I could tell by the way Ronnie's eyebrows lifted that I'd taken her by surprise. "Patiently sitting and waiting for the police to find the killer just isn't in my nature," I went on, "especially since Elise seems to be the primary person of interest right now. For that matter, my aunt and I are considered persons of interest too. What if every other suspect has an alibi that checks out, except for Elise, Tilly, and me?"

"You won't hear any laughing from me," Ronnie said. "Too many people spend years in prison for crimes they didn't commit."

Her words were a vote of support, as well as a scary reminder of what can go wrong in the justice system. I made a conscious effort to push away the dark thoughts and focus on the positive. Not that there was an overabundance of it at the moment. But working with magick required the right spells and potions, as well as the right mind set. Morgana and Bronwen had drummed that into my head right along with my ABCs. "Since the police don't have easy access to Jim's files," I said, "at least they won't have a ridiculous advantage over me."

Ronnie gave me a sly smile. "I know how *you* can have the advantage."

"I'm listening."

"Jim kept a thumb drive of client files at home, so he could work on them at night and over weekends. I have a feeling Elise will be glad to let you have it."

* * *

I stopped at the Harkens' house before heading home and caught Elise in the middle of making dinner. When I asked her about the thumb drive, she didn't hesitate. "Sure, anything that could possibly help. Besides, only you, Ronnie, and I know these duplicate files exist. The police never asked, and I never volunteered the information." She led me into the family room, opened the single drawer on the end table to the left of the couch and took out one of several TV remotes. I couldn't imagine what she was doing, but in less than a minute it became clear. She turned the remote over and slid off the little back panel that covered the batteries. Then she put her index finger inside and popped out a tiny thumb drive, catching it in her other hand. "I've been worried the police might get a warrant to search the house," she said. "If that happens, I don't want them to find the drive. If the killer was a client of Jim's, maybe the files can help us narrow it down." She handed me the drive. "If you want to speak to any of the clients, you'll have to be very careful about what you say and how you say it," she cautioned me.

I let her get back to preparing dinner. I still had to stop at the local market to pick up a few essentials like cat food, a salad from their salad bar, and a rotisserie chicken. Everything else I needed would have to wait for another day. On the way there, I was so preoccupied that I drove right past the mini mart and had to double back. When Ronnie had suggested I ask Elise for the drive, I'd been buoyed by the prospect. But now that I had it in my possession, I was having second thoughts. Although reading the files might not be a crime, it seemed at least unethical. I kept telling myself it was for a good cause. For a good cause. Focusing on that mantra, I grabbed what I needed in the mini mart and headed home.

When I unlocked my front door, I heard the cats yowling from the direction of the kitchen. By my watch, it was half an hour past their dinner time, but they all sounded as if they were starving. I dropped my handbag onto the table in the entry and toted the groceries into the kitchen to see what was going on. The cats were assembled on the floor looking up at Sashkatu who seemed to be leading the protest from the counter top. If the cats ever unionized I'd be in serious trouble. I made their dinners, still trying to convince myself there was nothing to feel guilty about. My intentions were pure, if not noble. I vowed that no one would suffer, because of anything I learned. Well, no one but the killer. I was more or less back on an even keel when the phone rang.

Five minutes later I was in my aunt's house with a hysterical Tilly and a befuddled Merlin. Tilly had been so incoherent over the phone that I'd raced right over to find out exactly what was going on. It took a few minutes before I was able to calm her down enough to explain the problem. We were sitting on the couch in her family room, while Merlin paced up and down and around in circles, eyes focused on the floor, lost in a world of his own. I wasn't sure if he knew I was there.

"It's my Isenbale," Tilly said, breathless and hiccupping her sorrow.

"What's wrong with him?" I asked, realizing he hadn't come to greet me. Unlike Sashkatu, he was a friendly cat, with no delusions of grandeur, and seemed to enjoy the company of humans.

"Merlin turned him into a bird," she said forlornly. As if on cue, a larger than average green parakeet flew into the room and perched on Tilly's shoulder. She absently put her hand up to pet his feathers. "I have nothing against birds, mind you, but I want my Isenbale back."

"Merlin," I called to get the wizard's attention. It took five tries before he finally stopped moving and looked up at me. I realized, for the first time, that his hair was no longer a tangled gray mess. It had been washed and combed, so he didn't look like a vagrant. With the proper clothing, he could actually pass for a citizen of the twenty-first century.

"Ah Kailyn," he said. "I was not aware of your arrival."

"Can you tell me what happened to Isenbale? Why is he a bird now?"

Merlin shook his head. "I was attempting to restore Tilly's powers to their full extent when the cat jumped into her lap and must have been touched by the spell I was casting. Why it would have transmuted the animal into another species is as baffling and upsetting to me as it is to your aunt." I somehow doubted that, but nothing would be helped by debating the point.

He went on. "I've been working on the problem, but have not as yet happened upon a solution. If you will excuse me, I'll get back to it." Without waiting to hear if I had more to say, he started his pacing again.

Apparently I was once again the cause of the problem. If I hadn't pressured Tilly into asking for Merlin's help, Isenbale would still be a big, furry cat. I turned to my aunt, who was sniffling beside me. "Tilly, don't worry, I'm sure Merlin will figure out how to reverse the spell. He's the most accomplished sorcerer ever born. Just think about how much experience he's had." I didn't remind her that he might be suffering from the same malady that had been playing havoc with our powers lately. If she hadn't made that connection on her own, she would soon enough.

"In the meantime at least you have the bird to keep you company," I added brightly. The words were barely out of my mouth when the parakeet issued a catlike yowl and promptly pooped on Tilly's shoulder.

She went into her bedroom to change into clean clothing, and I headed home. With Tilly now calmer in her misery, and Merlin on the problem, there was no point in my hanging around. Besides, my stomach was demanding to be fed.

Chapter 10

The moment my eyes opened the next morning, I had a kind of epiphany. While I'd slept, my subconscious had apparently been hard at work on Jim's murder and it had come up with a way to potentially take some of the suspicion off Tilly, Elise, Ronnie, and me. It would mean going to speak to Dr. Westfield and opening Abracadabra a little late, but if I was successful, it would be well worth any loss of revenue. I dressed quickly and fed the cats before running out the door. Sashkatu protested the fact that I'd left him behind. His disgruntled yowl followed me into my car. Since I couldn't explain that I'd be taking him with me later, he'd probably be in a feline snit when I did. My mother had done a fine job of spoiling him.

The drive to the county seat took less than an hour. I hadn't called ahead to find out if Dr. Westfield could see me, because I didn't want to be told he couldn't. If I simply showed up at his office, I could pretend ignorance about needing an appointment and try to worm my way in. At least that was my strategy, until I found out that the ME's office didn't take appointments. I entered the building that housed Westfield's office as well as the county crime lab and made my way over to the reception desk. I wasn't by any means stealthy with my high-heeled sandals beating a tattoo on the stone floor, but the receptionist didn't look up until I was standing directly in front of her.

"Oh hi," she said, immediately sitting up straighter in her seat and affixing a smile to her mouth. "How may I help you?" She was young and pleasant and, as it turned out, bored. From where I was standing, I could see over the high countertop to her work station below. I caught a glimpse of her cell phone before she had a chance to flip it screen down. She'd been playing Words with Friends. I wondered if she'd learned the hard way that it was easier to hide a cell phone screen than a computer monitor if one of your superiors happens to walk by.

"Hi Jessica," I said, reading the nameplate on the counter. "Is Dr. Westfield in?"

There was hesitation in her voice when she said "yes."

"I'm Kailyn Wilde. I was hoping he could spare a minute to see me."

"I'm sorry," she replied, her smile toned down to rueful, "but he doesn't really meet with the public. Just the police or like, government officials."

"That's okay," I said with more confidence than I felt, "I'm not the public. He knows me." I didn't mention that I'd only met him briefly, or that we'd exchanged maybe a dozen words. Or that he might not remember me. "In fact I saw him a few days ago." I really hoped he had a good memory for names.

"I'd like to help you," she said, "really I would. But I'd get into trouble." Her cell phone beeped, and she sneaked a peek at it.

"You should be careful," I whispered. "I got caught playing games like that at work and it wasn't pretty." Okay, not at work exactly, but in an economics class so boring it regularly put students to sleep.

"Yeah, I bet it happens to a lot of people."

"Especially that game. It's addictive."

"I know, isn't it?" Jessica agreed. She was beginning to sound less like the guardian at the gate and more like my co-conspirator.

"Do you think maybe you could buzz him and mention my name? Give him a chance to decide about seeing me?"

She shook her head. "He made it very clear that he's not to be disturbed unless the building is on fire or there's an emergency in his family."

I tried a different tack. "Do you get any bathroom breaks?"

She laughed. "Well sure. I could never sit here for eight hours straight without one."

"Does anyone cover the desk for you while you're gone?"

"No, I'm not gone for very long. And as you can see," she added with a sweep of her arm, "we're not exactly mobbed with visitors."

I could see by her expression that she had no idea where I was going with this new line of conversation. I'd have to spell it out for her. "I was thinking you might need to take one of those breaks pretty soon. No one can blame you for what happens when you're not here, right?"

Her face brightened. "Now that you mention it, I think I will need a break in about . . ."

"Fifteen minutes should do it." I'd noticed the security cameras when I walked into the lobby. Returning that soon might make me look suspicious, but it was probably enough time for her to be cleared of any collusion. I didn't want to be the reason she lost her job, but I couldn't afford to spend half the day loitering around the town either.

"You'll need the hallway to the right," she whispered after we'd coordinated the time on our phones.

I used the fifteen minutes to find a donut shop where I bought a cup of coffee and a glazed donut. My willpower is lousy when I'm stressed. The minutes dragged by. To prevent myself from buying another donut, I left the shop and spent the time exploring the town. If you'd asked me what I saw, I couldn't have told you. I was too pre-occupied with my little foray into crime. I was back at the ME's building at the appointed time. Before entering I gave myself a quick pep talk: *Walk with purpose, if you see anyone don't make eye contact, look like you have important business on your mind.* I squared my shoulders, lifted my chin and went in.

The reception desk was empty. I walked past it to the hallway. Jessica had told me to go right, but I suddenly realized she might have been using her position at the desk as her reference point, in which case I would need to go left. The longer I stood in the lobby, the greater the risk I'd bump into someone who'd ask a lot of questions. Once I reached the hallway, I had a better chance of looking like I belonged there. I decided to take her at her words. After all, she was there to help people find the office they needed.

Fortunately the hallway was carpeted, so my footsteps made no noise. I walked briskly, hoping no one came out of the closed doors I was passing. I'd forgotten to ask Jessica if I'd find Westfield in his office or in an autopsy room, but she probably wouldn't have known the answer anyway. I'd covered half the length of the hall when a door up ahead of me opened and an older woman walked out. She was focused on some papers she was holding. Maybe she would turn the other way and not notice me. But of course she turned toward me. As the distance between us closed, she looked up. I saw curiosity register on her face. If I was going to pull this off, I had to act like I was supposed to be there. I kept up my pace with my eyes straight ahead as if I had weighty matters on my mind. When we passed, she bobbed her head at me. With no time to decide how best to react, I returned the bob, but didn't slow down. *Nothing to concern you here, Ma'am.* I kept expecting her to double back to question why I was there. When that didn't happen, I had an overwhelming urge to peek over my shoulder to see where she was, but I knew that would be a red flag of guilt if she was watching me. When I reached the door with Dr. Westfield's name on it, I stopped and stole a sideways glance down the hall. The woman was gone, probably into another office. I'd had no idea that making it this far would be so tricky, but there was no time to relax and appreciate my small victory. I could still be booted out by the ME, himself. I knocked on the door, two short raps. No response. Next stop, the autopsy lab, wherever that was. I hadn't gone ten steps when I heard him say, "Come in, come in." He sounded gruff and harried, hardly the ideal time to have sneaked in to ask for a favor. Regardless, I was there and all I had to do was open the door. Showtime.

Westfield was seated at a sleek minimalist desk of Finnish birch and chrome. His computer was the centerpiece. Piles of papers and files were strewn across the remaining surface, making the computer look like it was under siege by the materials it was trying to replace. Several diplomas in simple, light wood frames decorated the walls, but aside from them, the one personal item I could see was a framed five-by-seven of the ME with his wife, three kids, and a Jack Russell terrier. The photo was standing at the edge of the desk, in imminent danger of falling off. Westfield himself looked markedly different than he had at the wake and on TV. His hair was sticking up as if he'd been raking his fingers through it, and his wire-rimmed glasses were perched on the tip of his nose, making him look like a cross between Einstein and the Nutty Professor.

"Hi, Dr. Westfield," I said, stepping closer to his desk, hoping that the farther I was from the door, the less likely he would be to order me out of it.

He stared at me, his brow furrowing as if he were trying to place me.

I smiled. "Remember me? Kailyn Wilde?" No flicker of recognition. "We met at Jim Harkens' wake." Still nothing. "I almost crashed into Detective Duggan?" I'd run out of reference points, so I stood there wondering what to do next.

"Aha, yes, I remember now," he said, but he didn't seem particularly pleased about it.

"There was no one at the reception desk, so I sort of showed myself in. I hope you don't mind. I only need a minute of your time."

"I don't accommodate visitors. If I did, I'd never get anything done." He looked back at the computer. "Think of it as not squandering your tax dollars."

Had I just been dismissed? His attitude got my back up, as my grandmother used to say. "Then I apologize," I said with some steel to my tone. "But since I'm here, perhaps you can make a small exception this time and permit me to ask you one question."

He tapped away at the keys while I waited, trying to decide how long to let our standoff continue before I took matters into my own hands and blurted out the question. According to my watch, almost three minutes passed before he looked up at me again.

"Fine, will you leave if I answer your question?" he asked with a heavy sigh.

"Absolutely," I agreed.

"I'd ask you to have a seat, but as you can see, there are no other chairs in here. That's by design. I don't encourage chitchat, not even with my colleagues."

"Clever," I said before I could stop myself.

Westfield scowled at me as if he wasn't quite sure how I'd meant it.

"Here's my question," I said quickly to distract him. "Did the position of the bullet wound indicate if the gun was fired by someone taller or shorter than Jim?"

Westfield sat back in his padded chair and wagged his head. "Don't tell me—you've always wanted to be Jessica Fletcher."

"Actually, Nancy Drew," I said. When was I going to learn to keep my mouth shut?

"The answer to your question is very simple. I can't release that kind of information during an ongoing investigation. So, if you'd please show yourself out." He looked back at the computer screen.

"Dr. Westfield," I said, "My aunt and I are considered suspects simply because we were the ones who found Jim."

"That's not unusual. And while I'm not unsympathetic to your plight, I can't change the rules for you."

"What if *your* wife were a suspect in a murder case, and you could give her some peace of mind by telling her that the gun had been fired by someone taller than she. Wouldn't you?"

For the first time since I'd walked into his office, the ME's mouth tugged up in amusement. It was far from a big old grin, but beggars can't be choosers. "You scoped out the place, saw the photo, and played to my weakness," he said. "And you didn't back down. I can respect that."

My heart lifted. "Enough to help me out?"

He leaned forward, his elbows on the desk, dislodging a pile of papers that cascaded onto the floor. "Even if I wanted to help you, I have nothing to tell you that would ease your mind." Hopes dashed, I thanked him stiffly and was opening the door to leave when he added, "Think about what I told you, Nancy Drew." On the drive back to New Camel I puzzled over his words. When it hit me, I smiled in spite of my dismay. Even if he'd been permitted to answer my question outright, it would not be what I wanted to hear. In other words, the trajectory of the gunshot had been upward. The killer was shorter than Jim. Given that Jim was five ten or so, Elise, Ronnie, Tilly, and I were shorter and still very much in the running as suspects.

Chapter 11

I went straight home to grab Sashkatu and open the shop, but I had trouble finding the wily old guy. After several minutes of looking under beds, checking closets, and mucking around in the basement clutter, I decided to stop playing the game his way and start using my brain. I picked up my keys with a lot of jangling and opened the front door. Before I could shout "goodbye," he showed his furry face. Although he was clearly put out at having been left behind earlier, he probably didn't want to spend the rest of the day with his kindred. He gave me an ingratiating "meow," but when I tried to pet him, he wriggled away from my hand.

The phone was ringing when we entered the shop. I turned off the alarm and picked up the receiver. Tilly was on the other end. She sounded more like her cheerful self, but I felt a pang of guilt. I should have called her earlier to find out how the second night with her houseguest had gone. She'd made my life a whole lot easier by offering to have Merlin stay with her.

"How are you? I asked.

"Better now that my Isenbale is a cat again. He's grumpier than usual, but I can hardly blame him."

Good news had been in such short supply lately that my spirits instantly lifted. "Merlin remembered how to undo the spell?"

"No, but it seems to have worn off. I think he's having trouble with his abilities here like we are. In this case, though, I couldn't be happier about it."

"How is our legendary sorcerer doing?" I'd been so caught up in other matters that I'd relegated the time traveler to the fringes of my mind. If I hadn't been trying to solve a murder, he would certainly have been front and center.

"Well, I found a way to keep him occupied and out of trouble."

I hesitated to ask her how, a bit afraid she was going to tell me about amorous activities. It wasn't a subject I was eager to discuss with her.

"I showed him the internet," she went on when I didn't respond, "and I haven't been able to pry him away from the computer ever since. This morning I found him passed out, asleep on the keyboard."

"Does he understand how to use it?" I asked.

"He already understands it better than I do, although that's not exactly a high bar to reach."

Despite Morgana and Bronwen's feelings about the technology, my aunt had bought a computer and was willing to learn. Or maybe she'd bought it specifically *to* spite them. No family is without its inner turmoil and ours was no exception. Before we got off the phone, Tilly invited me to have dinner with them. She was going to order pizza, another first for Merlin. How could I say no?

Felines fed, I walked over to my aunt's house. It was such a lovely summer evening it would have been a shame to take the car even though I was teetering on the brink of exhaustion. Since business had been slow, or more accurately, nonexistent, I'd spent the afternoon cleaning up the storeroom. I'd salvaged what little I could, tossed the rest, then mopped up the muck and glass. After order was restored, I'd made a list of products that had to be replaced. Too bad there wasn't a sorcerer's supermarket. That's when I recalled Merlin's offer to help restock my shelves, since he'd helped empty them. Fortunately it was summer and most of what I needed could be found growing in the wild. I could give him the list, and Tilly could ferry him around to find the items.

I arrived at Tilly's house at the same moment as the pizza delivery boy. After doing a little riff on "After you, no, after you," we wound up marching up her walkway together in a weird little wedding parody. While Tilly paid for the pizza, I went inside and found Merlin at the computer in the corner of the living room. He was so engrossed in what was on the screen that he didn't seem to notice me. Peering over his shoulder I understood why. He was reading about the space race and watching the grainy video of Neil Armstrong taking humankind's first step on the moon. I put my hand on his shoulder to let him know I was there. The poor man must have jumped three feet. When he spun around, his face had gone pale and his hand was pressed to his heart as if to keep it from popping out. My own heart took a dive to somewhere in the vicinity of my knees. I'd have to be more careful in the future. There was no telling what would happen to history if Merlin died in the twenty-first century. It was bad enough that he would return to his time babbling about computers, aircraft, and men on the moon. I apologized for scaring him, relieved to see the color return to his cheeks.

"Don't worry"—Tilly passed by on her way to the kitchen, pizza box in hand—"his ticker is fine. I've startled him a number of times too. When he gets involved with the internet, he might as well be in outer space."

I detected a note of disappointment, or maybe frustration, in her tone. Given her *druthers,* as Bronwen used to say, she would surely have preferred Merlin to be enthralled by her, not by electronics.

The heady smell of hot pizza must have reached Merlin's nostrils, because he rose without urging and followed the aroma into the kitchen. Tilly put the pizza box in the center of the table that she'd already set with paper plates, cups and napkins. Soda, seltzer, and water were on the counter along with an ice bucket. "Help yourselves," she said, holding the box top open. Merlin didn't need to be asked twice. He picked up a slice oozing with melted cheese and for a moment held it suspended in midair as if he didn't know what to do with it.

"Take a bite," I said, "but be careful—it's probably hot." I took a slice myself and bit off the pointy end. Merlin watched me, then tried it himself. His eyes opened wide with delight, the cheese dripping from his mouth into his beard.

He didn't say a word until he'd finished every last crumb of it. "What manner of comestible be this?" he asked, reaching for a second slice.

"Pizza," Tilly said, "bread dough with tomato sauce and cheese."

"Quite remarkable." He didn't speak again until he'd plowed through half the pie. "Never have I had a finer meal," he proclaimed, patting his stomach and burping with satisfaction. "But now to business. How far be it to London?"

I looked across the table at Tilly, hoping for some guidance, but she shrugged her shoulders. I was on my own. "It's far," I said, wary of causing a real heart attack. "Very far."

"You appear to be a smart young woman," Merlin said, "yet your answer is of no use to me. How many days travel is it? I imagine the journey is somewhat faster in a car than on horseback." He chuckled. "I much prefer the car. It is far kinder to the bones of an old man."

"You can't get there by horseback or car," I said. If he wanted the truth, there was no good way to put it.

"Why is that?" he bristled as if he suspected I was still dodging the question.

"Because it's across the ocean," Tilly replied bluntly.

Merlin frowned. "Such a thing is not possible."

I spent the next half hour trying to explain the New World to someone who believed the world was flat.

"That would explain a lot," he murmured after I'd finished. "Then I take it New London is not the London I know just spruced up a bit?"

"No," I said gently, hearing the pang of loss in his tone. "To reach London, England, it would take about six hours by plane, four or five days by boat." And you probably wouldn't recognize it at all, I added to myself.

He didn't say anything for a minute. Maybe he was trying to re-assess the enormity of his journey through time and space. When he spoke again, his voice sounded hollow and forlorn. "From what you have told me, were I to sail there or fly in one of those frightful con-traptions, I would not find the home I knew or the people I loved."

"I'm afraid not," I said.

"Then by Jove," he said, flinging off his sadness like a bother-some cloak, "I shall find a way back to my proper life. After all, I am Merlin!"

"That's the spirit," I said with all the enthusiasm I could muster, because I doubted even he could manage it.

"And until then," he went on, "I intend to enjoy the miracles of this new world of yours and help you girls recover from the strange affliction that has befallen you."

I didn't point out that he too appeared to be suffering from the same "affliction." Instead I wished him success, and while he was still in gung-ho mode, proposed my solution to restocking Abracadabra.

When I opened for business the next morning, I found a middle-aged woman asleep on my doorstep. She didn't look homeless. Her chin-length brown hair was well cut, and she was dressed in a stylish capri set and matching sandals. She didn't respond to my voice, so I gave her shoulder a gentle shake. When that failed to rouse her, I started worrying she might be dead. From there it was a hop, skip, and jump to imagining myself a suspect for another murder, a serial killer by accident of time and place. I really didn't want to call 911 again. I was still trying to decide what to do when she sprang up, wild-eyed and disoriented. For a moment we stared at each other, mouths gaping, but unable to speak. I managed to help her into the shop and get her settled in a folding chair I'd found and set beside the counter. By then she'd gathered her wits about her well enough to explain that she'd driven all night from North Carolina to reach me. I was her last hope. I almost groaned when she said that, because on its best days, magick doesn't come with a guarantee, and we hadn't seen our best days for some time now.

"What can I do for you?" I asked, hoping it would be something simple, something within my current ability to accomplish.

"Where should I begin?" she said vaguely.

I hopped up to sit on the counter. "Let's start with your name, since you already seem to know mine."

"Yes, yes, of course. I'm Lilly, Lilly Gould. So pleased to meet you." She started to extend her hand to me, but stopped when she realized we were too far apart.

"Nice to meet you too, Lilly. Why don't you tell me what brought you all this way?"

"Right. Here's the thing," she began, "over the years I've dabbled a bit in witchcraft—you know? But this . . . this is far beyond my ability to deal with."

"Okay," I said, wondering if she was ever going to tell me.

"Well, everything was going great until I opened my big mouth," she said, shaking her head. "You see, I was a widow for five years when I met Neal. He's everything my husband wasn't—kind, soft spoken, thoughtful, a real gentleman. I thought we'd be together for the rest of our days. But then I told his daughter the truth."

"Which is . . . ?"

"That she's a spoiled brat who's milking her father dry. She's thirty years old; she has a decent job, but she keeps asking Neal to buy her expensive things, things she doesn't need and doesn't want to spend her own money on. A three-hundred-dollar purse? No problem, sweetheart. A cruise to the Caribbean? Sure, honey. The poor man is incapable of telling her no. So I did it for him. At first I think he was actually relieved that I did it. But then she had a tantrum, stormed out of his house and now won't take his calls. Needless to say, I've become a pariah." Tears flooded Lilly's eyes and spilled down her cheeks, leaving dark trails of mascara in their wake. She opened her handbag and pulled out a travel pack of tissues. "You have to help me get him back," she pleaded, wiping her face. "It is possible, isn't it?"

"I think you've got a good shot at it," I said. Using a love spell or potion to make a stranger fall in love with you is wasted energy. I know from personal experience. Had it been possible, there would have been a number of boy bands camped out around my house when I was in my teens. On the other hand, using a spell to repair a relationship between two people who already loved each other was often successful. "I can tell you what to do, Lilly, but you'll have to perform the ritual yourself."

She was nodding so fast, she looked like a bobble-head on a bumpy road. "I brought a notepad," she said, rummaging in her purse again.

"The Silver Ring Love Charm is a powerful spell," I began once she was ready. "You'll need a silver ring that's never been worn, a white cloth, and a cup of white wine." I spoke slowly enough for her to write it all down. "As you probably know, love spells should be performed under a full moon. You start by blessing the silver ring. Then you wrap the ring in the cloth and bury it underground. Pour the wine over the place where you've buried it and recite these words:

> Blessed Goddess, fair and true,
> this silver gift I offer you.
> Bless this ring and let me see
> my lover coming back to me."

She seemed to be struggling, so I waited for her to catch up. "Leave the ring there for a month and dig it up under the next full moon. Then wear it until he returns to you."

Lilly stopped writing and looked up at me. "That's it?" She sounded disappointed.

"Yes, but you must believe in your heart and mind that it will work. There cannot be any doubt." For her to have driven up to New Camel as she had, I suspected that wouldn't be a problem.

After a moment's consideration, I decided to give her a second spell to try in case the first one didn't produce the desired result. I'd never before felt the need to do that, but my self-confidence had clearly hit an all-time low. I had to be careful about how I offered Lilly the extra spell, so I didn't pass my doubts on to her. "I almost forgot," I said, "we're running a two-for-one deal on spells this week." I hoped that hadn't sounded as lame to her as it did to me.

"Wow, I've never come across a sale on magick before," she said, quickly erasing that concern. Knowing that Lilly had two spells to try, gave me a certain peace of mind and I couldn't put a price on that. I gave her the details of the Lemon Love Spell. I was glad she'd be going back home to North Carolina to perform the rituals. She probably stood a better chance of success some distance away from me.

The rest of the day passed quickly, the shop busier than it had been for the past few weeks. A lot of local customers came in for their beauty products and the chance to gossip about the investigation into Jim's death. Every last one of them swore they knew Tilly and I were innocent. If called upon, they assured me, they'd be happy to provide sterling character references. Maybe recent events had made me paranoid, but I couldn't help wondering what they said when they weren't in my shop.

Chapter 12

Elise sounded troubled when she called to ask if I would accompany her to the bank where she and Jim had a safety deposit box. Of course she had good reason to sound that way even if no new concerns had surfaced in the past few days. But knowing her as well as I did, I detected a different timbre in her voice as if she was struggling to keep her wits about her. Had I been expecting a horde of magick-starved customers to arrive, I still would have closed the shop to go with her.

"Name the time and I'll be there," I said without hesitation.

"I don't want to disrupt your workday. Do you take a lunch break?"

"Sorcerers can't live on magick alone," I replied, although I usually brought lunch from home or grabbed something nearby so I could keep the shop open.

"Great, thanks. After the bank, I'll pick up lunch for us." We settled on noon.

After searching for fifteen minutes, I found the sign we'd bought years ago for those times we had to close the shop during the workday. It was hand-painted in an overwrought Victorian style with a picture of a clock whose hands could be moved to show the time we'd be back. Between Bronwen, Morgana, Tilly, and me, there'd always been someone around to cover if one of us had to leave. Now that Tilly's shop was closed, and she was wizard-sitting Merlin, there remained a grand total of me.

I set the hands at one o'clock and locked up. There was no point in taking my car, which was still back at the house. A brisk walk would bring me to the bank in less than five minutes. The Schuyler

Community was the oldest bank in the area and the only one located in the center of town. Two others were in strip malls several miles away to the north and east. The best part about the Schuyler was that everyone who worked there knew all of their depositors as well as their families. The worst part about the Schuyler was exactly the same thing. Familiarity of that nature was often a breeding ground for gossip. Over the years, the Schuyler had lost business to the other banks, simply because some people preferred to conduct their banking matters in a less homey, more clinical environment. My family had debated moving to another bank a couple of times, but in the end, convenience had kept us in town.

I found Elise waiting for me outside the bank. "I want to catch you up before we go in," she said after a hello hug. "When I called the bank after the funeral, I spoke to Debbie about having our safety deposit box unsealed and inventoried. She told me I'd have to get myself appointed administrator of the estate in order to do that, which I took care of yesterday." Elise paused to take a breath. "There's so much red tape to go through when a spouse dies, there's no time to grieve properly. You're expected to pick up and carry on as if everything is back to normal again. But it isn't. And at times I don't think it will ever be." She heaved a tremulous sigh. "Sorry." I nodded in understanding and let her continue. "I called Debbie this morning to make an appointment to take care of the box."

"She corrected me and said "boxes."

"Did you have more than one?" I asked.

"Not to my knowledge."

Now I understood the cause of her agitation.

"When I questioned Debbie about it, she said there were definitely two in both our names. At that point I pretended the second one had slipped my mind in all the turmoil. After I got off the phone with her, I immediately called Scott." I must have had a blank look on my face, because she went on to explain that Scott was a colleague of Jim's, his go-to attorney if he needed outside help. "He knew about the second box, but not why it existed or what it contained. He seemed totally surprised to learn that I had no knowledge of it. He said Jim would have had to forge my signature and photocopy my driver's license to open it in both our names."

"So Jim rented the second box without ever mentioning it to

you," I repeated, trying to make sense of it. If I was surprised, I could imagine how the unexpected news had hit her. "Can you think of any reason why he would do that?"

"Maybe he didn't want me to know about what was in it. But then why put it in both our names? I'm completely at a loss. That's why I wanted you to come along. By the time I got off the phone with Scott my thoughts were in a muddle."

"Don't worry," I linked my arm through hers, "We'll get to the bottom of it."

We marched in and headed straight for Debbie's desk. She popped right up when she saw us coming and met us halfway across the carpeted area where the bank officers had their desks. She was a slim woman in her forties, with basic brown hair in a bouncy wedge. Her clothes were bank conservative, with the exception of big hoop earrings. She pressed Elise's hand between her own two. "How are you?" Her grim smile reminded me of a funeral director.

"I'm okay," Elise replied, which was far from true. But answering any other way would have started a pointless exchange that would have wasted time and made everyone more uncomfortable.

"Good, good," Debbie said, releasing her hand. "We'll try to take care of this annoying business as quickly as possible. Do you have the papers naming you administrator of the estate?" she asked as she led us back to her desk. Elise produced them and Debbie took a minute to glance over them. Satisfied, she handed them back, then walked us over to the vault at the rear of the bank where we were met by a more senior bank officer. George Augales was a compact man who had to be flirting with fifty. He thanked Debbie and said he'd take over from there. It seemed like they'd choreographed this visit ahead of time to keep the bereaved from having to wait. I wondered if they'd synchronized their watches too. I berated myself for being cynical. They were probably trying to be considerate. Nope, the reasons notwithstanding, their studied compassion irritated me. I'd been spared this particular aspect of what I'd come to think of as "death chores." Morgana and Bronwen had never kept a safety deposit box. Instead they'd cast wards around the shop and house to keep anyone with malice in their heart from entering. Of course I now had the security system, so I didn't have to rely on the protection spells. But maybe it wouldn't be a bad idea to renew them anyway.

George was a by-the-numbers kind of guy. He asked Elise to sign both signature cards, which he'd already plucked from the files in anticipation of her arrival. The card for the secret box bore one supposed signature by Elise and three others by Jim. Elise spent a few seconds studying the signature that wasn't hers, before signing on the line below with a shaky hand. She handed George the one key she had, and he used it, along with the master key, to access the first box. Since Elise didn't have a key to the other one, George had to break the lock. I was surprised by the size of the secret box. It was one of the largest in the vault. Elise had to be wondering what on Earth Jim was keeping in there. I sure was.

George carried both boxes out of the vault and led us into one of the two small rooms where the bank's patrons could look though the contents of their boxes in private. George placed Elise's boxes on the table. Since he hadn't known I was coming, he excused himself to bring in a third chair.

When we were settled, Elise opened the small box first. In her place, I would have started with the secret one. Maybe she was putting it off, afraid what she might find out about the man she'd married, the father of her children. The first box held mostly papers, the deed to the house and titles to the two cars, her marriage license, the family's social security cards and birth certificates, plus a number of federal savings bonds in the children's names. George noted each item on a legal pad. The last thing was a black velvet jewelry pouch containing three gold bracelets, a sapphire and diamond cocktail ring and a pair of small diamond stud earrings. Judging by Elise's face, no surprises there. Before lifting the lid of the secret box, she turned to me. I nodded to let her know I was there for her no matter what she was about to discover. George was clicking and unclicking his pen, probably wishing we'd wrap things up so he could go for lunch. I looked pointedly at his hand holding the pen, and he was astute enough to realize his impatience was showing. He set the pen down and gave me a sour smile.

Elise lifted the lid of the box as gingerly as if she thought a rubber snake might pop out. Then her forehead bunched in a frown. The box was filled with bulging manila envelopes that seemed barely able to contain their contents. She withdrew one of them, opened the little aluminum clasp and peered inside. Her mouth fell open. It was the first time I'd ever seen someone actually look dumbstruck, but there was no better word to describe her expression at that moment.

"What is it?" I couldn't keep myself from asking. She upended the envelope, letting its contents fall onto the table. Ten neat stacks of hundred-dollar bills. George sat up straighter and retrieved his pen, while Elise counted the bills in one of the packs—one hundred. Easy math. The envelope contained one hundred thousand dollars. She pulled the other envelopes out of the box. There were five in all—a cool half million. She fell back against the chair shaking her head. George excused himself again and returned a minute later with a cash counter. The accounting had to be accurate, because the government was going to want its share.

Elise hardly spoke a word until we were back in her car. George had supplied her with a canvas tote in which to carry home the contents of both boxes. I'd taken care of the necessary thank yous, because she seemed to be operating on autopilot, minus the speech option. When we reached her car, she handed me the keys, acknowledging that she was too distracted to drive safely.

"Where to?" I asked, sliding into the driver's seat.

She took so long to answer that I was starting to repeat the question when she finally murmured, "Anywhere to get takeout—you choose." Less than fifteen minutes later, we pulled to the curb in front of Abracadabra with two turkey sandwiches, Russian dressing, pickles, bottled iced tea, and a small bag of potato chips.

From his window seat, Sashkatu greeted us with a disinterested yawn. I hiked myself onto the counter and started to unpack our lunch, while Elise stowed the tote under my desk, away from potential prying eyes. Then she joined me on the counter. The smell of turkey had caught Sashkatu's attention. He stepped down from the windowsill onto my desk chair to better view the proceedings and possibly wheedle a bite.

"I have no idea," Elise said in answer to a question I hadn't asked. Now that we were in the seclusion of my shop, she'd given up any pretext of composure, her shoulders slumped as if this were the final straw she could carry. "I mean, where could he have gotten all that money? And why keep it a secret? What did he intend to do with it?"

I'd been going over the same litany of questions myself. "One thing is clear," I said, addressing the most positive aspect I could find, "although Jim didn't want you to know about the money yet, he wasn't trying to keep it from you in the long run. It wasn't like he was squirreling it away because he was planning to leave you. If that were the case, he wouldn't have gone to the trouble of forging your signature and all to add you as a signatory." I unwrapped my sandwich and took a bite to make my stomach stop grumbling.

Elise perked up a bit. "You're right. I didn't think of it that way. But it still doesn't explain why he was keeping it a secret. He knew how worried I've been about having enough money for the boys' education. So why not tell me? Give me some peace of mind?"

"I'm afraid that part's got me stumped too," I said, which wasn't entirely true. But the one reason I'd come up with, pointed to criminal activity and I didn't want to go there. Once Elise had a chance to process everything, she'd figure that out for herself. Most people would have invested the money or, at the very least, secured it in a government-insured savings account. The fact that Jim had hidden the money away supported my fear that it was ill-gotten gains. Maybe he'd planned to keep it a secret until the statute of limitations ran out on whatever crime he may have committed. It was hard for me to think of Jim in that light, but based on the facts I had at the moment, there was no other light on the horizon. "You should try to eat something," I said to Elise. She was staring off into space, her sandwich on the counter still neatly wrapped up.

She unfolded the paper, took a bite, and chewed listlessly. "What am I supposed to do with all that cash now?" she mumbled around a mouthful. "I'm nervous just carrying it around."

I'd been so focused on the provenance of the money that I hadn't considered the more immediate concern of safeguarding it. "I guess you could rent a new box to keep it in, until you have a chance to talk to someone like a financial planner." I opened the chips and offered them to Elise, who dug in with more enthusiasm than she had the sandwich. Together we polished them off in no time, their salty, fried goodness as comforting in their own way as chicken soup.

"I don't think I'll rent the new box at the Schuyler," Elise said, after washing down the chips with her iced tea. "Now that they know how much money is involved . . ."

"Given the circumstances, you're entitled to a certain amount of paranoia." I assured her.

She tore a bit of turkey from her sandwich and held it out to Sashkatu, who considered it for a moment before deigning to take it. "Do you think the money has something to do with Jim's murder?" she asked.

That possibility had been running around in my head from the moment the first packet of bills hit the table. "We can't discount it, but until we know for sure, why not think of it as a windfall that will put your kids through college? Maybe that will help you sleep better."

Her mouth twisted into a wry smile. "A sledge hammer is about the only thing that might help me sleep better at this point."

"Do you remember the spell I gave you a couple of years ago to help calm and center you?" I asked.

"The one that's more like meditation than magick?"

"That's the one. Give it a try tonight."

"Thanks, I think I—oh no," she interrupted herself, "do I have to tell the police about the money?"

That question had also eluded me until that moment. "I think you need to ask Scott about that."

Elise nodded. "I'll call him when I get home. I'm afraid the money would give the police a motive to pin on me."

"Let me play the devil's advocate for a minute. What if they find out about it on their own? Won't you look guiltier for trying to hide it?"

"You're right," she said miserably. "It's a no-win situation. I can see the headlines in the tabloids—GREEDY WIFE KILLS HUSBAND FOR SECRET STASH OF CASH."

"It does have a certain ring to it," I said, eliciting a little laugh from her.

"You are bad," she said, glancing at her watch. "I'd better get going." She hopped down from the counter and stuffed her sandwich back into the bag to take home. "Thanks for holding my hand today."

"Anytime," I said, cleaning up the remnants of my lunch. She retrieved the tote from under the desk and was heading to the door when the phone rang. She mouthed a "goodbye" as I picked up the receiver.

Tilly was on the other end. "Kailyn, dear, we're having a bit of a problem." Although my aunt was given to hyperbole when things were going well, she tended to minimize when it came to trouble. Other itty bitty problems over the years had included a fire in her toaster oven that nearly roasted her shop and ours along with it, a large, rabid raccoon who'd gained entrance to her house through the fireplace flue, and an allergic reaction to peanuts that had landed her in the ICU. Given that history, I really wished I didn't have to ask her what was wrong.

Chapter 13

I closed up the shop for the second time that day, without waking Sashkatu, and ran home to get my car. According to Tilly, she and Merlin had stopped at The Rescued Pet several miles from town to buy Isenbale more cat food. It was the one pet store she or I would frequent, because the puppies for sale came from shelters and rescues, not awful puppy mills. While Tilly was paying for the food, Merlin wandered off to look at the puppies, and the next thing she knew there were puppies running everywhere. The manager and all the employees jumped into action, but before anyone thought of locking the front door, other patrons arrived, inadvertently providing the two dozen puppies with an escape route. Since Tilly wasn't much help in the running department, she called 911 and then me. In a high pitched, semi-hysterical voice she assured me that things were under control and that the police were on their way. She seemed to have forgotten that the police force of New Camel amounted to Officer Curtis. I told her I'd be there as soon as I could. The problem was that the puppy roundup had brought traffic to a standstill. By the time I made it to the strip mall where The Rescued Pet was located, there was one puppy still at large and he was in the parking lot surrounded by Merlin, Officer Curtis, the pet store staff, and half a dozen good Samaritans who'd pulled over to help in the rescue. All those people trying to catch one tiny beagle-mix would have been comical if it weren't for the danger the puppy was facing. The lot was large, cars coming and going, pulling in and out of spots, the drivers focused on getting to their next destination. To minimize the risk to the puppy, I positioned my car to block the entrance into the lot and jumped out to join the circle. I found myself standing opposite Merlin, who was almost unrecognizable. His long hair was pulled back in a rubber band

and he was wearing a pair of chinos and a striped polo shirt that had once belonged to Tilly's husband. Years ago when I'd asked her why she was keeping his clothes, she'd told me she was going to need them one day.

The puppy seemed to be having a grand old time. He would let someone get nearly close enough to grab him, before dodging under one of the parked cars. Tilly, who'd been watching from the sidewalk in front of the stores, disappeared into the pizza parlor next to the pet shop and reemerged with a slice that had been cut into small pieces. She handed bits of it to me and the others encircling the puppy. The smell brought him out from under the SUV where he'd last taken refuge, but in the end he chose freedom over food. A collective groan arose from the rescuers. Tilly was watching the drama from the sidelines, popping bits of pizza into her mouth as if she was eating popcorn at the movies. She looked surprised and a bit embarrassed when she realized she'd finished it all.

Across from me, Merlin made no effort to mask his feelings. He was clearly growing more impatient and disgruntled by the second. Alarms started blaring in my head, but before I could warn him not to use magick, the puppy suddenly appeared in his arms. Tilly and I were the only ones who understood what happened. Everyone else looked stunned, including the puppy. I tried to think of a reasonable explanation to offer them, one that didn't include magick, but nothing came to me. I told myself to be grateful Merlin hadn't accidentally changed the puppy into an elephant or a fire-breathing dragon. That would have caused a whole lot more consternation among the onlookers. As it was, instead of going about their business, they were talking to each other, trying to make sense of what they'd witnessed. I needed to put an end to their speculation, preferably before they decided to ask Merlin himself. It was one thing for people to buy my beauty products that worked a bit too well or to ask Tilly for a glimpse into the future. But asking them to accept that honest-to-goodness sorcerers were living in their midst would no doubt be pushing our luck. My grandmother had warned me from an early age not to ever give people cause to fear me. So I did the one thing I could think of to defuse the situation. I started whistling and applauding the puppy's safe capture. Tilly realized what I was doing and immediately chimed in. Soon everyone was clapping and whistling, their bewilderment temporarily forgotten in their triumph. Merlin handed the puppy to the store manager and executed a low bow with a flourish, from which he had some trouble straightening himself. Apparently old was old, even for the greatest sorcerer who'd ever lived.

Officer Curtis was working the crowd, reminding them that they were making it impossible for cars to enter or leave. When he reached me, he smiled and asked how I was doing, before pointing to my car, which still blocked the driveway. "I'll have to ask you to move it, so folks have access," he said pleasantly.

"I'm on it," I said, already on the move.

"Nice seeing you again," he called after me. I hopped into the car, pretending I hadn't heard him. I couldn't truthfully have said, "likewise," because seeing him was a troubling reminder of my suspect status.

With the puppies safely back in the pet store, I was torn between going right back to my shop or having a little chat with Merlin. The chat won. There wouldn't be much point in trying to keep my business alive if the three of us were eventually run out of town. I knew I was probably overreacting, but I wasn't willing to take the chance.

"You cannot practice magick like that out in public," I said sternly and without preface. The wizard and I were seated at my aunt's kitchen table. Tilly was in her pantry trying to decide which tea to brew. She believed that the right cup of tea could help you get through most of life's problems, especially when paired with freshly baked goods. She popped her head out of the pantry to give me a wide-eyed look that plainly said, *Good Lord, remember who you're talking to!*

But I was past trying to spare Merlin's sensibilities, past worrying that he might turn me into a toad. "I've told you before that this world is nothing like the world you came from, and you are going to get all of us in trouble if you're not more careful."

Merlin straightened his shoulders. "I have done nothing untoward," he said lifting his chin in stately indignation.

"You used magick twice today."

"Was it not your aim that the pup be saved?" he asked.

"Yes, of course it was."

"Well then, had I not intervened, we might still be standing there like a pack of imbeciles under the thrall of a one pound dog. So yes, I saw fit to use magick for everyone's benefit."

"The next time you think about using magick, you need to clear it with me or Tilly first. Do you understand?" I prayed he wouldn't contest the edict, because I didn't have an "or else" to throw at him nor any means of forcing him to comply.

He bulldozed right over my question with one of his own. "What other instance of magick would you accuse me of?"

"Those puppies didn't let themselves out of their cages."

"I had no part in it," he said, a smirk of satisfaction curving the edges of his mouth. "I was simply standing there, thinking how nice it would be to hold one of the pups when all the cage doors flew open."

I took a deep breath and let it out slowly, very slowly. I believed him. But if his errant thoughts could produce such results, we were in bigger trouble than I'd imagined. Over cups of Tilly's passionflower and red bush tea mixture, I told him what I suspected, and we went around and around that thorny bush without coming to any solution.

"How does one go about in the world without thinking?" Merlin finally demanded in exasperation. I had no answer for him.

"Oh dear," Tilly said, her brow furrowed. "I may not have put enough red bush in the mixture. I know, I'll make some apricot scones. They always give my spirits a lift."

"I'm sure they'll be delicious," I said, standing and taking my purse from the back of my chair, "but I'm afraid this is one time scones won't help solve our conundrum."

"Well they certainly can't hurt," she said brightly, already assembling the ingredients, the mixing bowls and baking pans. "I think better when my hands are busy."

"I wouldn't mind a scone or two," Merlin put in, "and apricot does sound delightful." I don't think they noticed when I left.

I parked my car in front of my shop. I hadn't bothered with the clock sign when I got the call about the puppies, because I didn't know when I'd return. As it happened, it was almost time to lock up for the night. I walked inside, surprised that Sashkatu wasn't asleep on his window seat. A moment later, he was snaking in and out of my legs as if he was on a slalom ski run. I was so unprepared, I tripped over him and lost my balance. It was a good thing the counter was there. I grabbed onto the edge of it and managed to stay upright. If I'd gone down, neither Sashki nor I would have fared well. Oblivious to his brush with disaster, he continued using my legs as a rubbing post. Once I was steady, I crouched down to stroke the length of his furry body and was treated to a rare purr of contentment. Maybe he'd been worried I was never coming back to feed him. Or maybe he'd finally made peace with the fact that I was in charge for the long haul and he ought to work his way into my good graces. Regardless of his motive, it was nice to connect with him again. He let me know our moment was over by stalking off to hide beneath my desk. I knew not to take it personally. He'd always been very much his own cat. I reset the alarm system, then came around the counter to my desk and scooped him into my arms before he knew what I was up to. He could be fussy about being carried, but this time he bore the indignity in stoic silence. Since I had my car there, I needed to drive back home, which meant going around the block to the front of the house. Sashkatu was dead set against getting in the car.

I opened the car door and tried to put him in the front passenger seat, but he grabbed onto my arms with his claws. He yowled. I swore. After several minutes of wrestling with him, I decided to use my brain. I started to put him down on the sidewalk, and the second he felt the cement beneath his back paws, he let go of my arm. Before he realized what I was doing, I grabbed him around the middle, tossed him gently onto the front seat and shut the door. So much for the detente in our relationship. At least his distress would be relieved in less than a minute when we arrived home. The scratches I'd received would take considerably longer to heal.

After I fed all my four-legged companions, I made myself some comfort food. Egg noodles with butter and cottage cheese was an old standby from when I was a kid. It was equally soothing to an ailing tummy or a troubled soul. I sat down at the kitchen table and turned on the small flat screen on the wall across from me. I'd bought it for company, now that I was eating most of my meals alone. I found a rerun of the *Bewitched* series from the long-ago sixties. It was always good for some laughs, mostly because the magick in it was so silly. I was a few forkfuls into my dinner, the muscles in my neck starting to unclench, when I suddenly found myself with company. In the form of two little energy clouds.

"There you are," my mother said. "Where have you been all day? You weren't in the shop when we popped in." For some reason, Morgana and Bronwen could travel through the ether to reach me at the house and the shop, but nowhere else.

"You have to actually open the shop in order for customers to come in and buy the merchandise," my grandmother added as if I'd become too addled to figure that out for myself.

"I spent half the day getting Aunt Tilly out of trouble," I replied. "And trust me, you don't want to know the details." In any case, I didn't want to rehash the whole story.

"My sister can be such a ninny," Morgana lamented.

"That may be," Bronwen said, "but you can't deny how talented she is."

"I've always been her greatest fan," my mother said crisply.

"Mom, Grandma, did you stop in to say 'hi,'" I asked, before they veered off on a tangent, "or is there something you wanted to discuss?" I immediately felt bad about the impatience in my tone; I was tired and my noodles were getting cold.

"Oh yes, yes." My mother said, back on track. "We've been discussing this murder investigation you're embroiled in and we agree that you should stop associating with Elise Harkins."

Where had that come from? "I've known Elise all my life. You hired her to babysit me. Now you've decided you don't trust her?"

"Well, circumstances change, and one has to accommodate to those changes or face the consequences," Bronwen said, clearly measuring her words.

"But nothing has changed," I replied.

"It's my understanding that she's a suspect in her husband's death."

"Tilly and I are too, in case my mother forgot to mention that."

"Statistically speaking, most murders are committed by people who are close to the victim," Morgana put in.

I was being double-teamed. My mother and grandmother didn't often agree, but when they did, it was usually easier to admit defeat than to argue with them. At least it was, back when the arguments were over my curfew on school nights and whether I could have a study date up in my room. This time the issue was too important for me to retreat or hoist a white flag. "Elise couldn't have killed Jim any more than I could have killed either of you. If she and I work together, we all stand a better chance of proving our innocence. I have no intentions of writing her off."

My mother's cloud had started pulsing with a disturbing maroon light I'd never seen before. "There are things you don't know about Elise," she said grimly.

"I'm listening."

"She had a little trouble with the law in her teens. It involved a boy."

"Doesn't it always?" Bronwen remarked. "Good girls fall for bad boys. Some things never change."

"Let's stick to the facts, Mother," Morgana said. "This is messy enough without a running commentary. Now where was I? Oh right, the boy ran with a crowd who were into drag racing, vandalism, shoplifting. Most of them had records. Then a new girl appeared on the scene, and the boy broke up with Elise. Her parents thought their prayers had been answered. But Elise was inconsolable. One night she threw a kitchen knife into her purse and went looking for them. She attacked the boy and the new girlfriend. She was lucky the rest of them pulled her away before she could really hurt them. Her parents agreed to send her for therapy in exchange for expunging the police report. Most of the town stood by the family. They knew it could just as easily have been one of their overwrought kids. So, the story got swept under the town's carpet, and life went back to normal."

"That must have been when I was really young," I said.

"*That's* what you took away from the story?" my mother asked incredulously.

"It seems to me that she's spent the last twenty-odd years living a decent, law-abiding life and raising two great kids, which doesn't happen by accident. She shouldn't have to keep answering for an impulsive moment back when she was a teenager. You knew all about it, and it didn't stop you from hiring her to babysit me. Weren't you worried she'd go crazy and hack me to death?"

Morgana was uncharacteristically at a loss for words. Bronwen stepped in for her. "Given Jim's death, perhaps we should have been more concerned."

"You have nothing to worry about," I said. "Elise is the most stable, ethical person I know." Since I didn't want their visit to end on such a strained note, I asked them how things were going in their new realm. They assured me everything was fine. We chatted for a few more minutes, before they left to do whatever spirits do on the other side of the veil.

My noodles were cold and starchy, beyond saving, and I didn't have the energy to make another bowl. Instead I finished off half a pint of chocolate-chocolate chip ice cream and crawled into bed. I hated to admit it, but that story about Elise's past was nagging at me. What if Beverly was right about Jim cheating? What if Elise found out, and it dredged up all of those painful teenage feelings again? I lay there staring at the ceiling, my heart beating a tattoo that asked— what if . . . what if . . . what if?

Chapter 14

"The wood must be elder," Merlin said, his arms folded over his chest in a pose that dared me to argue. He'd gone back to wearing the clothes he'd arrived in, which had benefitted greatly from a spin in Tilly's washing machine. With his hair once more untethered and wild, he could easily have played the part of Don Quixote. "Elder is a sacred wood," he went on, "and may only be used in the practice of white magick." We were in my shop, discussing the fact that he needed a new wand. In spite of being told about the problems my family had been having with our magick, he was convinced that his problems were due to not having his wand. Since he'd had no time to prepare for his sudden journey to the future, he'd left both of his seasoned wands behind. He'd tried a dozen times to summon one of them, only to end up with a pile of wood shavings in the palm of his hand. Rather than risk destroying the one that remained back in medieval England, he decided to create a new one.

I couldn't offer him mine, although I rarely used it. A wand was as unique and personal as a sorcerer's familiar. Bronwen had been a great proponent of their use and never went anywhere without hers. Mine, on the other hand, had never seemed to enhance my powers to any appreciable degree. "Elder wood it is," I said. "I'm sure Tilly will be happy to take you on a field trip. And while you're at it, you can gather some of the plants I need to replace."

"Why don't *you* take me right now?" he demanded petulantly. "That was my purpose in walking over here. Tilly was still asleep, and when I tried to wake her, she nearly bit my head off."

I knew he wasn't exaggerating; Tilly did love her sleep. I was trying to explain to him why I had to keep my shop open, when a customer walked in. I whispered a hurried reminder to Merlin to say as little as possible and not to focus his thoughts on anything in particular.

The customer was Beverly Ruppert of all people. After I told her off at the wake, I assumed I'd never see her in my shop again. So much for assumptions. When she came up to the counter, I nodded and waited for her to speak first. She gave Merlin a disparaging look, then nodded back at me. "Kailyn," she said, "I know we've had our differences, but I don't see why that should stand in the way of business. I need what you sell and, from what I hear, you can use the commerce."

"The last time you were in, you complained about the product you'd bought," I reminded her

"The one you gave me in exchange worked better," she said, "although it still wasn't up to Morgana's original standards. For the sake of your reputation, you might want to look into that."

Merlin was standing close enough to me that I could sense his body tensing like a cat gathering itself to pounce. I gave his shin a sharp, warning kick. "If you're here to buy something, Beverly, you should get on with it before I decide I don't need your business that badly." The reason I was tolerating her at all, was because she owned a popular hair salon that gave her access to the ears of most of New Camel and its environs. Essentially, she and I were locked in a strange *pas de deux*. She needed what I sold, and I needed good press. Without another word, she plucked a basket from the stack of them and spent the next ten minutes roaming the aisles. Merlin shuffled beyond reach of my foot, muttering under his breath. I couldn't make out what he was saying, but I sent him a "don't-you-dare" glare in case he was tempted to punish Beverly or me for that matter.

When Beverly returned to the counter, her basket was overflowing with multiples of everything from under-eye smoother to suntan lotion. She was probably stocking up in case I ever decided to bar her from the shop.

"I suppose you heard about Jim's interesting lunch date two weeks before he was murdered," she said in an offhand manner.

I kept ringing up her items without missing a beat. "I'm not interested in your gossip."

"Right, how could I forget? Well, rest assured you won't hear another word about it from me," she said dramatically. "My lips are zipped."

She'd said enough to bait me, but in spite of my curiosity, I had no intention of biting. I packed her purchases into two canvas totes with the store logo, maintaining my stance against the use of plastic. "Have a nice day," I said, forcing the words through clenched teeth.

"I didn't mean to offend," she said smugly. "But I know that if *I* had a stake in the outcome of the case, I'd want all the information I could get my hands on." She gave an exaggerated shrug. "People never fail to surprise me." She picked up a bag with each hand and was walking away from the counter when she froze in mid-stride and her eyes glazed over.

"Doreen waited on Jim and a young, blonde hottie at the Garden Grill," she said in a flat, robotic tone. "And they were awfully chummy." Then her mouth fell shut and she blinked rapidly, like someone startled from a nap. She looked at me with a bewildered expression, shook her head and walked out of the shop.

"Merlin," I said in a menacing tone, though I really wanted to kiss him.

"That hateful woman deserved some comeuppance," he said without a trace of regret. "And don't try to deny that you were curious. In deference to you, I applied considerable restraint. At least this way she'll never know she told you."

I had to admit that I liked the idea of picking Beverly's brain without her knowledge. Unfortunately, I wasn't too happy about what I'd learned. Evidence was definitely piling up against Elise. I had to find out if she knew about the not-so-discreet luncheon before Jim was murdered.

"Now will you take me or call Tilly?" Merlin asked, stuck on his own agenda.

I was punching in my aunt's number, when she hobbled up to us from her shop.

"There you are," she said to Merlin, clearly relieved to have found him. "I didn't know what to think when I got up and you were gone."

"And yet you found me," he said dryly. "I need wood for a new wand, and Kailyn has offered me your services. Shall we go?"

Tilly looked from Merlin to me. "Right now?"

I shrugged. "He isn't the patient type, in case you haven't noticed."

"But I haven't had my morning cup of tea yet," she protested.

"I know, why don't you two stop for breakfast along the way?" The suggestion immediately brought smiles to their faces. I handed Tilly the list of plants I needed and sent them merrily on their way, discussing breakfast options across the centuries.

The day flew by with a small but steady stream of customers. Some of them were locals whom I knew, but others had made the trip from as far away as Seneca and Cayuga counties. It was one of the best days I'd had in months. I attributed the uptick to the beautiful June day. It was finally beginning to feel more like summer, and folks were in the mood to go for a drive. I propped the shop door open with the three-foot-tall, brightly hued dragon statue that Morgana had bought for that purpose. The statue was a great attention grabber and also allowed fresh air to circulate through the shop.

Between answering questions and ringing up purchases, I didn't have time to eat more than a few bites of my peanut butter sandwich. Sashkatu didn't budge from his window seat all day, no doubt worried that someone might try to pet him. He had a firm no-strangers policy.

Although I'd been busy, the question of how to broach Jim's lunch date to Elise had apparently been simmering in my mind all day, my subconscious debating the pros and cons of various scenarios. The last thing I wanted to do was cause her more pain or distress. By the time I turned the sign in the shop window from OPEN to CLOSED, my decision was fully formed. There was no good way to ask Elise outright if she knew about the lunch date and, if so, when she found out about it. My one viable option was to call Ronnie again. Although she'd already told me that to the best of her knowledge Jim never cheated on his wife, maybe she could shed some light on who had shared that table with him. I was still holding out the hope that it was a perfectly innocent business lunch.

Tilly and Merlin returned from their day of plant picking as I was leaving the shop with Sashkatu. They hadn't been able to find everything on my list, but they'd accomplished quite a bit for one day. Tilly had stopped at a store for paper bags, in which to place the different flora, and a tote emblazoned with cute cat images to hold all of them. One by one, she pulled the plants out of the tote bag and piled them on my counter. There was Hobblebrush, Creeping Spike-Rush, Worm Seeded Spurge, and Northern Witchgrass. Some, like Calf's Snout, Eye of Newt, Hawk's Heart, and Gosling Wing, were fairly common plants, their fanciful names bestowed by sorcerers over the centuries to make them sound more mysterious. We'd never actually used the eyes of newts in our potions.

Merlin waited until Tilly was finished setting out the spoils of their trip, before showing me the elder branch that was destined to become his new wand. It was grayish-brown and slender, without knots or other blemishes. He held it along his right arm to demonstrate that it was the correct length, reaching from his elbow to his fingertip.

"Perfect," I said, since he seemed to be waiting for my reaction.

"Why of course it is," he said grandly.

Tilly declared that her feet were aching like rotten teeth. She was going home to soak them in warm water and a concoction that helped to somewhat ease the pain.

When I called Ronnie to ask if I could stop by, she said she was about to order Chinese takeout, so why didn't I join her? I offered to grab the food on my way there if she didn't mind waiting for me to feed the cats. Half an hour later I was in my car, headed to the China Castle. It was a grandiose name for a little storefront takeout place with four tables, but the food was always well-prepared. Another five minutes and I was pulling into the driveway of Ronnie's townhouse with the Moo Shu Chicken and Pork Lo Mein. It was a good thing I didn't have to drive farther with it, because I'm pretty sure the aromas filling my car were more powerful than the Sirens who'd beckoned to Odysseus. One more red light and I would have been shamelessly digging into those containers.

Although I'd known Ronnie most of my life, I'd never been inside her home before. When I'd seen her socially, it was generally at Elise's house or in town. From the outside, the townhouse was nothing special, but inside was a different story. There was a dramatic vaulted ceiling in the living room and dark, gleaming hardwood floors. I didn't know if Ronnie had used a decorator, but the place was elegantly furnished down to the smallest detail. I loved all the clean lines and contemporary style. Someday, when I was no longer a murder suspect and my business was once again flourishing, I intended to redecorate my home in a similar fashion. Maybe I'd ask her advice when the time came. But for the present, that was all pie in the sky, as Tilly liked to say.

Ronnie had brewed a pot of tea and set the table, so we sat right down to dinner. We chatted about safe things like the long-awaited warm weather, the newest fashions, TV shows and her job search. As if by prior agreement, we avoided more difficult subjects until the leftovers were stored in the fridge and the dishes were stacked in the washer. "So, what can I help you with?" Ronnie asked. We were back at the table with our tea cups replenished and an open box of Mallomars.

"Have you heard the latest gossip Beverly Ruppert's been spreading all over town?" I asked.

Ronnie frowned. "What is she spewing now?"

"Jim was supposedly spotted having lunch with a 'young, blonde hottie,' as she put it. If it's true, and Elise knew about it, the police are going to think it's an awfully good motive for murder."

Ronnie stunned me by breaking into a huge grin.

"Am I missing something here?" I asked, feeling as if I'd followed Alice down the rabbit hole.

"Jim was having lunch with his niece, Ella," she said, reaching for a Mallomar.

"Oh . . . oh wow," I stammered as her words sank in. "But are you sure we're talking about the same time and place?"

"Yes. He told me that Doreen's eyebrows nearly took flight when she saw them there."

"Then why didn't he introduce Ella to her to prevent this kind of gossip?"

"At the time, he thought it was funny. In fact we both had a good laugh about it. He certainly didn't expect to be murdered a couple of weeks later and have his whole life taken apart and scrutinized."

"Then I guess Elise knew all about it," I said, relieved that she wouldn't be blindsided by more of Beverly's malicious gossip.

"She said she wished she could have been a fly on the restaurant's wall." Beverly nudged the cookies closer to me. "You've got to have at least one or I'm going to feel guilty for indulging."

I was exhausted when I got home, but instead of going to sleep, I made myself some strong coffee and sat down at the computer. I was determined to start looking through Jim's files for other possible killers. If I waited for the perfect time to do it, I'd never get it done. After an hour's work, I was almost at the end of the Ds and hadn't found anything the least bit suspicious. Most of Jim's clients were local, their legal affairs as mundane and dull as I'd expected. From what I could tell, his practice dealt primarily with business contracts, tax issues, and estate planning. Of course I still had a lot of the alphabet to go through, but my fatigue was starting to win out over the caffeine, and if I didn't call it a day soon, I'd risk missing something important. That didn't turn out to be a problem though, because I was wide awake the instant I opened the last D file to find Detective Phillip Duggan's name.

Chapter 15

Adrenalin is definitely better than caffeine for keeping you on your toes. Although I didn't expect to learn that Detective Duggan was a closet serial killer protected for years by attorney-client privilege, I couldn't help being a little excited when his file popped up on my computer screen.

I skimmed through the file, then went back and read it more carefully. The detective had retained Jim's services in March of 2010 for the purpose of suing neurosurgeon, Robert Kane, for malpractice in the death of his wife. From what I could tell, it was one of those sad instances when the operation was a success, but the patient died. I couldn't make much sense of the detailed legal and medical jargon, but the verdict was easy enough to understand. The jury found the surgeon innocent of any wrongdoing. Based on the emails Jim and Duggan exchanged in the aftermath of the trial, it was obvious that Duggan blamed Jim for the outcome. In fact he went on to retain a second attorney to sue Jim for malpractice. And once again, Duggan lost. Feeling that he'd been twice denied justice, had Detective Duggan taken things into his own hands? It wouldn't have been the first time that an officer of the law committed a crime. There were plenty of cases in the news about police, lawyers, even judges who thought they knew the system and its loopholes well enough to get away with any number of crimes, including murder. But how on earth could I go about investigating the detective? If *he* was the killer, all he had to do was pick the most plausible suspect and frame him or her for the crime. The cards were clearly stacked in his favor. I doubted that he'd choose Tilly or me to be the fall gal. He would be too hard-pressed to come up with a believable motive. Elise, on the other hand, would fit nicely into his plans. And he knew enough about breaking and entering to have been the intruder who'd stolen Jim's gun from the house and planted it in the dumpster. I reached for the phone to call Elise, but set it down again before dialing. What was I doing? I had no proof of anything. The fact that Duggan had a good motive didn't automatically make him the killer, any more than ownership of the gun made Elise the killer. It was late, and I'd left tired in the dust hours ago, not the best combination for rational thought. Seven hours of uninterrupted sleep would surely give me a clearer perspective. At the very least it would be a salve to my nerves and keep me from being grouchy to customers. No business could survive for long with two grouches, and Sashkatu had cornered that market ages ago.

I fell asleep as soon as my head hit the pillow and didn't wake until morning sunshine streamed through my bedroom windows. I got out of bed with a more optimistic view of life. As much as I would have liked to place Duggan under citizen's arrest, read him his rights, and question him in a soundproof room beneath a naked light bulb, it was a pipe dream that wasn't going to happen. If I wanted to solve the case, I needed to be more proactive in my investigation. Since I hadn't yet pursued the lead I'd gotten from Ronnie, lunchtime seemed like a fine time to check that off my list. I was able to get an appointment with Dr. Silver to check out a molar that was hurting. I was a little troubled by how good I was at lying.

I used the morning to properly store the plant cuttings Tilly and Merlin had brought me, order new jars to replace the ones that had shattered on the storeroom floor and whip up some of the concoctions that had been in those jars. I was mixing a new batch of my grandmother's poultice for chest colds, when Tilly burst through the adjoining door from her shop. In my surprise, I lost my grip on the glass bowl, fumbling it like a novice juggler, before I managed to keep it from hitting the floor. Even if I had dropped it, I couldn't have been angry with her, because she was happier than I'd seen her in ages. Her eyes twinkled and her smile pumped up her cheeks, making her look like a middle-aged cherub in a muumuu.

"I'm fixed," she trilled, executing a neat pirouette of joy before losing her balance and wobbling like a top about to crash. Merlin, who'd followed her in, didn't waste a moment. With his new wand and an experienced flick of the wrist, he planted Tilly firmly back on both feet, a little winded, but otherwise unscathed.

106 • *Sharon Pape*

"Well done," I said with more enthusiasm than the feat probably merited. But my aunt was still upright, and I now had good reason to believe that Merlin could right our other magick-related woes." The sorcerer inclined his head graciously, every bit the entertainer acknowledging his due.

I turned to Tilly, who was still beaming. "How did you know for sure your ability was restored?" I imagined her going outside and summoning up the future of the first person who crossed her path.

"Easy," she said, "during my down time I felt like I was wearing blinders, the kind they put on horses so they can only see straight ahead. But as soon as Merlin the Magnificent cast his spell, the blinders vanished."

Merlin's chest pumped up with greater pride from her accolade. Then he turned to me and must have seen the concern that lingered in my expression. "Although Tilly assured me she didn't need a test to tell her she was once again whole, I insisted on one. Mayhap it will also bring you peace of mind. I asked her if I would live to see my home and time again."

"And I told him I could clearly see him back there. In fact, I was able to describe his home as if it were right here in front of me."

I was underwhelmed. Neither of them seemed disturbed by the fact that there was no way to verify if Tilly had accurately seen the wizard's future or a random image she'd plucked from his mind. I had no doubt it was what Merlin wanted to hear, but we might never know if she was in fact correct. I debated whether or not to bring up this glaring problem, but in the end I said nothing. They had the right to believe whatever they wished to believe. As my grandmother had never tired of telling me, "In this family, we are not in the business of subverting hopes or beliefs. We practice white magick, or no magick at all." By the gravity with which she'd weighted those words, I always had the feeling that she had taken such a misstep herself and that it had cost her dearly.

"What a fabulous day," Tilly went on. "I'm off to put a sign in my shop window saying that I will reopen at three this afternoon. Spread the word. Between now and then, if you need me, I'll be baking." Merlin's face lit up with a child's delight. "And I'm to be her taster," he declared, in no apparent rush to seek a way back to that home of his.

* * *

I parked my car in the lot that Dr. Brian Silver had shared with Jim Harkens. It still felt weird to be there now that Jim wasn't. His half of the building was dark, as if the structure itself was in mourning. Before leaving the car, I pulled down the sun visor and tried out a few expressions of pain in the mirror. They all looked phony. It was a good thing I didn't want to pursue a career in acting. I decided that grim and stoic would better serve my purpose. I locked the car and headed into the building. As I reached Silver's door, a woman and two whiney children were exiting. Inside, three other patients nearly filled the small waiting room. They were reading or playing with their phones, but they all looked up when I came in, probably hoping for some better distraction. I presented myself at the desk and received a set of forms to fill out. When I asked if the dentist was running late, the receptionist cocked an eyebrow at me and said pointedly that there'd been a couple of emergencies they'd had to squeeze in. Point taken. Although I wasn't an established patient of Silver's, they'd extended me that courtesy too. I murmured "thank you" and found myself a seat.

An hour later, Silver's dental assistant opened the door to the inner sanctum and called my name. As she led me down the hallway, she introduced herself as Patty. Judging by the pounds she carried around her midriff and hips and the gray roots that anchored her blonde hair, I put her at about fifty. She ushered me into one of the rooms off the hallway where an ergonomic dental chair was the centerpiece. Before sitting down on it, I did a quick survey of the room. All the equipment appeared to be state of the art. But what did I know? Patty's stomach gurgled as she clipped a dental bib around my neck. "Sorry," she said with a laugh, "serves me right for skipping breakfast." I felt bad about being the cause of her delayed lunch hour, but not too bad. I needed information if I had any hope of clearing Elise's name.

Patty sat down at the computer station that was on the right side of the small room. She clicked through several screens, then started asking me questions: What was the reason for my visit? Which tooth? When did it start to bother me? Did it hurt all the time or just when I ate or drank? Did it react to heat or cold? She was about to launch another question when Dr. Silver walked in. I'd never seen the man before, but since I knew he'd tried to steal Ronnie away from Jim, I'd imagined him to be unctuous and glib, a man accustomed to getting his way regardless of whom he steps on in the process. I was pleasantly surprised to find that he was an affable, down-to-earth guy with a balding pate and an early paunch lapping at his belt. Although he might have been as hungry as his assistant, he introduced himself and spent a couple of minutes chatting with me about mundane things like the weather, my shop, his cat. It was easy to relax around him. I found myself thinking I should switch to him for my dental care—unless of course he turned out to be the killer. That thought quickly knocked me back on track.

"It must feel strange in the building now that Harkens is gone," I said, using Jim's last name to minimize my ties to his family.

"It is a little creepy," Patty replied, a frisson causing her shoulders to twitch. "I mean I feel sorry for his family and all, but it's scary as hell that he was murdered right here. I wish they'd hurry up and find the killer already."

"Everyone's been paranoid since that day," Silver said. "I've been walking Patty and the rest of my staff to their cars when they leave at night." He pulled a pair of latex gloves from the dispenser on the wall.

"Ah, but who walks *you* to *your* car?" I asked wryly.

Silver smiled and shrugged. "I'm a fatalist. I don't worry about what might happen. I take sensible precautions and I try to be mindful of my surroundings. But in the end, whatever's going to happen is going to happen regardless of whether I worry about it or not."

"I wish I could learn to be like that," I said, thinking that the one person who didn't need to be concerned about a killer at large was the killer himself. But I was having a hard time picturing the dentist with a gun in his hand. "Did you hear the gunshot from your office?" I asked.

"I heard it," Patty said, "but I thought it was a car backfiring. In this town, gunshots are the last thing anyone thinks of. Though I guess that's not true anymore."

I looked up at Silver, eyebrows arched to make it clear I was waiting for his response. "I wasn't here," he said. "I'd left early to take care of some banking." He didn't sound like he was lying, but I barely knew the man. Even a lie detector analyst depended on establishing a baseline before testing a subject. Unfortunately I had no way to check out his alibi. If I was lucky enough to hit on the right bank, the bank officials would never release information on a client's comings and goings, except to the police. It occurred to me that Duggan might not know about the feud between the two men. Wasn't it my responsibility as a concerned citizen to make sure he had all the pertinent details regarding the case? If he did know, and I played my cards right, I might be able to find out if Silver's alibi had stood up. Until then, I was adding the dentist's name to my list of suspects.

While I was following my thoughts, the dentist had decided to get on with the business of my molar. Patty briefed him on my problem as he pulled on the gloves with the snap of latex. Now came the tricky part, trying to keep him from actually doing any work on me. I didn't know anyone who liked having a dentist poke around in their mouths and I was far from an exception. I sure hoped Elise appreciated what I was risking for her.

Silver gave my teeth a quick look-see, then took two x-rays of my lower left jaw where the painful molar was supposed to be. The results popped up on the computer screen, and he studied them for a minute, Patty on her tiptoes peering over his shoulder. When he turned back to me, his brow was lowered in a frown that was probably puzzlement, but made him appear sinister. Maybe trying to investigate a potential murder suspect with so many instruments of torture close at hand wasn't the brightest idea I'd ever had.

"I don't see any problem in that area of your mouth," he said, his tone as pleasant as ever. "Would you describe the pain to me."

"Well, it's sharp. Sometimes it hurts when I eat cold stuff, but other times it doesn't."

He nodded as though he'd come to a conclusion. "It does sound like the tooth is somewhat sensitive, but there doesn't seem to be anything fixable at this point. You can try one of the toothpastes for sensitivity issues; they do a pretty good job. This type of problem sometimes vanishes on its own, but if it gets worse or more constant, give us a call and we'll bring you right back in."

"Thank you," I said, relieved that he didn't suggest a root canal or something equally awful. "I'm embarrassed to have taken up your time with this." Too bad I couldn't blush on demand. Silver assured me things like this happened all the time. Better safe than sorry and so forth. After he left the room, Patty unclipped my bib and brought the chair upright.

I swung my legs onto the floor. "I'm sure Dr. Silver isn't going to miss dealing with Harkens anymore," I said.

"You mean the dustup over Ronnie?" She rolled her eyes.

I smiled. "I heard it was getting to be like the Hatfields and the McCoys around here."

"Harkens was a real jerk about the whole thing," she said dismissively. "Silver made Ronnie an offer, she declined. No big deal. Harkens acted like he'd been stabbed in the back."

"Just business, nothing personal," I summed up, as though I sided with team Silver.

"Exactly," she said, one foot already out of the room. "Give us a call if that tooth acts up again."

By the time I paid my bill and jumped into my car, I'd been gone for over two hours. Not that I expected anyone to have missed me. Tilly would still be baking; Merlin was probably in a sugar coma, and Sashkatu had always believed that the lull between breakfast and dinner was best spent asleep. So when I pulled to the curb in front of my shop, I was shocked to find a man about my age sitting on the sidewalk beneath my I'LL-BE-BACK sign that was off by an hour.

Chapter 16

"I'm so sorry I'm late," I said, fumbling through the keys on my chain and then dropping them. "I had sort of a dental emergency, and the dentist was running late. He's not my regular dentist, but he squeezed me in, so I couldn't just up and leave." I realized I was babbling to a perfect stranger. I shut my mouth before I embarrassed myself any further.

"Dental emergencies rank right up there with cardiac emergencies in my book," the man said, wincing for effect. He scooped up the keys as he stood and held them out to me.

"Thanks for understanding. And for waiting." Up close, I found myself thinking he might actually be the perfect stranger. He had to be six feet tall, with hazel eyes and dark hair that the breeze kept tugging onto his forehead. Even his clothes passed muster—a navy polo over tan chinos, Topsiders on sockless feet. I did something I'd never done before—I checked his ring finger. *Seriously?!* I chided myself. But in spite of the reprimand, I was dismayingly glad to see that his finger was bare. "I'm Kailyn Wilde," I said, holding out my hand. I had the odd feeling that I'd met him before, but I had no idea when or where.

"Travis Anderson." He took my hand and squeezed it tightly for a moment instead of shaking it. I studied his face, but didn't see any spark of recognition there. Maybe I knew him as the man of my dreams. Good lord, I sounded like a girl in a bad romance novel. Thank goodness Tilly wasn't there to read my thoughts.

Once I got the door open and disarmed the security system, I invited him in. An invisible cloud of sugar, cinnamon, and butter was wafting through the shop, courtesy of my aunt's baking frenzy. She must have left the connecting door ajar, which she often did to encourage my customers to pay her a visit too. Not that I minded, but I hadn't eaten lunch, and the smells were making my mouth water.

Sashkatu wasn't on his usual perch at the window, but I had a pretty good idea where to find him. The only thing that trumped sleep in his book was food. I excused myself to check next door. At the rear of the shop, I poked my head into Tea and Empathy and found him in a sunny corner, nibbling on a piece of scone. He didn't bother to look up. I could hear Tilly and Merlin talking in the kitchen. Satisfied that all was right, I went back to attend to my customer.

Travis was sniffing the air appreciatively. "Exactly what is it you sell in here?"

"The heavenly aroma you're enjoying is from my aunt's shop next door."

"I didn't notice a bakeshop."

"It really isn't one. She's a psychic who also serves a mean English Tea."

"Does she sell the baked goods separately?"

"Sorry, it's a package deal."

He shrugged. "Too bad." I must have looked curious, because he went on to explain that he didn't believe in psychics.

I'd heard that from plenty of people over the years, most of them men. "But you *do* believe in magick?" I couldn't help asking.

He produced a lopsided grin that added to his appeal. "I enjoy the occasional magic show, purely as entertainment of course." My perfect stranger was starting to tarnish before my eyes.

"Then what brings you to my door?"

"To be honest, my mother." At least he had the decency to look embarrassed.

"Your mother believes in magick?" I asked, enjoying his discomfort probably more than I should have.

He shook his head and laughed. "You don't make it easy for your customers, do you? Will I be required to sign an affidavit stating that I'm a believer before you'll sell me anything?"

"Lucky for you, around here money talks."

"In that case, would you point me in the direction of the shampoo and conditioner for thinning hair?" Clearly not a problem he had.

"Second aisle on your left, bottom shelf. If she colors her hair, you should get the purple bottles." He returned to the counter with two bottles of each. "How did your mother hear about Abracadabra?" I asked, ringing up the purchase.

"One of her friends was here last summer. According to my mother, the woman's hair doubled in volume after a few months. This stuff's legal, right?"

"To the best of my knowledge, and no one has suffered any unwanted side effects from the products over the past few millennia."

Travis chuckled. "That's how long your shop's been around?"

"No, don't be silly. This shop has barely been here for three hundred and fifty years."

"Touché. I get it. You have to keep up the mystique of the place."

"You have no idea," I said, tempted to give him a taste of that "mystique." But if I tried a little magick and failed, I'd wind up proving him right. What if I stuck to something simple, without any hoopla beforehand? That way if it didn't work, he wouldn't know I'd made the attempt. I put his products into a canvas tote. If I wanted to wow Travis, it was now or never. I focused my mind on the shop brochures piled neatly at the end of the counter. I tried to lock onto the top one and lift it off the stack, but I kept losing it before I had any real traction. Travis didn't seem to be any the wiser, but if I kept staring at the brochures, he was sure to wonder why. I was on the verge of giving up when I finally felt my mind hook onto the brochure and lift it free. Once it was off the stack, it was easy to propel through the air and drop gently into the canvas bag. In light of our recent magick woes, I was a bit amazed that I'd succeeded. Maybe having Merlin around was healing me too. In any case, I didn't dare celebrate my success in front of Travis. I had to act like it was a common thing to see in a real magick shop.

"Okay," he said, clearly nonplussed. "How did you do that? Is there a button under the counter or what?"

"Magick," I replied. "I don't know any other way to do it." In spite of my best intentions, I was finding it hard to contain the smile that spread across my face. It felt like it reached from ear to ear.

He stepped over to the brochures and passed his hand around them, no doubt checking for a wire too fine to be easily seen. "Neat trick, but I'll figure it out," he said, hefting the tote off the counter. "I was a total magic nerd as a kid."

"I'd be interested to hear what you come up with."

"You'll be the first one I call."

"The number's on the brochure."

"Right, thanks." When he reached the door, he turned back to me. "I may not be a convert yet," he said, "but I *am* glad I waited for you."

The door had barely shut behind him, when my mother and grandmother appeared simultaneously, two clouds of stormy energy hovering over the counter at eye level. News sure traveled fast on the other side. "I'm afraid I've been a very bad girl," I said, in hopes of preempting them with a cute confession to take the edge off their pique. I should have known better.

Sparks flew from Morgana's cloud. "You think this is funny? This is not a joking matter."

"I didn't say it was. But it's also not the end of the world."

"It could be," my mother said, no doubt hoping to add gravitas to her claim.

"Anything *could* be," I replied. "And by the way, I'd like to know why you think it's okay to spy on me whenever the mood strikes you."

"I wasn't spying," she said indignantly. "I wanted to stop in for a visit, but I always check first to be sure you're alone."

"We're simply concerned about your future," Bronwen said, entering the conversation for the first time.

My mother wasn't ready to get off her soapbox yet. "You were showing off for that young man, weren't you?"

"When someone has a closed mind, I can't help trying to pry it open," I said in my own defense.

"You've always liked proving people wrong."

"Well I wonder who I got that from," I muttered before I could stop myself. If my mother heard me, she chose to ignore it in pursuit of her own agenda.

"You were using magick to flirt with him," she said. I had to admit she was partly right, but I didn't have to admit it out loud. Again in my defense, I'd never been self-confident enough to flirt with my ordinary skills. The couple of times I'd tried had been awkward and downright laughable. My college roomie and I still double over with laughter whenever we talk about my feeble attempts. If I was smart, I would take my mother's verbal drubbing and get it over with. Sadly, time had proven I wasn't that smart.

"Kailyn," my grandmother said in that way she had of sounding stern and understanding at the same time, "I'm sure you haven't forgotten why it's best not to flagrantly remind people that we're not quite like they are; that we have certain, shall we say, advantages over them. I know how easy it is to feel bulletproof at your age. But beneath the thin veneer of this modern age, people are essentially the same as they have always been." She succeeded in talking me down to a low simmer.

Although I understood their concerns, hiding my powers had always been a sore subject for me. When I was a child, I didn't see any point in having special abilities if I had to keep them hidden. Superheroes were always flaunting theirs. Adding more fuel to my confusion was the fact that my aunt worked openly as a psychic. I'd pointed out this glaring double standard many times during my early years. Bronwen always gave me the same answer. "There were times when your Aunt Tilly would have been hanged or drowned for correctly predicting the future or reading someone's mind. One day real magick will find greater acceptance too." But children are nothing if not impatient. There were some incidents at school that required Morgana's intervention. After a while I got better at doing things on the sly. With adulthood had come rational thought and a sense of responsibility for my "gifts." Before meeting Travis, I couldn't remember the last time I'd taken my telekinesis out for a spin in public. According to Bronwen, the definition of "in public" was in view of anyone other than family.

"People are afraid of what they don't understand," my mother said now, her tone immediately raising my hackles again. What was it between mothers and daughters that was so easily resolved by *widening* the gap by an additional generation? "And they're envious of what they will never have or ever hope to attain."

"Okay, Morgana, no need to beat a dead horse," Bronwen said. I could have kissed her for that, but I didn't know how to go about it in her present form.

"Oh by all means," my mother grumbled. "Once the great Bronwen has spoken, everything else is superfluous."

My grandmother sighed. "Get a grip, dear."

Listening to them spar, I wondered if my mother's relationship with *her* grandmother had been easier too. They went at it for a few more minutes, without any sign of their emotions cooling. At that point, I interrupted them with a reminder that a customer could walk in at any moment. They vanished on the spot, still embroiled in their eternal combat.

I managed to get through the rest of the afternoon more upbeat than I had any right to be, given the *Sturm und Drang* with my elders and the fact that I was no closer to finding Jim's killer. If the police were the only ones who could elicit customer information from the bank, then logic dictated I pay Duggan a visit. If he already knew about the feud between Jim and the dentist, maybe I could get him to reveal if Silver's alibi had held up. I'd been wanting to talk to the detective now that I knew he and Jim had not parted amicably. I would have to be careful about what I said and how I said it, though. If Duggan suspected I had access to Jim's confidential files, things would quickly become worse for both Elise and me. I was thinking this when the phone rang and Elise's number appeared on my caller ID. We spoke so often these days that our phone etiquette had evolved into verbal shorthand: "Hi, you okay?" "You?" Sometimes we didn't bother with responses before jumping right into the meat of the conversation.

"I need to see you." Elise's voice was ripe with unspoken words.

"Six?" That would give me time to feed the cats and check on Tilly and Merlin. I didn't know exactly why I felt the need to check on them. Maybe it was because the sorcerer's recent track record hadn't been great. He'd turned the cat into a bird and was responsible for the great puppy escape. Of course he'd also changed the bird back into a cat, helped round up the puppies, and restored Tilly's abilities. In the final tally, though, there was still too much potential for disaster to give me peace of mind.

"Pizza?" Elise asked.

"Half mushroom?"

"Done."

I had the kitchen table set with paper goods when she arrived. We took time for a quick hug before tearing into the pizza. Before *I* tore into it anyway. I was so hungry I didn't come up for air until I'd downed most of my first slice. "No time for lunch today," I said in explanation.

"Were you busy sleuthing?" she asked, taking her first, dainty bite.

I told her about the faux dental emergency and how I hoped to learn if the bank verified Silver's alibi. I poured each of us a glass of citrus-steeped water and reached for another slice.

"I realized where the money in that safety deposit box could have come from and why Jim never told me about it." I froze with the pizza halfway to my mouth as if chewing might compromise my hearing. "When we were first married, Jim occasionally played poker with his friends. The stakes were low; it was mostly a chance to hang out with his buddies and have a beer or two. As everyone got married, started families, the game fell apart. Then Jim found another game through one of his clients."

"That high stakes game you told me about?"

She nodded. "The more he lost, the more fixated he became on winning it back. When I confronted him, he claimed it was entertainment, not an addiction. I didn't talk too much about it to you, my sister or anyone. I couldn't spend all my waking hours dwelling on the problem. I became an ostrich. If I stuck my head deep enough in the ground, he would miraculously be cured."

I put the slice of pizza down on my plate. "I remember there was one point you threatened to take the kids and leave if he didn't go for help. But he did, right? I thought you guys were in a better place after that."

"So did I. But where else would he have gotten all that money? He must have started gambling again. And winning." Tears gathered in her eyes. "The money is going to be a huge help, I can't deny that. But I feel betrayed, like our marriage was built on deceit." The tears wobbled on her lashes, then ran down her cheeks, murky with mascara.

I reached across the table to squeeze her hand. "He probably convinced himself he was protecting you by keeping his relapse a secret."

"Or he kept it a secret, because he didn't want to give up the whole roller coaster ride of gambling and he didn't want me on his back about it." She sounded wounded and angry. I couldn't blame her. She took a half-hearted bite of her pizza, before putting it down again. "There's something else I wanted to tell you," she said. "This may be grasping at straws, but there are two other people who could have taken Jim's gun."

"Who?" New avenues to pursue equaled good news in my book.

Elise took a sip of her water. "Anna, my cleaning woman, and Ronnie." My hopes deflated. I couldn't imagine any scenario in which Anna or Ronnie would steal Jim's gun and try to frame Elise for his murder. "The way things are going," she went on, "I decided I can't afford to overlook anyone."

I tried to think dispassionately, the way the police would. "Did they both know where Jim kept the gun?"

"I wouldn't be surprised if Anna saw him take the gun out or put it away at some point over the years. We trusted her implicitly. Not to mention that the woman is afraid of her own shadow. Ronnie definitely knew where the gun was. Jim showed it to her when she was thinking of buying one for protection. You know, a woman living alone. She even went target shooting with us a couple of times."

"How about opportunity?"

"I leave Anna alone in the house all the time, and Ronnie comes over when we're away to water the plants and bring in the mail. They both have keys."

"Given the stakes, you're right—we can't afford to automatically dismiss them." I debated taking a third slice, but decided two was my limit, or should be. "You can't be the one to confront them," I said, "because you won't push hard enough. On a subconscious level, you'd be worried about destroying your relationships with them. You have to tell Duggan what you've told me and let him take it from there."

"It feels like I'm throwing them to the wolves," she said miserably.

A loud rap on the front door made her jump in her seat. It was immediately followed by the creaking of the hinges, which reminded me they needed oiling. "Kailyn," she whispered, "I think I heard someone walk in the front door, but I know you locked it after me."

"Tilly's here," my aunt called out before I could explain. "Merlin's with me, so you'd better be decent."

"In the kitchen," I yelled back. "She knocks before she lets herself in so she doesn't startle me," I told Elise, who still looked unsettled.

"I smell pizza," I heard Merlin say. A moment later they both appeared in the kitchen doorway along with my cats, all milling around Merlin's feet. Sashkatu stayed at the periphery of the mob. Oblivious to everyone, furred and not, Merlin made a beeline for the box in the center of the table, causing the cats to scramble out of his way. After helping himself to a slice, he sat down with barely a glance at Elise or me. If we ever figured out how to send him home, it might have to be with a pizza oven. The cats were vying for a place beside him, which led to a lot of hissing and hackle raising. Elise watched all this with a bewildered expression.

"This is Merlin," I said, "a distant cousin of ours, visiting from England. He's a bit . . . um . . . eccentric and he has this weird connection with cats." I hoped that introduction would be enough to satisfy her curiosity. Of course if he changed one species of animal into another in front of her, it probably wouldn't suffice. Since Merlin didn't show any interest in finding out who she was, I decided to stop the meet and greet there.

"Merlin isn't a name you hear every day," Elise said, her own slice of pizza left to languish on her plate.

I shrugged. "We don't actually know that side of the family very well."

Tilly had shuffled her way around the table to give Elise a motherly kiss on the top of her head. "How are you holding up, dear?" she asked.

"To be honest, I have no idea."

"I promise you, it will get better. Time is a healer as well as a thief." I'd never thought of Tilly as a purveyor of wisdom. My mother had always filled that slot, after Bronwen of course. It made sense that Tilly, being younger, had had to carve out her own niche in the family. So she was the fun one, the lamp-shade-on-her-head one, the one who marched to the beat of her own whimsy. Silly Tilly. Maybe I'd underestimated her.

She lowered herself into the chair between Elise and me. "Baking is hard on the body, especially the feet," she said with a soft groan. "I've tried to do it while sitting, but I'm up and down so often that my knees start aching." She reached into the box and tore off a piece of the pizza crust, her favorite part of the pie.

"Did you come by to chat or was there another reason?" I asked.

"A reason," she repeated, her thinly penciled eyebrows knitting together. "Yes, I'm fairly sure there was a reason . . ." She took a napkin to wipe away the crumbs on her chin. "Oh, I know!" She reached for her purse on the floor beside her. It was large enough to tote around a week's worth of clothing or a litter of tiny dogs. When I was a kid, I'd dive into her huge handbags in search of the hard candies she always kept there. I still marveled at the variety of things she felt obliged to carry around. This time she withdrew a plastic container and set it triumphantly on the table. "I brought dessert."

I opened the lid to find mini pastries and scones from the day's baking. "I had to hide them from *the mouth* over there," she said, looking pointedly in Merlin's direction. "In the interest of full disclosure, I mean this as a bribe."

I bit into the frosting of a pink petit four. My aunt knew her way around a bribe. I slid the container across the table to Elise, who selected a mini orange-cranberry scone. "Okay," I asked, licking my fingertips, "what do I have to do now that I've ingested the bribe?"

"Here's the thing," Tilly said, "it's impossible to do readings with Merlin around. No one wants a third party present when we're discussing private matters. I was hoping you could keep him with you when I have clients."

I could hardly say no. Merlin had shown up in my storeroom, not hers, and she'd been kind enough to let him stay with her. She might not have expected the care and feeding of a legendary sorcerer to be as demanding as it was, yet she hadn't dumped him back on my doorstep. At least not until now. "We'll work it out," I told her with a lot more confidence than I was feeling.

Chapter 17

The squad room looked a lot like the ones I'd seen on TV, although somewhat smaller. The flooring was tile, the lighting fluorescent, the desks utilitarian steel, each holding a computer terminal. It would have been hard to make the room more drab. Duggan was one of two detectives there. He was in shirt sleeves, his tie loosened around his neck.

"Miss Wilde," Duggan said, looking up as I approached his desk, Merlin trailing behind me. I'd asked the sorcerer to change into the jeans and shirt Tilly had given him, but he'd refused. Comfort meant more to him than fitting in. A sentiment to be applauded if he were a teenager, but problematic, since we didn't want to draw unnecessary attention to him. I worried about the questions his appearance would raise. Where did he come from? Was he destitute? Homeless? Crazy?

"Good afternoon, Detective," I replied.

Duggan was frowning in Merlin's direction. "Is he with you?" He seemed poised to leap over the desk and muscle him outside if I denied any connection to him.

"Yes, he is." I enjoyed watching the detective's expression try to accommodate to this unexpected news.

"Relative?" he asked, no doubt thinking that had to be the reason I was in the company of an elderly man who looked like a vagabond.

"His name is Merlin," I said to skirt the issue. Telling the detective that I didn't know, would only lead to a round of twenty questions and a series of lies that would eventually trip me up. "He's from England," I added. "Merlin this is Detective Duggan."

Duggan extended his hand, looking like he'd prefer to shake hands with a serial killer. Merlin bowed slightly from the waist, which left the detective in an awkward position with his arm in midair. I'd personally taught Merlin that a handshake was the norm in our society, so I knew he was having a little fun at Duggan's expense. I shot him a glare, which he pretended not to notice.

"Is there a place we can talk in private?" I asked Duggan.

"Yeah, I suppose," he said grudgingly, letting his hand fall to his side. Merlin and I followed him out of the squad room and down a narrow hall. He stopped at the first open door, with the lettering IN-TERROGATION ROOM 1, turned on the light switch with the swipe of his palm and waited for us to file in. Compared to this room, the squad room positively sparkled. There was a table in the center with two chairs, all gray metal. I was surprised there wasn't a naked light bulb suspended above the ensemble. Duggan told us to have a seat and ducked out long enough to locate another chair and drag it into the room. Opting to be contrary, Merlin eschewed the chair to pace around the small room as if there was something of interest to be found on the scuffed and dirt-smudged walls. Duggan sat down opposite me, arms crossed at his chest. "What can I do for you today, Miss Wilde?"

"It occurred to me that you might not know about the feud that was going on between Harkens and Silver, the dentist who shared the building with him. Given the fact that Harkens was murdered, I thought you might appreciate the heads-up."

"Do you?" he said, not looking the least bit appreciative. "I wouldn't be very good at my job if I didn't already know about that. Not to mention the fact that they both called us to complain about each other on a weekly basis. Curtis handled the calls, but the paperwork came across my desk too."

"Sorry. I was trying to be a good citizen," I murmured. "Didn't mean to step on any toes." It hadn't occurred to me that Duggan might take offense at my input. He'd asked the public to call the hotline if they had information pertaining to the case. I almost said as much, but given his foul mood, I decided against it.

"Anything else you wanted to get off your chest?" Duggan asked, pointedly looking at his watch.

"Just that Silver told me he was at the bank at the time Harkens was killed. Of course I have no way to find out if that's true or not."

"Maybe you think I should deputize you, so you can poke your nose into more places where it doesn't belong?" His face was as impassive as stone.

"No, of course not," I replied, trying to remain polite in spite of his jabs. "May I ask if the bank corroborated his story?"

"Ask away, it's a free country," he said expansively, "but you ought to know that I have zero intentions of releasing that information at this time."

"Well, I guess I should let you get back to work then," I said, standing. I was getting dizzy from watching Merlin circle the room anyway. Why had I ever thought I could trick the detective into revealing whether or not the alibi panned out? Hubris, plain and simple. Duggan pushed his chair back from the table, the legs screeching across the tile as he rose. Halfway up he froze, his flinty eyes glazed over. I whipped my head around to find Merlin. The sorcerer had stopped pacing and was staring straight at the detective.

"Merlin, don't you dare!" I snapped, hoping Duggan couldn't hear me in his present state. "No black magick—you promised."

"Nary a soul will suffer by my actions," he replied calmly, still holding the detective in his thrall. "You have a lot to learn, my dear. Not all magick is distinctly black or white. As in life, most magick falls within areas of gray."

"No!" I filled the word with all the gravitas I could muster. I couldn't afford to let Merlin run wild. He was far too powerful, and I'd be setting a dangerous precedent. The world he came from had vastly different rules about what constituted acceptable behavior. "You play by my rules," I said, "or you can find someplace else to live." If he called my bluff and went off on his own, he'd have no one to guide him through the mine field of the modern world. There was a good chance Tilly and I were all that stood between him and disaster. Was there even a penal code for crimes of magick? Merlin must have reached the same uncomfortable conclusion, because he released Duggan a moment later. He did it so abruptly that the detective pitched forward and almost succumbed to gravity, before regaining his balance. He looked at me, then at Merlin, with questions he clearly couldn't put into words. Instead he straightened his shoulders, hardened his jaw, and strode out of the room. He was standing at his desk when we caught up to him.

"I want to apologize if I overstepped the bounds, Detective," I said, feeling that I needed to do some damage control. "I hope you'll write it off as an innocent desire to help."

He gave me a stiff nod. "Leave the investigating to the police, and you and I will get along real fine."

"Got it."

He sat down in his swivel chair and turned to face his monitor, which most people would have taken as a dismissal. But I still had one card left to play and I was too stubborn to leave bad enough alone. "There's been so much death in my life lately," I said, "first my mother and grandmother and now Jim. Not that I can really compare losing a friend with the loss of my family. I think it's a matter of reaching a tipping point."

Duggan nodded again without looking at me. He was probably hoping if he didn't engage me further, I'd run out of steam and leave.

"You know what it's like, Detective. Losing your wife the way you did was so awful. My Aunt Tilly was telling me that Jim helped you sue that doctor for malpractice."

Duggan turned back to me, eyes narrowed, jaw tight. "You've been checking up on me?" he demanded, more like an accusation than a question.

I did my best to appear taken aback, as though I had no idea this would be his reaction. "Checking up on you? No, not at all. Tilly mentioned it in light of Jim's death. You know, she was thinking about all the people whose lives he'd touched over the years." I left it at that. If I added the rest of what I'd discovered, it would be as good as saying, *you had a dandy motive to murder Jim. Shouldn't someone be investigating you?*

Duggan's face was flushed a deep red, and a vein in his temple was pulsating. "Harkens and I parted company years ago," he said through clenched teeth. "Count yourself lucky he won't be around to screw up your affairs." And there it was. Years had passed, but the detective still carried a deep and abiding hatred for Jim. In other words, a perfect motive for murder. But who had the guts to say that to Duggan's face or place him under investigation? For now I intended to tuck the information away in a well-lit corner of my mind. It was ammunition to be used if Duggan decided to arrest Elise, ammunition to be given to a defense attorney and private investigator. Elise was the only one I planned to tell about this exchange with the detective. I hoped it might give her some much needed peace of mind. I had one more thing to do before I left the police station. A bit of fence mending.

"I . . . I am so sorry, Detective," I said. "I seem to keep putting my foot in my mouth today. My grandmother used to call it hoof-and-mouth disease," I added with a thin, nervous laugh that I didn't have to fake. "I'll let you get back to work."

Duggan didn't say a word, but I could feel his eyes boring into my back as Merlin and I walked out of the squad room.

Once we were in the car, I slumped back in my seat, wilted. The bravado that had enabled me to stand up to Duggan left my body in one long, shaky breath. Merlin, who seemed completely unperturbed by his first encounter with modern law enforcement, gave me a wholehearted and enthusiastic thumbs-up. It was one of the many things he'd learned from watching TV, not all of which were as commendable.

"If your goal was to enrage the man, your aim was true." He clearly meant it as a compliment, but it made me laugh. I hadn't thought about it in quite that way before, but I suppose that had been my goal. Make the man angry enough to ignore discretion and he might let something slip that I couldn't have pried out of him under normal circumstances. I turned on the engine and backed out of the parking spot.

"Don't forget, you promised not to repeat anything you saw or heard in there," I reminded Merlin. It was a promise I'd extracted from him on the long ride to the county seat.

"You have naught to worry about, dear girl. My word is my bond. Ask anyone who knows me." Not the best guarantee, since everyone he knew had been dead for centuries. As I drove home, my initial sense of victory lost its luster. With the clarity of hindsight, I knew that I had not just tested Duggan's feelings about Jim; I may also have added my name to the top of the killer's hit list.

Chapter 18

Providing daycare for Merlin turned out to be a more difficult assignment than I'd imagined. He was like a toddler, endlessly curious about his new world. But unlike a toddler, he had an arsenal of magick with which to explore it. In other words, he required a lot of supervision. I had to keep finding jobs to occupy him, because a bored sorcerer can be a dangerous thing. The first problem cropped up with my customer, Marge Stucky. She'd moved to the area from out-of-state about a year ago and had visited my shop on several occasions. A recent widow, she'd traded the climate of Florida for the comfort of being near family. She was friendly and chatty and short; the latter should have set off a warning in my head as she chirped "hello" on her way past the counter where I was ringing up another sale. Too late I realized she might need assistance in reaching the upper shelves. In the past, she'd come to me for help, but that was before Merlin's arrival. As it happened, he was in the aisle she went down, restocking the various teas we make. Having lived in an era when chivalry was second nature to men of the upper classes, he gallantly offered his services when he saw her trying to get a jar off the top self. Unfortunately the product was pushed too far back and beyond the reach of his long arms. Frustrated, he did what came naturally and floated the item off the shelf and into his hand.

"Good lord," I heard Marge exclaim. She had an unexpectedly loud voice for such a diminutive person. "How did you do that?" My heart sank. At that point, I didn't know exactly what had happened, but since it involved Merlin, I was pretty sure it also involved magick. I didn't have long to wait. Marge strode up to the counter with a jar of depilatory cream in her hand. Merlin must have gotten it down for her without bothering to grab the stepstool or telescopic arm, both of which we had for that purpose. Now I had to come up with an ordinary explanation for the extraordinary stunt Marge had witnessed. I handed the first customer her receipt and tote bag and wished her a nice day. She stepped away from the counter, but lingered at a nearby display of healing crystals. It was obvious she was sticking around to hear what had caused Marge's outburst.

"What a clever trick," Marge cooed at Merlin, who'd followed her up to the counter, looking like he expected to be named employee of the month for helping her. "You have *got* to tell me how you did that. My grandson loves magic, and if I can teach him that trick, I'll be his favorite grandma." Great, I thought, and tomorrow the other grandmother will be in to learn a better trick.

Merlin opened his mouth to respond, but I cut him off. "It's actually a complicated thing," I said. "It's not something you can easily duplicate at home." Marge's smile evaporated. "You wouldn't want us to give away trade secrets, now would you?" I cajoled her. "It could put us right out of business."

She issued a sigh. "No, I suppose not. I don't know what I'd do without your creams and lotions."

After she and the other woman left the shop, I went over the rules again with Merlin. Although he didn't argue with me, he was huffy for the next couple of hours. By the time Tilly closed up and came to fetch him, I was mentally and emotionally exhausted. The constant worrying about what he might do next was like living on an active volcano that could blow at any moment. Tilly was better at dealing with him, no doubt because she wasn't much of a worrier. I'd inherited that useless trait from my mother who'd had plenty to spare. And no amount of logic or clever spells had proven sufficient to banish it.

That evening I dragged myself home. I made the cats their dinner in slow motion, which netted me a chorus of yowls. Once their bellies were full, I made myself a sandwich of peanut butter and apricot preserves. Much as I wanted to collapse on the sofa and watch some mindless TV while I ate, I marched myself over to the computer to resume going through Jim's files.

The phone startled me awake. Who would be calling in the middle of the night? With that thought, a shot of adrenalin kick-started my brain. I must have fallen asleep at the computer, which was in hibernation mode, with one of the cats out cold on the keyboard. My neck was stiff, my right hand numb from bearing the weight of my head. When I tried to use that hand to pick up the receiver, I knocked it off the base and onto the floor, waking the cat, who took off for safer quarters. I swiveled the chair around and grabbed the receiver with my left hand. "What's wrong?" I said tersely, positive either Tilly or Merlin was on the other end with a tale of woe.

"Is this Kailyn Wilde?" a man asked tentatively.

I didn't recognize the voice. "Yes, who is this?"

"Travis Anderson."

It took me a moment to match the name with the voice. "Oh hi. Why are you calling so late?" My sleep-addled brain was having trouble catching up to real time.

He laughed. "Late? My grandma doesn't even go to bed at eight-thirty. Are you okay?"

"Yes, I'm fine," I said, finally realizing that the sky was not fully dark yet. "I was working on the computer and I must have dozed off." I couldn't remember how much I'd accomplished before my eyelids brought the curtain down.

"Glad to hear you're all right," he said, more relaxed. "For a second there I was worried one of your magic spells had gone awry and changed you into a unicorn or something."

"Like I said, I'm fine." I didn't mean to sound testy, but his remark had punched a particularly sensitive button of mine. I made a conscious effort to soften my tone. "Are you calling to tell me you've figured out how to do my magick trick?"

Travis laughed again. "No, I'm afraid I haven't had any success so far."

"I'm not surprised."

"But I'm not giving up yet. As a general rule, I don't give up easily. On anything."

"Then you called to give me a progress report?" I asked dryly.

"No, I called to ask you out for coffee."

"You should know upfront that I can't be bribed or maneuvered into revealing any secrets." After all, there was nothing but magick involved.

"I'll spring for the coffee," he said. "Maybe a donut too."

"In that case, how can I say no?" As soon as the words left my mouth I regretted them. Why did I want to spend more time with someone who mocked the possibility of real magick? Whose mind was slammed shut to anything he couldn't quantify? The irritating answer was that my heart seemed to have a mind of its own, doing a little somersault when I realized Travis was the caller. Well, maybe chatting at length with him would cure my heart of its ill-conceived desire. This wasn't the first time I'd been infatuated with the wrong kind of man. In fact it had happened often enough that I called it my personal catch-22. By their very nature, cynics attracted me, daring me to prove them wrong. But there was the rub, as Shakespeare might have said, because I wasn't supposed to let on that I came from a family of honest-to-goodness sorcerers. I felt like Captains Kirk and Picard of the *Starship Enterprise*, arms always tied by the Prime Directive.

"Name the time and place," Travis said, "keeping in mind that good, strong coffee is a must."

I decided to get our mini date out of the way as soon as possible. "How's eight o'clock Wednesday at the Morning Glory?" The kitschy little breakfast place was close enough to my shop that I wouldn't be late opening, they were well-known for their coffee, and I was hooked on their Morning Glory muffins.

"Sounds like a plan," Travis said. "And in case you're harboring any thoughts of standing me up, remember—I know where to find you."

By the time we said goodbye, I was wide awake. I tapped my computer back to life. The file that came up had to be the one I was reading when I fell asleep. I'd made it all the way into the Rs, which was impressive, but I hadn't jotted a single note on the legal pad I kept beside the computer. Boredom must have been the culprit that sent me into dreamland. It would have succeeded again an hour later if Beverly Ruppert's file hadn't popped up on my screen, instantly reenergizing me.

Her professional relationship with Jim had begun in May of 2000 with a consultation about estate planning, which struck me as odd. She was probably in her thirties at the time, single with no dependents. Maybe she stood to inherit a large sum of money and wanted to make sure it went to the person of her choice should she die suddenly. Jim had met with her several times over the wording of the will. I could tell by the tenor of his notes that he became increasingly annoyed with her nitpicking changes. After three months, the will was finally signed, witnessed and notarized. She went back for another consultation less than a year later. I wondered if Jim cringed when he saw her name in his appointment book. This time she wanted to sue her neighbor, because his dog barked incessantly. Jim advised her to file a complaint at town hall. There was no need for her to pay attorney's fees. But Beverly insisted he take care of it. The upshot was that the neighbor couldn't leave his dog outside barking for more than half an hour three times a day. As I read on, I could see a pattern emerging. Beverly was clearly manufacturing reasons to spend time with Jim. From what I could glean, her feelings were not reciprocated. On multiple occasions, Jim referred her to other attorneys better suited to her various issues. She refused to deal with any of them. It seemed to me that a psychiatrist would have been better suited to her needs than any attorney. Her file ended with the sixth, and most ridiculous, of her trumped up legal problems. She wanted Jim to sue her dentist, because he didn't get her teeth as white as the model in the ad. She claimed it caused irreparable damage to her self-confidence. According to Jim's notes, he told her outright he was too busy to take her case. Although Beverly was not the sharpest knife in the drawer, as Morgana used to say, she must have finally gotten the message. And since unrequited love was often a hop, skip and jump away from unqualified hatred, her efforts earned her a spot on my hit parade of suspects.

Chapter 19

Tilly was all aflutter when she called early the next morning and told me to put on the news. The medical examiner was about to release his final report on Jim's death. I turned on the TV, to see journalists and cameramen staking out their territory in the same press room where the ME had given his preliminary report. Off to one side of the fray, stood Travis Anderson. It was one of those smack-your-forehead moments. Now I understood why he'd looked familiar, but hadn't shown any signs of recognizing me. He was dapper in a summer gray suit, peach gingham shirt, and peach-and-gray striped tie. Professionally coiffed and made up, he looked like a plastic, more perfect version of the man who'd come into my shop. I turned up the volume. He was using the lag time before the ME took the stage to refresh viewers' memories on the particulars of the case. Jim was still so front and center in the minds of our small community it was easy to forget that to the rest of the nation he wasn't much more than a statistic.

I was watching for less than a minute, when Travis cut himself short to announce the arrival of the ME. The room went from noisy to hushed in an instant as the camera swung away to focus on the podium where Police Chief Gimble was once again introducing the ME. Westfield joined him on the stage, wearing a white lab coat over blue scrubs as if he was headed straight back to the autopsy suite the moment he finished with this annoying speed bump in his day. He thanked Gimble and took a moment to adjust the microphone. "I'm here today to present my final report on the death of James Harkens," he said without inflection. "Mr. Harkens died of a single gunshot to the forehead. The bullet entered the cranial cavity at an upward angle, passing through several critical structures of the brain, killing him instantly. There were no other significant findings." The hands of a dozen journalists shot up. Westfield pointed to a reporter in the third row.

"Why is the angle of the bullet important?"

"It indicates that whoever fired the shot, did so from a position lower than the victim's head."

A reporter in the back of the room: "Did you find anything noteworthy in Harkens' blood?"

"As I said, there were no other significant findings."

A woman midway back on the left side: "Would his death have been instantaneous?"

"Yes, most certainly."

A woman in the fifth row: "Did he have any cuts, bruises, or other signs of violence?"

"I'll say it once more—there were no other significant findings." My heart went out to him. If people kept asking me the same, repurposed question, it meant they weren't paying attention. He showed a lot more patience than I would have.

A man in the front row: "Did he have any enemies?"

"I don't have that sort of information, so I'll let Police Chief Gimble respond." Gimble, who was standing at the back of the stage, hustled up to the microphone. Westfield switched places with him, left the podium, trotted down the steps, and was out the door before the reporters and cameramen could intercept him. I had to admire his style. Some of the reporters appeared torn between staying to hear what Gimble had to say and running after the ME with more questions. From what I could see, the police chief won out.

"I believe the question was with regard to Harkens having any enemies. I'm afraid I can't get into any particulars about that, since we're still conducting our investigation. Suffice it to say that there's a good chance he had at least one." Although Gimble's tone was entirely professional and serious, his last remark was met with a low buzz of laughter from those in attendance. He fielded another half dozen questions that provided little more in the way of new information, before ending the press conference.

As soon as Sashkatu and I arrived at my shop, Tilly toddled in through the connecting door. In deference to the warm temperatures, she was dressed in one of her frothier muumuus, but her feet were clad in sneakers for what had to be the very first time. Over the years

Bronwen, Morgana, and I had each tried to coax her into buying a pair as a compromise for her aching feet, because she'd steadfastly refused to consider orthopedic shoes. I suspected Merlin had something to do with her sudden change of heart. If so, way to go, Merlin! I made a big deal over how stylish and youthful they made her look. Of course I might have suggested a tamer color than turquoise with racy, orange laces, but I kept that thought to myself.

"They're so comfortable," she said as though she was the one who'd discovered them. "I got Merlin a pair that are almost identical."

I struggled to suppress a laugh at the thought of the two of them in the wild, matching footwear. "What did you think of the press conference?" I asked, to change the subject before the laughter won out.

"Disappointing," she said. "A lot of waiting to be told nothing new. I don't know why they bothered to trot Westfield out for the event."

Sashkatu chirruped impatiently, looking from me to his steps and back again. "Oops, sorry, your majesty," I said, moving them into position and locking the wheels, so he could ascend to his window throne. I turned back to Tilly. "Maybe we're jaded from all the cop shows on TV with their plot twists and melodrama."

"I suppose," she said with a sigh. "I was really hoping he'd find something that would point the investigation in a new direction, away from Elise."

"You and me both. But I found something in Jim's files last night that will interest you. It seems our friend Beverly was a client of his." I spent the next few minutes filling her in on the details.

"The photo!" she exclaimed with the passion of a miner discovering gold. "I'd forgotten about it after all this time."

"What photo?" Sometimes talking to Tilly was like walking in late on a movie.

"Do you remember a number of years ago when Beverly started that book club and invited me?"

If she'd told me, it hadn't made a blip on my radar at the time. "Okay," I said, waiting to hear where she was going. Tilly always got to the point eventually, but the trip there often required a lot of patience on the part of the listener.

"I quit after a couple of meetings, because Beverly led the discussions and she loves nothing better than the sound of her own voice. But that's beside the point. At the last meeting I attended, I got so bored I excused myself to visit the bathroom. When I came out, I could still hear her yakking, so I wandered into her bedroom. That's where I saw this photo of her and Jim, you know, one of those selfies. She'd tried to use a black marker to obliterate him from the picture, but it didn't work very well. The photo paper was probably too glossy to hold onto the ink. I guess I put the whole thing out of my head. But after what you've just told me, I wonder if she decided to erase him in a more permanent fashion."

"Back up a minute," I said. "Beverly left that photo out in the open?"

"Yes and no," Tilly murmured, suddenly busy brushing some invisible lint off her sleeve.

"It was either out in the open or it wasn't," I said, although I already knew the answer.

Tilly raised her head to look me in the eye. "If you must know, it was in the top drawer of her nightstand. Under a pile of other stuff. In an envelope. But that doesn't change the fact that it's turned out to be an important piece of information, thank you very much." She straightened her shoulders as though she'd been vindicated. "For all we know my psychic ability lured me to that drawer."

"What lured you to that drawer, Aunt Tilly, was pure nosiness. And I'm afraid one day it's going to lure you into something dangerous, not merely unethical."

"You worry too much, dear," she said, pulling me into a smothery embrace of bosom and chiffon and the potent floral scent she'd worn since I'd drawn my first breath. "So, what do you think?" she asked upon releasing me. "Could Beverly be the killer? It would be sort of wonderful if she was. I don't think there's a single person in all of New Camel who's overly fond of her. For that matter, I doubt she'd be missed if they sent her off to prison."

Tilly had already tried and convicted her. But although she'd won a place on my list, she wasn't at the top of it. "I don't know if she's smart enough to plan and carry out a murder like this," I said. "Don't forget, she would have had to sneak into Jim's house to steal the gun too."

"You may be underestimating her, Kailyn. She's a lot craftier than you think." I took my aunt's words to heart. She knew Beverly better than anyone in my family did. I glanced at my watch, and it dawned on me that we'd been talking for fifteen minutes and Merlin hadn't yet made an appearance. "Is our time traveler still asleep?" I asked.

"Hardly, he's in my shop, polishing off the last two cucumber and watercress sandwiches. Having him around, I don't have much garbage anymore. Oh, I almost forgot why I came in here. You don't have to watch him today. I don't have any appointments, so I thought we'd forage for the plants we didn't find for you the last time. With my new sneakers, I'll be able to cover a lot more territory. I packed us a picnic lunch to make a whole day of it. Can't remember the last time I was on a picnic."

I didn't let on how glad I was to be without Merlin for the day, but on the inside, my heart was doing a happy dance. A day alone in my shop, without the stress of trying to keep our elderly ward out of trouble felt like summer vacation when I was a kid. I saw them off in Tilly's convertible and went back inside to order more organic, non-GMO food for my cats. If big business kept messing with our food supply, every healthy alternative would need a name ten words long. I was finishing up when the first customer of the day came through the door. He was a large, florid man, on the cusp of fifty. He strode in like he was hurrying to catch a train. He was wearing pants that looked like they came from a suit and a long-sleeved dress shirt, the buttons straining to stay closed over the substantial mound of his belly.

I was still at my desk behind the counter, when the door chimes announced his arrival. "Is this the magic shop?" he called out as he crossed the threshold.

"Yes, Abracadabra is a magick shop," I said, rising to greet him.

"Yeah, I think that's the name she gave me." His voice was deep and loud, the accent definitely New York City, although I couldn't pinpoint the borough.

"What can I do for you?" I asked, wondering if he'd made the trip for his own purposes. I didn't get many men in my store, unless they were dragged in by wives or girlfriends. I couldn't count Travis, since he'd come at his mother's behest.

"I need a spell or a potion or whatever you call it."

"I'll be happy to help you, Mr. . . . ?"

"Dutch, call me Dutch." He stuck out a large, beefy hand that swallowed up mine like a starving Venus flytrap.

"Nice to meet you, Dutch. I'm Kailyn," I said, waiting a respectable few seconds before rescuing my hand. I didn't want to be rude, but I've always found it awkward to continue a conversation with my hand still trapped in someone else's. "Why don't you tell me what the problem is."

"I can sum it up quick. Things were going fine until a few months ago, then all of a sudden everything dropped into the crapper."

"I think you'll need to narrow that down a little more," I said.

He checked his watch as if he'd already spent too much time in the shop. "Okay, here's the deal. I'm heavily invested in the market—the stock market. From my early twenties, when I bought my first stock, until recently, I've had the old Midas touch, if you know what I mean. Couldn't pick a bad stock if I tried to, and believe you me, I tested that theory a few times." He coughed up a chuckle that made his double chins jiggle. "But I woke up one morning a month ago and my mojo was gone, gone like some gypsies came and stole it in the night. Now I know that's not possible." He paused and looked at me as if for confirmation.

"No," I said soberly, "I doubt gypsies were involved." Or any other ethnic group.

"So, can you help me get things back on track or not?"

"I can certainly provide you with the means to regain your winning abilities, but how well it works will depend to a large degree on you."

"No problem. You tell me what I've got to do and I'll do it."

"I'm afraid it's not quite that simple. Do you believe in magick?"

"If you mean like the guys who saw girls in half—no. But I'm willing to believe in real magick if that's what you're selling here."

"Belief plays an important role in how well magick works," I said. Dutch was coming at this all wrong. "It comes from within, it can't be bought and taken for a trial spin."

"Got it."

I had some serious doubts about that, but there was just so much you can argue with a customer who's bull-headed. I forged on, hoping I'd get through to him on some level. "You should also know that while magick can bring you prosperity, it won't work if greed or malice are at the core of your intentions."

"No problem. I'm a good person," Dutch said, standing up a bit taller. "I donate to charities. I even worked at a soup kitchen a couple of Thanksgivings back. There isn't an evil bone in my body."

"You don't have to prove anything to me," I said. "It's really none of my business. I'm simply explaining how white magick works."

"Are you trying to tell me that I'd be better off with black magick?"

"Absolutely not. Trust me when I say you don't want to mess around with black magick or anyone who uses it."

"Noted. We're good to go then. Lay that old white magick on me."

I asked him to have a seat in the chair near the counter, and since he didn't seem to have brought pen and paper with him, I handed him the ones from my desk.

"No thanks," he said, pulling his phone out of a holder on his belt. "I'll put it into an email to myself. Much easier that way."

"Sorry, no electronics for this." I'd thought about putting the most frequently requested spells into the computer, so I could print them out with a click of the mouse, but I'd decided against it. Something intimate, intrinsic was lost when computer technology was inserted into the process. I'd found that magick worked better when the would-be practitioners wrote the instructions the old-fashioned way, the words flowing into their ears, through their brains, and out through their fingers onto actual paper. Morgana and Bronwen were right about keeping to the old ways in some things.

Dutch didn't look too happy about my rule, but he stowed the phone and accepted the pen and pad. "Ready when you are, but it feels like I'm back in *Little House on the Prairie* days."

I ignored the remark. No amount of explanation was likely to meet with his approval. "You'll have to perform this spell on a clear night with a full moon," I began slowly. "Place a silver coin into a non-metal bowl and pour fresh rain or spring water over it. Place the bowl where the moonlight can shine on it, then drop seven fresh basil leaves into it one at a time as you say these words three times:

> By the light of the moon
> Bless me soon.
> Water and silver shine
> Make wealth mine.

Leave the bowl where it is until morning, then pour out the water and leaves and carry the coin on your person."

"That's it?" Dutch sounded disappointed and skeptical. "That's all I have to do?"

It was a common reaction, one I'd come to expect from people who were new to magick. "Yes, as long as you've met the requirements about belief and good intentions."

"Oh yeah, right," he said, his eyebrows bunching together in a frown as if it had finally dawned on him how important those requirements must be if the spell itself was so simple. Clearly lip service wasn't going to suffice. He tore the page with the spell off the pad, folded it carefully, and tucked it into his shirt pocket. "I don't suppose this spell comes with any kind of money-back guarantee?" he asked, handing the pad and pen back to me.

"I'm sorry. Its effectiveness relies too much on the person using it."

"I kind of figured, but it was worth a shot."

We took care of the financial end of the transaction and I wished him good luck. The phone started ringing before he was out the door. Tilly was on the other end and she didn't sound at all chipper.

"Is everything okay?" I asked warily, hoping I'd read her mood wrong.

"No," she said, "everything is not okay."

I felt my body tensing. "What's the matter?"

"We've had a bit of an accident."

"Are you and Merlin all right?" I asked.

"I suppose we are, in a strictly physical sense."

I could hear angry voices in the background. "Was anyone else injured?"

"No, but perhaps you should come meet us here." A police siren nearly drowned out her words. So much for my lovely day of freedom.

"Where are you?" I had to yell over the noise.

"Outside Watkins Glen," she yelled back. "I've got to go talk to the police."

The thought of Tilly and Merlin dealing with the police filled me with dread. I grabbed my purse and said goodbye to Sashkatu, wishing I could change places with him.

I had no trouble finding the scene of the accident. Tilly's red car was easy to spot in the middle of a lovely front yard. Or more accurately, what had been a lovely front yard. Deep, muddy ruts marked the tires' path from the road through a thick hedge of evergreen bushes and into a decorative waterfall with an intricate arrangement of rocks and flowers. Evergreen branches and shredded flowers were snarled in the car's grill, making the vehicle look as if it needed to floss after having a salad. There were two police cars parked at the curb. One officer was talking to the homeowners, the other to Tilly and Merlin. They reminded me of coaches chatting up their boxers in opposite corners of a ring.

I parked behind the police cars and headed over to team Tilly. She brightened up when she spied me coming. "Here's my niece," she announced. "She'll be able to clear all this up in no time."

And how exactly was I supposed to do that? I introduced myself to the officer who looked like he was reaching the limits of his patience.

"I've been trying to ascertain how this accident happened and who was at the wheel," he said to me. "Ms. Wilde's license, registration, and insurance information are in order, but the gentleman with her doesn't appear to have any ID."

"I can vouch for him," I said, keeping my voice low so Merlin wouldn't be able to argue the facts. "He's our cousin. Unfortunately he suffers from dementia."

"The problem is that it appears he was the one driving the car when it wound up in this yard—"

I didn't hear anything after he said Merlin was driving. I wondered if I was too old to run away from home. "May I have a word with my aunt?" I asked.

"I wish you would," the officer said shaking his head.

I grabbed Tilly's arm and drew her a few feet away. "Please tell me Merlin wasn't driving,"

She looked puzzled. "Well, if you really want me to, but I've never liked lying. It always trips me up and gets me in more trouble."

"That might not be possible in this instance," I said through clenched teeth. "Why on earth would you let him drive?"

"He said it looked simple enough and he insisted he wanted to try it. It's hard to say no to him. He's not just some ordinary old man."

At that moment, I would gladly have taken an ordinary old man in his stead. Talking to Tilly was getting me nowhere. If there was any way to keep the police from arresting Merlin, I had to figure it out and figure it out fast.

"Officer," I said, walking back to him, "we'll be happy to make complete restitution to the homeowners for the damages they've incurred. But if we involve the insurance companies and lawyers this could drag on until winter. As long as the owners don't press charges, they'll have their money in a lot less time."

"Problem is, I'm going to have to write up a report on the incident."

"Can't your report state that the parties involved agreed to a settlement and that no charges will be filed?"

He scratched the back of his head. "If the homeowners do agree to that, I might be able to make it work. But you can count yourselves lucky no one was injured or you'd find yourselves in a very different situation."

"Believe me, Officer, we know that, and my aunt promises this will *never* happen again, right Tilly?"

"Well," she started, no doubt about to tack on a caveat of some kind. I shut her down with one steely glare. "Yes, fine," she said, "I promise."

By the time I drove Bonnie and Clyde home and returned to my shop, it was midafternoon. As I was exiting my car, Lolly walked over to let me know that several tourists had told her they were disappointed to find Abracadabra closed. I thanked her for the heads-up, but there was no way I could have let Tilly and Merlin handle the landscaping crisis by themselves. It was one of the problems with being the shop's proprietor and sole employee. There didn't seem to be any immediate remedy for the situation either, since I couldn't use ordinary venues to advertise for a sorcerer to work part time.

I flopped down in the chair at my desk, tired, hungry, and frustrated. Sashkatu regarded me for a moment before offering up a gentle trill that may have been meant to soothe my tattered nerves. He could be intuitive and sweet when he wanted to be. I took the plastic bag with my lunch from the shelf beneath the counter. I was about to take my first bite of the peanut butter and jelly sandwich when I realized there was mold on the bread. Terrific.

Chapter 20

After closing the shop for the night, I didn't go straight home. My car was still parked out front, so I drove to the EZ-Pick Grocery and Gas on the edge of town. To get Sashkatu into my car without a struggle, I lured him with an open can of tuna. Although it worked like a charm, I was never going to try it again. For a good two weeks afterward, my car had a distinctly fishy smell, no matter how much air freshener I used or how many spells I tried.

I filled the gas tank, then parked and left Sashki in the car with the engine running and AC on for his comfort, while I ran inside to grab a few items for dinner. I threw a package of low-fat Swiss cheese into my basket, along with whole grain bread and a premade salad. But since I'd once again missed lunch, I was a sucker for the impulse items near the counter. A bag of chips and a chocolate bar wound up in the basket too. I could have been the spokesperson for a "never go shopping when you're hungry" campaign.

Rushing out, I bumped into Ronnie, who was on her way in. We stopped for a quick hug. I would have hugged and run with a promise to talk soon, but she looked too pale and distracted to dismiss that lightly. "Are you all right?" I asked.

Her shoulders slumped as if she'd been trying to keep up a facade of normalcy, but my concern had cut right through its underpinnings. She shook her head. "Do you have a minute?"

"Sure," I said, in spite of my gurgling stomach. "Come talk in my car." I unlocked the doors, and Ronnie slid into the passenger seat. I stowed the groceries in the back, snagging the bag of chips to take up front with me. Sashkatu was stretched out on top of the dashboard, sunning himself in the oblique rays of the lowering sun. He assessed the situation through half-closed eyelids, but didn't come to attention until he heard me crinkling the chip bag. It was rapidly approaching his dinner hour too. I offered the bag to Ronnie first, but she declined. Then I broke off a tiny piece of one for Sashki, who sniffed the offering, but decided to go back to sleep until real food was available. I didn't know if it was bad etiquette to eat something crunchy while listening to a friend's problem, but it was either that or a concert of stomach noises.

I poured some chips into my palm. "Tell me what's going on," I said, tucking one into my mouth and sucking quietly on it.

"Out of the blue this afternoon, Duggan called me down to the New Camel precinct house."

That explained her distress. "What did he want?"

"To question me again, at length. He seems to think I had access to Jim's gun."

"Did you?" I asked, although I already knew the answer.

"Not really. I mean, I knew where he kept it, but I didn't have the combination."

"What did Duggan say?"

"That a lock box isn't much of an obstacle for someone with murder in mind."

"Does he know you sometimes babysit for the family?"

"Yes and I admitted I have a house key, so if he finds out on his own, he won't catch me in a lie."

"That was the best thing to do," I said. Especially since Elise had told him that too. I wasn't happy about my role in Ronnie's misery, but after Tilly, my loyalty was first and foremost to Elise. Even though Ronnie and I had spent more time together recently than in all the preceding years, I still didn't know her all that well. And in a town the size of New Camel, it was likely that the killer would turn out to be someone I knew. By the time the case was closed, New Camel was going to be awash in social casualties.

"Listen," I said to Ronnie, "it's not only a matter of having had access to the gun. They have to prove you're the one who stole it, and that you had a motive to murder him. From what I can see, you didn't stand to gain anything from Jim's death, except an unemployment check that won't even cover your bills." Ronnie digested my words in silence. "Duggan hasn't trumped up some kind of motive, has he?" I asked.

"No," she said, "but I don't have as much faith in the system as you seem to. I keep thinking about all the people who've rotted away in prison for crimes they didn't commit."

"You need to put those thoughts out of your head," I said, trying to lift her spirits in spite of everything I'd told myself. "I happen to know people who had actual motives to want Jim dead."

"Who?" she asked, hope supplanting the worry in her eyes.

"I'm not ready to say yet. Once I'm sure about my suspicions, I'll go to the police. Or the media. But until then," I said, locking eyes with her, "you can't mention this to anyone." One of these days I was going to bury myself with good intentions.

She put her hand to her heart. "I won't. I swear." She leaned over the center console and grabbed me in an awkward hug. "I'm so grateful I bumped into you."

When Sashkatu and I walked into the house, my foot immediately flew out from under me. I landed so hard, I felt the floor recoil beneath me. The groceries and the contents of my purse flew everywhere. If it had been a different sort of day, I probably would have laughed at my graceless entrance. But I was tired and hungry and my left hip hurt from bearing the brunt of my fall. I'm pretty sure I caught a smirk on Sashkatu's face as he side-stepped me to sniff the package of Swiss cheese that had landed a few feet away. I looked around to see what had sent me sprawling. The culprit appeared to be a sheet of white paper, tri-folded like a business letter, which had come to rest near my right foot. With the grocery bag in my arms, I hadn't been able to see it on the floor. I sat up and retrieved the letter. A single line was printed in a large, bold font on the otherwise empty expanse of white: KEEP YOUR NOSE OUT OF THE INVESTIGATION OR YOU'LL BE THE NEXT CASUALTY.

I read the note three times, not because I didn't understand it, but because I couldn't decide how I felt about it. The wording of the threat was far from intimidating. In fact I found it cheesy, like something out of an old movie. But I knew better than to dismiss the threat for that reason. Someone who has killed once, might not find it difficult to kill again, whether or not they excel at writing threats. What bothered me most about the note was that the killer had brazenly come up to my house and slipped it through the old mail slot in the front door, instead of into the mailbox at the curb. In broad daylight. Which also meant he or she knew I wasn't home. Had they been watching me, following me? A chill crept along the length of my spine. I couldn't remember ever feeling so exposed and vulnerable. I looked around, as if I might see the killer's shoes sticking out from beneath the living room drapes. I heard my mother's voice in my head telling me to stop the nonsense and pull it together. I'd had to unlock the door and disarm the security system, hadn't I? And there was more I could do to protect myself. I would place new wards around the house. Before Morgana and Bronwen died, our magick had become so unpredictable that it had seemed pointless to try to maintain the protective spells. But given these new troubling circumstances and Merlin's beneficial effect on my powers, it was definitely time to put new wards in place. I'd remind Tilly to do so as well.

Lost in my thoughts, I'd forgotten my own hunger, but the cats hadn't forgotten theirs. They'd formed a semi-circle around me to voice their displeasure. Sashkatu marched through their ranks with the swagger of a five-star general, came straight up to me, turned, and swatted me in the face with his tail. Message received.

After everyone else was fed, I made a Swiss cheese sandwich with a good, grainy mustard. The salty chips were the perfect accompaniment. Dessert was the candy bar. Fortified, I went hunting for the embroidered satchel in which my grandmother kept the materials for the warding ritual. I found it on the top shelf of her bedroom closet. Although months had passed since she and my mom died, I still felt like I was invading their privacy when I went into their closets. One day I'd have to go through their things, but I wasn't ready to tackle that yet. Maybe it would be easier if Tilly and I did it together. Besides, she might want to keep some personal items of her mother's and sister's. But this night I needed to focus on renewing the protective wards and then finishing the remainder of Jim's files.

Bronwen's satchel reminded me of the one Mary Poppins carried. It had a deep red background with an elaborate design of gold and black fleur de lis. I'd always thought it was the most magickal-looking item in our home. I opened the bag warily, because Bronwen was known to cast exotic spells over her possessions to discourage would-be thieves. I'd seen the bag sprout rose thorns and porcupine quills and on one occasion harbor a live bat. This time nothing flew out but the stale, musty odor of disuse. I peered inside. Satisfied that everything seemed fine, I reached in and pulled out the bell. Holding it brought back memories of when I was little and used to hide in my bedroom closet with my hands over my ears, because the chiming of the bell was so painfully loud. Bronwen had explained that it had to be loud enough to clear the negative energy out of the house. But knowing the reason for it didn't stop my ears from hurting. The years since then had apparently whittled away at my hearing, because I didn't feel any discomfort as I walked through each room of the house, ringing the bell. With the exception of Sashkatu, the cats took off to find refuge from the siege of noise. Sashki slumbered on blissfully atop the living room couch, proof that old age has its perks.

With the house purged of negative energy, I went back to the satchel and took out the symbols of the four elements. Bronwen used sand to represent earth, sea water for water, and a burning candle to represent air and fire. I found all three materials stored in the bag along with a small, fragrant sandalwood tray on which to place them. Once everything was ready, I carried the tray outside. I slowly walked the perimeter of the property and the footprint of the house itself. I envisioned the elements forming an unbreachable barrier around the space as I murmured Bronwen's chant:

> With earth and water, air and fire,
> Guard this place from all who'd harm us.

Then I walked the perimeter of the house again, pausing at the windows and doors to pass each of the elements around their framework. For the upstairs windows, I followed Bronwen's example and placed the wards from inside the house. We didn't own a tall enough ladder to do it any other way, because no one in my family was fond of heights. Once the ritual was finished and the materials stored away again, a gentle wave of safety and peace washed over me. The cats must have felt it too, because they returned from their hidey-holes and settled in their favorite spots around the living room. I would have liked to join them, but they didn't have a murder to solve, and I did. Picturing Elise in prison for a crime she didn't commit was all it took to fire up my motivation. I sat down at the computer, pulled up the files from Jim's flash drive and got to work.

I found more than fifty clients under S and T, but none of them set off any alarms in my head. They ran the gamut of humdrum issues from real estate to estate planning, contracts to leases, and prenups to divorce proceedings. Some attorneys were experts in one field of the law; Jim had been more of a dabbler. U and V were easy to whip through, and I was thinking I might make it to bed before the late night news. But W proved to be a game changer. I was already so bleary-eyed that it took me an extra moment to process the name when it popped up on the screen. Roger Westfield. The county ME. I shook my head to clear away the cobwebs and started reading.

Westfield had hired Jim within a month of moving to the area. His file was small. It contained the wills Jim prepared for the ME and his wife, which looked pretty standard to my layman's eyes. Whoever died first left the entire estate to the living spouse. If they both died, the estate went to their children once they reached the age of majority. Mrs. Westfield's sister and brother-in-law were named legal guardians for the children until that time. The one other thing in the file was a brief notation Jim made a few weeks later, which said that the ME had brought him a sealed, standard-size business envelope, to be given to his wife should he predecease her. I wondered what such a letter might say. A declaration of his love for her? A confession of an affair? A motivational essay encouraging his family to persevere without him? A map to the Lost Dutchman's mine? I definitely needed some sleep. But not before I looked through the last few clients on the disk.

It was well past midnight when I finally crawled into bed, contorting my body to fit around several slumbering cats. But as tired as I was, I couldn't put that letter out of my mind. Where would Jim have put it for safekeeping? Possibly in the paper files he kept as backup, which meant that the police must have it by now. It occurred to me that he might have told Ronnie about it in case he wasn't able to fulfill the request himself when the time came. I made a mental note to talk to her about it the next day. With that decided, I must have relaxed enough for the combined delta waves from my feline bedmates to lure me off to sleep.

Chapter 21

I took Sashkatu with me and deposited him in my shop before meeting Travis, so I wouldn't have to go back home to fetch him before I opened up for the day. Instead of twiddling my thumbs until the appointed hour, I walked into the Morning Glory Café seven minutes early. Travis had beaten me there. He was seated in a booth toward the rear of the restaurant, talking on his cell phone and jotting notes on a little pad. He was concentrating, completely plugged into what the caller was saying, his brows drawn together so tightly they forged a vertical crease over the bridge of his nose.

At that early an hour on a weekday, the restaurant was half full, the patrons all town residents. I exchanged nods and waves as I passed their tables. Without glancing behind me, I knew that every one of them turned to see whom I was meeting for breakfast. In a town the size of New Camel, I would have been surprised if they didn't.

Travis clicked off his call and looked up as I reached his booth. The tension in his face instantly softened into an easy grin.

"Hi," I said, sliding in across from him before he had a chance to stand and greet me. It seemed like the least awkward way to handle things, since I didn't know him well enough for a kiss, and a handshake would have been too formal.

He slipped his phone into his pocket. "I see you're a fan of punctuality."

"Always have been," I said.

"Me too. Irritates the hell out of some people, though," he added with a laugh.

"Sounds like you enjoy doing that."

"Irritating people? You don't? Be honest now." He skewered me with his eyes, daring me to lie.

I couldn't help but laugh. "Okay, maybe a little." Sitting there with him, I remembered why I'd first been attracted to him that day in my shop. You could read all the magazine articles and self-help books about not judging a man by the way he looks, but you can't help what attracts you. And I was attracted to him like crazy. He had a sly, confident smile like he'd read the ending of our story and was waiting for me to catch up. But his eyes also showed elusive flashes of the boy he'd been. I was glad he'd chucked the on-air suit to go with a polo and chinos again. I definitely preferred this casual Travis to the up-and-coming TV journalist. I could picture him on the deck of a sailboat, hair streaked lighter by the sun. *Seriously?* I asked myself. Have you forgotten that this is the man who scoffs at magick and essentially considers you a fraud who earns a living by duping people, including his mother?

My internal rant was cut short by the young waitress who'd come to take our order. I'd never seen her before, but college kids from neighboring towns often found jobs in New Camel when the tourist trade spiked in the summer. I asked for a Morning Glory muffin and tea. Travis wanted coffee, black, and after a moment's hesitation, seconded the muffin.

"Their Morning Glory will knock any others you've had out of the water," I said.

He shrugged. "This is going to be my first one. Figured I'd give it a try."

"Ah, so you're impulsive as well as punctual."

"It's important to be open to new experiences."

"As long as it's not magick." The words slipped out before I knew they were on my tongue.

"It's not exactly a proven science," he said wryly.

"In the right hands, it's actually more of an art."

"Touché." He held his hands up in mock surrender. "I propose a truce. Let's agree to disagree for now. I've been looking forward to seeing you too much to spend the time sparring."

How could I say no when he put it that way? "Truce," I agreed, although it seemed like we were merely kicking the ball farther down a bumpy road. Sooner or later we'd have to decide if our opposing views were a deal breaker. But I decided to live in the moment and enjoy the time with him. It wasn't as if I was signing on for the long haul; it was nothing more than tea and a muffin. "You never mentioned you were a big shot TV newsman," I said to steer the conversation into more benign waters. Anything he asked about me was bound to lead right back to magick.

"Hardly a big shot up here in the boonies," he said in an aw-shucks tone. He paused for a moment. "I know this is going to sound really awful, but the truth is, the Harkens murder has been a huge break for me."

"You're right; it does sound awful," I said, although I hadn't intended to make it sound quite so harsh. After all, he hadn't pulled the trigger or hired a hit man in order to further his career ambitions. "Sorry," I murmured, "I guess that hit too close to the bone."

"No, I'm sorry. I get it. Too soon after such a traumatic event to be talking about personal silver linings. Especially when I don't know if you were close to the victim."

"Jim Harkens was our family's attorney, but I've always been a lot closer to his wife, in spite of our age difference."

He nodded. "I should have asked, before opening my big mouth."

"Apology accepted." I didn't know what more to say. Apparently neither did he. The silence was piling up between us like bricks building a wall. I glanced around the restaurant as I tried to come up with a new topic, but we had no history to fall back on. No, "hey, remember the time" or "how's old so-and-so?" Travis was staring out the window, probably engaged in the same futile exercise. Luckily the waitress arrived with our breakfasts.

I added sweetener to my tea and spent a ridiculous amount of time cutting my muffin into quarters. How was it possible that two intelligent people couldn't think of anything to talk about? Then it hit me—Travis's coverage of Jim's death could be a silver lining for Elise and me too. If he was good at his job, he probably knew more about the case than anyone beside the police and the killer. And if he didn't, at least it would serve to break the silence. "Have you done a lot of research on the Harkens case?" I asked.

"I'm still at it," he replied, grabbing for the lifeline I'd tossed him. "I need background material on all the players to add color and filler to my reports." He broke off a piece of the muffin and studied it. "What's in this thing?"

"Walnuts, carrots, raisins, coconut, and sometimes pecans and dates. Bakers add different things. Your basic kitchen-sink recipe."

He took a bite and chewed thoughtfully. "It's good." He sounded surprised. "I don't normally go for a hodgepodge like that, but it really is good."

"Has your research turned up anything interesting?" I asked to get him back on topic.

"Possibly." He stopped to drink his coffee. "I don't usually talk about a story I'm working on," he said, when he realized I was waiting to hear more. "Okay, can I can trust you to keep your lips zipped?" I nodded. "Here's what I know—your ME, Westfield, made it to the top in the Manhattan medical examiner's office at a young age. His resume was impressive, Ivy League, consistently placed in the top two on every civil service exam he took. He was definitely on track for Chief ME of the entire city. So why pack it in and move to a little backwater up here?"

"To get his family away from the crime in the city, the threat of terrorism, the overcrowded schools, the pollution?" I said. It made perfect sense to me.

Travis frowned as if he'd caught me cheating on a test. "That's his response, almost word for word, every time he's asked the question."

"I think he did the right thing for his family. And I wouldn't be surprised if his wife played a major role in the decision. Not everyone needs money and fame to be happy." I thought of telling him how Tilly had turned it all down too, but I suspected he'd discredit the source.

Travis finished his coffee and beckoned to the waitress for a refill. "You think I'm looking for intrigue and melodrama where none exists?" his voice was oddly hollow. It was as if I'd taken a pin to his balloon and all his enthusiasm had fizzled out.

"Look," I said, "you asked my opinion, so I gave it to you. But you're the one in the news business. Your instincts are bound to be a lot better than mine."

He laughed, but it sounded forced. "Yeah, you're right. What was I thinking?" The waitress came by with the coffee and hot water carafes. She refilled Travis's cup, but I declined more water for my tea.

"Did you uncover anything else in your research?" I asked, catching him with a mouthful of muffin. While I waited for him to finish it, I picked at the second half of mine. I always took a piece home with me and this time would be no exception. They were as filling as steak.

"I don't know if you've already heard this," he said, "but it seems the guy who monitors the camera for Harkens' building told police he was called away on a bogus emergency and when he got back, he realized someone had shut down that camera."

"Do you know the guy's name?"

"No. The police said he didn't want to be identified. A smart move on his part. Not so great for those of us in the news business." He drank his coffee. "Now that you've picked my brain, how about a little reciprocity? Anything you can tell me about this quiet little town of yours? Aren't little towns supposed to have dirty secrets? How about some lurid details that could pump up my ratings?" This time his smile made it all the way to his eyes.

"If there's any lurid stuff going on around here, no one's thought to include me," I said. I was sure Travis would love to hear about the bad blood between Duggan and the victim, but I'd promised to keep the material on the flash disk confidential, unless and until Elise needed it to prove she was not the most likely suspect. I didn't take that vow lightly and I certainly didn't know Travis well enough to trust him with such sensitive material. Although I'd made no such promise to my aunt concerning Beverly's unrequited love for Jim, it felt wrong to put a reporter on her trail when I had no proof she'd done anything more than try to erase him from a photograph. Besides, Tilly had invaded Beverly's right to privacy in her own home, which made me feel dirty about passing on the information, no matter how much I disliked the woman.

I stole a glance at my watch, thinking I should make my exit while the conversation was easy and before one of us managed to put a foot in a mouth again. I was glad to see it was nearly ten o'clock. Travis wouldn't think I was making up an excuse to run. In spite of the awkward period we'd muddled through, I wanted to see him again. The heart wants what the heart wants, or more accurately, what the hormones want.

Travis consulted his watch too. "I didn't realize it was that late. I know you have to go. I'll take care of things here." I thanked him and slid out of the booth. "Kailyn," he said with his off-kilter smile. "I think I enjoyed this. Maybe we can get together again?"

I laughed. "I think that might just be a possibility."

Chapter 22

The phone startled me awake at eight a.m. The woman on the other end was speaking so rapidly that I didn't catch her name or the reason for her call.

"Excuse me?" was all I could manage as I tried to extricate myself from a convoluted dream in which I was stuck back in Merlin's time.

"I'm sorry. Let me start again," the woman said, clearly making an effort to slow down and speak more distinctly. "My name is Natalie Catapano. Your aunt Matilda and her companion drove onto my front lawn the other day?"

Uh-oh. I'd given the Catapanos my phone number instead of Tilly's, in an effort to stay on top of things. "Yes, of course, Mrs. Catapano," I said, "how can I help you?"

"It's beautiful, absolutely magnificent," she blurted out. "Tony and I, well our mouths fell open when we looked outside this morning. We can't get over it. How on earth did your aunt arrange all this? And in so little time. She must have had a crew of elves working here all night. Didn't even wake us. Or any of our cranky neighbors. It's nothing short of magic."

"I'm so pleased to hear you like it," I said, thinking they'd hit the nail on the head. No one could have set the Catapano's landscaping to rights so fast without a healthy dose of magick. "I'll be sure to let my aunt know."

Natalie wasn't ready to let go of the subject yet. She gushed on for another few minutes in mind-numbing detail, ending with a request for the name of the company Tilly hired.

"I'll ask her to give you a call," I said. New Camel was about to have another murder to solve. But this one would be a cinch.

* * *

I left for work early, intending to stop first at Tilly's house. I didn't call to say I was coming, because I wanted to catch her off guard. Instead I was the one surprised that no one was home. I drove on down to Main Street where I found her car parked in front of our shops. At least she and her accomplice weren't off somewhere getting into more trouble. I pulled up behind her mustang and played a brief, but spirited, game of "catch the cat" with Sashkatu, who was feeling unusually chipper. After opening Abracadabra, I set Sashki on the floor and the two of us marched straight back and through the connecting door to Tilly's place. I'd been so preoccupied that I hadn't immediately noticed the smells of baking. Baking was my aunt's go-to when she was overwrought, worried, or depressed. Over the years, the level of her baking frenzy had proven to be a fair measure of the state of her nerves. That day I put it at seven out of ten.

There were trays of pastries and scones cooling on every available surface. Merlin was watching the action from a stool at the entrance to the kitchen. Sashki rubbed his face against the sorcerer's pants leg, then curled up around his feet, the smell of baked goods making his tiny nose twitch with anticipation.

"Good Morning, Mistress," Merlin greeted me as if nothing were amiss. But then his perspective with regard to magick was worlds apart from mine.

"Is it?" I replied, sidling past him to enter the kitchen at the same moment the oven timer started to chirp. I stepped into Tilly's path as she turned away from the sink to answer its call.

"Kailyn," she said, clearly not as delighted to see me as she usually was. The timer kept chirping for attention. "Excuse me, dear, I have to see to the strudel."

I stood my ground. "I got a phone call from Natalie Catapano this morning."

"Oh really?" Her voice was a full octave above its normal range. She looked from me to the oven and back again, like a criminal trying to decide if she should make a run to save the strudel. When had she started baking strudel for her teas anyway?

"She's thrilled with how beautiful her yard turned out," I said.

"Isn't that nice?" Tilly stepped to the side to get around me, but my reaction time was too good. "Kailyn," she said impatiently, "the strudel is going to burn."

"According to Natalie, the work was done so fast and noiselessly, it was nothing short of *magick*."

"It wasn't my doing," Tilly said with a defeated sigh. "Let me get the strudel out, and I'll tell you everything."

I went back to my shop to wait. Sashki stayed with Merlin. Big surprise. When Tilly came to talk, she was holding a plate of apple strudel as a peace offering, wizard and cat close behind her. She set the plate on my counter and collapsed into the chair beside it, looking exhausted. "I meant to take care of the Catapano's landscaping the proper way," she said. "I got some estimates, but the numbers were staggering. You'd think we drove a semi through the gardens of Versailles."

When she paused, Merlin picked up the narrative, no hint of apology in his tone. "Matilda was so upset, how could I not take pity on her? It is simply not in my nature to stand by and do nothing in someone's time of distress."

Since it was pointless to argue with the man, I turned back to my aunt. "Why didn't you come to me? We could have figured something out together. Now Natalie will be telling everyone in the county how you transformed her yard overnight. And by the way, she wants the name of the company you hired to do it." The color drained from Tilly's face.

"And how would you go about helping her with that?" I asked Merlin, who was clearly stumped.

"I could . . . we might . . . there are a number of spells and potions that can fiddle with one's memory. But they can be tricky."

Wow, why didn't that suggestion calm all my fears? "There's also her husband's memory," I pointed out. "And the memories of all the people who happen to see the property or speak to the Catapanos." Not even the great Merlin could hope to stuff this particular genie back in the bottle.

Tilly was wagging her head in silent misery, possibly realizing for the first time how deep and muddy a hole she and her Clyde had dug for us. The ringing of my phone provided them with a chance to retreat to the warmth and sweetness of her shop. A tour bus was scheduled to arrive soon anyway, and there was nothing to be gained by rehashing the matter *ad nauseam*. When I picked up the phone, I found Ronnie on the line.

"Kailyn, I need to talk to you," she said grimly. "In person."

"I have to speak to you too," I said, wondering what grave, new problem had landed on her doorstep and, by extension, mine.

"An early dinner at The Caboose?" she suggested. We agreed on five-fifteen at the restaurant, which was technically in an old train car, not a caboose. Of far more importance was the fact that they made the best burgers, fries, and shakes in the county and quite possibly the state. Minutes after clicking off the call, the tour group descended on New Camel. It was a lively bunch of women from the Boston suburbs who kept me jumping, which was exactly what I needed in order to make it through the workday.

Chapter 23

The day had been hectic and profitable, so I didn't feel guilty about closing up ten minutes early. Besides, the hour before closing was notoriously slow in the touristy part of town. Those few minutes allowed me to drop Sashkatu at home and feed everyone. It also meant I could enjoy my own dinner without constantly checking the time. Driving to The Caboose, all I could think about was one of their cold, thick strawberry shakes. That's when it dawned on me I'd had nothing to eat since breakfast.

I pulled into the half-filled parking lot. Although five-fifteen on a weekday evening was a good time to eat at The Caboose, a mere half hour later the lot would be full and it would be difficult to get in the door. With six booths on either side of the center aisle, The Caboose had never had enough seating. The result was a booming takeout business.

I parked in the spot next to Ronnie's car and went inside. The restaurant wasn't big on decor. When it had first opened in the eighties, its claim to fame was a Lionel train that rode the inside perimeter on a track that went by each table. Several of its freight cars had been outfitted with cup holders, so that shakes and other beverages could be served by train, captivating children of all ages, myself included. Unfortunately, the restaurant was sold a decade later, and the new owner didn't have the patience for a gimmick that was often in need of repair. He did, however, have the smarts to retain the original kitchen staff and assure their loyalty by giving them a substantial raise. The trains were gone, but the kitchen still turned out consistently great, if not heart-healthy, food.

I spotted Ronnie in a booth on the right, halfway back, drinking iced tea. I slid in across from her at the same time the waitress arrived to take my drink order. Service was never lagging at The Caboose; turnover was the name of the game. I ordered my strawberry shake and turned to Ronnie. My heart dropped at the bleak look in her eyes. She made an effort to paste on a smile, but it was like putting a little Band-Aid on a gash from a machete. My own smile instantly evaporated.

"Are you all right?" was the first thing to pop out of my mouth. A downright stupid question given her expression. "What's wrong?"

"No, you first. You said you had a question."

I thought about arguing that she should go first, but it was easier and faster to get on with it. "Jim's file on Roger Westfield mentioned a letter he wanted Jim to give to his wife in the event of his death."

Ronnie nodded. "It was sealed when Westfield gave it to us."

"Do you know where Jim put it for safekeeping?"

"Ordinarily he would have put it in Westfield's paper file, but for some reason, he shredded it."

It was hard to keep the frustration out of my tone. "Couldn't he have been disbarred for doing that?"

Ronnie shrugged. "As long as money isn't involved, you'd be surprised what lawyers can get away with in this state."

My head filled with a dozen related questions, all of which were beside the point for now. "What makes you think he shredded the letter?"

"I did all the shredding in the office—part of my job description. In fact the shredder was always right next to my desk. He hated wasting his time on it. A few months ago, I left early, forgot my glasses and had to go back in. I found Jim at my desk, feeding the letter into the shredder. I knew it was Westfield's letter, because he'd dropped the envelope that had his wife's name on it. He jumped six feet when he heard the door closing behind me. It's possible he was startled, because he wasn't expecting anyone. If I'd been in his shoes, I might have reacted the same way."

"Did you ask him why he was shredding it?"

"Yes, and he got angry. Told me to mind my own business. In all the years I'd worked for him, he'd never spoken to me like that before." I could tell by her voice that the incident had shaken her at the time.

"Another dead end," I murmured with a sigh. "We'll never know what was in that letter."

The waitress stopped at our table to set down my shake and take our order—two cheeseburgers with fries, no onion on mine. Once we were alone again, I tried to put the letter out of my thoughts and listen to what was on Ronnie's mind.

"Here it is," she said, punctuating the words with a heavy sigh. "When I told you about Duggan calling me down to the police station again, it wasn't just about my having had access to the gun. Someone came forward with new information." She stared at her iced tea, poking at the lemon wedge with her straw. "I didn't tell you the truth when you asked me if Jim was having an affair." She couldn't seem to look me in the eye. "This person claims to have seen Jim and me in a . . . a compromising situation that—"

"Hold on. What are you saying?" Although I'd heard her words, my brain was having trouble making sense of them.

"I'm saying *I* was the one having an affair with Jim," she said bluntly, her words quickly swallowed by the general hubbub.

"Wait—you and Elise are friends, really good friends." I wanted her to take it back. Tell me it was a joke. That she'd misspoken.

"We didn't mean for it to happen. I know that's what everybody says when they're caught. But it's the truth. It wasn't some thoughtless, frivolous fling. We'd managed to keep our feelings under lock and key for a long time. And then one day we couldn't anymore. I'm not saying any of this to excuse my behavior. There is no excuse for it. I was hoping to at least spare Elise more pain, let her memories of Jim remain untainted. But that's not likely now. I wanted you to hear it from me. That way you can be there for her when . . ." Her last words caught in her throat.

In the space of a minute, she'd rendered me senseless, too numb to react. I couldn't come up with a single thing to say. Not one expletive to spit at her.

"Here you go, ladies," the waitress said brightly, parking our plates in front of us. "Enjoy!" she called as she moved on to another table.

I rummaged in my handbag for money. I found a twenty, tossed it onto the table, and stood up on shaky, Gumby legs. Ronnie rose too. We both started to talk at the same time. "I've gotta go," I mumbled, amazed that my voice was working.

"No," she said, low and determined as she dropped another twenty on the table. "I've done enough damage. Please stay and eat." She walked away before I could argue. I didn't want to stay, but I also didn't want to follow her out like I was running after her, so I sank back down in the booth. My stomach recoiled at the thought of biting into the burger, despite the fact that I'd been looking forward to it all day. I reached for the shake instead and took a sip. Cool and creamy, it slid down my throat without effort, although the taste barely registered in my brain. I drank most of it and once I was certain I wouldn't see Ronnie in the parking lot, I got up and left. The forty on the table would cover the bill and a hefty tip. I didn't want to signal the waitress to bring the check, because then I'd be forced to explain why our food went untouched. She'd ask if my friend was okay, if I'd like a to-go bag or if I'd prefer to order something else. Questions I didn't want to answer. Questions I wasn't sure I could answer with any degree of normalcy.

I parked in my driveway and went inside, unable to remember how I actually got there. A part of my brain must have directed my driving, while another part was busy sorting out my tangled thoughts and feelings. One realization I'd come to was that in addition to all of Ronnie's sins, she was a coward. She should have been the one to tell Elise. To stand there and take whatever Elise would say or do to her. But Ronnie had made me her flunky. All that babble about not wanting to cause Elise more pain was pure garbage. Ronnie didn't want to grovel or deal with any more pain herself. For Elise, hearing this news would be like losing Jim all over again. A second death that robbed her of even the sustaining memory of being loved. And Ronnie had me the messenger.

I turned on the TV in hopes of distracting myself. It was hard to find a show that wasn't about murder or adultery. I tried a couple of sitcoms, but they were more irritating than amusing. Sleep was probably the one thing that would quiet my thoughts, if I could manage to fall asleep at such an early hour. A cup of Tilly's Sweet Dreams tea might help. She made it from a mixture of chamomile, valerian, lemon balm, and lavender. I'd never been crazy about the flavor of valerian, but Tilly maintained that it was the most potent herb in the concoction. While I waited for the tea to steep, I checked to be sure the cats' communal water bowl was full.

I was headed from the kitchen to the stairs, teacup in hand, when the phone rang. I backtracked to the kitchen for it, glancing first at the caller ID. I was afraid Elise might be on the other end and I wasn't up to destroying her world quite yet. I breathed a sigh of relief when I saw Travis's name.

"Hi there," he said. "I assume I'm not intruding on your bedtime again."

I squelched a laugh. If he only knew. "Hi, what's up?" I asked, reaching for my most wide-awake voice.

"I thought you might want to hear the results of my latest research."

"Sure."

"If you're not busy, I could swing by in . . . say . . . ten minutes." Oops, I hadn't realized he meant in person. He sounded so eager, I didn't want to shoot him down. Not to mention that my heart had started doing a little jig at the thought of seeing him again. I gave him directions to the house, then ran upstairs to pull a comb through my hair and put on some lip gloss. I told myself I would have done that if it was a girlfriend coming over too. But I didn't buy it.

Chapter 24

Travis was at my door almost to the minute. The cats, who'd been sleeping on various ledges and furniture tops, took off at the first whiff of a stranger entering their space. Only Sashkatu remained. He opened one discriminating eye to appraise the situation and decided there was no need to further trouble himself.

I offered Travis a drink, hot or cold, but he declined. I'd left my own tea in the kitchen. I could always reheat it later if I still wanted it. For now sleep was the last thing on my mind. We sat on the couch, angled toward one another, with enough distance between us to satisfy a dueña.

He certainly wasn't a sweep-you-off-your-feet kind of guy. I was torn between finding it a refreshing change from other men I'd known and wishing I knew if he was interested in me as more than a casual friend.

He frowned at me. "What's wrong? You don't look so hot."

"Wow, that's what every woman wants to hear." It really was the last thing I needed to hear at that moment. Then again, a lot of men wouldn't have even noticed. Maybe it wasn't such a bad thing for a guy to be able to key into your emotional state. At least Travis had the good sense to look abashed.

"Hey no, I'm sorry, I didn't mean it that way," he said, stumbling over his words. "But you look stressed. Like something happened to upset you. Shut up, Travis," he muttered to himself, "before you shove your foot any farther down your throat."

I couldn't help but laugh. He did have a charming, boyish way about him, what my grandmother would have called *winsome*. "You happen to be right," I admitted. "Something did happen. But word of advice—don't ever use that as a pickup line."

"Got it," he said with a wry smile. "Look, if you want to talk about what's troubling you, my ears are at your disposal."

I did want to talk about it, especially to someone who could be objective. The problem was, in his line of work, information, gossip, innuendo were all grist for a very hungry mill. "I need to know that you won't disclose anything I tell you to anyone. That I won't see it on the late news or in tomorrow's paper."

He came off the back of the couch and sat up straight. "You can trust me," he said soberly. "I know that's what a lot of reporters would say to ease your mind, while trying to worm their way into your good graces, but I can't think of any other way to put it."

"Even if what I tell you could be a bit of a scoop?" I pressed him.

"You can trust me no matter what it is. If you have a bible handy, I'll swear to it."

I wanted to believe him and I'd always been a good judge of character, until my instincts went belly up with Ronnie. I told myself her confession was going to come out, probably sooner than later, whether or not I said anything. At least this way I could vent and find out how trustworthy Travis was. Two birds, one stone. I filled him in about Ronnie and Jim.

"It does put a new spin on the case," he said.

"Please tell me you're not sorry you made that promise?"

Travis shrugged and grinned. "If I don't cut it as a reporter, I can always go to work for my uncle's construction company. Seriously though, it looks like the police have a new contender for the killer's crown."

"But why would Ronnie kill the man she claims to have loved?" I'd come up with a few scenarios myself, but I wanted to see if he could add anything."

"Maybe she got tired of waiting for him to leave his wife and marry her. Maybe he replaced her with a newer model. Maybe he broke off the affair and fired her, a lethal double whammy for a woman of a certain age."

"All good reasons not to own up to the affair unless the police found out about it," I said. "If Ronnie did kill him, she might have gotten away with it, if not for that one witness."

"One is all it takes," he said, "unless the witness had a vested interest in destroying her or is too old and dotty to be credible." He paused. "Can I still take you up on that offer of a drink? Water would be fine."

I was already on my feet. "Is water with citrus okay?"

"Sure, we reporters like to live on the edge."

I returned with a tall glass and a napkin and sat down a little closer to him this time. It takes two to tango, as they say. "Okay sir, you have the floor. I assume you're here to shoot down my theory on why Westfield left the big city."

Travis took a long drink of the water, then put the napkin down on the end table and set the glass on it. "Not necessarily," he said, lounging back against the cushions. "I admit I'm more cynical than the average person. In my line of work, I can't afford to take things at face value."

"I would never have guessed," I said, rolling my eyes.

"Hey, if you're not cynical, you don't dig, and if you don't dig, you can't find buried secrets. I read through the police reports and the ME's findings for the six months preceding Westfield's resignation. Sadly, what stood out was how many kids died due to gun violence. I knew it, of course, but the statistics are always hard to read."

"In other words, I was right. Westfield wanted to get his family out of Dodge."

"Possibly. But a good reporter doesn't find one statistic and call the job done. I also found a number of the usual eyebrow raisers—people who died young from medical conditions that had previously gone undetected."

"Like high school athletes dropping dead on the football field?"

"Or forty-year-olds dying during their morning jog. They tend to be mostly undetected heart conditions, but it's far from a common occurrence. The media, with the exception of me, pounces on cases like those and plays them up until it seems like a new plague is erupting.

"And?"

"So far nothing seems questionable."

"Do I get to gloat now?" I asked sweetly.

"Not quite. I want to poke around some more. Think you can hang in there?"

"Do I have a choice?"

"I promise not to keep you waiting too much longer." He covered a yawn. "Sorry, not bored, just sleep deprived." He glanced at his watch "I should probably let you put on your jammies and get to bed too."

Now that he was about to leave, I was consumed by the need to tell him about the threatening letter. "If you have a moment, there's something I'd like to run by you."

"Sure, I'll assume I'm still under oath."

I told him about the letter and explained that I couldn't bring it to the police, because I considered Duggan a suspect. And I if I told Tilly or Elise, they would worry, which would make me feel worse and do nothing to help the situation.

"I'm glad you told me," he said when I was done. "It could be an empty threat, someone playing with you. But it could also be the real thing if the killer is worried that you're getting too close. You never want to back a killer into a corner. Any chance you'd be willing to stop your investigation and leave it to the police?"

"How can I? If Duggan is the killer, it's in his best interests to let Elise take the rap. I may be the only person working to prove her innocence." Hearing my own words out loud made them scarier than thinking them.

"Hopefully, a good lawyer would."

"I can't let it go that far. Her kids just lost their father. If she's arrested and tried for killing him, it will destroy them completely."

Travis was silent for a minute. "I think you're making a mistake," he said finally, "but I can't fault your loyalty. Any chance you'd consider taking on a partner?"

A partner would mean having someone to discuss clues with, bounce ideas off. Not a terrible idea. But I did have a couple of concerns. "I guess I wouldn't mind a partner as long as that partner isn't volunteering his services merely to protect me."

"No way. I'd be in it for my own selfish reasons. Breaking this case could get me a few rungs higher up the news chain."

I couldn't tell if he was messing with me or being totally honest. "You should also know upfront that I'm not great at playing second fiddle."

"Now there's a big surprise. I wouldn't be much of an investigative reporter if I hadn't figured that out by now. So, what do you say—partners?"

"As long as either one of us can call it quits at any time."

"That's what I like—a firm commitment," he said wryly. "I guess I'll have to live with that for now." He stuck out his hand, and we sealed the deal. Another part of my brain was busy wondering if we were ever going to get past the handshaking stage. "I'm sure you realize that as much as I'd like to, I can't pursue this case full-time," he said. "My producers have their own ideas about how I should spend the hours I work for them."

"You mean because they pay you a salary, they think they own your time?"

"I know, they have a lot of nerve. Seriously though, I will keep after it whenever I'm free. Meanwhile, Kailyn, please try to stay out of trouble. Don't ever forget, this isn't a mental exercise; you're trying to take down a killer."

"I couldn't forget it if I wanted to. My best friend lost her husband, and her children lost their father. That's about as real as it gets."

"I imagine it is," Travis said.

"Now that we're partners, do you think you could do some checking on the other suspects on my list too?" I asked as I walked him to the door.

"Sure, but it will cut into the time I spend on Westfield."

"I can live with that." What I couldn't live with was letting the killer get away because I was chasing after the wrong person.

Travis turned to me when we reached the door. "If this partnership has any chance of working, we have to keep each other in the loop. You can't pick and choose what you tell me. Nothing is too small to mention. That includes any other threats."

"Agreed," I said, not ready to let him leave yet. Not with my heart and hormones still demanding answers. I rose up on my toes to kiss him goodbye. At the same moment he bent to kiss me. We banged heads hard and dissolved into silly laughter fueled by fatigue and awkwardness.

"Okay," he said, rubbing his forehead, "how about we try that again, with you standing still this time?" Before I could answer, his mouth was on mine and, in spite of my throbbing head, it was clear that my heart and hormones were definitely on to something.

Chapter 25

I went to bed, but sleep eluded me. Between my evolving relationship with Travis, the meaning of our new partnership, and my fears for Elise, my mind was ablaze. Although Travis never spelled it out, I knew he expected me to be careful and patient while he shouldered the bulk of the investigation. But even though I'd promised to keep him in the loop, I hadn't agreed to sit idly by. That would be a short drive to crazy. There had to be something I could do from my end, while he was in the city chasing down other leads. What if I could sneak in to see Westfield again? Maybe he wouldn't mind telling me the story of why he moved his family to New Camel. *Really, Kailyn? Are you basing that on how pleased he was the first time you snuck in?* I could say I was doing an article for the local newspaper about why people move to Schuyler County. Most people like to talk about themselves. Unless they're guilty of murder. Even if he declined my offer, he might slip and inadvertently give me information. Back and forth I went, arguing both sides of the question well into the early hours of the morning, before finally succumbing to sleep.

I opened my eyes to the first light of dawn seeping in around the edges of the window shades. The idea of going to see the ME popped right back into my head. I was definitely still game for the trip to Watkins Glen. No surprise. I've always preferred action to inaction, apprehension to boredom. I threw back the covers with hearty determination, upsetting the two cats on whom it landed. You'd have thought I poured ice water on them instead of a light summer quilt. They leapt up and ran for their lives, trampling the other cats, as if they were nothing but inconvenient speed bumps. Rudely awakened, the others jumped up to join the mass exodus. Sashkatu, curled on the high land of his pillow, slept on, undisturbed by the fray.

After showering, I dressed in beige capris, a beige T-shirt and an old pair of flat, beige sandals I found in the back of my closet. I liked beige well enough when paired with other colors, but a solid uniform of beige was not at all my style. That day I wasn't dressing to impress. I was dressing to get lost in the background. For that same reason, I didn't put on makeup and I pulled my hair back in a simple brown elastic band that virtually disappeared against the brown of my hair.

I was too wired to be hungry, so I made myself some calming tea and fixed the cats' breakfast. One by one, they left their hidey-holes, slinking into the kitchen, wary of what other terrors awaited them. Once their bellies were full, they seemed to regain their equilibrium. I left them to their morning ablutions and drove over to the shop, where I set the clock in the window to let customers know I'd be opening at noon. Then I locked up and headed for Watkins Glen. I wanted to be at the ME's office shortly after it opened, to minimize the chance of missing Westfield if he took a coffee break or left for an early lunch. I would still have to contend with the receptionist gatekeeper, but I'd already decided to use a little harmless magick to get past her.

A spell of invisibility is difficult to pull off at the height of one's powers and under the best circumstances, even more so with the problems I'd been having. The one time I'd performed the spell, I'd gotten into big trouble. I was in the fifth grade at the time and had forgotten to do my homework, because I'd been caught up in a Nancy Drew mystery yet again. I was afraid the teacher would call on me with a homework question I couldn't answer, prompting her to send another note to my mother. I figured I had nothing to lose by giving the spell a whirl. At the time, I'd read the spell once, over my grandmother Bronwen's shoulder, but I've always had a great memory. Except for homework, that is. The spell had worked better than I could have hoped, until my teacher actually thought I'd gone missing. The principal had come running to the classroom, only to find me in my assigned seat, where I'd been all along. Laughter had done me in. My concentration faltered and the spell was broken. There I was, plain as day. To my teacher's dismay, and my regret, the faculty and students had teased her about it for the rest of that school year and for several years afterward. Although it had pained me to be the source of her discomfit, admitting the truth would have incurred far-reaching consequences. To say that Morgana and Bronwen had not been pleased with me was the understatement of the century and the reason I never thought of trying the spell again. Until now. I briefly considered taking Merlin along as a sort of backup battery, but after tallying the pros and cons of enlisting his help, I'd decided to go it alone.

I'd be lying if I said I wasn't nervous on the drive to see the ME. But what, I asked myself, was the worst that could happen? Westfield could call security and have me thrown out or he could get an order of protection to keep me away in the future. The fact remained that the last time I snuck in there, he *had* come around and answered my question. It was enough to keep my foot on the accelerator.

I parked in the same municipal lot I'd used on my first trip there and walked the two blocks to the forensics building. On my way, I started working on the spell. It required intense concentration, blocking out all the sights and sounds around me. I focused on drawing light particles to me and through me. I imagined the feeling as they passed through my body, until I didn't have to imagine it anymore. In my head, I chanted,

> Light pass through me.
> No one see me.
> Light pass through me.
> No one see me.

Over and over, I repeated it, until I became as one with the photons and could no longer feel them as an outside force. Maintaining my concentration was the hardest part. I reached the building as two men in suits were exiting. Instead of holding the door open for me, they let it slam shut in my face. So far so good. I risked a quick glance at the reception desk. It was occupied by the same young woman as the last time.

> Light pass through me.
> No one see me.

I moved slowly, staying close to the perimeter of the lobby. I avoided any sudden movements, kept my arms as still as possible, and my eyes riveted to the ground because eyes are the hardest to conceal. Someone walked toward me, a man, judging by the trousers and shoes. He was coming too close. I automatically made a quick course correction. He called out a goodbye to the receptionist, causing her to look in my direction.

> Light pass through me.
> No one see me.

"Take care, Steve," she said. I held my breath. A second passed, then another and another. I'd dodged a bullet. A few more steps and I reached the farthest corner of the lobby, where it intersected with the hallway. I turned right. I had to resist the temptation to drop my guard and consider myself safe. The hallway held as many opportunities for failure as the lobby, maybe more. The last time a woman had popped out of an office doorway. She'd assumed I belonged there, but someone else might not. Focus.

> Light pass through me.
> No one see me.

Westfield's office was the fifth one down. I'd considered the possibility he might be in the autopsy suite. An additional set of problems. Door one, door two, three, four—

"Hold it." The voice came from behind me, male, deep, and reeking with authority. Could he be talking to someone else? I looked down the hallway and saw no one. I knew precisely where I went wrong. I'd lost my focus the second I started thinking about how to find the autopsy room.

I pasted a pleasant expression on my face and turned around. The man was tall, with wide shoulders and substantial girth, maybe an ex-football player gone to seed. He was in the gray-and-black uniform of a security guard. There was a gun holstered on his hip. His hand hovered over it, at the ready.

He stopped a few feet from me. "Who are you here to see?" he asked.

I hadn't heard an alert from the receptionist, but she might have pressed a silent alarm. It didn't track right, though. If she'd seen me in the lobby, she would have questioned my presence back there. I decided the guard must have happened upon me by luck, good for him, bad for me. If I played this right, I might still have a shot at seeing Westfield.

"Hi, Officer," I said. "I'm Kailyn Wilde." He wasn't a police officer, but it never hurt to pump up someone's ego before requesting their help.

"Ms. Wilde," he said, "what is the nature of your visit today?"

"I'm here to see Dr. Westfield." I held my chin high and dug deep for every bit of confidence I owned. I could tell he was weighing my answer, my potential for making trouble.

"I'll be happy to see you to his office."

Not the answer I wanted to hear. I knew the office was ten steps away, but I allowed him to lead the way. He rapped on the door. Westfield's muffled voice said, "Come in." The guard cracked the door enough to accommodate his head. "A Ms. Wilde is here to see you, Dr. Westfield. Are you expecting her?"

I heard the muted noise of a chair being pushed back on carpeting. Moments later the door was opened from inside and Roger Westfield was standing in the doorway. "Well, if it isn't Nancy Drew. Groupies are such a problem in my line of work," he said sardonically.

The guard seemed unsure about how to react. "Do you want me to escort her out?" he asked hesitantly.

"Yes, Gus, please do. If I took time out for every fan, I'd never get any work done."

Gus gave him an appreciative chuckle. "You've got it, doc. Sorry to have disturbed you."

Westfield gave me a hard look. "I'm a happily married man, Ms. Wilde. Don't let there be a next time, or I'll call the police and press charges." The guard hooked his hand around my upper arm.

"One question?" I begged the ME. "Just one. I swear."

"What is it this time?"

"Why did you leave the city and move up here?"

"That's your big question? That's why you snuck in here?" He shook his head. "It's simple. I didn't want to find my wife or kids on the autopsy table," he said, tilting his head in a sign to the guard, who promptly marched me away. I'd no doubt have the imprints of his big fingers on my arm as a souvenir of the trip.

Chapter 26

L olly was the first one into my shop after I turned the CLOSED sign to OPEN. One of her signature pink aprons was tied around her waist and a smudge of chocolate accented her rosy left cheek. The ruffle-edged aprons, available in every pastel of the color wheel, sold almost as well as her fudge. Seeing her in the apron was usually enough to make my mouth start watering for her candy. Pavlov would have loved me. But that day, not even my favorite fudge would have cheered me up. My trip to Westfield's office hadn't netted me much more than his irritation and possibly an order of protection against me. Although he'd confirmed my guess as to why he moved his family up to Schuyler County, there was a good chance he said the first thing that popped into his mind in order to get rid of me. And now, in the spirit of my partnership with Travis, I would have to tell him about it. I shoved my misery to the back of my mind to stew and dredged up a smile for Lolly.

Sashkatu had barely installed himself on his windowsill throne, but when he saw her come in he didn't waste any time trotting back down his stairway and executing a small leap onto the counter to greet her. They shared a brief session of scratches and cuddles while he licked at the candy on her cheek. He'd always had a soft spot for her, or maybe it was a sweet spot.

"You smell like chocolate," I said appreciatively. "You must be making candy day and night." I couldn't imagine how else she kept her display cases full. Her shop drew the largest number of customers by far.

She smoothed back the wisps of hair that had sprung free of her bun. "I think I've even been making chocolate in my sleep. This time of year it's hard to keep the supply equal to the demand."

"Then I'd better get you right back to work or my life will be forfeit when the fudge runs out. What can I do for you?"

She laughed. "Not to worry. I've been meaning to come talk to you, but then I get busy and forget. Mind if I park myself in that chair? I've been on my feet for hours."

"That's why it's here." How had Morgana and Bronwen managed without a chair all those years? It was fast becoming the most popular item in the shop. As soon as Lolly settled herself there, Sashkatu joined her, curling into a ball in her well-padded lap.

"When I was watching the ME's press conference the other day," she said, rhythmically stroking Sashki's back, "I recognized the man I'd seen racing out of town the day Jim died."

My friendly interest zoomed to intense focus in a split second. "What do you mean?"

"About four thirty on the day he was killed, I needed my late afternoon coffee. It helps me make it through until closing. I left my niece in charge of the shop and was crossing the street when this car came out of nowhere like a bat out of hell. If I hadn't jumped back, he would have mowed me down and probably kept right on going."

Could it be that simple? Could Lolly have seen the killer leaving the murder scene? "Who was it?" I prodded her when she paused to coo to Sashki.

"Well I don't know his name, but at the press conference he was wearing a suit and standing in the background next to Police Chief Gimble. I imagine he's someone with clout."

"Can you describe him to me?"

"Tall, broad shoulders, gray buzz cut. He looks like an army drill sergeant."

It had to be Duggan. "Did you notice the kind of car he was driving the day he nearly hit you?"

She nodded. "It was a Jeep, a black Jeep. I wanted to get the plate number to report him, but by the time I got my wits about me, he was gone."

I'd seen the unmarked car Duggan drove when he was on the job, and it wasn't a Jeep. What had he been doing in New Camel so close to the time of the murder and why had he been in such a big hurry to leave that he almost ran over Lolly? The answer that best fit those questions was that he'd just shot Jim and was making his getaway. But I needed more proof than Lolly's memory of a traumatic incident, before I could take my suspicions up the ladder to Gimble. "I'm glad you told me," I said, the wheels in my head spinning like mad.

"When I recognized him at that press conference, I was afraid to go to the police," Lolly went on. "I mean, what if he's somebody high up in government? But I didn't feel right not telling anyone. I know you've been doing some investigating of your own, so I thought maybe the information could help you."

I thanked her, and we chatted about town stuff for a few minutes. Then she made me promise to stop by later to taste her newest fudge sensation—chocolate maple walnut twist. Sashki was sound asleep on her lap, so she took great care to pick him up and place him gently back down in the center of the chair. His snoring barely missed a beat.

After Lolly left, I couldn't stop thinking about this major new wrinkle in the case. Although the prospect of paying the detective another visit didn't fill me with warm, fuzzy anticipation, it had to be the next thing on my agenda. I'd promised to keep Travis in the loop, but if I told him what I was planning to do, he would surely shut me down. He'd say that if Duggan was the killer, the odds of learning anything useful by confronting him were close to zero, whereas the odds of provoking him into killing me also, approached one hundred percent. I wrestled with my conscience. It wasn't as if I was going to accuse the man outright. I'd be much more subtle. Plus I had the weaponry of magick to protect me, more or less. Hardly a convincing argument. My conscience won out. I'd made a pact with my partner and I was obliged to honor it.

When I reached Travis, he was on assignment, covering a suspicious fire in the next county. He hadn't been down to Manhattan yet. "There's a better way of going about this," he said, after hearing me out. At least he hadn't gone all alpha male on me, forbidding me to do it. Maybe he suspected such a tactic would not be well-received.

"Okay, I'm listening."

"Most of the businesses along Main Street, including Harkens's building, probably have security cameras. See if you can get the property owners to let you view the video footage from that day. You may get lucky and find proof that it was Duggan's Jeep tearing down Main Street, or better yet, proof of him entering and leaving Jim's office building. Of course Duggan probably had all the video in his hands within minutes of Jim's death," he added as an afterthought.

"Do you think he might have tampered with it? I mean, if he was the killer?"

"I wouldn't rule it out. But security video is time-stamped. You should be able to tell if there's missing footage. It's definitely worth a shot."

How had I not thought of checking the cameras? I was turning out to be more like Inspector Clouseau than Nancy Drew. As long as I had Travis on the phone, I decided to bare my soul and get it over with. I gave him a brief summary of my trip to see the ME, emphasizing the comical aspects of my failure and Westfield's dust-dry humor. Travis didn't find it funny. But then neither did I. That might come some months or years down the road. Or maybe not at all. "One more thing," I said. "Do you think one of your cop friends would check with the DMV and find out what kind of car Duggan drives when he's not on the clock?"

"Already on my list of things to do."

Travis proved to be right about the security cameras. Abracadabra and Tea and Empathy were among the few businesses that didn't have them. When Morgana had reluctantly added the alarm system, cameras had seemed like overkill. She'd read Orwell's *1984* at least a dozen times in her youth and abhorred the idea of what she called "big brother cameras." However, if asked her opinion of them now that New Camel had had its first homicide, I suspect she would reconsider the idea, much as I was.

I contacted every shop owner in town and asked if I could view the video footage of the day Jim was murdered. Not a single one refused. They told me the old footage was stored by the security company for a month, in case it was needed in an investigation or lawsuit. Nearly all the systems had been installed and were monitored by Third Eye Security. The company had apparently offered a group discount at the time, but Morgana and Tilly had declined.

When I called Third Eye, I had to go through a receptionist, a low-level sales rep, a customer service rep, and a harried woman from the billing department before finally reaching a supervisor. For the fifth time that morning, I introduced myself and explained what I wanted. The supervisor tried to brush me off, saying that the police had already viewed all the video from that day. I told him that since I had the necessary waivers from their customers, I wanted to see the footage for myself. We went back and forth about it for another minute, until he snapped at me to be there at ten the next morning and hung up.

Tilly was free to take over at Abracadabra for me. She only did readings three or four days a week, because, as she put it, she needed to spend quality time in her own head too. Then I called Elise to tell her about the incident with Lolly and the security footage I was going to see.

"Let me come with you," she begged. "I need to do something constructive. I've already cleaned out every closet, twice. I know I'm driving the boys crazy, and they have enough to deal with." Her voice cracked on the last words.

How could I say no? With her help, I'd be able to get through the tapes more quickly. She might even catch something I missed. It was a win/win situation. But by the time we agreed to meet at Third Eye the next morning, my stomach had twisted into a painful knot and I knew exactly why. I still hadn't figured out how to tell her about Jim's infidelity and Ronnie's betrayal. As much as I wanted to protect her from the added distress, I had no right to keep the information from her. If only magick could rewrite the past.

Chapter 27

I picked up Elise on the way to Third Eye Security at nine-thirty in the morning. Their headquarters were located between New Camel and Watkins Glen, a twenty-minute trip from her door. According to the large white sign with green lettering at the driveway entrance, Third Eye was the only occupant of the one-story brick-and-glass building. Petunias and marigolds, in eye-catching purples and yellows, crowded around the base of the sign, bobbing their flowery heads at us as we turned in. I followed the driveway into the parking lot, which faced the front entrance. The back of the lot was full, most likely with employee cars. In the front row, two spaces were designated for the handicapped. The next three bore signs that said they were reserved, although not for whom. Then came the visitors' spaces, all of them empty. They clearly didn't get much walk-in trade. When I'd checked out the company website, it was easy to see why. Their homepage said they'd be happy to make an appointment to come to your residence or place of business to give you a free estimate on the best security system to fit your needs.

I pulled into the first visitor spot, and Elise and I entered the building through a standard set of double glass doors, without so much as a buzzer system to stop us. I'd expected some sophisticated security setup to impress potential customers with the need for protection. If Third Eye had no qualms about their own safety, why should anyone else? If I'd been running the show, I would have tricked out the place with every technological gadget at my disposal to show people what they needed in order to rest easy.

The receptionist hadn't been told to expect us, which didn't surprise me, given how poorly the company had handled my phone call. We waited fifteen minutes while the young woman tried a dozen extensions in her effort to locate the supervisor. When he finally appeared, he produced a syrupy smile at odds with the chill in his blue eyes. He introduced himself as Scot Avery, the man I'd spoken to the previous day. I said I was Kailyn Wilde, but before I could finish introducing Elise, he turned on his heel and asked us to follow him. I opened my mouth to tell him he could use a course in public relations, but Elise caught my eye and shook her head. She was right, of course. It wasn't the best strategy to antagonize the person who was about to show us what we wanted to see. It still took a lot of restraint on my part not to say anything and even more not to tiptoe over that old black-magick line to give him some richly deserved comeuppance. Something simple like making him slip on the polished tile and crack his tailbone, a very painful injury for which there is no cure but time. I knew a lot about it, because Tilly had cracked hers the first and last time she went ice skating.

Avery showed us into a cubicle that was too small to have been anyone's work station. It was possible they used it for storage, because there were file boxes and folders stacked high along every wall. In the center of the space was a table you couldn't rightly call a desk. It was more like the folding tables people keep in their basements for times when there are too many people to squeeze around the dining room table. Avery had provided us with two chairs, positioned side by side in front of a computer monitor. When we'd talked on the phone, I'd given him the date and the specific hours, three p.m. until seven p.m., in which we were interested. Since Jim wasn't murdered until the late afternoon, it would have been a waste of time to look for his killer earlier in the day. Avery had the requested footage ready to go and, after showing us how to access the time period in question, he left us to it. At least he wasn't going to be hovering. With the three of us in the room, along with his hefty attitude, it felt like there was barely enough air to breathe.

With Elise at the controls, we found images of Duggan's black Jeep driving along different segments of Main Street around four thirty, the time Lolly said he went speeding by her. We couldn't find any convincing evidence that he was doing more than the posted limit of thirty. The Jeep did appear to be moving slightly faster than the few other vehicles around it, but one had to keep in mind that Main Street, New Camel had never been a hotbed of speeders or drag racers. Most locals were content to obey the posted speed limit, and tourists tended to crawl along, scoping out the shops and looking for a place to park. It was possible Lolly had looked down at her phone for a second and when she looked up again, the Jeep seemed to come out of nowhere. But speeding aside, we wondered why the detective had been in town at all that day. He didn't live in the vicinity and he didn't ordinarily have reason to check things out at the precinct substation in town, at least not until after Jim was murdered. Of course it was pure conjecture on our part. We had no way of knowing if Duggan had come into New Camel for other, perfectly legitimate reasons.

We moved on to the footage from the camera outside Jim's building. The ME was the first one we saw entering after three that day. Four fifteen by the time stamp. We didn't see Jim or Dr. Silver enter, presumably because they'd come to work in the morning. But right before four o'clock, Elise popped into view, carrying her purse and a manila envelope. I hadn't expected to see her in the video. Before I could ask her about it, she hit pause and slumped back in her chair. "It still doesn't seem real," she murmured. "I didn't go to Jim's office a lot, but that afternoon when he was getting ready for your appointment, he realized he'd left some of your paperwork at home. He called and I dropped it off. Everything was so normal, so ordinary. He asked me what I was making for dinner."

I put my arm around her shoulders for a one-armed hug. "If this is too hard for you, I can drive you home and finish up here by myself."

"No, no, I'm fine, really," she said, sitting up and squaring her shoulders resolutely. "I need to be doing this."

I didn't try to change her mind. If she was determined to stiff-upper-lip it, I would support her choice. "Okay then, back to work," I said, all business. But after a couple of minutes, the screen went black. We exchanged a brief look of bewilderment, before she hit fast forward. The recording didn't resume until four fifty-five. We watched Tilly and me arrive shortly afterward. But by that time, Jim was already dead.

"What the hell happened there?" Elise said. "Some kind of power outage?"

I shook my head. "That would have to be the most convenient power outage I've ever seen. And the most localized. I didn't lose power at my shop, and the traffic light on Main was working when Tilly and I drove over there."

"Then someone's responsible for shutting down the security camera and turning it back on."

"If we can find that someone, we may have our killer."

"Wait a minute," she said. "What about Duggan? And Beverly. We didn't see them in the footage."

"You're right. I didn't consider the possibility that the killer might have entered *and* left while the camera was down."

"You still think Duggan's the one, don't you?" Elise asked.

"As far as motives go, revenge is a powerful one."

"So what's next? Where do we go from here?"

"We have to narrow the field somehow," I said.

"Westfield, Silver, Beverly, and Duggan—is that it?"

I opened my mouth to add Ronnie's name to the list, but managed to swallow it in time. I'd been so preoccupied with the video footage, I'd actually put the whole sordid mess out of my mind while we'd been in Third Eye. I couldn't keep procrastinating, waiting for a good time. There was never going to be a good time. I had to tell Elise today.

"It might help to find out if Westfield was in the building for a dental appointment," Elise mused.

"That's a good idea," I said, trying to refocus on the work at hand "It won't be easy with the HIPAA privacy law. Let me see what I can do."

"If we're done here, we ought to get going," she said.

"You mean before Mr. Personality comes back to kick us out?"

"You're an evil temptress," Elise said with a smile. "Who has a chocolate shake for lunch?"

I pulled out of the drive-thru lane and into the parking lot. "Protein and calcium," I replied. "What's wrong with that?" I'd suggested stopping at the fast-food place on the trip back to town. I needed courage for what I had to tell her and my comfort foods were ice cream and chocolate. Put them together and you had a shake. My Aunt Tilly had introduced me to the concept of ice cream for lunch when I was seven and even my conservative grandmother saw no harm in the occasional indulgence. I found a shady spot under an old elm tree to park, opened the car windows and turned off the engine.

"I guess, when you put it that way," Elise said, taking her first swallow and groaning with pleasure. "My boys would have a fit if they knew what I was doing."

"You've never let them have anything a little crazy for lunch?" I asked. I knew she'd always been careful about what she gave them, but I didn't realize how strict she'd been about it.

"Does pizza count?"

"Nope. It's not fried or filled with sugar."

She took another long pull on her straw. "I've got to do this with them one day," she said when she came up for air. "I want to see their reactions when I tell them what's for lunch."

We drank in silence for a minute, then I set my shake down in one of the cup holders between us. "Listen," I said, "we have to talk."

Elise let the straw pop out of her mouth. "Uh-oh, now I know how my kids must feel when I start a conversation like that." She put her shake into the other cup holder. "What is it?"

I was having trouble getting the words past my lips. Elise was finally beginning to show a spark of life after Jim's death, and I was about to snuff it out. It didn't help to remind myself that I was merely the messenger. The result was going to be the same.

"Kailyn, you're beginning to scare me," she said.

"Jim was having an affair," I blurted out. I hadn't meant to say it quite that bluntly, but I couldn't ask for a do-over.

Elise sat there strangely still, with no expression on her face. I'd expected anger and tears, a full-blown storm of emotions. She's in shock, I told myself. This is what shock looks like. "Are you okay?" I asked, which had to be one of the most inane questions ever. How could she possibly be okay after what I'd told her?

"How did you find out?" she asked, bypassing my question. Her voice was tight, but steady.

"Ronnie told me."

Elise's face remained blank, unreadable. "Did she tell you who the woman was?"

"She admitted being the one."

Elise didn't speak for a moment. I waited, giving her time to absorb it all. "Have you told anyone else?" she asked finally.

"No, of course not."

She nodded, as if confirming something to herself.

"You're handling this awfully well," I said cautiously, still expecting the inevitable meltdown.

She uttered a sharp, grim laugh, more like a bark. "You should have been there when I found out."

"What?" It was my turn to be shocked. "You already knew?"

"Yes. Jim thought he was covering his tracks. But wives know. I think we always know, if we're willing to admit it to ourselves. To be certain, I hired a PI. He took photos of Jim going into her condo, others through the half-open blinds of her bedroom. You get the idea."

"Why didn't you say anything to me?" I asked, trying to wrap my head around this unexpected turn of events.

"I was afraid if I told you, if I said the words, the dam would burst and I wouldn't be able to stop it. I had to stay strong and get all my ducks in a row, before Jim found out I knew. I had to put money away, retain a good divorce attorney. I was going to tell you before I told anyone else, before I served him with the divorce papers. But then the bum went and got himself killed, and I didn't dare tell anybody." Tears flooded her eyes and cascaded down her cheeks. The dam had finally burst.

"You know my lips are sealed," I said solemnly. I would resort to black magick without hesitation if that was the only way to keep my promise.

Elise was fumbling in her purse for tissues. She pulled one out of a travel pack and blew her nose. "That was never my concern. At that point, I wanted to keep you as far out of the loop as I could, so that if the police suspected me, they wouldn't think you were complicit in Jim's death."

She certainly had a right to her qualms. Duggan would arrest her in a second if he learned that she knew about the affair. He already had the gun with her prints on it. Opportunity was a slam dunk. She wouldn't have had any trouble finding a time when Jim was alone in his office. All Duggan was missing was a motive. And this would give it to him on a silver platter.

I dropped Elise at her house, after making her promise to call if she needed anything. She assured me she'd be fine; she had to be for her boys.

On the drive back to my shop, I tried to sort out my thoughts. There was one huge question I had to ask myself, although it was repellent. Was it possible Elise was the killer? The answer was immediate. No way. I'd known her most of my life, and she'd never shown the slightest inclination to violence. Not that she was a saint. She got angry like everyone else, said and did some things she wasn't proud of. But to the best of my knowledge, she'd never intentionally hurt anyone, with the exception of that ex-boyfriend when she was in her teens. As a child, she'd been known for rescuing every stray animal that crossed her path. Her mother used to complain that they were supporting the veterinarian. The Elise I knew was simply not killer material. However, it was easy see how anyone else looking at the evidence might come to a different conclusion. The clock was ticking down. I had to find the killer and soon.

Chapter 28

Tilly and I paid Beverly a surprise visit at five thirty in the afternoon based on the assumption that she was more likely to be home around dinnertime. I needed to find out if she had an alibi for the time of the murder. If she did, I could drop her from my suspect list. I took Tilly along, because she knew Beverly far better than I did and might be able to provide some insight on what she told us.

Beverly came to the door in shorts that were too short and a tank top that was too revealing. To her credit, though, she looked better in the outfit than a lot of women her age would have. Tilly gave me a quick roll of her eyes.

"Sorry to drop in on you like this," she said to Beverly, "but we were in the neighborhood and wanted to stop by to warn you."

Beverly fell back a step as if the unexpected words had knocked her off balance. "Warn me? About what? I don't understand." She sounded frantic.

"Maybe *warn* is a bit strong," I said. "Give you a heads-up is more like it."

"Well okay, please come in." She held the door open. "A heads-up about what?" she asked, her voice still shaky. The fragrant smell of frying chicken instantly enveloped us. Although Tilly had wanted to take the lead, she seemed distracted by the aroma. Beverly's eyes were flitting back and forth between us as she awaited an answer.

Since I couldn't get my aunt's attention without being obvious, I took over. "We were out running errands and overheard some people speculating about whether you were a suspect in Jim's murder." We hadn't heard anything of the kind, but it was the most expedient way to ferret out the information I wanted. Although I didn't like lying, given the serious business of murder, I'd decided I could live with it.

"Me? Why me?" Beverly exclaimed, her hand pressed to her chest. "What motive could I have? Jim wasn't even my attorney anymore."

Tilly finally remembered we were there for answers, not chicken. "Everyone knows you were smitten with him, but he rejected you," she said, clearly taking more pleasure than she should have in needling her.

"I don't know if I'd characterize it quite that way," Beverly said huffily. "Plenty of women have loved and lost, or suffered unrequited love. If that were a reason to commit murder, there'd be more dead men than living ones." Beads of sweat were percolating on her forehead and upper lip. She was certainly afraid, but of what? Being found out? Being wrongly accused?

Being a topic of gossip herself?

I threw my aunt a stern look. We didn't want to give the woman a heart attack or a stroke. At least I didn't. I took Beverly's hand. It was cool and damp with sweat. "Please, try to calm down," I said in a soothing tone. The last thing Tilly and I needed was another body to report to the police.

"Calm down?" she squeaked. "How can I calm down? It's not every day someone tells me I'm a suspect in a murder case."

"It was probably idle speculation by gossips," I said.

"Think back to the day Jim was murdered," Tilly said, "do you remember what you were doing between four and five in the afternoon?"

Beverly stared at the floor for a minute. "Okay . . . I think . . . I think I was working in my garden." She looked up triumphantly. "Yes, that's what I was doing. It was a hot day, so I waited until the sun was lower in the sky."

"Did anyone see you out there during that hour?" I asked. Beverly shook her head. "Maybe a neighbor walking a dog? The mailman or a delivery service? The ice cream truck?" I'd run out of options, and she was still wagging her head.

"There's no one who can vouch for me," she said forlornly. "How am I supposed to prove what I'm saying if I live alone?"

"I think your chicken is burning," Tilly said, sniffing the air. Beverly's eyes widened and she took off for the kitchen. We heard the banging and clanging of cookware, followed by the vent fan roaring to life, after which she returned to the foyer where she'd left us.

"Is everything okay?" Tilly asked sweetly.

"Of course not," she said. "I've burned my dinner and I might wind up in jail."

"I think we should get out of your way," I said, taking Tilly firmly by the arm.

Once we were back in the car, I turned to my aunt. "You didn't have to be so hard on her."

"Why not?" she asked petulantly. "She's a malicious gossip. You don't know the half of it."

I turned on the engine. "I don't doubt that, but she's not a killer. You saw how she reacted. She would have had a heart attack before she could pull the trigger. For that matter, can you see her breaking into Elise's house to steal the gun?"

Tilly snorted. "I suppose you're right. But you can't blame a girl for hoping."

Chapter 29

I sat up in bed, wrenched from a deep sleep. The red digital numbers on the clock-radio bored through the darkness—1:33 a.m. My head felt fuzzy, wisps of a dream evaporating beyond my reach. I couldn't figure out what had awakened me. The cats were all up too, looking as confused as I was. Then I felt the vibrations in the air, wave after wave of troughs and crests like the ripple effect of a stone cast into a pond. They were subtle. Most people wouldn't have noticed them, but the cats and I are more sensitive to disruptions in the plane. Something had disturbed the wards around my property. I grabbed the cotton robe from the closet and punched my arms into the sleeves as I ran down the stairs, flipping on lights as I went. I wasn't worried about coming face to face with an intruder. If someone had actually managed to get inside, I would have been feeling a lot more than slight vibrations from the wards. For that matter, the electronic security system Morgana had had installed would have tripped an ear-shattering siren by now too. Tying my bathrobe closed around me, I unlocked the front door, hit the switch for the porch light and stepped outside. I didn't realize I was barefoot until I felt the spongy grass beneath my feet and the cool dew seeping up between my toes. In seconds I was able to home in on the source of the vibrations. In the amber glow of the streetlamp there was a rock roughly the size of a baseball. The good news was that the wards had worked as intended, stopping the object before it could reach my property. The bad news was that someone had hurled that rock at my house, no doubt intending to break a window and frighten me. It wasn't until I picked up the rock that I saw the paper tied to it with twine. The twine had loosened enough for me to maneuver the note free and leave the rock where it had landed.

I padded back inside and sat on the bottom step of the staircase to read it. I expected it to be in the same cheesy genre as the first one and I wasn't disappointed: IF YOU INSIST ON PLAYING WITH FIRE, YOU'RE GOING TO WIND UP BURNED. My first instinct was to call the police, but I stopped myself before picking up the phone. It might be a whole lot more useful to report the incident to Duggan in person, to see his reaction up close and personal. In spite of the detective's absence from the video footage, I hadn't eliminated him from my list of suspects. It occurred to me that I should bring along the rock to have it tested for prints. Since I didn't have the thin latex gloves police used in crime scene investigations, I did the next best thing. I grabbed a gallon plastic bag and went back outside. I stuck my hand into the bag, picked up the rock and pulled the bag inside out, freeing my hand and leaving the rock inside. Since I'd touched it briefly, I'd have to ask Duggan to take my prints in order to eliminate them from the results.

After resetting the security system, I went upstairs, hoping for a few more hours of sleep. I crawled back into bed, but the cats remained restless for a while longer. When they finally resumed their places on the bed, they were sound asleep in seconds. I was less successful. My brain, still on an adrenalin high from my little adventure, refused to quiet down. It was busy coming up with a workable, if not foolproof, plan to find out if Westfield had been to see the dentist the day Jim was murdered. A dental alibi at the right time could mean he hadn't been in the building for nefarious purposes.

Sashkatu and I went to my shop an hour before it was time to open. I brought the evidence along in a small shopping bag and locked it in my desk drawer behind the counter. Then I made the first of two phone calls. I didn't know what time Dr. Silver started seeing patients, but I waited until nine, figuring that most of his staff would be in by then, and things should be humming along. The busier the office, the better my chance of wangling private patient information.

"This is Monica, how may I help you?" asked a cheerful voice, after I'd made my way through the maze of their automated menu.

"Good morning," I said, "I'm calling from Dr. Westfield's office. He asked me to schedule his next appointment for a cleaning. He forgot to do it when he was there. He said his hygienist gets booked so far in advance, he was concerned she wouldn't be available if he waited too long."

"I'll be happy to take care of that for you," she said. "When did he want to come in?"

"Well, that's the only problem. He doesn't recall exactly when he was last in, and when I looked back on his calendar, I couldn't find it. You know how it is with these geniuses," I said with a low, conspiratorial laugh. "My boss can pinpoint the exact cause of any death, but at times he can't tie his own shoelaces."

"I'm afraid I can't discuss his last appointment or any other private patient information with anyone other than the patient or his authorized representative," she said, clearly not taken in by my attempt at camaraderie.

"Right. That would be me."

"*Authorized* representative," she repeated, her cheery tone dialed down a few notches. "I'd need a signed waiver or verbal okay from him along with his social security number."

"He's in the middle of performing an autopsy," I explained. "He can't possibly come to the phone."

"We'll be happy to accommodate him when he's available. Have a good—"

"If Dr. Westfield didn't authorize me to call you," I interrupted her, "how would I have known which dentist to call?" Monica didn't answer for a moment. Maybe they hadn't covered that question in her privacy training. I could only hope. "Look, I'm not trying to be difficult. We're both working girls. I don't know what kind of boss Dr. Silver is, but I can tell you that Dr. Westfield has no tolerance for the words *didn't* or *couldn't*. He's gone through four secretaries in two months. I'm a single mom and I *really* need this job." I managed to say it with a catch in my voice. I was getting disturbingly good at lying. But it was either lie or use a little of Merlin's "gray magick." One way or the other, I wasn't getting a gold star in ethics for this conversation.

Monica whispered a date so softly that I barely heard her, then resumed her normal volume. "Six months brings us to December 8th. Would you like me to schedule him with his usual hygienist, Carol?"

"That would be great." Maybe I should have taken up acting.

"Same time?" she asked.

"Four o'clock, right?"

That was the time he was clocked in on the video.

"Yes. He's all set then."

I thanked her and clicked off the call. I decided I couldn't cross the ME off my list quite yet. Although he had been in the building to see the dentist, I could hardly count it as a perfect alibi, because he'd apparently left during the time the camera was down. I had no way to figure out exactly how much time he'd had between seeing Carol and getting back in his car. For all I knew, he could have hidden out in the bathroom in the shared hallway, waiting for the safest moment to walk into Jim's office, kill him, and then leave without being seen. It would have been a difficult way to plan a murder though. He would have had to know that Ronnie generally left early every Wednesday and that was the easy part. What if the dentist was running behind that day? What if the procedure took longer than he expected? A killer would have needed nerves of steel to deal with the stress from all those ifs. It was a good thing I'd never contemplated a life of crime. I would have folded from the pressure before I ever left home.

My last call of the morning was to Detective Duggan. He seemed surprised to hear from me. But then I was somewhat amazed to be making the call. Up until last night, I couldn't have imagined a reason why I would want to speak to him again.

"I need to see you as soon as possible," I said after identifying myself. "It's about the case." As if it could have been about anything else.

"Aw, and for a moment I thought you were asking me out."

"This is important."

"Okay, talk to me."

"I have some evidence for you." I was determined to play this by my rules. I wanted to see his reaction, read it in his eyes and his body language, not try to judge it from the tone of his voice.

"I don't have time for games."

"Believe me, it's no game. I'll drive over to see you in Watkins Glen, if you prefer."

"I'm on the road, trying to do my job," he snapped, clearly exasperated with me. He didn't say anything for the next few moments. I waited for him to go on. There was nothing to be gained by pushing harder. You have to know your adversary. "I'm not too far from New Camel," he said finally. "I'll stop by your shop within the hour. This better be good." He hung up without a goodbye, his warning hanging over me. I didn't have long to worry about it, though. No sooner had I put down the phone than the first customers of the day walked in.

Unless we were a stop on a bus tour, there were generally lulls between customers. That morning there were no lulls. Locals came in, needing refills of cosmetics and potions. Our products did seem to be working better since Merlin was around. Newcomers were arriving by the minute too. A lot of families with children. After a brief appraisal of the merchandise, a good deal of which was breakable, most of the parents chose to park younger kids outside with husbands or friends. The few who'd come alone with kids spent more time scolding them than looking at the products. I kept expecting to hear the crash of glass onto the hardwood.

One intrepid mother brought her three-year-old along, without benefit of a stroller or tether. She looked vaguely familiar to me, but before I could figure out if I knew her from somewhere, her son pulled his hand free of hers and took off. She chased him all over the shop without success, until a sympathetic patron and I joined forces with her. We blocked his access to the aisles, but that made him head for the hallway. I caught up to him where the closed storeroom door had him stymied. I plucked him off the floor, before he could double back and passed him to his embarrassed mother, who was a few steps behind me. She thanked me, apologized, and promptly exited the shop, her son launching a tantrum in her arms.

Although I was thrilled to have so many customers, the timing could hardly have been worse. Duggan would be arriving any minute. I poked my head into Tilly's shop to beg for help. She listened to my predicament, beaming like a car with its brights on. Merlin stood beside her wearing a sly smile that made me nervous.

"I'll be happy to help," she said.

"I as well," he echoed.

"What is it with the two of you? You look like the cats that ate the canary *and* the goldfish." I must have been rattled by the upcoming visit with Duggan, to have missed the signs from the get-go. "Okay, what exactly have you been up to?"

"Some harmless advertising, my dear," Tilly said. "Merlin wanted to help your business, so I explained what a billboard was and in no time at all, he whipped up a great ad."

I had a lot more questions, but I wasn't at all sure I wanted to hear the answers. The noise issuing from my shop was growing in volume. "We'll talk about this later," I said. "Now I need you in there to help with the results of your advertising campaign. And Merlin, no more magick!"

Duggan arrived in the middle of the chaos. He stood in the doorway, clearly bewildered by the number of people in the shop. I was standing at the counter, watching for him. When I spied him, I waved for him to follow me past the crowded aisles to the storeroom. I closed the door behind us to drown out some of the noise.

"What's going on here today?" he grumbled.

"My Aunt Tilly's been trying her hand at marketing," I said.

"From the looks of the place, she has a knack for it." He pulled a little pad and pen out of his shirt pocket. "Okay, now that you got me here, where's this so-called evidence?"

"Let me start at the beginning. Someone's been threatening me." I watched for his reaction and didn't see any signs of surprise. But then cops probably dealt with threats all the time and knew they were rarely carried out.

"How?" He sounded bored.

"The first time it was a note slipped under my door when I wasn't home."

"The first time? How many incidents have there been?"

"Two so far. The second was last night. Someone threw a large rock at my house with a note tied to it."

Duggan's brow gathered into a frown, the sharp lines on the bridge of his nose digging in deeper. "Do any damage?" He was either a fine actor or he wasn't the person behind the threats.

"No, fortunately." I didn't mention that the wards had stopped the rock before it could reach my property. Adding magick to the mix would only have muddied the waters.

He paused to write in his pad. Flipping it closed, he retired it and the pen to his pocket.

"I have the notes and the rock with me. Do you want to see them?"

"Wasn't that the whole point of my coming down here, Ms. Wilde?" he asked with a sigh of forbearance.

"Yes, yes of course," I said, tripping over my words. "I meant, did you want to see them right *now*?" Not a great save. I'd been so busy monitoring his reactions, I wasn't paying enough attention to my own words.

"Now would be terrific, unless you were going to offer me tea and crumpets first."

"I'll run inside and grab them," I said, turning on my heel and squelching a less polite rejoinder.

I was only gone a minute, two tops. In that time, I must have fielded ten questions from customers. Tilly and Merlin were doing their best to help everyone, but Tilly looked frazzled, and Merlin's face told me he was reaching the limits of his tolerance. I had to get back out there before he took control of the situation in his own, inimitable fashion.

I did a slalom run around my patrons and found Duggan leaning against the wall in the hallway. I handed him the shopping bag with the evidence.

"I'll send this over to forensics, see if they can come up with anything," he said taking it from me. "You'll need to stop by the local substation and have them take your prints," he said, exactly as I'd expected. He started to walk past me to the sales floor.

"Wait. Will you let me know what they find?"

He stopped and turned back to me. "I can't promise anything that could compromise the investigation." I was about to argue the point, but the grim set of his mouth warned me to let it go. "And in case I didn't make it clear before, Miss Wilde, I'll tell you one more time. Keep your nose out of police business." He enunciated each syllable like my mother had when I was a kid and she'd caught me doing something expressly forbidden. "Got it?"

"Yes, I've got it," I said with a healthy dash of attitude myself.

"Good. Because it's obvious you don't take orders well."

"So I've been told."

He skewered me with a parting glare and strode off, telling everyone in the shop to make way. Following in his wake, I couldn't resist calling out to him in a lilting tone, "have a nice day now!"

Chapter 30

After Merlin "took down" the billboard, business in my shop returned to its usual level of highs and lows. I didn't even have to tell him to do it. He'd come to that sensible conclusion himself, after the Commissioner of the New York State Department of Transportation announced in a TV news bulletin that the perpetrators were being sought and, when found, would face a hefty fine and possible jail time. It seems Merlin had magickally "installed" the ad over an official transportation department sign on the thruway. He'd also infused it with properties similar to post-hypnotic suggestion. He could never be accused of doing things by half measure.

Although the sign vanished as magickally as it had appeared, I expected a visit from the police. After all, it was my shop being advertised on the sign. They did not disappoint. But I was pleasantly surprised when it turned out to be Curtis who stopped by, instead of Duggan or another detective.

"Your shop was the logical place to start," he explained a bit sheepishly. I told him I understood, but that I'd had nothing to do with it, which he translated to mean that I didn't know who had done it. Given the circumstances, I had no intentions of pointing out his error.

"It could have been a prank," I said, "someone trying to cause trouble for me." Curtis pounced on that possibility as if he were the one in jeopardy. He jotted a few notes on a pad and left clearly more lighthearted than he'd arrived. I was pretty sure he was planning to ask me out, once the murderer was caught and I was no longer under any suspicion. In that eventuality, I'd have to let him down gently. I know some women enjoy juggling boyfriends, but I've never been one of them.

With things back to what passed for normal at work, I was able to concentrate on the investigation again. Ever since Elise and I went to Third Eye to look at the security footage, I'd been bothered by the timeline. The one invariable, immutable fact I had to work with was that Jim was dead when Tilly and I arrived at his office shortly after five. I knew what time most of the suspects entered the building, but due to the video's down time, not when they left. The big question in my mind, the question in flashing neon lights, was quite simple. Who was the last person to leave Jim's office before we got there? Answer that and you had the killer.

Although I couldn't drop in on Westfield or Silver and question them as to the precise minute they left the building that day, I could ask Ronnie when she left. Could I trust her response? Once upon a time, I would have said "yes." Now, not so much. I decided it was still worth trying. Put on the spot, she might make a mistake. I waited until the late afternoon to make the call, so there'd be less chance of being interrupted by customers. Moms had to be home for children returning from school, and tourists were apt to be on their way to motels or hotels for the night. I dialed Ronnie's number, wondering what tone our conversation would take.

"Kailyn?" she said warily. Although I liked caller ID as much as the next person, it did eliminate the sometimes important element of surprise.

"Do you have a minute to talk?" I asked, skipping the customary greetings. There was no point in pretending we could go back to our pre-confession relationship.

"Of course. Is something wrong?"

There was so much wrong I wouldn't have known where to start. But I knew her question was a knee-jerk response. "I keep thinking about Jim," I said, diving right in.

"Me too," she murmured, more to herself than to me.

I almost got sucked into the trap of expressing my sympathy. She had no right to it. "Were you still in the office when Elise got there with our paperwork that day?" I asked.

"Yes, we chatted for a couple of minutes before I left. Wednesdays I leave a little early to visit my mother in the nursing home."

"I know. You're a good daughter." A lousy, backstabbing, adulterous friend, but to the best of my knowledge, a good daughter. "I heard you put her in that great new facility . . ."

"Lakeside," she supplied. "It's expensive, but she gets the best care there.

"Yes, right." I knew from Elise that Ronnie had had a difficult time when her mother was diagnosed with Alzheimer's.

"Were you with your mom when you heard about Jim?"

"No, I always turn off my phone during our visits. I heard the news when I played back my messages on the way home and I . . . I lost it." Her emotion sounded genuine to my novice ears. Maybe Duggan would have known for sure if she was telling the truth. I was learning it wasn't as easy to detect lies as I'd once thought. "I was shaking so badly," she went on, "I had to pull over to the curb. I didn't trust myself to drive for close to an hour. I was in such a state, I could have killed somebody."

Or did you kill somebody and then fall apart? I wondered. I thanked her for talking to me, and she said she was glad to help. Our parting words were more uncomfortable than the rest of the conversation had been. What can you fall back on when the vocabulary of polite, social interaction is no longer appropriate? *We should get together soon. When are you free for lunch? Regards to the family.* All useless phrases. I was left with "Okay then, Ronnie, bye."

I clicked off the call and Googled Lakeside Nursing Facility. The receptionist was well-spoken and pleasant. Yes, they have a sign-in sheet to keep track of who is in the building at all times. Unfortunately not everyone remembers to sign out when they leave. No, she couldn't share that information with me. She said she was sorry and wished me a lovely day. Having a badge would definitely have helped when it came to requesting records. I briefly entertained the idea of asking Merlin for help, but then I came to my senses. If we kept exhibiting our various powers, how long would it take before the population of New Camel, and possibly all of Schuyler County, decided to start burning witches again?

I wandered up and down the aisles of my shop, unable to settle into work. There were bills to be paid, shelves and products to dust, windows to clean, but none of those chores motivated me. What I needed was some good news, something to smile about. I picked up the phone and called Travis to see if maybe he'd been more successful with the investigation on his end.

He answered on the first ring. "Please, tell me something wonderful," I begged.

He chuckled. "Yes, Ma'am, I'll do my best. As it happens, I do have some information for you."

"I'm hanging on your every word."

"Not over the phone."

My spirits sank. "Seriously? Why not?"

"Because I'm at your door." It took me a moment to absorb what he'd said. When I looked up from my phone, he was walking in. He gathered me into a hug, making me realize how restorative such a simple act could be. Hugs were definitely not celebrated enough in story or song. "Better?" he asked, tipping my chin up to look me in the eye.

I exhaled a peaceful sigh. "So much."

"Then I'll be sure to keep that in my repertoire. Now, are you ready for your briefing?"

I hopped up on the counter, leaving the chair for him. "Ready."

"I did some checking on your suspects. Duggan was suspended once when he was a cop on the beat, for the use of undue force. He had to complete a course in anger management as a condition of his return to work. And that drill sergeant persona you mentioned—it came from being a marine."

"If you consider his background in the light of his history with Jim, it's not a stretch to believe he finally erupted and killed him. The video proves he was driving through town at the right time."

"Yes, but don't forget," Travis said, "he would have had to get in and out of that building within the time the video was down and not be seen by Ronnie or Elise. There wasn't much room for error."

"If the killer got someone at Third Eye to shut down the camera, who would have had more clout to do it than a well-respected detective?"

"I'm afraid I'm about to complicate things for you."

"Ronnie?"

"She's got a juvie record from her high school days. Nothing terrible. She and another girl got into it over a boy. It was pretty brutal, but because no one saw who threw the first punch, it was basically a case of she said, she said. In the end, the judge made them both shoulder the blame with court-mandated community service and counseling. Ronnie seems to have kept her nose clean since then."

"I'm impressed. How did you find out all this?"

Travis grinned. "A reporter needs to have confidential sources. Friends in high *and* low places."

"Any more goodies for me?"

"Now you're getting greedy. I'm still working on Silver and Westfield."

It struck me that he didn't know about Elise. "I've got one more to add," I said, my upbeat mood instantly snuffed out by my misery over her confession. "It's Elise."

I could tell by his expression that he saw the shift in me. But he didn't say a word, until I'd emptied my heart to him. And he didn't try to jolly me up with false cheer. He reached up and put his hand over mine on the counter. "Do you think she could have killed him?"

"No," I said immediately. "Yes." My throat was tight, making it hard to push the words through. I shook my head. "I don't know. I've always believed that anyone is capable of murder, given the right circumstances. But that was an easy thing to believe, when it was only a theory. I can't bear to think of Elise as a killer."

"Okay," Travis said. "We'll leave her for last. I won't put out any feelers, unless we run out of other options. Or Duggan cracks the case."

"Thank you," I said.

"For what?" He gave me a wink. "I'm just trying to rack up points with the boss."

I smiled. "Hey, I never claimed to be the boss. We're partners."

"Yeah, but some partners are more equal than others. I know my place. And I'm not complaining."

"Can I run something by you?" I asked.

"Sure."

"I think someone needs to go back to Third Eye."

"You want to find the person in charge of monitoring that building."

"It's the best way to get some solid answers instead of all these *ifs* and *maybes*."

"I'm sure Duggan already tried that."

"Then why hasn't he arrested anyone yet? Someone clearly shut down that camera on purpose," I insisted. "It can't possibly be that difficult to figure out who did it. There are a limited number of people who work at Third Eye."

"It's not quite so simple. Although we can probably assume that someone was bribed or threatened into shutting down that camera at a specific time, we can't be sure it was the individual at that monitor bank. What if he or she refused to cooperate with the killer? Then the killer would have had to find someone else to do it. That would explain the bogus emergency call to get the uncooperative employee away from his monitors for an hour or so."

I snapped my fingers. "And if the first employee did cooperate, the emergency call would have been his alibi if the police questioned him."

"Exactly," he said. "I'd be surprised if the call wasn't made on an untraceable throwaway cell."

"So you're telling me it isn't worth going over to Third Eye again?"

"No. I'm telling you, it won't be as easy and straightforward as you seem to think."

"Not to mention, I can't be the one to do it."

"All right," Travis said dryly, "what haven't you told me, partner?"

"Nothing . . . really. You know Elise and I went there to view the camera footage. I guess I didn't mention that the supervisor and I didn't exactly hit it off."

"As much as I would love to help out, the odds are someone there will recognize me from TV. Is there anybody else you can enlist?"

It had to be someone I trusted implicitly. My mother and grandmother were gone from that short list, and under the circumstances, I couldn't very well ask Ronnie or Elise to help out. My plan seemed doomed, until I realized I still had one option.

Chapter 31

The plan was simple. At least until I added Tilly to the mix. I couldn't have asked for a more loyal, trustworthy, or enthusiastic helper. But whenever my aunt is involved, there's always the potential for disaster. The plan was for her to go into Third Eye and say she was thinking of hiring the security firm for her business, but first she wanted a tour of their monitoring center. On my first visit there with Elise, I'd taken a couple of minutes to do some reconnoitering. I was mainly interested in the configuration of the monitoring center. Rather than one large, open space with all the monitors, it was divided into cubicles. Each cubicle held one person and a small bank of monitors. The setup made it easier for a worker to hide inappropriate behavior on the job. But it also cut down on too much chitchat among colleagues, a definite bonus when it came to the bottom line of a business.

"I think you should walk with a limp," I told Tilly. "It's a good excuse to go slowly. That way you'll have time to find the Harkens monitor."

"With my poor feet, I was made for this assignment," she giggled. In preparation, I'd taken her back to Jim's office building. We stood beneath the camera for her to get a good view of what she would see when she found the correct monitor.

"Once you find it, be sure to take a good look at the person at that console," I said.

"What if their back is to me?"

"Make an excuse to walk up to him or her to get a better look."

"I know. I'll pretend to recognize the person and go over to say hello. Then, when I'm closer, I'll apologize for the mistake."

"Perfect."

"I told you, dear, no worries."

If only. "When you're done, come back to the car, and we'll wait for lunchtime. With any luck, the person at that monitor will leave the building, you'll point them out to me, and I'll try to convince them to answer a couple of questions."

"If they're not willing, I can always try rummaging around in their heads a bit," Tilly said with a hopeful twinkle in her eyes.

Although I wasn't thrilled about letting her take advantage of anyone that way, the potential good it could do far outweighed the bad. It seemed like everything in life boiled down to an equation in the end. And Merlin was right. Most things fell in the vast gray areas between black and white.

The next morning I drove to my aunt's house for our visit to Third Eye. It was a beautiful day. Thunderstorms had swept through overnight, taking the heat and humidity with them. The air was dry, the sky a crisp, cloudless blue. If the person we were after didn't go out for lunch on such a day, he had to be related to a mole.

Merlin glared at me from the doorstep, while I maneuvered Tilly and her lavender muumuu into the passenger seat of my car. When he'd heard where we were going, he'd offered to help us and was greatly offended when I'd nixed the idea. There were only so many variables I could handle at one time. I'd make it up to him at dinner with pizza, extra mushrooms, and for dessert, an ice cream sundae at the Confection Connection. Ice cream had nearly unseated pizza as his favorite food.

Tilly and I arrived at Third Eye at ten o'clock. I helped her out of the car at the main entrance in deference to both her real foot woes and her supposed limp. She'd brought along a cane that once belonged to her late husband, claiming it was hard to limp convincingly without something to lean on. After she went inside, I parked in the second row of the lot, a location we'd agreed upon. I didn't want to leave the engine running for however long Tilly would be gone. Instead I opened all the windows to let the fresh breeze waft through. Time dragged. I'd never realized how difficult waiting could be without a distraction. Especially when it was coupled with anxiety for my aunt's well-being. I told myself that everything must be going okay, because I hadn't received any panicked phone calls from her or heard police sirens heading this way. When was I going to learn not to count those unhatched chickens?

Five minutes later the main doors opened and out came Tilly, suspended between two beefy security guards. They each had her by an arm and, being so much taller than she, were carrying her so neither her feet nor the cane touched the ground. She was struggling wildly to get away, wielding the cane like a weapon, but only managing to swat at the air. It took a lot to make my aunt angry. Compared to fire-breathing dragons like Morgana and Bronwen, she was an absolute lamb and usually assumed the role of peacekeeper when they had their backs up. But if you pushed Tilly to the limits of her patience, you were not going to get off unscathed.

When I saw the three of them emerge from the building, I chose my feet over the car as the most direct route to them. I jumped out, sprinted across the lot and the near side of the circular driveway, through the grass island in the center and then across the far side of the driveway to the walk where they were standing. During the fifteen seconds I was racing to her aid, I tried unsuccessfully to imagine what she could have done to deserve such ignominious treatment. As I drew closer, I could hear her demanding to be put down and threatening retribution of epic proportions. What the guards didn't know, couldn't know, was that she actually could wreak real havoc in their lives. Plus I had no doubt Merlin would be glad to lend his efforts to her cause.

I'd almost reached them when they set her down on the pavement. My heart lurched into my throat as I watched her sway precariously back and forth, before finding her balance. At least the guards had the decency to stay beside her, until she appeared to be steady on her feet. They were turning to go back inside when I ran up to her.

"Are you okay, Tilly?" I asked. Her face was beet red with anger and indignation. I wouldn't have been surprised to see steam venting from her ears.

"I'm fine, in spite of those two oafs," she said loudly enough for them to hear. "If they had half a brain between them, they'd realize what I could do to them." Thankfully the guards didn't bother to turn around. They shook their heads and shared a laugh as they disappeared inside. I would have loved to give them a proverbial piece of my mind too, but I knew I had to be the reasonable one, the calmer of stormy seas. I asked Tilly if she wanted to wait for me to come around with the car.

"I don't want to spend another second at this godforsaken place," she said, still projecting her voice for the benefit of anyone in the zip code.

"All right, that's fine." I offered her my arm to lean on, but she stalked off ahead of me, clearly angry with the whole world.

"I'm perfectly capable of moving under my own steam," she said, her chin thrust upward in a petulant, so-there manner.

I knew Tilly needed to recover from her rage at her own pace. The best thing I could do was give her the time and space. I followed her back to the car without another word. I slid under the steering wheel, and she more or less fell into the passenger seat. We sat there beside each other in unhappy silence. I glanced at my watch. A quarter past eleven. Lunchtime was quickly approaching. In planning this little adventure, I'd taken into account the probability that the staff took their lunch hour in shifts. Otherwise the monitors would go unmanned for a period of time. The first lunch hour might begin as early as eleven thirty. If Tilly had fulfilled her mission before the debacle, I'd need her to point out that individual. I gave her another five minutes to sulk, and when she still hadn't said anything, I dove in.

"Aunt Tilly, the first lunch shift could be leaving any minute. If you found the person at the Harkens monitor, I need you to point him or her out to me." Tilly was staring out the windshield, eyes glazed over. If I knew my aunt at all, she was busy planning her revenge. First things first, I told myself. I'd tackle the revenge issue later. I reached over the center console and gave her arm a firm but gentle shake. "Tilly."

She exhaled a long sigh and turned to me, her eyes finding their focus and her face relaxing into a much more Tilly expression. "I'm fine, dear," she said, "and I got a good look at our mark. In fact, from the moment I walked in there, I sold my act like a pro." Her chest puffed up with pride. "I had no trouble recognizing the view from the Harkenses' building on the screen. There was a man at the console, his back to me as I'd feared. I used my little mistaken identity ploy to get a closer look and was into my apology when a mouse scurried out from beneath his desk, headed straight for me. Well, you know how it is with me and mice." I did. Only too well. "I screamed and ran like the dickens. Avery called for security and after they caught me, he accused me of industrial espionage. But the important thing is that I shouldn't have any trouble pointing the guy out to you. His name's Todd Spivak, going by the name plaque on his desk. I noticed it right before the mouse . . ." She shuddered at the memory.

I was having a hard time not laughing at the image she painted. A giggle escaped my efforts, which made her start giggling too. From there it was a runaway train. We were doubled over, until tears were rolling down our faces and my stomach ached. I had trouble catching my breath. "What would I do without you?" I said, keenly aware that we were the sum total of family in this world.

"Did you bring along something to nibble on while we wait?" Tilly asked hopefully. "It seems acting and doing the fifty-yard dash can work up an appetite." I apologized for not thinking to bring refreshments. "That's okay," she said, opening her purse. "I think I have a muffin somewhere in here." Before she was able to find it, the doors to Third Eye opened, and employees started trickling out and heading for their cars.

We'd almost given up on our guy being part of this first wave, when he came through the door a few minutes after the rest of his colleagues, moving like a man on a mission. "There he is," Tilly said. "In the blue shirt and black pants." An unnecessary description, since he was the only one leaving the building at that point.

He'd already reached the first row of cars by the time I climbed out. I had to run to intercept him. "Excuse me," I called out.

He slowed his pace, but didn't stop. "Yes?"

"I wonder if you can help me out?" He looked more annoyed than curious, but he stopped. Tilly had clambered out of the car and was making her way toward us, no doubt ready to steal the answer if need be.

He glanced in her direction, frowning as if he knew something was up, but couldn't put it together. "I'm late for an appointment," he snapped, "I don't have time for this."

"One question," I begged. If I'd known how to bat my eyelashes, I swear I would have. "Please, if you could answer one question."

Suspicion narrowed his eyes. "You a reporter?"

"No, I have a small business in New Camel."

"All right. What is it?"

Since I couldn't ask outright if he'd helped the killer, I asked the one question he might answer. "Do you know why you were targeted with that phony emergency call?

"You sure sound like a reporter," he grumbled, starting to walk away. Although Tilly had reached us, she looked as if she was running out of steam.

"I swear to you, I'm not a reporter. I'm here trying to keep my friend from being arrested for murder."

"I don't know what you're talking about," he said, quickening his pace.

I fell into a trot to keep up. "Why were you targeted?" I don't know if it was the desperation in my voice, but he stopped and turned to me, so abruptly that I almost plowed into him.

"I have no idea," he said, his words clipped with anger. "For all I know she pulled the number out of a hat. And if you don't leave me alone this instant, I'm calling the cops." He plucked his phone from his shirt pocket to back up the threat. Tilly must have put on her after-burners, because she caught up to us at that moment, wheezing and sputtering.

"Okay, okay," I said, backing away from him. "Sorry to have bothered you. I didn't mean you any harm." Of course I couldn't speak for Tilly. She was concentrating on the man with such intensity, I was worried she might give herself, or him, a stroke in the process.

"Stay away from me," he said, wincing as though in sudden pain. He stumbled away from us and down the next row of cars.

"He's definitely trying to hide something," Tilly said between labored breaths. "He's built the equivalent of a moat with alligators to thwart any intrusion. Did he tell you anything useful?"

I put my arm around her shoulders and we headed slowly back to my car. "Not as much as I would have liked, but more than he thinks he did."

Chapter 32

" A re you sure Spivak said *she*?" Tilly asked. We were in my car
on our way home from Third Eye. She was searching her
purse again for the elusive muffin.

"There isn't a doubt in my mind," I said. However, now that I'd
had a few minutes to think about it, I *was* having doubts about the
importance of the word.

With a little cry of triumph, Tilly pulled the sandwich bag containing the muffin from the depths of her purse. She opened the plastic bag and held it out to me. "It's carrot, have some."

I glanced at the bag. The muffin hadn't fared well in her purse,
disassembling into a pile of muffin crumbs. I declined, not hungry
enough to try to eat it while driving. She shrugged and popped a piece
into her mouth. "If the caller was a woman, wouldn't that eliminate all
the men on your list of suspects?" she asked after swallowing.

"At first I thought so," I said. "It seems to me a smart killer would
try to limit the number of people involved in his plot. The more people involved, the greater the risk. Based on that, the killer is most
likely the one who bribed or threatened the employee into helping
and later called in the fake emergency to provide him with an alibi."

"Makes sense to me," Tilly said, having finished off the muffin in
record time. She brushed the crumbs from her hands. "So why don't
you sound so sure about it now?"

"When it was just a theory, I was totally onboard with it, but now
that I'm trying to apply it to real life . . . I don't know."

"You're worried the killer isn't necessarily all that smart," she
said, hitting the nail squarely on the head. "I can't believe I forgot to
bring along the thermos of iced tea."

"You'll be home in a few minutes," I promised. She was right. I had no way of knowing if the killer was, in fact, smart about his crime. Emotions can make anyone act stupidly. I'd read stories about police committing crimes and making the same stupid mistakes as the average criminal. I decided my theory was toast. But instead of being upset about it, I was relieved. Eliminating the men from my suspect list would have narrowed the field to Ronnie and Elise. And no matter how I looked at it, Elise had the more believable motive for committing murder. So, welcome back, guys.

After dropping Tilly off at home, I went straight down to Main Street to open my shop. Sashkatu would have to cope with sleeping away the afternoon at home with the other cats, instead of on his tufted window seat in the shop. I peeked into Lolly's shop and found her alone, restocking empty trays in the display cases.

"It looks like you had a busy morning," I said, after a quick cheek-to-cheek greeting. "Unfortunately I forgot to put my clock sign in the window before I left this morning." Some people, like Beverly, would have asked where I went, but Lolly wasn't one of them. She respected boundaries. It was one of many things I liked about her.

"Not to worry. I fielded a lot of inquiries about your shop. Since it's not like you to be gone the whole day, I told them to try again this afternoon."

"Thanks, you're such a good friend."

"Hey, it was good for me too. I've never known a customer to come in here to ask a question and leave without making a purchase." She took a plump, sugared apricot dipped in dark chocolate from the tray she was working on and handed it to me in a small square of tissue paper. "I bet you haven't had time for lunch."

I laughed. "This should have enough calories to keep me going until dinner." I thanked her again and walked across the side street that separated our shops. While I waited for customers to arrive, I made my way through the aisles, dusting and moving products that were out of place. Most shoppers were good about putting items they'd decided not to take, back where they found them. But there were always the few who couldn't be bothered.

With my hands busy, my mind was free to problem solve and the most immediate problem I had involved Elise. When I'd asked Ronnie if she left the office before Elise on the day Jim was murdered, she claimed she had. I had yet to pose that same question to Elise. I dreaded asking her more than I dreaded a root canal. Make that ten root canals. Without benefit of Novocain. Asking her would be akin to saying I had my doubts about her innocence. How did you mend a friendship after that? She might claim to understand my reasoning, but the damage would be done. Things would never be the same between us again. That simply wasn't acceptable. I needed a more subtle way to find out, without actually posing the question. If that failed, I might be desperate enough to consider letting my aunt poke around in her mind.

I finished primping the shop, but I was no closer to a perfect solution for my talk with Elise. I was headed back to my desk to tackle the books when Morgana and Bronwen popped in for a visit. I told them about my dilemma with Elise, then gave them a rundown on how the investigation was going, including the information I gleaned from visiting Third Eye.

"Maybe we should have installed the cameras when we added the alarm system," Morgana said.

"No need to worry," I assured her, "the new wards I put in place seem to be holding."

"Even so," Bronwen said, "when it comes to safety, one must do all one can."

"Technologically as well as magickally," my mother put in.

"That goes without saying," my grandmother added.

"It never hurts to reiterate and reinforce." Morgana's tone had taken on a sharper edge. If I was any judge of my progenitors, sparks were about to fly.

"Reiteration can be tiresome and result in losing one's audience," my grandmother said with a snap to her words.

"Okay, hold it!" I said with my own punch of attitude. "Why do the two of you still spend all your time together, when it's clear you get on each other's nerves? Surely you can put some distance between yourselves and stop the endless bickering." A stunned silence followed my outburst, and it occurred to me that I'd never spoken to them in such a way. I never would have dared. But they no longer lived on this plane, and the balance of power was shifting in our relationship. I thought about apologizing, but I wasn't entirely sorry for what I'd said. It was Bronwen who wound up breaking the ice.

"Although I didn't care for your tone, Kailyn, you may have a valid point."

"It's true," Morgana acknowledged, "we have a lot of issues to work on. We've been avoiding them, because it means letting go and moving on." Her voice cracked, "and we are so deeply tied to you and Tilly."

My mother had always been self-possessed. I couldn't remember ever hearing her sound this vulnerable. "I know it's been hard for you," I said gently, "dying the way you did. But losing both of you has been hard on me too."

"Of course it has," Bronwen said. "All our unfinished business, the difficulties with our magick, dumped on your young shoulders. Then the murder. You've handled it all better than we could have hoped."

"Better than we would have," Morgana said generously.

"Well, I don't know if I would go *that* far," Bronwen muttered.

Morgana's cloud flashed red with anger. "If you have something to say, mother, by all means—" And they were gone.

I was bewildered by their departure, until I heard a voice coming from the doorway behind me. "Incredible—was that magick or a hologram?" Although the voice was soft in tone, it was unexpected. I must have jumped a good ten inches. Had I been a cat, I might have forfeited a life in the process. I came up with a smile and turned around. The woman in front of me was elderly and petite, dressed in classy beige linen pants and a white silk blouse. Her eyes were fixed on the spot where my family clouds had been.

"A hologram, exactly!" I said, glomming onto her word as if it was a lifeline. "We're experimenting with new advertising techniques."

"Oh," she said with a sigh, "I was hoping it was real magick." She held out her hand. "Nice to meet you. My name is Cecelia."

"I'm Kailyn," I said, taking her hand in mine. She looked so deeply disappointed that I found myself saying, "Cecelia, can you keep a secret?" If Bronwen and Morgana knew what I had in mind, they'd be horrified. But this was my time and I wanted to flex my muscle.

"I've kept more secrets than you can imagine," she said with a sly smile and a wink, "but that's all you'll get out of me."

I went to the doorway and poked my head outside. There were people out on the street, but no one on my block. I had a few minutes. I came back in and looked around the shop, deciding on the chair next to the counter about four yards away. I focused my mind on it and tugged. Nothing happened. I hadn't moved anything of that size and weight before, but I wanted to give Cecelia more of a show than levitating a little pamphlet. This was clearly going to take more concentration. I blocked out all the external distractions: the hum of the air conditioner, the buzzing of a fly, the ticking of the clock, the rumble of a car driving by, until nothing existed in time and space but the chair and me. I visualized my energy as a brilliant spear of light. I threw it across the room to the chair and after three tries, I hooked into it. I tried pulling it toward me, pulling it, pulling it . . . When it shuddered and inched forward, I nearly lost my focus in the brief second of triumph. But I held on. The chair moved again, slowly at first, then with increasing speed as if it were barreling down a hill at me. I tried to stop it or at least slow it down, without success. I stepped out of its path, but the chair made a course correction and continued straight for me. I'd set it in motion with me as its target and it was sticking to that program. I had no choice, but to wait for the chair to reach me. Although I put my hands out to act as a buffer, the chair slammed into me with such force, it knocked me to the floor.

Cecelia was cheering and applauding like a child at her first circus. She probably thought the crash at the end was an intended part of the act. "Amazing! Simply amazing! I always believed real magick existed, yet after all these years of searching for it, I'd all but given up on ever finding it. What a pity my late husband wasn't here to see this. The fool was always telling me I was nuts." She laughed and chattered on in that vein, as I pulled myself to my feet. "Oh my goodness," she interrupted herself, "you're bleeding. Are you okay?"

I looked down at my right leg. A trickle of blood was oozing from my shin where the chair had slammed into it. A small enough price to pay for my victory. I pushed the chair back to its spot by the ordinary method. I found a tissue behind the counter and wiped away the blood, which had stopped flowing by then.

After my little command performance, Cecelia was eager to try all the products her friends had been raving about. I totaled up her bill and filled three of the tote bags with her purchases. She'd bought more than anyone, at least in my lifetime.

"I'll help you get these into your car," I said. "Is it parked outside?"

"Give me a minute," she said, walking out the door. She returned with her chauffeur, a large man with a jolly face, dressed in formal livery. He picked up the heavy bags as if they were filled with pop-corn. Before Cecelia followed him out, she turned to me and whis-pered, "Thank you for entrusting me with your secret. Now, if you don't mind a bit of advice from an old lady, you ought to work on some magickal brakes, before you try that again."

I was still laughing when my mother made an encore appearance. Great, I thought, here comes another lecture on the perils of showing off my magick.

"Kailyn," she began, "I've been thinking about your situation with Elise and I have a suggestion for you." My mother hadn't seen me doing battle with the chair? "Let Elise know about Ronnie's claim that she left the office first. That way you're providing Elise with information she needs for her own defense. And how Elise re-acts to the news may give you some insight into the truth."

"That might work," I said. I'd forgotten how good my mother was at problem solving, at seeing the trees as well as the forest. I missed having her in my life. The crazy, impromptu visits from her and my grandmother only served to emphasize the difficult side of our rela-tionship. I thanked her for coming back and sharing her wisdom.

"You're welcome. I wish you'd take more of my advice to heart." So she *had* seen me perform for Cecilia. "Don't worry," she added quickly, "that's all I intend to say on the subject." She wished me good luck and was gone. Apparently my earlier take-charge attitude had made an impression. Made her realize that I was in charge now and would decide things for myself. Although she might not think I was ready, Fate had already taken the reins from her hands and passed them into mine.

I pulled to the curb at Elise's house. Her boys were outside shoot-ing hoops on the driveway with friends. When I'd called Elise to ask if I could stop by after work, she'd asked me to stay for dinner. I used the excuse of having to run home to feed the cats, but the truth was that my stomach was churning with anxiety and the mere thought of food was making me queasy.

We hugged each other in the foyer. Since Jim's death, our hugs had become more than a greeting. They were a pledge of support and loy-alty, which made me feel like a hypocrite that day.

Elise had made tea for us, one of my aunt's special blends. I sat on the kitchen banquette that was like a wraparound booth. Elise strained the tea she'd had steeping on the counter and brought it to the table. She'd set out mugs, spoons, and napkins before I arrived.

"I've been dying of curiosity since you called," she said, going back to the counter for a dish of lemon wedges and a jar of honey. She slid into the nook across from me and poured the tea.

"Sorry, I didn't mean to sound mysterious," I said. I was sure she could hear the tension in my voice. "It's nothing more than my usual updates to keep you in the loop. Plus, it's a good excuse to stop in to see you."

If Elise thought anything was amiss, she hid it well. "Gotcha," she said. "I'm no longer expecting anything momentous. You're officially off the hook."

I stirred a teaspoon of honey into the tea. It was now or never. "It seems Ronnie is claiming she wasn't the last one to see Jim alive that day." It took an effort for me to put the spoon down and look up into my friend's eyes. As a kid, I'd had the same difficulty looking at my mother when I was lying. "She's saying you were still in the office when she left. I have to assume she's told Duggan as much."

"It happens to be the truth," Elise said, calmly squeezing lemon into her cup. I was there for another five or six minutes after she left."

"Oh okay, as long as she's not lying about it," I said. I felt ashamed for having doubted her innocence and thrilled that she didn't consider Ronnie's claim a problem.

"But remember," she added, "during the hour that security camera was down, anyone could have walked in, including Ronnie. If she's the one who arranged for the blackout, she knew how much time she had. All she had to do was wait for me to leave."

"She worries me," I said. "She doesn't know we're aware of the blackout. And she could easily be the one trying to frame you. She knew where you kept the gun and she had a key to your house."

"Believe me, I haven't crossed her off my list yet either."

What now? Unless I planned on asking my best friend outright if she killed her husband, I'd played out my hand. Instead I asked how the boys were doing.

She sighed. "Up and down. When they're with friends or engaged in sports, they do better. Nights and weekends are hard. And it's not helping that they're constantly bombarded with news about the investigation. It's on the internet, on TV. There's nowhere to hide from it. I think once they catch the killer and the news coverage winds down, it will be easier." I couldn't help thinking that if she was the killer, she was also one hell of an actress.

As if on cue, Zach and Noah ran into the kitchen, pink and perspiring. But they weren't trying to beat each other to the refrigerator for a cold drink as they always did. They stopped short at the banquette. "Ma," Zach said, "Detective Duggan is outside. He asked me to get you."

Elise pushed back from the table, her brow pinched with worry. I followed her to the front door. The boys trailed behind me like kids watching a horror film with their fingers partially covering their eyes. They clearly wanted to know what was going to happen and afraid to know. When we reached the door, I could see that their friends were no longer playing in the driveway. Duggan and Curtis were waiting on the porch. Except for the day of the murder, I'd never seen the two of them together. My heart clenched. I knew what was coming and prayed I was wrong.

Chapter 33

"Don't worry about the boys," I told Elise as Curtis guided her into the backseat of his patrol car. She'd been cooperative from the moment they said they'd come to arrest her for the murder of her husband, Jim Harkens. It sounded so formal and final, it made my legs go rubbery weak. Elise remained ramrod straight and listened stoically as she was read her rights, but when Curtis reached for his handcuffs, she shook her head and begged him, in an urgent whisper, not to put them on her in front of the children. Curtis had looked at Duggan to make the call. The detective nodded, probably thinking she couldn't cause much trouble anyway.

"Don't worry about anything here," I said to Elise, doing my best to sound calm for both her sake and the kids'. "I will call your sister the second I walk inside. But regardless of when she can get here, the boys will be fine with me." At least as fine as they could be under the circumstances. I'd watched them go from an overheated pink to a deathly white in the space of a few minutes. I had my arm around Noah, who was crying and clinging to my side. Zach was struggling to maintain his composure, but his lower lip was quivering and he was blinking rapidly, trying to hold back tears. Some ancient maternal instinct etched into my DNA told me not to try to comfort him in public or he would crumble.

"Call John Casper too," Elise reminded me, angling her head so she could look up at me from the open car door.

"Right away. Take care of yourself. You'll be back home in no time. It's going to be okay." I seemed to have an endless supply of trite phrases.

Duggan folded himself into the passenger side of the car. "Detective, wait," I said, realizing none of us had had the presence of mind to find out where they were taking her, "where . . . ."

"Watkins," he replied curtly and closed the door without looking at me. I wanted to believe that meant he was feeling guilty about arresting Elise, but I knew it could also mean he was tired of dealing with me or a thousand other things. Curtis shut the rear door, sealing Elise off from us, walked around to the driver's side and slid behind the wheel. He backed the patrol car into the street and drove away. The children and I stood rooted to the driveway until they were out of sight. Then Zach turned and ran into the house. I could hear him thundering up the stairs as Noah and I walked inside still joined at the hip.

I asked Noah if he wanted to watch TV. He shrugged, but followed me into the family room. He picked up the remote from the side table and dropped onto the leather sectional facing the flat screen above the fireplace. "Do you want something to eat?" I asked. He shook his head. I didn't blame him. I couldn't have swallowed anything either.

I took Elise's address book from the ledge above the sink. My first call was to her sister Karen, the second to John Casper. I knew that he and Jim were business colleagues more than chums, but that Jim had always told Elise to call on Casper if he wasn't "around." We love our euphemisms, even if they're not fooling anyone. I tried his business phone first, but was shunted to voice mail. Instead of leaving a message, I called his home number and caught him as he was walking in. He didn't sound overly surprised to hear about Elise's arrest, which didn't win him any points with me. How good would he be at defending her, if he already believed she was guilty? But I had no alternatives at the moment. I gave him Duggan's name, and he promised to call the precinct in Watkins Glen immediately and get down there as soon as possible. I figured that meant he was going to eat dinner before he went anywhere. I hung up and dialed my aunt. After giving her a brief rundown on what had happened, I asked her to go to my house and feed the cats. Then I went upstairs to check on Zach. I found him lying on his back in bed, eyes closed, listening to his iPod. I decided not to disturb him. I was on my way downstairs again when I heard a key jiggling in the front lock. I reached the foyer as Karen walked in. I filled her in on the status of the boys and told her about the attorney. She thanked me for everything and sent me on my way. The boys would be fine in her care.

Back at home, my stomach wanted nothing to do with dinner. I grabbed a pint of Ben and Jerry's Chunky Monkey from the freezer and a spoon from the utensil drawer. I went into the living room to curl up on the couch and call Travis. It didn't escape me that I'd reached for both the ice cream and Travis for comfort. Not long ago, I would have wanted only the ice cream.

"Our stars must be aligned," he said, "I was about to call you."

"So you believe in astrology, but not magick?" I couldn't help teasing him. How did talking to him have such an immediate salutary effect on me?

"If you're not careful, I won't tell you the hot news I have."

I scooped out a spoonful of Chunky Monkey and slid it into my mouth. "No fair. I'm in real distress here."

"Why?" His tone was no longer playful. "What's going on?"

I told him about Elise.

"Maybe this can distract you a bit." I took another spoon of ice cream and waited for him to wow me. "I talked to a couple of cop friends," he began, "and it seems that by the time Westfield left the Big Apple, he wasn't exactly well-liked by the boys in blue."

That got my attention. "What do you mean?"

"The anti-mob unit was sure they finally had a case that would stick against one of the Rigosi family lieutenants. They arrested him for the murder of one of the family's competitors, a man who conveniently dropped dead at the age of thirty-two—no history of medical issues. Not unheard of as you know, but certainly not common."

"And Westfield did the autopsy," I said.

"Yup. According to his report, the guy died of a garden variety heart attack, no evidence of foul play. Needless to say, the DA's case went down the toilet and there was more than enough embarrassment to go around."

I put the ice cream on the coffee table with the spoon stuck in it. "The cops thought he'd been injected with chemicals to make it look like a heart attack?"

"Exactly."

"But wouldn't the chemicals have shown up in his blood?"

"Right again. Except the blood test was clean."

"What about the markers that normally show up in the blood after someone has a regular heart attack?" I asked.

"They were present, according to the report."

"Wait, the medical examiner doesn't test the blood and tissue himself. There's a forensics lab for that." I was speaking like some kind of expert, but my experience was limited to watching TV.

"I believe that's true," Travis said. "So Westfield, or someone in the lab, may have substituted blood from a person who died naturally from a heart attack."

"Or," I said, "someone lied about the results. Wasn't there an investigation?"

"If you can call it that. Nothing was found. My friends think it was all brushed under the carpet, to protect some big mucky-muck on the take."

"Do you think Westfield left town, because of his deteriorating relationship with the police? Or was he actually fired as a sacrificial lamb to save someone else's hide?"

"Your guess is as good as mine."

We were both quiet for a minute, following our separate trains of thought. "While this is all very interesting," I said, breaking the silence, "I don't see how it helps Elise's case. A bullet in the head is a pretty straightforward cause of death." My spirits slumped again. I picked up the ice cream and filled my mouth with a spoonful of melting comfort.

"I'm still waiting to hear from one guy with some high-end connections," Travis said. "And I've got feelers out on Silver too. You never know."

"Thank you," I said. "I don't mean to be such an ingrate. You don't know Elise, yet you're working hard on her behalf, and all I do is complain that it's not enough."

"Hey, don't make me out to be some kind of saint. We're partners, remember? I'm doing this for you and me as well as for Elise. If we crack the case before Duggan, I'll be able to name my price."

"Seriously?"

"No," he said with a laugh, "but I might be able to beg the network for a raise."

"When will you be back up here?" I was thinking that if I had to wait too long, there was a real chance I might overdose on ice cream. Not the worst way to go, all things considered.

"By the weekend, at the latest."

"With Elise being arrested, I'm surprised your boss doesn't want you in Watkins Glen today. After all, this case is your baby."

"He knows I'm down here investigating, and he knows there's always a chance other information will surface that turns everything we think we know on its head. In my opinion, the DA doesn't have an airtight case yet. I think Duggan was told to make the arrest to appease the voices demanding action."

"Won't the mayor or police chief be holding a press conference?" I asked.

"No doubt, but I can cover it from here. Viewers won't realize I'm not onsite. Except for you of course."

I was out of ideas to lure him back. We said goodnight, but I hated to hang up. Without his voice to distract me, my fears for Elise would consume me. And my nagging doubts about her innocence would taunt me from the sidelines.

Chapter 34

My eyes popped open at five o'clock. All around me the peaceful breathing susurrations of my six sleep-mates taunted me. I think my mother had a spell to cure insomnia, but the daunting task of going through her papers again to find it, made me procrastinate. Since there was no point in staring at the ceiling and wishing I was feline, I crawled out of bed. Carefully this time, to avoid another stampede.

I was on my way downstairs to brew a cup of tea and watch the early news, when I heard the low hum of an engine. The residential streets in my neighborhood are lightly traveled and people are generally respectful of the posted speed, but this driver was going well below the limit, virtually rolling along as if searching for something or some place. But at five o'clock in the morning? The first possibility that came to mind was the rock thrower. Was my nemesis back with a new projectile? A new threat? The hair on the nape of my neck prickled at the thought. There were plenty of ordinary explanations, I told myself. But it was too early for garbage pickup or the mail. It would be hours before the camp buses rumbled through to collect their campers. Maybe it was a police car patrolling the area to keep us safe from Jim's killer. Or keeping an eye on my house in particular for less pleasant reasons? I wasn't normally given to paranoia, but after recent events it was hard not to be skittish.

I continued down the stairs, leaving the lights off. If I wanted to look outside, the indoor lights would make it harder to see. Besides, I didn't want the driver to know I was awake and aware. When I heard the engine rev slightly and move away, I sighed with relief and scolded myself for tilting at windmills. But before I could enter the kitchen, I heard the engine again. I couldn't explain how I knew it was the same one, but I did. Not enough time had passed for the driver to have gone around the block. He or she must have made a U-turn.

I stood frozen in place, listening, the sound of my heartbeat throbbing in my ears. This time the vehicle didn't drive by. It came to a stop. I heard the faint squeak of brakes being applied. I stepped over to the living room window and peered carefully around the edge of the blinds. It was pitch black, but the light from the street lamp showed me a black SUV idling at the curb near my mailbox. As I watched, the driver opened the door and stepped down. I couldn't tell if it was a man or a woman, but something about the way the individual moved made me think it was a woman. She had on a baseball cap pulled low over her eyes and a windbreaker with its collar pulled up along her jawline. The streetlight caught the flash of a white envelope in her hand. I needed to find out who she was and put an end to her threats. I had Travis's voice in my head, begging me not to be a hero. But I couldn't stand there and do nothing when I had the chance to unmask Jim's killer.

I considered going out the back door and sneaking around to the front to take her by surprise, but I nixed the idea. She would be out of sight for half a minute or more and I might miss something crucial. I talked myself into watching and waiting, until she put the envelope into my mailbox. I needed all the evidence I could get. But if I wanted to get the license number before she drove away, timing would be critical. The crazy thought popped into my head that it would have been really helpful if I had a flying broom. Lacking that option, I had to do what I could to shorten my response time. I checked to be sure I had my cell phone in the pocket of my bathrobe. I unlocked the front door slowly, worried the click of the tumbler would make too much noise in the stillness. But the driver didn't react, didn't look in the direction of the house. She reached out tentatively past the mailbox as though she was aware of the force field and was trying to determine if it was still active. Then she jerked her hand back as if she'd been shocked. The wards don't involve an electric current, so her reaction had to be a product of fear.

Apparently satisfied that she couldn't get closer to the house, she opened the mailbox and slid the letter inside. Now! I threw the door open and sprinted across the lawn. I ran faster than I'd ever run, my bare feet hardly touching the ground. It was close. But the woman climbed back into the SUV and slammed the door shut as I reached the curb. She gunned the engine and sped off. But not before I'd gotten a photo of the license plate. Unfortunately she must have realized that when she saw the flash of light.

I was shaking so hard, I couldn't move for a few seconds. After I regained some control over my limbs, I walked to the mailbox, grabbed the envelope and went inside. There was a time when my first instinct would have been to dial 911, but I didn't know whom I could trust at the police department. Instead I called Travis. He answered with a sleep-dazed mumble, but the moment he heard my voice, he came fully awake. "What's wrong?"

I raced through the salient points of what happened, determined to sound strong and in control. No damsel in distress here, thank you very much. "Can you get one of your buddies to run the plate for you?" I asked hopefully.

"I can certainly try."

I read off the numbers and letters. "I think it was a black SUV."

"That doesn't matter. With a little luck, we'll have the owner's name soon enough."

"Fingers crossed."

"What was in the envelope?" he asked.

"I didn't get around to opening it yet. All I could think about was giving you the license plate."

"Open it, please. I want to know what it says before we hang up."

I'd dropped it onto the kitchen table when I sat down to make the call. I put the phone on speaker and tore the envelope open. Inside was a single sheet of printer paper. "It's one line," I said. "Is INVESTIGATING THIS CASE WORTH YOUR LIFE?"

Travis didn't speak for a few moments as if he was carefully weighing his words. "Kailyn, promise me you won't go after any more potential killers or their henchmen on your own. That little stunt you pulled could have ended very differently if that person had had a gun and felt threatened enough to use it."

I promised, without argument, which probably surprised him. Although I'd thought of that possibility, hearing him say it in his solemn reporter's tone, unsettled me more than I cared to admit. I'd been too caught up in fury and frustration to properly assess the danger. But he was right. I could have been shot. I might now be lying dead right there on the quiet street in front of the house where my family had lived for hundreds of years.

* * *

I showered, dressed and fed the cats, all in slow motion, physically and emotionally drained from the adrenalin-charged beginning to my day. I was locking up to go to work when I remembered with a groan that I'd promised Aunt Tilly I would wizard-sit. She had several readings scheduled, and if I canceled at the last moment it would turn her day upside-down. At the very least, it would require an explanation. I didn't want to tell her about the latest visit and threat from the killer. She was already anxious enough.

When I arrived at my shop, the aroma of warm apple strudel permeated every corner. The strudel had been such an instant hit that it quickly earned a regular place on Aunt Tilly's tea menu. As with everything she baked of late, she made extra and stashed it away for me, before Merlin could devour it all. He'd filled out a lot since his arrival in the twenty-first century. His cheeks were no longer slack, but nearly as full and rosy as Tilly's. His scraggly, white hair had a healthy shine to it and his green eyes a sharper twinkle.

To keep him busy, I'd decided to have him help with a thorough inventory. I needed to know which items to reorder, which herbs and plants to gather and which cosmetic and grooming products to whip up. I took him into the storeroom, gave him a pen and a mini legal pad and told him to note the name of each item along with the quantity of them on the shelf. I figured it would take him an hour or two. At the same time, I'd inventory the retail space, so I'd be available to customers. Merlin grumbled mildly about doing work that was far beneath his abilities, until I placed ear buds in his ears and strapped my iPod onto his arm. I'd made him a mix of country, rock, and pop with a smattering of show tunes and some classical pieces. I'd customize it once I knew more about his preferences. He seemed enchanted by the variety of music, as well as the fact that it was issuing from such a tiny box. For a man of his advanced years, he'd taken to modern technology with the alacrity of a child. While I was showing him how to use it, Sashkatu meandered in. I couldn't remember the last time he'd had any interest in checking out the storeroom. I knew I wasn't the reason he'd left his prized perch. To underscore the point, he headed straight for Merlin. When I left them, Merlin was tallying products and swaying to the music, while Sashki wove in and out of his legs, with a beatific look on his furry face. It looked like an interspecies dance routine.

* * *

I had a nice flow of customers throughout the morning and into the middle of the afternoon. They were mostly tourists, who didn't know about the murder investigation, or didn't care. They asked a lot of questions regarding my stock and magick spells and kept me engaged, with little time to dwell on darker matters. When Merlin finished the inventory, he was content to sit and listen to the music until Tilly came for him. I suspected I wasn't getting my iPod back anytime soon.

With thirty minutes left until closing time, it wasn't likely I'd have any more customers, so I started my end of business routine. I was counting the register receipts when a middle-aged woman ran in, relieved to find the shop still open. She'd come all the way from Elmira and had taken a wrong turn, driving for an hour in the wrong direction, before realizing her mistake. I invited her to have a seat, so she could catch her breath, but she assured me she was fine. "My niece raves about your wonderful products," she said, "and I desperately need an eczema cream that works."

"We have a few different items that should help," I told her. "I'll be happy to go over their properties with you." I led her to the last aisle of the shop and pointed out the three remedies. She was trying to decide which would best suit her needs, when a younger woman walked in. I invited her to explore the shop and promised I'd be with her shortly. Five minutes later, the woman from Elmira decided to take all three eczema products. I rang her up, handed her the tote with her purchases and wished her a safe trip home with no wrong turns.

I found the younger woman studying a shelf of ointments, creams, sprays and unguents for insect bites and stings. "Sorry about the wait," I said. "How can I help you?"

She turned to face me, and now that I was up close to her, I realized she was the woman who'd looked familiar to me the crazy day of Merlin's ad campaign. But I still had no idea who she was. "Your shop has some fascinating things," she said with a brilliant smile. Her hair was long, straight, and platinum blonde. I wondered if she'd been a cheerleader back in high school. She definitely had the look. I knew, because I'd envied that look during my teen years. "I'm not in a hurry," she said. "I mean, if you have other customers to take care of..."

"There's no one else," I assured her. "I'm all yours."

"Oh great," she said, "maybe you can help me with this." She held out a piece of lined notebook paper she'd had in her hand.

"Sure." It was always easier when a customer brought along a list, even a generic list of grooming or health problems they wanted to address. Otherwise we wound up playing a version of twenty questions while I tried to figure out what they needed. I unfolded the paper and glanced at it, then looked up at her. "I don't understand."

"It's simple, Ms. Wilde." Her smile was gone, along with the sweet, cheery voice. "I want you to lock the front door and put the CLOSED sign in the window," she said, pulling a gun out of her purse. "And I don't have all day."

Chapter 35

"If this is a robbery, you can have whatever is in the register, but it's not a lot." I couldn't recall there ever being a robbery in the tourist part of New Camel. We didn't sell many high-end items. And a magick shop seemed like the least likely target of all. But the customer is always supposed to be right and this one had a gun, so she could take whatever she wanted.

"Move it," she snapped.

My brain finally made the connection that had eluded me for too long. She looked familiar, because I'd seen a newspaper photograph of her with her family when they moved to the area. She was Ginny Westfield, the ME's wife. No wonder robbery didn't interest her. The stakes were significantly higher. She'd killed Jim, although I didn't have a clue as to why. And now she was here to wrap up a few loose ends, namely me. The threats had not been empty after all.

I walked to the door slowly, trying to come up with a plan to defend myself if things went farther south. As I was approaching the counter, the shop phone rang. "Don't even think about answering it," she warned me.

"If it's someone who knows I'm supposed to be here, they'll come check on me if I don't answer." After one missed call during the workday? Not likely. Unless I came up with some better ideas, I'd be dead by closing time.

"Let me worry about that," she said. "Keep walking."

I considered trying to flee instead of locking the door. She might not have any qualms about shooting me in the back, but I had to try something. There was no cavalry on its way to rescue me. With my body positioned to block the doorknob from Ginny's view, I turned it slowly, until it was free of the jamb. I started to fling it open, but she'd already realized what I was up to and was on the move. She body-slammed me into the door, knocking it shut. I was going to have a mess of bruises later. If there was a later. It didn't escape my attention, though, that she could have shot me, but chose not to. Maybe I was wrong about what she was after. Or maybe she was worried that a gunshot at the open door would prompt some panicked 911 calls.

She ordered me out of the way and took care of locking the door and turning the sign herself. I considered screaming, but that was guaranteed to bring Tilly running and put her in danger too. "Now what?" I asked.

"We'll go into your storeroom."

"I don't have one," I said, trying to punch a hole in her plan. She was probably thinking the storeroom was far enough back from the street that a gunshot in there might not be heard. Then she could run out the rear door and be long gone before anyone knew what she'd done.

She narrowed her eyes at me. "Do I look stupid to you? I know everything there is to know about this shop."

So she'd come in that first time to reconnoiter. Too bad hindsight wasn't great at solving murders.

"The storeroom," Ginny repeated. I led the way down the short hall with her behind me, the gun most likely pointed at my head. When we turned into the storeroom, the theme song from *Game of Thrones* filled the air. She jammed the barrel of the gun against the back of my skull. "Where's that coming from?"

"It's the ringtone on my cell," I said. "It's on my desk up front." The explanation seemed to appease her. She ordered me to the back of the storeroom where the rear door is located and unlocked it.

"That took long enough," Roger Westfield snapped, shutting the door quickly behind himself. Killing was apparently a family activity. Ginny handed the gun to her husband and gave him a brief rundown on what was what, after which he told her to leave. She seemed happy enough to oblige, letting herself out the way he'd come in. Seconds later, Tilly's voice rang out loud and clear from the direction of her shop, which meant the connecting door was open.

"I can't believe you ate it all." She sounded like she was scolding Merlin. "It's a good thing I hid a piece for Kailyn!" Judging by the

volume of her voice, she was coming closer. I tried to send her a tele-
pathic message to stay away. It had never worked in the past when
we'd tried it, but I was desperate.

A frown creased Westfield's forehead. When his wife had cased
the place, she must have missed the connecting door between our
shops. A nasty little fly in the ointment.

"Not a word," he said, "or you'll get her killed too."

I nodded, but my brain kept screaming, *Tilly, stay away. Please
stay away.* A moment later she appeared in the doorway of the storeroom, a plate of strudel in her hand. She looked from me to the ME
and back again, no doubt trying to figure out what she'd walked in
on. When she noticed the gun, the color drained from her face and
her breathing became rapid and shallow. She started swaying on her
feet, woozy as a drunk on a trampoline.

"Aunt Tilly," I said, "get a hold of yourself. Fainting isn't going
to help anyone." I knew from having seen Bronwen handle Tilly in
crisis mode that firm direction was the only way to reach her. She
blinked rapidly and clenched her jaw as she tried to oblige me, but
she was having trouble finding her equilibrium. By that time, I'd
started second-guessing my words. If she fainted, at least she wouldn't
be afraid. Where were Morgana and Bronwen when we could have
used them? The sudden appearance of two talking clouds, complete
with lightning bolts, would have provided the kind of distraction I
needed to try to take Westfield down.

"How did you get in here?" he rasped at Tilly, who was teetering
on the brink of consciousness.

"I . . . we . . . I mean—"

I could see he was losing patience with her. "There's a connecting
door between her shop and mine," I explained.

"Get over there next to your niece," he said, using the gun like a
pointer. Tilly managed to wobble over to me, the plate of strudel still
in her hand.

"Tilly," Merlin called out from her shop, "what would you have
me do with the leftover tea?" If the situation had been on a TV sit-
com, it would have been silly and entertaining, but this was all too
real and could easily end up with all of us dead.

Westfield glared at us. "Tell him whatever you have to, but keep
him from coming in here if you value his life."

Tilly looked at me for guidance, so I nodded. "Stay there," she called back, her voice as wobbly as she was. "I'll be back in two minutes." Westfield seemed satisfied with her performance. But he didn't know Merlin. Telling the sorcerer not to do something was as good as handing him an invitation to try it. It was one of his less endearing charms.

A moment later, Merlin was standing in the doorway, followed closely by Sashkatu. "What kind of nut farm is this?" Westfield was getting himself worked up. Not a good thing as long as he was holding the gun. "Is anybody else going to show up?"

"No," Tilly whimpered. "I locked the front door after my last reading." Great, I thought. So much for any chance of being rescued. No, I wasn't giving up that easily. I turned my thoughts to strategy. The ME had to have a breakpoint, the maximum number of people he thought he could control by himself. Or kill. How many bullets were in his gun? Did he have more in his pocket? Maybe not. After all, he'd planned on killing one person today—me.

"Get in here, old man," he ordered Merlin.

"Do you know to whom you're speaking?" the wizard demanded regally. "What exactly is the meaning of all this?"

"Get in here and shut up. Does that work better for you?" Westfield was getting angrier and more agitated by the minute. He clearly hadn't planned on a mass execution, but now he was stuck. How could he let any of us leave the room alive?

Although he could be arrogant, Merlin was hardly a fool. Without another word, he made his way over to us, Sashkatu as good as Velcroed to his leg.

If we had any chance of surviving this ordeal, we needed a plan and we needed it fast. What if all of us charged at him? No, the odds were good that he'd get off a couple of shots and they could be fatal. I wasn't willing to risk it. Maybe our best chance was to try to reach Westfield on a personal level. That was how I'd connected with him that first time in his office. I knew one thing about him for certain. He adored his wife and daughters. "Dr. Westfield," I said, "have you considered the consequences of what you're doing? For your children's sake, put the gun down. There has to be a better solution, no matter what the problem is."

"I tried other solutions, but you don't scare easily. And you were getting too close."

"Too close to what?" I asked naively.

"Drop the dumb act. You're as clever as they come. You played the staff in my dentist's office to get information on me."

How could he have found out about that? "I don't understand."

"They called to change the appointment you supposedly made for me. Ring a bell now?" There was nothing I could say that would help my case, so I kept my mouth shut. "And you probably got my license number last night."

"I tried, but it was too dark out."

"I have no reason to believe you. The real question is whether or not you've convinced Duggan to run the plate for you. He isn't your biggest fan."

You don't say. I was about to bring up the subject of his family again, when Merlin cleared his throat. "My young man, by any civilized code of conduct, threatening to slaughter unarmed people, especially ladies, is a cowardly and despicable act."

"Merlin, don't," I pleaded, without any real hope of stopping him. "You're only making matters worse."

"Nonsense, this fellow is sorely in need of instruction."

"You ought to listen to the 'lady,'" Westfield shot back.

Merlin ignored both of us. "Although I am not privy to your complaint with Miss Wilde, the honorable way to correct a perceived wrong is to challenge your enemy to a fair duel. Since it would not be seemly for you to issue such a challenge to a lady, I will act as her second and meet you at a time and place of your choosing." I felt like I was watching two cars about to collide and I had no way to stop them.

"What's wrong with this guy?" the ME asked.

"He suffers from dementia," Tilly piped up.

Merlin wheeled around to look her in the face. "I most certainly do not. Why would you say such a thing?"

"To save your hide," she rasped under her breath.

"Enough, all of you," Westfield snapped, waving the gun at us.

"You have such beautiful children," I said softly, trying to turn the conversation back to personal matters. "Do you have any idea what this will do to them?"

"Do you think I wanted to kill Harkens?" he asked incredulously. "Do you think I want this?"

"No, I'm sure you don't," I said. "Maybe Jim was an accident? With a good lawyer—"

"It wasn't an accident; I simply reached the end of my rope. Everyone thinks you get to choose how you live your life, but it's not true. Life backs you into corners, into impossible choices."

"I know." The moment the pointless words slipped out, I regretted them. This wasn't a little chat between friends about mundane disappointments. Every word mattered. No do-overs.

His expression hardened. "You don't have a clue."

"Then do the decent thing and at least explain this to us."

He didn't say anything for the length of a minute. I figured my attempt to reach him had failed. I was trying to come up with another tactic, when he finally broke his silence. "The decent thing, huh? Okay, but only to prove my point. I was the ME for Manhattan before I moved up here. I did my job well and went home to my family with a clear conscience every night. I did right by my wife and children. In other words, I lived a good life, an exemplary life, some might say. Then one night the cops brought in a body for autopsy. It was getting late, so I put it in cold storage to work on in the morning. But bright and early the next day, I was visited at home by a man who said he was associated with the Rigosi family. Said they were prepared to pay me half a million dollars to do them a little favor. Easy stuff. All I had to do was lie about the cause of death for the body that came in the night before. I was ridiculously naive. I thanked the man for the generous offer, but said I couldn't accept. He asked me if I would prefer to visit my wife and daughters in the cemetery."

Tilly gasped.

"He said it calmly," Westfield went on, "didn't so much as raise his voice. At first I thought I hadn't heard him correctly. So he repeated it in the same casual way. Then he said I had two minutes to decide. It was the easiest choice I ever had to make. I chose to keep my family alive." His voice started to tremble on the last words.

"Oh dear, how awful," Tilly said, shaking her head. "You poor boy."

"Truly terrible," I said, meaning every word of it deep down in my gut. "But I don't understand what Jim Harkens had to do with it."

"I took the money," he continued, "gave up the position I'd worked hard to attain and moved my family up here to the sticks, so I would never be a target for people like that again. I didn't tell my wife the truth, because I didn't want her to live in fear. I told her I wanted to leave the city to raise our family in a safer environment. She didn't need much convincing. She grew up in the suburbs and wasn't much of a city girl at heart. After we were settled here, I hired Harkens to write my will. I also gave him a sealed letter to be given to my wife, should I predecease her. The letter explained the truth about our move and told her where to find the money. But Harkens was too curious for his own good. He betrayed me and opened the letter. He decided he could use some of that dirty money himself. He started blackmailing me. If I didn't cooperate, he threatened to tell the authorities, my family and the rest of the world what I'd done. I couldn't let that happen, because my family would be right back in jeopardy from the Rigosis. So I paid him what he asked for. But he was a gambler and he kept needing more. I finally told my wife the truth. Every miserable grain of it. Then I went to Harkens's office and killed him." He heaved a deep sigh. "The scary part was that I didn't feel remorse. All I felt was relief."

We were all silent, trying to digest what we'd heard. In spite of myself, I couldn't help feeling a certain kinship with him. Given those same circumstances, I might have done the same thing. Yet that didn't make it right. And if the ME was arrested and tried for murdering Jim, the whole sordid mess would come to light and the threat against his family might still be carried out. The police could promise to protect the Westfield girls, but if someone wanted them dead badly enough . . .

"If you kill us too, you'll be looking at four counts of homicide. And when they bring you to trial, the truth will come out. You'll spend the rest of your life in prison. Your wife will be tried for abetting you. What about your daughters' safety then?"

The ME shrugged. "I've thought about this long and hard and I've come to understand the mean truth. I lost my family the night that corpse landed on my autopsy table. It's just taken me all this time to realize it." He sounded resigned, defeated, but he wouldn't have come here to kill me if he didn't also harbor some hope for a future. Even if it was only for a future on the run.

"I have a question," I said, aware I was treading on dangerous ground.

"Sure, why not?" he said expansively. "But make it quick, because I've wasted enough time here and we have to get down to business."

Chapter 36

"Why were you trying to frame Elise Harkens?" I asked him.
"It seemed like a good idea at the time," he said wryly, as if
he was actually beginning to enjoy the dialogue. Venting, even brag-
ging about the secret he'd kept for so long. "I needed to direct the investigation away from me. Wives and husbands have been killing
each other since the dawn of time. If you dig deep enough into any
long-term relationship, you can probably find a motive for murder. I
chose Elise when I bumped into her and Jim at the shooting range.
They actually had the kind of gun I wanted to use. It was like I had
Fate's blessing."

Without thinking, Tilly clucked her tongue in disapproval. I held
my breath, afraid Westfield would cut his narrative short to make her
his first victim. But he ignored her. "Turns out, you can talk yourself
into believing pretty much anything."

Caught up in the story, Tilly wouldn't let it go. "How did you get
into their house to steal the gun?"

"Fate to the rescue once again. My cleaning lady is their cleaning
lady. She had their house key."

I tried to shush my aunt before she said anything else, but she was
a runaway train on the downhill. "The cleaning lady gave you the
key, just like that?"

The ME gave a grim chuckle. "You don't go through what I have,
without learning that everyone has their price, be it money or the life
of someone they love."

The casual tone of his words made my skin crawl. Whatever empathy I'd felt for him turned to ice and shattered. The man he'd been
the night that corpse arrived was not the man who was holding the
gun on us today. Reasoning with him was not going to save us.

I don't know if Sashkatu was reading my mind or the mood of the room, but he chose that moment to make a run at the ME. Before any of us realized what he was about to do, he launched himself at the ME's gun hand. The weapon flew out of his grip, clattering to the floor. But he recovered too swiftly and with one swipe of his arm, caught Sashki in midair and knocked him halfway across the room. I winced as I watched his arthritic legs absorb the shock of his landing. Tilly shrieked in horror. I ran to help him, but he shook off the pain with an angry yowl, a small but stoic hero. Unfortunately his efforts were in vain. The gun had landed less than a foot away from Westfield. He had it in his hand in seconds and ordered me to get back to the others.

"The cat tries that again," he said, "and he won't have enough lives left to—hey," he interrupted himself, "what's going on with the old man?"

I looked over at Merlin, who was standing on the other side of Tilly. His eyes were closed and he was mumbling words I couldn't distinguish. But I knew he was casting a spell. "He's praying," I said. "Just an old man praying for his life."

"Well it's creepy. Tell him to cut it out."

"Merlin," I yelled to get his attention, "Merlin, stop it. Stop it this second."

"Tell him to cut it out or he gets the first bullet." Westfield cocked the gun to prove his point.

"Merlin, stop!" I pleaded. "Stop!" He was so completely focused on the spell that he was beyond hearing me. I turned to the ME. "You can see that he suffers from dementia. He's a harmless old man."

Westfield wasn't buying it. "He either stops the mumbo jumbo right now or he's dead."

Tilly's eyes bulged with panic. Without a word, she reached over and grabbed the skin on the wizard's forearm, pinching and twisting it with every bit of her strength. Merlin's eyes flew open. He screeched as if a hawk had ripped a chunk out of him. "What possessed you to do such a thing?" he demanded of her, rubbing the bruised arm.

I did it to save your life, you old fool," she said.

"I have never suffered anyone calling me a *fool*," he responded indignantly, "and I do not intend to start now."

"Shut up, both of you!" The ME growled at them. The gun was still cocked. It wouldn't take much for the first bullet to fly. We were down to last resorts. I tried to quiet my mind, which, under the cir-

234 · *Sharon Pape*

cumstances, was harder than anything I'd ever done. I focused my
energies on the gun. I tugged at it and tugged at it until I felt as if I
were twisting myself inside out with the effort. But the gun didn't
budge. If I could move a chair, moving the gun should have been
easy. The problem had to be my state of mind.

Westfield was talking, but I blocked out his voice. I couldn't
allow him to distract me. I grabbed Tilly's hand, hoping somehow
she would strengthen me. She immediately understood what I was
trying to do. She still had the plate of strudel in her other hand. After
a second's hesitation, she let it drop to the floor. Merlin yelped and
was bending to retrieve it, when Tilly seized his hand. With the three
of us linked, the boost from their energy nearly rocked me off my
feet. If this had any chance of working, it had to be *now!* I locked my
eyes on the gun in the ME's hand and tugged at it with every ounce
of my being. But instead of drawing the gun to me, I somehow drew
myself to it. I was standing inches from the ME. Before he could
process what was happening, I yanked the gun out of his hand. He
was a quick study, though. Ignoring the whys and hows of what I'd
done, he was determined to retake the weapon. As we struggled over
the gun, it fired. All of us jumped. Tilly shrieked. I looked up, afraid
she'd been hit. "I'm okay," she sang out. "It hit the wall." But in that
moment of distraction, Westfield got a better grip on the gun. I was
seconds away from losing it. In desperation I stomped on his foot,
grinding my stiletto heel into it. He howled, the pain causing him to
loosen his grip on the gun. I opened my hand too, letting the gun fall
to the floor. Then I kicked it across the room to Merlin and Tilly, before sprinting back to them. Tilly grabbed the gun off the floor and
was pointing it at the ME with shaking hands. She passed it over to
me as soon as I reached her, apparently forgetting that I'd never
learned how to shoot either. But one of us had to convince Westfield
we knew what we were doing or he'd be on us in no time.

From across the room, he glared at us with feral anger, cornered
yet again. One thing was clear. If he took a single step toward us, I
would have to shoot him, pull the trigger without hesitation, without
thought. All of our lives depended on it.

"No one move." The order came from the rear door, which the
ME had left unlocked for his escape. The voice was deep and com-
manding—detective Phillip Duggan. I wanted to turn and look, but I

didn't dare take my eyes off Westfield, until I knew for sure we were safe.

"Thank goodness you're here!" Westfield said. "Wilde is the one you're after. She killed Harkens and in another second she would have killed me too."

"He's lying," Tilly cried out before I could. "He's the one who killed Jim. He confessed. We all heard him." Merlin lent his voice to the fray and soon they were all shouting over each other.

"Quiet, all of you," Duggan snapped. "Put down the gun, Ms. Wilde."

"Not until you've got him in handcuffs," I said, although my arms were aching and I didn't know how much longer I could hold the gun extended in front of me the way they did on TV. Duggan must have given Curtis the nod, because the younger cop walked past me, holding a pair of plastic cuffs. He crossed the room to Westfield and in less than a minute, the killer's hands were cuffed behind him. I lowered the gun.

Duggan was holstering his weapon as he came from behind me. He held out his hand. "I'll take that now."

My fingers were locked so tightly around the gun that for a moment I had trouble releasing it. Once it was in Duggan's hand, relief surged through me, making my limbs go weak. In the next instant, Tilly threw her arms around me with such enthusiasm that she nearly sent both of us crashing to the floor. Somehow we managed to stay upright, swaying together like a couple trying to dance on a ship in heavy seas. Merlin joined us and had to make do with patting the part of my back that was free of Tilly's embrace. "I commend you," he said, solemnly. "You were as courageous as any knight of the realm." I thanked him. "Although," he went on, "had I been allowed to continue with my spell, things would have come to a more satisfying and entertaining conclusion."

Tilly released me and turned her twinkling eyes to the sorcerer. "You were going to turn him into something, weren't you?"

"I had not as yet decided between a rat and a beetle, when you stopped me by nearly tearing the skin from my body." He was clearly not over his pique.

I left them and went hunting for Sashkatu. He wasn't between the rows of metal shelving. I finally found him in the closet with the broom and cleaning supplies. I knelt down and held my arms out to him. Had it been an ordinary day, he would have ignored me. But there was nothing ordinary about this day, and he knew it as well as any of us. He struggled to his feet and came to me, favoring his left rear leg. He didn't put up a fuss when I scooped him up and cradled him in my arms. I promised him his own salmon fillet for dinner and carried him over to Merlin and Tilly, who welcomed him like a conquering hero. Curtis was reading the ME his rights as he escorted him out of the storeroom.

"I'm going to need statements from all of you," Duggan said. "Take some time to compose yourselves, then come down to the station, the one right here in New Camel."

"Detective," I said as he turned to leave. "A huge thank you, from all of us."

"You're welcome, Ms Wilde, but you seemed to have things under control before we arrived."

"How did you know what was happening here?"

"I didn't actually. You should thank your boyfriend. He's very persistent. When he couldn't reach you on your business phone or your cell, he called me. I told him the police were not in the habit of tracking down people who didn't answer their phones for a few hours. He explained what he'd found out about Westfield and why he was worried about your safety. He wouldn't let up on me. By the way," Duggan added dryly, "you might want to impress on him that threatening to throw a police officer *under the bus,* even figuratively, is a good way to wind up in jail."

Chapter 37

After we gave Duggan our statements, I took Sashkatu straight to Dr. Hudson. He, and his father before him, had been our family vet for as long as I could remember. He gave Sashki a thorough exam, never an easy job, and proclaimed him to be in fine shape overall. The X-ray showed that his leg was badly sprained, but not broken. Hudson prescribed plenty of rest and no more feats of derring-do. No problem. Sashki preferred couch-potato mode.

On the way home, I stopped to buy two salmon fillets. One for Sashki, which I'd dole out over the next few days and one for the other cats to share as an apology for making them wait so long for dinner. I had finally collapsed on the couch when Morgana and Bronwen popped out of the ether. I nearly groaned out loud. The day been long and emotional enough. I was weary to the marrow of my bones.

"You were magnificent," Morgan proclaimed.

That got my attention. "Wait—you saw what happened?"

"We certainly did. Most of it anyway. I think we missed a bit in the beginning."

"Your mother is right," Bronwen chimed in. You were magnificent. You and Sashkatu both!" They gave me a round of applause with claps of thunder.

"Thank you," I said, though I didn't feel grateful. "Why didn't you try to help us? We were minutes, seconds, away from being murdered right there in front of you." My outrage was foaming in my mouth.

"We're not allowed to interfere," Bronwen said without apology. "It's that simple."

"Otherwise, don't you think we would have done whatever we could to help?"

"How could I have known that?" I said. "You never mentioned it before."

"Clearly an oversight," Bronwen replied. "But now you know. It happens to be the primary law on this side of the veil. The consequences for disobeying it are . . . suffice it to say—formidable."

"One last thing before we go," my mother said. "Was this your first instance of teleportation?"

"Yes. But at the time, I didn't realize I was doing it."

"Now that you're aware of this ability, you must practice it, cultivate it," Bronwen instructed. "Strengthen it as you would a muscle. It is the rarest power in our bloodline. I know of only one distant aunt who possessed it generations ago." Once they were satisfied with my promise to comply, they took their leave.

A split second after their departure, the doorbell rang. I opened the door to find Travis on the porch, holding a bag of something that smelled wonderful. He walked in, put the bag on the floor and pulled me into a hug and a lingering kiss, although we'd connected at the police station less than an hour before. When he bent to retrieve the bag, I hooked my mind into it and with one good tug lifted if off the floor and sailed it up to my waiting hand. On the short drive home, I'd decided that if Travis was going to be in my life on more than a temporary basis, he needed to know my magick was real. The bag of food provided the perfect opportunity. He'd brought it, and it hadn't been out of his sight. There was no way I could have tampered with it.

Travis didn't say a word at first. His expression was a strange combination of confusion, fear, and amazement. With that one act of telekinesis, I'd turned the immutable rules of his world upside-down. I had no intention of revealing my teleportation to him or Elise, until I'd had time to explore it in depth.

"No tricks," he mumbled, as though trying to absorb what he'd seen.

"No tricks."

"You know it's not possible."

"And yet . . ."

"It may take me a while."

My heart unclenched. I'd known there was a chance he would see me as a freak, as evil, as alien. That he would leave and never come back. But he wasn't running for his life. It sure sounded like he wanted to make us work. "In every other way, every important way, I'm still me," I pointed out. "Think of it as a talent I have that you don't. Like playing an instrument, or painting or crocheting."

"Crocheting? Now there's a talent I've always coveted." Although he said it with the barest of smiles, it was a step in the right direction. Maybe it wouldn't take as long as he thought to come to terms with this other side of me. In any case, we had to drop the subject, because a car had pulled to the curb, and Elise was jumping out of the passenger side. I had no reason to hide the fact that Travis knew the truth about me, but he deserved the time and space to adjust to it, safe from anyone else's expectations.

Elise ran up the walk and the steps to my house and burst through the doorway. We shared a happy, teary, girl greeting, after which I introduced her to Travis. She handed me a bag she was holding. "I made my lawyer stop on the way, so I could pick up ice cream. You can't celebrate properly without it."

Travis pointed to the bag of food I was still holding. "Pulled pork sandwiches, because man can't live by ice cream alone."

"Yeah, but I'm pretty sure woman can," I chimed in.

We sat at the kitchen table and divvied up the goodies. I didn't realize how hungry I was until I took the first bite of my sandwich. I could tell Travis was loosening up by the minute. I knew he and Elise had to be bursting with questions, but they waited until dessert to demand the details of my close scrape with the killer.

"Disappointed it wasn't Duggan?" Travis asked me.

"Not really. He may be a curmudgeon, but I suspect he's got a nicer side buried somewhere in there."

"I'm reserving judgment on him," Elise said dryly. "Arresting me didn't exactly win him any points." She scooped up some vanilla fudge ice cream, dropped it into her dish, then passed me the container. "Here's what I don't understand. How did Westfield figure out it was you who called his dentist's office?"

"From a little fact I failed to consider," I said, embarrassed to admit it. "Caller ID."

Travis chuckled. "A novice mistake. I've made my share of them."

"When the girl from Silver's office called to change the appointment I'd made for Westfield, he asked her who'd made it in the first place. That's when she remembered seeing the caller ID and wondering why it was from a cell and not from his office number. But she was so short-staffed and swamped with calls that day, she never pursued it."

Elise grinned. "It's a good thing you have your day job to fall back on."

"You know," I said, "in spite of the danger and all, it was kind of fun trying to figure out who the killer was."

Travis nearly choked on his ice cream. "I don't like the sound of that."

"Hey, there's nothing to worry about," Elise assured him. "The odds of there being another murder in this town have to be less than the odds of winning the lottery, twice."

"In that case," he said, "I've still got some celebrating to do. Pass the ice cream."

"Did you ever find out why Duggan was leaving town around the time of the murder?" Elise asked.

"No," I said. "That's something we may never know. It's not easy to check on the whereabouts of a detective who's apparently done nothing wrong."

"Or it may come to light when you least expect it," Travis added.

By the time Tilly and Merlin popped in with a batch of peanut butter chocolate chip cookies, we swore we couldn't eat another bite. I introduced Travis to my aunt and Merlin. Travis' eyebrows hitched up when he heard Merlin's name. I gave him the standard explanation—strange side of the family, all with odd names. He seemed to accept it without question. Then again, what's a peculiar name compared to learning your girlfriend is a sorceress?

In spite of our protests, Tilly passed around the tin of cookies, and we somehow managed to nibble our way through half of them. "Merlin has something to tell you," she announced, her eyes dancing like a little kid who's got a secret about to explode inside her. "He's been researching the history of our town and he believes he knows the truth about its name."

"That camel story is sheer poppycock," Merlin began. "One need look no further than the place-names all over this country. New this and new that, followed by a name from England: New England, New York, New Jersey, and so forth." He looked around the table at us. We all nodded in agreement, waiting for the punch line. "Well," he said, clearly relishing the drama of the moment, "there is no place in England now, nor at any time in its rich past, by the name of Camel. There is, however, I mean there was"—he quickly corrected himself—"a place known as Camelot. It is my belief that New Camelot was the name bestowed upon this town by those who journeyed here from the original Camelot, centuries ago. Over time the name lost a few letters and an important chunk of its history." He sat back in his chair as pleased with himself as I'd ever seen him.

Looking around the table, I could tell by their expressions that Travis and Elise found the theory clever and fanciful, nothing more. That was fine. They both had enough to deal with for now anyway. But when I looked at Tilly, her eyes gleamed with the same certainty that I knew burned in mine.

Acknowledgments

A big thank you to my husband, who critiques the chapters as I write them; my daughter, who reads the finished book and makes sure I haven't missed the forest for the trees; my son, who gets the kinks out after I've been sitting at the computer for too long; and the furred ones, for providing pet therapy when the going gets rough.

Thanks to Donna and Gloria at the Park East Literary Agency for their help.

Thanks to all my friends for their continued support and encouragement.

Don't miss the next bewitching novel in the
Abracadabra mystery series
That Olde White Magick
Coming soon from Lyrical Underground, an imprint of
Kensington Publishing Corp.

Keep reading to enjoy a sample excerpt . . .

Chapter 1

"Every living soul in this town must be here tonight," my Aunt Tilly remarked as I pulled into the last parking spot at the New Camel elementary school. It was the school I attended as a child, the school my aunt, mother, and grandmother had attended, as well as generations of Wildes before them. It had started out as a one-room schoolhouse and expanded over the years to accommodate fourteen classrooms—kindergarten through sixth grade. It still sat on the crest of Johnson's Hill at the eastern end of town. I loved the tradition and continuity it represented, the warmth of hometown I felt whenever I passed by.

"I'm not surprised," I said, turning off the engine. "Everyone I talk to has an opinion on the matter. A very definite opinion."

"We'd better hustle our bustles and get in there before all the seats are taken."

Tilly took off her seat belt and opened the car door, nearly sliding right out, courtesy of her silk muumuu-clad bottom. I reached for her arm to stop her, but I was still in my seatbelt and she was too far away. At the last moment, she grabbed the door jamb to stop herself.

"Whoops," she said with a gasp and a giggle, "that was like a carnival ride. I need to stop wearing such slippery fabrics or you'll be scooping me off the pavement one day."

Merlin emerged from the backseat, grousing. "I cannot fathom why I am being compelled to attend a meeting, in which I have neither interest nor purpose. I am not a citizen of this town. Or, for that matter, of this state, this country, or this particular period in time."

My aunt and I let him grumble on without comment. It wasn't the first time he'd serenaded us with that particular tune. We joined the stream of people entering the school and heading down the hallway to the gymnasium. Everyone was calling out hellos or stopping to share quick hugs, which caused everyone else to detour around them like water around a jetty. As a result, the normally short walk to the gym was taking far longer than it should have, but I had no right to complain. I was as guilty as everyone else. That's what happens when the residents of a small town congregate in one place. Merlin, on the other hand, griped enough for both of us. He knew only a few people and he regarded the traffic snarl as a plot to keep him from his TV shows.

In spite of all the open windows, the building had a stale, musty odor from being closed most of the summer, and the late August heat wave was making matters worse. At least there was some decent cross ventilation going when we reached the gym. Rusty Higgins, the sum total of the school's custodial staff, had propped open the two large emergency exit doors in the back.

The gym had always been big enough to host the town board meetings, but that night it was overcrowded, the walls bulging with people. The air vibrated with tension and the loud droning of all their voices made me feel like I was walking into a massive beehive. In hindsight, not the best place to have brought Merlin, who was twitchy and out of his element under the best of circumstances. Tilly and I had debated for days about whether or not to take him. Despite the jeans and shirt we bullied him into wearing, his raging white hair and beard set him apart from the local population. There was no way around it. He was already drawing blatant stares of curiosity. On the other hand, leaving him home alone, where the deadly combination of boredom and magick might lead him astray again, wasn't a comfortable option either. In the end, keeping an eye on him had won handily.

"Let the gawkers gawk," I said. If anyone asked nosy questions, they'd get our now standard reply. Merlin was a distant English cousin, from the eccentric side of the family, here on an extended visit. *Extended* barely covered it. He'd be staying until I figured out how to send him back to his own time and place. Although he'd been with us for two months, I was no closer to reaching that goal than I had been the day he crash-landed in the storeroom of my magick shop.

Apparently no one had told Rusty to expect a larger than usual turnout, because there were less than two dozen folding chairs set up facing the mobile podium. By the time we arrived, they were all taken. I spied a few empty spots in the bleachers, but I knew my aunt would have trouble reaching them. I had visions of her stepping on the hem of her silk muumuu and either pitching forward onto her face or tumbling backward to the floor, taking others with her like a human avalanche. The safer option was to remain standing in the empty area behind the chairs with everyone else who found themselves seatless. There were plenty of disgruntled comments about the situation, but I didn't see one person leave.

This was my first town board meeting. According to Tilly, neither she nor my late mother and grandmother had ever attended one either. But she knew that the town's charter, which had originally called for monthly meetings, had been changed to quarterly meetings decades before I was born, once it became clear there wasn't anything the board needed to address that couldn't wait a few months. Until now. Our mayor, Lester Tompkins, had called this meeting as a special session.

At precisely seven o'clock, three of the five board members, including the mayor, trooped into the gym from the adjoining supply room and stepped onto the podium. They took their seats behind a cafeteria table, grandly draped with the town's insignia, a camel on a verdant field.

"A camel," Merlin muttered when he noticed it. "And yet I am not permitted to tell these people the true name of their town. I should think they would welcome the knowledge."

"Some people don't deal well with change," I explained for the twentieth time. "We have to wait for the right moment." I didn't harbor much hope it would happen any time soon.

"I disagree. This is the perfect time, given that the whole town is here."

"Everyone is too divided over the hotel. I can't imagine a worse time to throw another change at them."

He glowered at me, but stopped arguing.

"I'm surprised the board members aren't down here, glad-handing the crowd, banking votes for the next election," Tilly whispered loudly enough for people within twenty feet of us to hear. As if on cue, Beverly Ruppert, the newest member of the board, swept into the gym with the aplomb of a Broadway star making her grand entrance. She was dressed for the part in a sleeveless beige sheath that was straining across her hips and stiletto heels that caused her to walk like a novice on stilts. Tilly rolled her eyes at me as Beverly threaded her way through the crowd, stopping to greet everyone with a handshake or an air kiss. It looked like she would miss us on her current trajectory to the podium, but at the last moment she spied us and changed direction. Tilly groaned.

"Well, look who's here." Beverly flashed her broadest political smile for us. "We finally got you two to attend a meeting." Since she'd been on the town board for all of four months, I was tempted to ask how many meetings she'd attended before discovering her political calling. But I held my tongue. We needed Beverly on our side, at least until the Waverly proposal was decided. She was against it as much as Tilly and I were.

"Hi, Bev," I said. Tilly gave her a nod of acknowledgement.

Beverly homed in on her. "I guess there's no point in asking you which way the vote will go tonight, is there, Tilly dear?" she said with syrupy condescension. "Everyone knows your track record has been abysmal lately."

I felt Tilly's anger flare and wished that telepathy was one of my stronger suits. Then I could have talked her down and urged her not to take the bait.

"My aunt is too ethical to try to influence the outcome with a prediction," I said, before my ethical aunt could come up with a more caustic response. As I spoke those words, I realized it wasn't Tilly's reaction I should have been worried about. Merlin was glaring at Beverly, mumbling something unintelligible, his lips grim and all but hidden in the bird's nest of his beard. He was too far away for me to stop him with a discreet jab to the ribs, and Tilly, who stood between us, seemed content to allow him free rein for the moment.

"Don't they need you up there so they can start the meeting?" I asked Beverly in a last-ditch effort to get her away from Merlin. She'd still be within reach of his powers on the other side of the gym, but if I could break his concentration on her, it might buy me the few seconds I needed to talk some sense into him.

Beverly gave me a dismissive wave of her hand. "Amanda's not here yet any—" her voice cracked and was gone. When she opened her mouth, no sound emerged. Not a croak, not a rasp, not a whine. Her hand flew to her throat, her eyes widened with dismay and bewilderment. The harder she tried to speak, the more frustrated she

248 of Sharon Pape

became. She was opening and closing her mouth like the goldfish I'd had as a child. I turned to Merlin. He was wearing a beatific smile, as if all was right with the world. Tilly didn't seem troubled by Beverly's predicament either, or the fact that the wizard had gone rogue right under our noses. Of course, as apt punishments go, I had to admit that Merlin nailed it.

Panic was rising in Beverly's eyes, the corded muscles in her neck standing out with the prolonged strain of trying to make her vocal chords work.

I had to do something before she had a stroke or a heart attack. I slipped behind Tilly, grabbed Merlin's arm and squeezed. "Stop it!" I yelled into his ear to be sure he heard me. I threw in the worst threat I could imagine. "Or no pizza for a month."

In a matter of seconds, a blood-curdling scream rocked the gym. It ricocheted off the walls, the floor, the ceiling and the wooden bleachers. Conversations stopped dead. All eyes turned to Beverly. Merlin had released her from the spell once he understood his pizza would be forfeit, but he'd timed it to coincide with her effort to force sound through her vocal cords. Even she seemed stunned by the horrific noise she produced. Her cheeks turned crimson.

"Sorry, sorry—everything's okay," she called out, scowling at the three of us as if she suspected we were to blame for the fiasco. Muttering that she needed fresh air, she turned on her wobbly heels and stalked out of the gym with far less composure than when she arrived. I locked eyes with Merlin. If steam had been shooting out of my ears it wouldn't have surprised me.

"Yes, I know," he said, preempting me in the sullen, world-weary tone of a teenager. "We need to talk. Again."

"Well, we do," I said, my thunder stolen. We'd been letting him watch way too much TV. More important, although we made it clear that he must not go about randomly casting spells, he'd done just that. He was an old man with the abilities of a master sorcerer and the attitude of a teenage rebel. Disaster was always on the agenda.

Tilly pulled a tissue from her purse and dabbed at her forehead and upper lip. "It's sweltering in here. I'm going outside to cool off." When she caught the hitch of my eyebrow, she added, "Don't worry, I'm not chasing after Beverly to give her my two cents, even if she deserves it and more. I'll go out the back way. I won't be long."

I watched her shuffle through the crowd and disappear through the emergency doors. She couldn't have been gone more than a minute or two, when another scream pierced the air. I knew that scream. It was Tilly's. But it sounded like part of a duet, or how I imagined a duet of screams would sound. Grabbing Merlin's hand, I ran for the rear doors. Having been closer to the gym's entrance, we were among the last to make it outside. By then, sirens were blaring in the distance, whipping my anxiety to a frothy peak.

Once we made it outside, all I could see were people's backs. I elbowed my way through the crowd, pulling Merlin along with me, excusing ourselves as we charged ahead. I fielded a lot of dirty looks, but that wasn't going to stop me. Tilly had screamed and the situation was serious enough to bring the local emergency squad. I had to find out why.

Merlin and I broke through the ring of onlookers, and found ourselves directly across from Tilly. Her eyes were wide, her face bleached white. Beverly, who was standing a few feet away, didn't look much better. They were both focused on a woman's body lying prone on the grass between us. So many people were standing and kneeling around her that I couldn't venture a guess about her identity. Dr. Bronson, Tilly's rheumatologist, was at her side along with an off-duty EMT and a nurse who looked familiar. They must have all been in the gym when the screaming erupted.

Dusk was already descending, courtesy of the mountains to the west. It was becoming harder to see by the minute. The interior lights in the school didn't reach around to this side of the school grounds. People were calling for flashlights; two men ran to find Rusty. Though it seemed like forever, it couldn't have been more than a couple of minutes before the exterior floodlights flashed on, instantly turning twilight back into day.

With the help of the EMT, Bronson turned the woman over. Wasn't he supposed to wait for the ambulance to bring a spine board? I wondered. As they lay her on her back, the answer was easy to see. There was no need to stabilize her. Her neck had been slashed from ear to ear. She was probably dead before anyone got to her. Gasps and cries rose as those in the front passed this information to those behind them. The victim was Amanda Boswell, the missing board member.

Sharon Pape is the author of the popular Portrait of Crime and Crystal Shop mystery series. She started writing stories in first grade and never looked back. She studied French and Spanish literature in college and went on to teach both languages on the secondary level. After being diagnosed with and treated for breast cancer in 1992, Sharon became a Reach to Recovery peer support volunteer for the American Cancer Society. She went on to become the coordinator of the program on Long Island. She and her surgeon created a nonprofit organization called Lean On Me to provide peer support and information to newly diagnosed women and men. After turning her attention back to writing, she has shared her storytelling skills with thousands of fans. She lives with her husband on Long Island, New York, near her grown children. She loves reading, writing, and providing day care for her grand-dogs. Visit her at www.sharonpape.com.